ANOTHER DAY, ANOTHER DUNGEON

GREG COSTIKYAN

ANOTHER
DAY, ANOTHER
DUNGEON

Book ONE of
Cups and Sorcery

A TOM DOHERTY ASSOCIATES BOOK
NEW YORK

ANOTHER DAY, ANOTHER DUNGEON

Printed in the United States of America

Quality Printing and Binding by:
THE MAPLE-VAIL BOOK MANUFACTURING GROUP
Pine Camp Drive
Binghamton, N.Y. 13902 U.S.A.

for Elizabeth

Cast of Characters

The Adventurers

Timaeus d'Asperge, *Magister Igniti:* an aristocrat and fire mage, financer of the expedition.

Sidney Stollitt: partner in Pratchitt & Stollitt, a firm that specializes in theft, divorce work, and assembling expeditions into the caverns. She is far more reliable than her partner.

Nick Pratchitt: Sidney's partner.

Father Geoffrey Thwaite: a priest of the god Dion, patron of drunkards.

Kraki Kronarsson: barbarian and illegal alien.

Garni Ben Griwi: dwarf and experienced adventurer.

The Caverns

Lenny the Lizard: tour guide.

Drizhnakh, Garfok, and Spug: assorted orcs.

Fragrit: orc priest.

Dorog: another orc.

Rog: large person with claws and an unpleasant disposition.

Corcoran Evanish: customs official.

The Boars

Wentworth Secundus Jorgensen, *Magister Alchimiae:* Master Alchemist and Fullbright of the Loyal and Fraternal Sodality of the Boar.

Jasper de Mobray, KGF, *Magister Mentis:* a flying, largely invisible adept of the mental arts. Member, Order of the Golden Fleece; Order of the Green Flame. Fullbright of the Boars.

Morglop Morstern: cyclops, Fullbright of the Boars, swordsman.

Manfred: the Grand Boar.

The Court

His Grace, Mortimer, by the Grace of the Gods Grand Duke of Athelstan, Lord of Durfalus, Defender of the Faiths, etc., etc., etc.: enthusiastic mycologist.

Sir Ethelred Ethelbert: his foreign minister.

Jameson: Sir Ethelred's secretary.

General Carruthers: Commander of the Ducal Guard.
Major Yohn: Commander of the Fifth Frontier Warders, recently returned from the suppression of the Meep Banditti.

University Faculty
Doctor Calidos: Timaeus's don, Senior Professor of the Department of Fire.
Doctor Macpherson: Adjunct Professor of Imperial History.

Bad Guys
The Right Honorable the Baroness Veronee, *Magistra Necromantiae:* Baroness of the Realm, necromancer, and spy for Arst-Kara-Morn.
The Lich: powerful dead guy.
Rupert: Veronee's butler.
Cook: Veronee's cook.
Ross Montiel: elven gangster.
Micah: his lieutenant.
George, Fred, and Billy: assorted thugs.

Neighborhood Fixtures
Mrs. Coopersmith: Nick and Garni's landlady.
Elma: mistress of number 11 Cobblers Lane, the house that Montiel commandeers.
Vic: senile old geezer.
Madame Laura: successful madame, in hock to Montiel. Mother of "Priscilla."

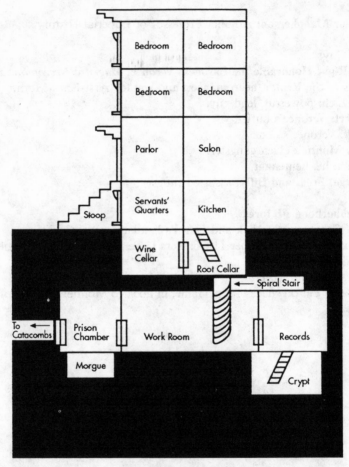

VERONEE'S TOWNHOUSE

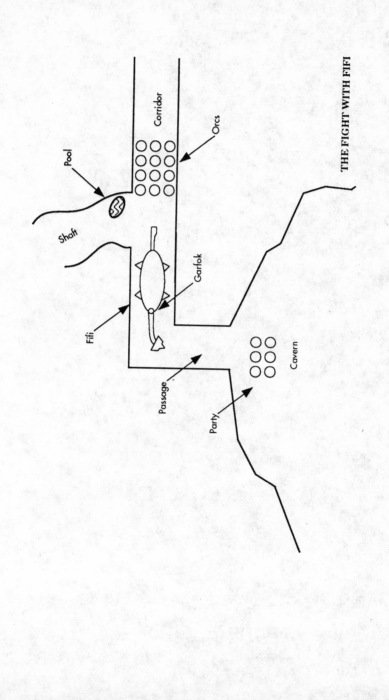

THE FIGHT WITH FIFI

Part I.

ANOTHER DUNGEON

I.

Timaeus d'Asperge was comfortably ensconced in his favorite armchair at the Millennium Club. One hand held his ancient meerschaum, stuffed with Alcalan black leaf. By his other hand, on a small serviette, stood a decanter of Moothlayan single malt.

"Now that you have your Master's," the man with the monocle asked Timaeus, "what will you do?"

"Hah!" said the Colonel. "Go to Ish and join the army, that's what, eh?" He struck Timaeus on the knee with a clenched fist. "Show those damnable orcs what for, eh, boy? Good man."

Timaeus cleared his throat with slight embarrassment. "Actually," he said, "I was thinking about opening a practice—"

"Go into trade?" said the man with the monocle with undisguised horror. "My dear boy, that will never—"

"No, no, the military life, that's the ticket," said the Colonel. "By Dion, I envy you! Marches in blistering heat, hostiles sweeping out of the hills . . . university makes a gentleman out of you, but the service makes you a man, what, what?" The Colonel reached over and slapped Timaeus's slight paunch. "Lose that in the army, that's for certain." His eyes gleamed over his gray mustache. Timaeus puffed on his pipe to avoid having to respond.

"What about adventuring?" said the man with the monocle.

"Hmm?" said Timaeus.

"A traditional way for a young nobleman to win fame and fortune," the man with the monocle continued. "Slaying dragons, rescuing damsels in distress, that sort of thing." He waved a hand airily.

"Well," mused Timaeus, "I had thought about it, but I wouldn't know where to start. I mean, what, advertise for quests?"

"Start with the Caverns of Cytorax," suggested the man with the monocle. "They're not far. Scads of monsters down there, I'm told."

"Mmm," mused Timaeus. "But where would I find companions?"

"What about your mates at the university?" asked the Colonel.

"Mostly out of town," said Timaeus. "Back at home or joining the
army. Besides, I'd need more than wizards. Men at arms, spelunkers, cler-
ics . . . you know."

"You need a staff officer," said the Colonel. "Take care of these petty
problems for you."

"If you don't know how to do it yourself," said the man with the monocle, "hire it done." He coughed delicately into a handkerchief. "I know
just the firm."

"A group that assembles expeditions into the caverns?" said Timaeus.

"Umm, rather . . . a firm that handles—matters of delicacy. I should
think they could assemble some experienced adventurers with fair ease.
Pratchitt and Stollitt, Stollitt and Pratchitt. Something like that. I'll give
you the address."

Garni was sweating into his beard. Dwarves weren't used to city sum-
mers. Their native mountains were usually cool.

At least it would be cool in the basement apartment he and Nick Pratchitt shared. It wasn't in the best part of town, but it did have the distinct
advantage of being cheap.

Garni walked down the hall to the apartment door. The door was bolted
shut. He heard giggling on the other side.

Garni knocked. "Nick," he said. "It's Garni. Open up."

There was silence for a moment. Then, through the door Nick said,
"Uh, Garni? I'm busy. Could you come back later?"

Damn. "Look, Nick," said the dwarf, "I just want to get some lunch."

"Just a sec," said Nick. There was a shuffling sound, then a bang. The
door opened a crack. Two hands held out a salami, a loaf of bread, and a
wine jug. "Here," said Nick. He didn't have a shirt on.

Garni sighed. He took the food. Nick closed and bolted the door.

Garni sat down in the hallway by the apartment door. At least he was
out of the sun down here. He munched on the salami and listened to the
giggles.

Personally, he didn't find human women attractive at all. Too gangly.
No facial hair. Garni wondered what Nick thought he was doing. Sidney
would find out. It was only a matter of time. And Nick certainly acted like
he cared what she thought about things.

Oh, well. It wasn't his business. His business was to find a job. Garni was a decent blacksmith, but the guild here in the city had that racket sewed up. Manual labor was about all that was left. He wasn't having any luck finding work. And the rent was three months overdue.

"Mrs. Coopersmith," said Garni. He got to his feet and brushed crumbs off his jerkin. "How nice to see—"

"Where's my money, dwarf?" said the woman. Her arms were floured to her shoulders. Sweat spread in semicircles around her armpits.

"Umm, in just a few days . . ."

The woman scowled. "Dwarves and single men," she said bitterly. "I should have known."

"I'm terribly sorry, but—"

"I want my money Tuesday."

"Of course, Mrs. Coopersmith. We'll . . ."

She turned on her heel and climbed back up the stairway.

Giggles came from the apartment.

Garni sighed and climbed after his landlady. He'd go down to the docks and see if any ships had come in. Maybe he could earn a few pence unloading cargo.

Kraki Kronarsson leaned on the bar. His dirty blond hair hung down around a face that hadn't been shaved in days. The bar creaked under his bulging thews. "Ale," he told the innkeeper.

The innkeeper was walleyed. "Well, honorable," he mumbled, smearing a greasy rag across a tankard under the misapprehension that this was improving the tankard's looks, "there's the matter of your tab, sor."

A group of fishermen at one of the tables was singing loudly. Kraki had been listening to the song and hadn't really heard the innkeeper. He did notice, however, that he wasn't getting any ale. "Vhat?" he said, touching the haft of the broadsword slung over his back—a nervous gesture.

"Three weeks stay," said the innkeeper. "Sixpence a night. Meals and drink. You owe—"

"You qvibbling little snit," shouted the barbarian, standing away from the bar.

The fisherman stopped singing.

"Hoy," said a man at the bar. He wore a workman's apron. His thews bulged almost as much as Kraki's. "No call for such language. Dere's ladies present." An overage and rather blowsy whore hung on the workman's arm.

Kraki reached across the bar and grabbed the innkeeper by the shirt. "I am Kraki, son of Kronar," he shouted. "I grace your sty vith my presence. Be grateful you may show hospitality to so great a lord!"

The workman walked over and put a hand on Kraki's arm. "We do things different 'ere, barbarian," he said. "Yer owes the man."

Kraki punched him in the jaw. The workman stumbled back.

The fishermen rose from their table. The whore dived for the exit.

The workman grabbed a bar stool and broke it over Kraki's head. Kraki didn't bat an eye. "You dare lay hands on the son of a chief?" he bellowed. He grabbed the workman by the waist and hurled him onto the fisherman's table. It collapsed. Tankards of ale flew. The fishermen converged on Kraki.

The innkeeper cowered behind the bar and moaned. Why was it always thugs and barbarians? Why couldn't he have a nice, quiet clientele consisting solely of spinsters and maiden aunts?

Father Thwaite stopped singing when they pushed him through the door to the abbot's office. It was cool in the office. A little chilly, even—at least if you were naked.

"Brother," said the abbot.

Dion help me, I'm in for it now, thought Thwaite. He released his penis. He swayed a bit. He was drunk. Very drunk.

Well, it had been fun.

"I suppose," said the abbot, shuffling some papers on his desk, "that you can explain why you were pissing on the chancellery bell?"

"Yes, Reverend Father," said Thwaite. "See, there was this li'l—" He hiccupped. He continued determinedly, enunciating clearly. "Little spot of tarnish. And urine is acidic. So I . . ."

The abbot sighed heavily. "What am I to do with you?" he said.

Father Thwaite hung his head. "I'm sorry, Reverend," he said. "But the spirit moved me—"

"Spirits, rather," said the abbot. "They say you've been into the brandy again."

"Wine is a susss . . . a sacrament," said Thwaite.

"In vino veritas, yes, Brother," said the abbot. "One of the precepts of our order. Yet moderation is also virtue. Why are you naked?"

"It was . . . warm in the garden," said Thwaite. "An', I thought, why do we clothe ourselves? The Creator gave us skin. So . . ."

The abbot took off his spectacles and folded them up. "Since you refuse to abide by the rules of our order—"

"I'm sorry," said Thwaite, suddenly realizing the depth of his predicament. "I promise I'll—"

"It's a little late for that," said the abbot, rubbing his eyes with thumb and forefinger. "Go to Brother Mortain. He will issue you a begging bowl. Depart from here into the streets of the city."

Thwaite sat down. The flags were chill on his thin, middle-aged buttocks. "You're expelling me from the order?" he said, suddenly sober.

"Not at all," said the abbot. "You may return when you have learned moderation."

"And until then?" said Thwaite, head bowed.

"Leave us. Beg for your living. Live only off the largesse of others. If you obtain more than sixpence, give it to the poor. Drink when you are offered drink; but purchase none yourself."

Father Thwaite rose, bowed, and shuffled backwards to the door, continuing to bow. After the door closed, he stuck his tongue out.

He visited the kitchen before he left and stole a bottle of cheap wine. Dion, he told himself somewhat defensively, permits theft to those who are in need.

The goon's name was George. He looked like a George. His shoulders were nearly as broad as the doorway.

Sidney Stollitt leaned back in her chair. Surreptitiously, she opened the top drawer in her desk. She fished around in the drawer for a dagger. She thought there was one there. She hoped so.

George was picking his teeth with a stiletto. "Nice joint you got," he said, looking around. The drawer of one of the filing cabinets hung off its rails. A roll of flypaper hung from the ceiling, covered with dirty specks. "You wouldn't wanna lose it, huh?" said George.

"All this?" said Sidney. "I'd be devastated." They could torch the place for all she gave a damn. There wasn't a lot invested in the furnishings.

"Ross says you guys been bad," said George. He wandered into the office and over to the file drawer. He studied it with apparent interest.

"Sorry," said Sidney. There didn't seem to be a dagger in the desk drawer after all. Nick had probably done something with it. Where the hell was Nick, anyway? He should have been here hours ago.

"Ross just wants you to know," said George, turning back to face her. "Ross says he wants to be friends."

"I know about Ross," said Sidney.

George looked at her. "You don't know nothing," he said. With a sudden, brutal motion, he punched out the glass in the door. The glass that said PRATCHITT & STOLLITT. It had cost them several shillings to get it etched. Sidney winced.

"If you're going to rip up the place . . ." she said in a menacing tone.

"Friends help out friends," said George. "That's what Ross told me to say."

"Sure," said Sidney. "And we know who our friends are."

George shrugged and disappeared.

Sidney slumped back in the chair. Damn.

Last week, she and Nick had robbed a house on Nob Island. They'd gotten away with a nice little box of jewels. They hadn't fenced the goods through Ross Montiel, who controlled half the fences in this part of town. He was obviously upset; he expected Sidney and Nick to take their business to him.

But she was damned if she'd work with the little scumbag. Maybe it was time to take on an honest proposition or two. Lay low on the burglary.

Where the hell was Nick, anyway?

A face peered in through broken glass. It bore an uncertain expression, red hair, and an unkempt beard. A lit meerschaum pipe stuck out of the middle of it. "I say," it said. "Is there a Mr. Pratchitt or Mr. Stollitt about?"

"No," said Sidney. "I'm Stollitt."

"There must be some mistake," said the face. "Are you Mr. Stollitt's wife?"

"I'm Stollitt," she said. "Sidney Stollitt." The face's accent was aristocratic. It was probably connected to a mark, Sidney thought. "Why don't you come in?"

"Ah," said Timaeus. "Thank you. Sidney's an unusual name for a girl, isn't it?" He turned the doorknob. It came off in his hand. He stared at it for a moment, then pushed on the door, which opened. He came into the office, set the knob on Sidney's desk, and looked around.

"No," said Sidney in complete defiance of the facts, "it's not." The mark wore a red tunic with gold trim. He had sandals on his feet. He was a little pudgy, not too old. The tunic and the pipe screamed fire mage. Sidney hoped he didn't get upset. The building was a firetrap.

Timaeus was dismayed. This Stollitt wench looked tough enough, certainly. She had a long scar on one cheek. Her black hair was tied back in a silver ring; it wouldn't get in the way in combat. She was lean and moved as if she could fight.

But the office was dismal. The glass in the door was broken. There were holes in the plaster. There were mouse droppings on the floor.

"What can I do for you?" asked Sidney, rising and motioning Timaeus toward a chair.

Timaeus sat on the chair gingerly. It hadn't been reupholstered within living memory. Horsehair stuck him through his clothes. "I wish to engage your services to assemble an expedition to venture into the depths of Cytorax Caverns," said Timaeus.

He wanted to go into the dungeon? What did she know about dungeons? She belonged in the city.

Still, anyone who wanted to go to Cytorax was clearly a fool. And you know what they say about fools and their money. "I'm your woman," Sidney said.

II.

"**W**hat *is* all this crap?" asked Nicholas. He lay on an unmade bed, his boots off and his hands behind his head. The morning sun slanted into the basement apartment. Clothes were strewn across the floor. On the rug in the center of the room, Garni had assembled a veritable mountain of equipment.

"This?" said the dwarf, waving at the pile.

"Yeah, that."

"The caverns are dangerous, young Nick. One must be prepared."

"Prepared for a six-month siege?" There were weapons, flasks, pouches of stuff, hand tools, boxes, torches, food, clothing, pieces of cloth. It looked, Nick thought, like the odd lots from an estate sale. "It'd take a week just to catalog it all. You got anything to eat?"

"Hardtack and pemmican."

"Yuck," Nick said.

"It's all I can justify taking," said Garni. "I need the room for more important things."

"Like what?"

Garni picked up an item. "This."

"A mirror? What do you want a mirror for?"

"I don't know. To see around corners, maybe."

"Yeah? I'd take a couple of roast chickens instead. How are you going to fit all this stuff in, anyway?" It was a fair question. The pile stood higher than Garni.

Garni shrugged. He maneuvered objects into his pack, trying to fit everything into the smallest possible space. He'd put something in the pack, move it around, decide it didn't fit precisely right, and try something else. "I'll manage," he said.

Nick noticed a long pole sticking out of the pile. He pried it out; other objects slid and tumbled.

"Be careful!" Garni said.

"Sorry. You'll never get this in, anyway." It was more than double Garni's height.

"Yes, I will," said Garni, taking the pole. He disassembled it; it came apart into four segments.

"What is it?" asked Nick, as Garni strapped the segments to the side of the pack.

"An eleven-foot pole."

"Why eleven feet?"

"There are some things I wouldn't touch with a ten-foot pole," said Garni.

Nick chuckled. "You really think all this stuff is necessary?"

"Some of it we may not use. But any of these things might save our lives."

"If you say so, Garni. Tell me something, though."

"What?"

"How much does all this weigh?"

Garni hefted his pack. "I'd guess about a hundred pounds, all told."

"You're really going to carry a hundred pounds of kit into the caverns?"

"Yes."

"I thought the whole point was to bring stuff *out* of the caverns. Treasure. Jewels. Magic items. How are you going to carry anything out?"

Garni ran his fingers through his beard and smiled. "You'll just have to carry my share of the treasure, Nicholas."

It was morning in the city of Urf Durfal. The houseboy of the Inn of the Villein Impaled staggered out into Roderick Square, carrying two buckets. In the center of the square stood the equestrian statue of Grand Duke Roderick, father of the current ruler of the city; and around the statue was a fountain, spouting water borne from the hills by the city's aqueducts. The houseboy went to the fountain and filled his buckets. The floors of the inn badly needed mopping, as they did every morning: the inn's clientele tended to carouse in particularly messy fashion—nor were they all capable of keeping down the rotgut the taproom served.

Around the square, merchants put up awnings to protect perishable merchandise from the fierce sun. The day looked to be a hot one; there was nary a cloud in the sky. Except, perhaps, for a figurative cloud gathering over the head of Sidney Stollitt.

She stood in the shadow of Roderick's statue. With her was a mule cart and a drover. The drover was reclining with his straw hat pulled down over his eyes. Sidney, unable to contain herself, was pacing and scanning the faces of passersby.

Dawn, she had said. And here it was half past seven.

Garni, at least, had been prompt. She'd sent him out after Father Thwaite; Timaeus had advanced them each a small sum to purchase equipment, and Sidney was reasonably certain that the cleric had found a way to turn his into booze. Garni was under orders to examine every body he found in the gutter. Odds were, one was Thwaite.

Nicholas Pratchitt approached. He was wearing black leather—enough to turn a footpad's blade, but not heavy enough to qualify as real armor. Sidney scowled; that might do for the city streets but was hardly appropriate for a dungeon expedition. As he neared, she saw that he had circles under his blue eyes and his black hair was mussed. He looked as if he hadn't slept all night. He was whistling a sprightly tune.

"Where the hell have you been?" snapped Sidney.

"Am I late?" Nick asked unrepentently.

"*Garni* was here on time," Sidney said. "*Garni*'s reliable. *Garni* keeps his commitments."

Nick winced. The unspoken corollary was that, since he shared a flat with Garni and had not appeared at the same time as the dwarf, he'd spent the night elsewhere. In another bed. Someone *else's* bed. A bed, to belabor the point, that was neither his own nor Sidney's. With some relief, he saw Kraki lumbering out of the inn. The barbarian held a large mug of ale in one hand, which he drained in three neat gulps. "Hallo," he said. "Ve go now?"

"You're late," said Sidney.

"Late?" said Kraki. He looked around. "Vhere is everybody?"

"They're late, too," said Sidney.

Kraki shrugged. "Late," he said, "is if everybody else gets there first. So I not late." He raised his head and sniffed. One of the vendors at the edge of the square had fired a charcoal grill and was cooking something. "Am hungry," said Kraki, and lumbered away.

"Keep an eye on him," Sidney said to Nick. "Keep him out of trouble." Nick grinned at her and followed the barbarian.

There was an explosion. A brilliant flash lit the square. Sidney Stollitt hit the ground and rolled across the cobblestones into the cover of the rim around the fountain. The mules neighed and bucked; the drover came alive and yanked at the reins. Muffled screams came from the merchants' stalls.

Timaeus d'Asperge, *Magister Igniti,* stood in the fountain. Smoke billowed about him. The water hissed, quenching the flames of the explosion in which he had appeared.

"Good morning, Stollitt," he said, peering at her prone form over the lip of the fountain. "Sorry I'm late." He stepped out of the fountain, shaking his legs.

Sidney sat up. "Is this how you usually get around?" she asked. "Because if it is, I may change my mind about this deal."

Timaeus fumbled for his pipe in a mildly embarrassed way. "Mmm, well, no," he said. "Usually not. Teleportation takes a certain amount of power. I wouldn't have used it, but . . . well, I overslept, I'm afraid, and I was running a bit late. Where is everybody?"

"Good question," said Sidney, brushing herself off.

"There's no one here but you and me," Timaeus said, peering about petulantly.

"Nick and Kraki are over there," she said, pointing toward a vendor's awning. Timaeus looked nearsightedly in that direction; he didn't see them but took her word for it.

"And what of the others? I commissioned you to assemble a group, and yet I find us standing here, two hours after we were supposed to have departed, with nary a soul to be seen."

"You didn't show up," sneered Sidney. "Why should they?"

Timaeus colored. "As to that," he said, "I *am* financing this expedition, after all. My hirelings may expect to wait on my presence; but I, hardly, on theirs. Now—"

"Hireling, am I?" said Sidney nastily.

"In a manner of . . . I say . . . is that the dwarf?"

Garni was trundling a wheelbarrow toward the statue. Thwaite lay in the barrow, legs flopping over the front, his tonsured pate banging against the barrow's metal surface as the wheel bumped over stones. The cleric was obviously unconscious.

"Here we are," said Garni cheerfully. "Ready to go?"

Timaeus stared at the brown-robed cleric, apparently dumbfounded. He stuck a finger into Thwaite's ribs experimentally. "What's wrong with the man?" he inquired.

"He's unconscious," said Sidney.

"I can see that," said Timaeus. "Is he subject to regular fainting spells?"

Garni chortled. "Yup," he said. "He regularly faints when he's downed a hogshead or two of wine."

There was a long moment of silence. "Are you certain," Timaeus asked Sidney unhappily, "that this potted priest is the only cleric you can find who will accompany us?"

"Look," Sidney said with irritation, "priests sit in temples and collect gold from suckers. Why go wander around a hole in the ground looking for more gold? Especially when the hole is populated by nasty monsters with large, pointy teeth. Sitting around's a lot easier. Finding a cleric willing to risk the caverns wasn't easy."

Timaeus sighed and shook his head.

"Thwaite's okay," said Garni. "When he's sober."

"Which, judging by available evidence, is never," said Timaeus. "Ah, well, *ad praisens ova cras pullis sunt meliora,* as the poet says."

Charcoal smoke swirled into the air and an interesting aroma with it. Several little pastries warmed on a grill over the brazier. The vendor turned them with his one good hand; the other arm ended in a cloth-bound stump.

"What's your pleasure, good sirs?" said the vendor.

Kraki pointed to one of the pastries. "Vhat is that?" he asked.

"Greep tart," grunted the vendor.

"Vhat?" said Kraki. "Vhat is greep?"

"Huh," said the man, waving his spatula. "You don't know what greeps are? Well, when the air goes chill . . ."

GREEP TART

"Well, when air goes chill and the leaves begin to turn, that's when the greep flocks gather. They turn, turn above the painted leaves, wheeling in their thousands, their thousand thousands. The sky is dark with them, the flocks, the many greeps. Their tiny call is magnified so that it becomes a constant honk, the cry of a god, blanketing the woodland with the sound.

"I remember it still, that constant honk, that bleating, that call. . . .

"We fled, my family and I, from our homestead in the hills of Cordonia. Mayhap we lived foolishly close to the Eastern Realm, but our homestead was old, ours for generations, and we farmed rich bottomland we would not readily abandon.

"But when the trolls began to move, we had no recourse but to flee, lest we be butchered as our neighbors were. So we fled, fled into the Cordon Wood, with naught but the clothes on our backs and a tool or two. We left our fields, our home, our comforts.

"The elves granted us refuge. They gave us acorn meal, and said that we might live within the wood if we so wished. We were grateful, for we had nowhere else to go, no way to win our livelihood. But the conditions they placed upon us, oh, the conditions were onerous.

"We were not to slay a single animal within the elvenwood, though there were beavers in the streams and deer among the trees. We were not to cut a single tree, though we might burn such branches as were already dead. Certain mushrooms and plants, also, were forbidden us; they were too precious, we were told.

"They stood there in their merry green, their damnable big eyes twinkling, peering at us, and expecting us to kowtow to them, our protectors, our benefactors.

"We could not sow a crop, for the earth lay in the shade of the trees, and no crop would grow on such ground. We could not cut the trees to clear a field, for the elves forbade it. We gleaned a meager sustenance from the forest—mushrooms, berries, acorns, and nuts. But the deer we could not touch, nor the squirrels, nor any of the abundant life that flourished about our little hut.

"The winter was cruel. We cleared the forest round about of dead branches; each day, I was forced to forage farther and father afield for tinder. And our tiny store of nuts and dried berries rapidly diminished.

"We lost our youngest child that winter, my wife too starved herself to nurse him adequately. And all of us were lean.

"The spring brought some relief. Ferns sprang up anew, and herbs. We ate the tender shoots on the trees, anything at all that we could stomach. Gradually, we regained some semblance of health, though always we were hungry.

"But as the weather cooled toward autumn, and as the greeps gathered for their migration, we faced another winter, a winter we knew we could not again survive. . . .

"In Alcala, they string nets among the trees. The greep flocks come down to rest and are caught. Then they gut the birds and roast them. . . . In Alcala, the greep migration is a festival time, a time for celebration.

"But the elves would not countenance the death of a single bird.

"The flocks darkened the skies, and the honks rang counterpoint to the grumbles of my stomach, the stomachs of my children. . . .

"And so I fashioned an awkward bow and strung it with my daughter's hair. I shot seven of the birds, seven small birds, to feed us. And I made them into tarts.

"They were delicious. The gods' ambrosia cannot taste so fine. The flesh was sweet, satisfying, the finest thing we had ever tasted.

"We slept well that night.

"But the following morning, the elf-lord came. He grinned up at me, his pointy ears poking beside his crown of laurel, and told us we had been naughty.

"Then his soldiers took me and struck off my hand in punishment for my theft. For that is what the elves termed it, a theft from nature, a violation of their covenant with my family.

"They drove us from the elvenwood. Perforce, we found our way to this city. Now, I make a meager living selling my greep tarts and gain a meager measure of revenge from knowing that with each tart I sell, another of the birds dies.

"Come, taste the flesh. It is sweet and delectable. There is no taste to compare with that of the greep, the greeps that sweep the skies above the elvenwood, their numbers so great that they darken the sun."

"Is good," said Kraki. Nick shuddered. He'd nibbled on one tart, decided it had all the consistency and none of the culinary attractions of stewed rat, and had offered the rest to an alley cat. The cat had given him a contemptuous glare and had taken off for parts unknown.

"Are we all quite ready?' said Timaeus impatiently.

The drover clucked and the mule cart began to move, eastward into the sun, toward the Caverns of Cytorax.

The mouth of the caverns was blocked by a striped, red and white gate. To one side stood a small building. The travellers entered it and followed the signs that pointed to the customs post.

Inside a small chamber, a bureaucrat wearing an elaborate and ill-fitting blue uniform sat on a stool. He stamped Sidney's papers and motioned her on. Kraki walked up to the bureaucrat, who held out his hand.

"Your papers, sir?" said the bureaucrat.

Kraki yanked the official half over the counter. "LET ME PASS, PIG, OR YOU VILL TASTE THE BITE OF MY STEEL!" he roared. His mighty thews bulged alarmingly.

"Let him down, Kraki," Sidney said.

"Guards! Guards!" screamed the bureaucrat, clawing at Kraki's hands.

Kraki threw the official across the room, whirled, and drew his sword. The side door smashed open. Soldiers poured in. "Drop the sword, barbarian!" shouted one. They spread out along the walls, ringing the party.

"I am a free man!" shouted Kraki. "I vill not be herded like sheep! I spit on your papers!"

"Better do what he says, buddy," said Nick.

"No!" shouted Kraki. "I kill them all. Then ve go."

"Impractical," said Timaeus.

"Come on, Kraki," said Sidney. "What happens when we come back?"

Kraki glanced at her, then turned back to keep an eye on the soldiers. "Hah?"

"We go in the caverns. We slay lots of monsters. We come back with piles of loot. We're tired and beaten up—and we have to fight our way out through dozens and dozens of soldiers. Why not show him your papers, huh, pal?"

Kraki thought about this for a moment, then sheathed his sword. The soldiers looked relieved. The bureaucrat got up slowly, checking to make sure nothing was broken. "Don't got none," said Kraki sullenly.

There was silence for a moment.

"No papers?" said the bureaucrat. "That's impossible."

"In vild North, ve have no need for papers," insisted Kraki. "I say I am Kraki, son of Kronar; any who say different, I kill for the lying cowards that they are. That is how ve identify ourselves in Northland!"

The bureaucrat cleared his throat. "Quite. However, all foreigners are issued letters of transit when they cross the border."

"Yah?" said Kraki. "I valk across border. No vone give me papers. No vone stop me." He pulled his sword about two inches out of its scabbard and let it fall back. "No vone try." He glared at the bureaucrat. "You vant to try?"

"Er . . ."

"Surely, good sir," Timaeus intervened, "there are regulations to cover this eventuality. The discovery of an undocumented alien within the Grand Duke's realm can hardly be an unique occurrence."

"Oh, yes," said the bureaucrat happily, "there is a . . . regulation . . ." His voice trailed off. An expression of dismay passed across his face. He backed toward the soldiers.

"What is it?" asked Timaeus.

"When an undocumented alien is found within the Grand Duchy of Athelstan . . ."

"Yes?"

The soldiers tensed.

"He must be jailed—"

Kraki roared a challenge and drew his sword. Hastily, the soldiers prepared for combat.

"*Unless!*" shouted the bureaucrat. The tableau held.

"Unless vhat?" said Kraki.

The bureaucrat spoke rapidly. "Unless he is within ten miles of the border, in which case he must be escorted across it."

Kraki considered this for a moment. "Vell, then," he said, sheathing his weapon and smiling slowly. "I vill go qvietly."

"Yes," said the bureaucrat unhappily, "but I believe the provision is intended to apply to raiders or people who wander across the border by mistake—not to those who have been living illegally in the grand duchy for some time. . . ."

The captain of the guards eyed Kraki's heavily-muscled torso. "If regs give us a choice between fighting *that* and escorting him ten feet into the caverns, guess what my choice is."

There were mumbles of agreement from the other soldiers.

The cavern was a great gash in the earth, far wider than it was tall, like the mouth of some vast creature. At one end was daylight, blinding compared to the dimness within. At the other end, the chamber broke apart into shafts and passageways, tendrils extending off into the depths. Within the chamber, not far from the customs post, lay the village of Gateway.

"Why did we have to go through customs, anyway?" Nick asked Garni.

"The earth below thirty cubits belongs to us—to the dwarves," Garni said.

"That's right," said Timaeus hefting the wheelbarrow containing Father Thwaite over the rocky floor. "Although the Caverns of Cytorax lie entirely within the boundaries of Athelstan, by ancient treaty with the Dwarven Kings, the grand duchy extends only thirty cubits below the surface of the earth. Below that depth is dwarven territory."

Gateway was built of rock quarried from the chamber walls, limestone loosely mortared together. The buildings were small, the walls somewhat rickety; but then, no weather penetrated here, and the cavern remained always at the same chill temperature.

Shops lined the street. An orc wearing an apron stood in one; behind him stood bottles of liquor and bales of weed. "Duty free?" the orc grunted. Sidney smiled and shook her head. She had been here before. Since Gateway lay wholly within the caverns, it was outside Athelstani jurisdiction. It was sometimes convenient to do business beyond the reach of the grand duke's justice.

A smallish lizardman bounded up and zeroed in on Timaeus, the most prosperous looking of the group. He tugged on the wizard's robe. "Welcome to cavernth, honored thir," the lizard said, hopping rapidly to keep up. "Need hotel? Know all good rethtauranth. Act ath guide? Thee many hithtoric thights? Rent thithter? Hourly rateth."

"Get lost," Nick said menacingly. The lizardman hopped away from him a little.

"No, no," said Timaeus. "None of us is familiar with the depths of Cytorax Caverns. An experienced native guide could prove invaluable."

"Yeth! Yeth!" said the lizardman, hopping closer. "Lenny knowth all about cavernth! Lenny show you! Lenny take you to good treasure, yeth! Lenny ith good guide! Reathonable rateth!"

"This is a mistake," Sidney said.

"What do you mean?" said Timaeus a little huffily.

"Just look at the little reptile," said Sidney. "Give him the opportunity, and he'd sell you as quickly as his sister."

Lenny looked at her with wounded eyes. "Not true! Not true!" he whined. "Lenny honetht lithard! Honetht!"

"Really," said Timaeus, "I hadn't expected racial slurs from you, Miss Stollitt. Given trust and support, I'm sure this young creature—"

"Yeth!" said Lenny. "Trutht Lenny! Lenny find treasure! Big treasure!"

"Look," said Nick to Timaeus, "forget it. It's a dumb idea. Okay?"

Timaeus bristled. "Nonsense. None of us is familiar with Cytorax. We need a guide. I'm sure this fellow will do us proud." He patted the lizardman on the head; Lenny looked back adoringly.

"Twenty thilver pennies per hour?" Lenny said.

Timaeus cleared his throat. "Sidney, please take care of the details, if you will." He wandered across the street to look at one of the stalls.

Sidney gritted her teeth. She glared at the lizardman. "Two pennies an hour, you little bastard," she said, fighting to keep control of her voice. "And not a penny more."

The lizard looked disappointed that he wasn't bargaining with Timaeus. "Three," he said. "And one perthent of any treasure."

"Two and a half—and no part of any treasure, you reptile. And if you abandon us down there, I'll hunt you down and kill you—and your sister, too. Got me?"

Lenny looked at her with wounded eyes. "Lenny not do that," he said sadly. "Lenny good guide. Lenny help. Need three pennieth. Thtandard rate."

Sidney sighed. "Three pennies," she said. Lenny bounced up and down in joy. He bounded off after Timaeus.

"Thir! Thir! Not shop here. Lenny show you better thtore. Duty free itemth. Good pritheth."

"What are we getting into?" said Nick.

Kraki grunted and picked up the handles of the wheelbarrow. "Don't vorry," he said. "If lizard con us, I tvist head off." He strode off down the street.

"That's very reassuring," said Garni doubtfully. He hoisted his gear and followed.

Sidney shook her head and sighed.

Nick patted her on the bottom. "Don't worry, kiddo," he said.

She glared at him. "And why the hell not?" she muttered.

III.

The passageway, Garni thought, had obviously been a mine shaft at one time. He raised his lantern and studied the beams that held up the roof; they looked several centuries old. He doubted they were entirely sound.

Up ahead, Lenny had stopped at a thick wooden door. Light seeped out around its edges. "Thththth!" Lenny said, putting one finger to his crocodilian snout. The others joined him.

"Okay," said Garni in a low voice. "Everybody ready?"

The others readied their weapons. Timaeus nodded.

Garni threw himself against the door. It slammed open. He stumbled into the room beyond, waving his battle-axe and shouting a battle cry.

Swords swiped through the air above Garni's head. Two trolls stood inside the room, one on either side of the door. They'd been prepared for intruders—but obviously expected someone taller than the dwarf.

Unable to stop himself under the weight of his pack, Garni staggered all the way across the room to fetch up against one wall. One troll turned to charge the dwarf, while the other kept a wary eye on the door.

Kraki stood blocking the doorway, studying Garni's axe work. "Well?" said Sidney, prodding him from behind.

"Hah?" Kraki said. "Oh! Ve kill things now?"

"Yes, you idiot!"

"Hokay, hokay," said the barbarian huffily, drawing his sword. "You don't have to get upset." He hurled himself into the room. "YAH HA!" he exclaimed, plunging his sword into one troll's torso, whipping it out, and hacking off the head of the other.

Both trolls fell.

Kraki flexed his muscles heroically, looking pleased. He posed with one foot atop a trollish body. Garni lowered his battle-axe to the ground and stood panting, leaning on its haft.

The troll under Kraki's foot reached up and ripped open the barbarian's calf. It rolled for its sword. Kraki, astounded, stood with one foot in the air, bleeding from his leg wound. "Vhat going on?" he complained.

"Shut up and fight," panted Garni. The troll stood up clutching its sword. Snarling, Kraki ran to it and hacked off both its arms, then both its legs for good measure.

The limbs began to inch across the floor toward the glaring, limbless torso. Garni fumbled with an arm, trying to keep it away. The other limbs began to heal back in place.

"Vatch out!" shouted Kraki. Behind Garni's back, the other troll, blindly fumbling across the floor, had found its head. Kraki charged across the room and kicked the head out of the troll's hands. The head bit him on the foot.

"Ouch!" said Kraki. "I kill you now." He stabbed at the head gingerly, trying to avoid his foot. He hopped on his free leg. The head gnawed on his toes.

"Those things can regenerate," said Sidney worriedly from the doorway. She tossed a dagger at one trollish arm, trying to keep it from getting back to its torso.

"Quite so," said Timaeus.

"How can we kill them?" asked Nick, peering intently at the trolls, his face ferretlike in the torchlight.

"If I recall my natural philosophy," Timaeus said, "only fire or acid will do."

"Great," said Nick. "I'm all out of Greek fire, I'm afraid. How . . . ?"

"Leave it to me," said Timaeus, as Kraki hopped around the room stabbing at the head on his foot. "Stand back." Timaeus cleared his throat, held his pipe, and gestured, speaking Words of mystic power. A ball of flame appeared in his hand; he hurled it into the room.

The ball exploded.

There was a blinding flash.

There was a tremendous, thundering boom.

Flame splashed out of the room, billowing up and down the corridor for dozens of yards.

Sidney, Nick, and Lenny were hurled down the corridor like straws in a wind.

The caverns shook with the boom. Dust and pebbles fell from the corridor roof. Beams creaked and shuddered.

Father Thwaite fell out of the wheelbarrow. "Where am I?" he said faintly.

"Well," said Timaeus happily. "That certainly did the trick."

The magician was completely untouched by the explosion and breathed the thick smoke without discomfort. By touch, he found Garni's lantern, which the blast had snuffed, and relit it.

The room was devastated.

The rug on the floor was burnt to a cinder. The wooden table at the back of the room was burning merrily. The trolls were charred and motionless. Garni was unconscious on the floor, his clothing smoking. Kraki's skin was covered with soot. He stood with an idiot grin on his face, one leg in the air with a charred trollish head on the raised foot. As Timaeus watched, the barbarian's eyes turned up into his head, and he tumbled to the floor. The floor shook.

"Oh," Timaeus said. "I say."

Nick stumbled into the room, supporting himself against one wall. His hair was singed. "I think I've seen the spell before," he said hoarsely. "Fireball, wasn't it?" He coughed and waved the smoke away from his face.

"Er . . . yes."

"What's the diameter of a fireball?"

"Ah . . . thirty feet or so."

"Hmm." Nick eyeballed the room. "I'd say this room is about ten by ten."

"Er . . . Yes," said Timaeus. "Given the volume of the spell, a certain amount of splashback was to be expected."

A green snout peered around the edge of the door. Lenny looked in hesitantly.

"A certain amount?" Nick said incredulously. "You're an educated man. You figure it out. The spell's volume of effect is *ten times* as big as this room."

"Ah . . ."

"We're lucky to be alive! Have you looked at the corridor? I just hope the support beams hold long enough for us to get out."

Timaeus was turning pink.

Sidney pulled herself into the room. She moved gingerly, as if unconvinced that she was still alive. "Nifty spell," she said sarcastically. "Real neat."

"Look . . ." said Timaeus.

Thwaite staggered into the room. The cleric looked haggard, hung-over, and queasy. He stopped and peered around. He noticed the charred corpses, the unconscious bodies, and the gore that had splashed everywhere. Thwaite looked even queasier. He staggered back out of the room. There was a retching sound from the hall.

Timaeus sighed. "Look," he said softly, "I'll be more careful next time. Fire doesn't much affect me, you see, and sometimes I forget what it can do to others. I'll try to give you some warning. Is that acceptable?"

Nick and Sidney looked at each other. "It's your expedition," said Nick. "You twit," said Sidney.

Timaeus bristled. "Madam, I've given you my apology—"

"Don't call me madam," snarled Sidney.

Thwaite staggered back into the room. He fetched up against a wall. "Hello," he asked the wall, "do I know you?"

"As a matter of fact—" said Timaeus.

Sidney sighed. "It's Sidney, Father," she said. "And this is Magister d'Asperge, the leader of the expedition I was telling you about." She glared at Timaeus.

"Hmm?" the cleric said, studying the wall. "I vaguely recall . . ."

"The expedition into the Caverns of Cytorax," Timaeus said. Thwaite shuddered. "Which you joined by signing the papers of enlistment in my office not forty-eight hours ago."

"The Caverns of Cytorax?" Thwaite said in horror. "What in Dion's name did I do that for?"

"You must have been drunk," said Timaeus dryly.

Thwaite cleared his throat. His head was pounding. "A state I much prefer to my current one," he said. Glancing around the room, Thwaite noticed Garni's sprawled body. Blisters were beginning to form on the dwarf's face. "Oh dear," Thwaite said. "Hmm." He pushed off the wall, staggered over to the dwarf, and dropped to the floor. Timaeus made an abortive gesture to catch the priest, then realized Thwaite had merely fallen to his knees.

Thwaite studied the dwarf. He held a wrist, thumped Garni's chest, and felt the dwarf's forehead. Thwaite closed his eyes and concentrated for a moment.

"Yes," he said faintly. From within his robes, he produced a silver aspergillum and a stick of incense. He leaned over and lit the incense at the burning table, then wafted the stick over the dwarf's body, murmuring a prayer. He stood the stick on the floor and sprinkled the body with water from the aspergillum, praying as he did.

Under the cleric's ministrations, Garni's blisters began visibly to recede.

Perhaps, Timaeus thought, the cleric would be of some assistance after all. He scratched an ear and surveyed the blasted room and his injured companions with embarrassment. "Idiot," he muttered to himself.

The room was carved from the rock; sedimentary banding along the walls plunged at an odd angle toward the floor. The table, no longer burning, stood at the rear of the room. Underneath the table lay a trunk, bound with leather. Straw ticking lay in a clump against one wall.

Garni was still too weak to rise, but that didn't stop him from directing the search. "Righto," he said. "Nick, lad, search the bodies. Sidney, take a look at the chest. If you would be so kind, Magister d'Asperge, do you think you could examine the table? Father? The straw . . . ? Thank you."

Kraki propped himself up against the wall, put both hands behind his head, and grinned, watching the others work. Thwaite had bound up the barbarian's leg, but his injuries excused him from the labor, at least for now.

Nick went over the body of the man the trolls had killed. "A purse," he said. He poured its contents into his hand. "Four shillings and—um— eight pence ha'penny." Lenny came over and stared at the silver avidly. Nick poured it back and fixed the purse to his belt. "A dagger—a cheap one."

"Pockets?" asked Garni. "Are the clothes worth anything?"

"They're sliced up," Nick said, "and kind of bloody."

"Never mind. Slit open the belt."

"Hey, what do you know! A gold sovereign, sewn into the leather." Garni grinned into his beard.

Timaeus yanked open the table's only drawer. A cockroach crawled out. "Zounds," he said, and jumped back. He pointed at the cockroach and started muttering a spell. Before he could complete it, the roach had disappeared into a crack. Timaeus stopped muttering; smoke curled from his finger as the aborted spell dissipated. He shook his finger painfully and cursed under his breath, then reached into the drawer. "Empty," he reported, "save for this paper." He pulled it out. "It appears to be a note of some kind. Written in—I believe it is orcish script."

"Lenny read! Lenny read!" said the lizardman, bounding up and down. Timaeus handed it to him. Lenny puzzled over it. "Heat oil in heavy thkillet," he read slowly. "Fry one pound thalted manthflesh—"

"Yoiks," said Timaeus in disgust. "A recipe."

"If you would, Magister d'Asperge," said Garni, "the rest of the table."

"What rest? There's only the one draw."

Garni sighed. "Anything behind the drawer?"

"Hmm?" Timaeus pulled it out. "No."

"Does the drawer have a false bottom?"

"Ah . . . no."

"Does the top of the table lift off?"

"No."

"Flip it over. That's right. Now, pry out the table legs."

"Is this necessary?"

"Professionalism, Magister! We must be thorough! Does the leg sound hollow?"

"No."

"Test it."

"Eh? What do you mean?"

"I've known magic wands to be disguised as table legs," Garni said.

"Ye gods . . . All right." Timaeus pointed the table leg at a wall, and said *"Klaathu . . . Proujansky . . . Moshalu!"*

Nothing happened.

"The other legs."

With mounting impatience, Timaeus tried the other three legs. Nothing.

"Knock all over the tabletop."

"I say, this is a bit thick."

"Wouldn't you feel like an idiot if we passed up a treasure just because we weren't thorough?" said Garni.

"I suppose, but—"

"Professionalism, my dear Magister! Professionalism! Knock, my good man!"

"Non omnia possumus omnes," Timaeus muttered—but he knocked on the tabletop. It sounded like solid, slightly scorched oak.

"All right, hand me the legs." Timaeus did so. Garni took out his boot knife and started whittling.

"What the devil are you doing?"

Garni shrugged. "There might be secret compartments . . . items glued into the wood . . . anything. You never know."

Timaeus rolled his eyes and reached for his pipe. He started tamping it with pipeweed.

"Ah . . ." said Father Thwaite.

"Yes, good cleric?" said Garni.

"Ah, this straw seems to be matted together with . . ."

"Yes?"

"Well, from the stench, I would venture to guess that it's . . . troll urine."

"Indeed. Well, persevere, Father! Persevere!"

"Yes," said Thwaite faintly.

"Nick, lad?" said Garni. He'd reduced one table leg to shavings and was working on the second.

"Yes, Garni?" Nick said, grinning.

"The troll bodies."

"What about them? They don't have any clothing . . ."

"You never know what might be in the stomachs."

Nick lost his grin. "Stomachs?"

"Yes. Trolls are not very bright, you know. They've been known to swallow the most extraordinary things."

Grimacing, Nick moved toward one of the trolls, dagger in hand.

Timaeus had finished tamping his pipe. He brought one finger toward the bowl . . .

There was an explosion.

Everyone dived for cover.

Flames raged around Timaeus's head for a moment, then dissipated in smoke.

Unscathed, Timaeus puffed contentedly on his pipe. He looked around the room and noticed that everyone was hugging the floor. "Oh, really," he said. "Can't a man smoke in peace?" He puffed some more.

"How are you doing with the trunk, Sidney?" Garni asked.

"Just a minute," Sidney said. She pressed an ear to the steamer trunk and tapped over it with a finger. She drew back, stood up, and took off her pack. She took an ear trumpet out of the pack and tapped over the chest again, listening with the trumpet.

Then, she brought out a Y-shaped silver wand and, holding the forked end of the wand in both hands, moved it over the chest and down all four sides. The wand remained stable.

She stepped back and looked at the chest, thinking for a moment. Then she took a coil of rope from her pack. She looped it around the chest and moved as far across the room as she could. She gave the rope a tug. The chest moved slightly. Nothing else happened. She yanked harder. The chest moved a little farther.

She coiled the rope and looked at the chest thoughtfully.

"Yust open it," said Kraki.

She glanced at him. "It could be trapped."

"Bah," said Kraki.

"Everyone out of the room," said Sidney.

"This is silliness," said Kraki. "Ve are vasting time."

Nick stumbled out of the room, green trollish ichor dripping from his sleeves. He looked rather greenish himself. The others followed him, Kraki last and reluctantly.

Sidney dragged the heavy oak tabletop up to the chest. She tipped it up along its long edge and crouched behind it. She laid a metal rod, several feet in length, over the tabletop. The rod had a claw at the end; carefully, she used it to pry open the chest lid.

The lid opened. Nothing else happened.

Sidney peered over the tabletop and into the chest. She probed the interior with the rod.

Nothing happened.

She stood up and let the tabletop fall with a bang.

Everyone rushed into the room. "Are you all right?" Nick asked.

"Sure," she said, peering in the chest.

Lenny bounded up and down. "Lenny lead you to good treasure! Magic! Thilver! Jewelth!"

"Two bags of pemmican," she said, "and a jar of—" she sniffed, and took a swig "—rather flat ginger beer."

Lenny stopped bounding up and down.

"Well," said Timaeus scathingly. "It was certainly foresighted of us to bring the wheelbarrow along. How could we ever get this munificent treasure out otherwise?"

Kraki fingered the edge of his sword and eyed Lenny thoughtfully.

By the time they left the room, they'd reduced everything in it to flinders. "Now that," said Garni happily, "is what I call a professional job."

IV.

Where water had run into the terrestrial depths, it had left a slantwise crack in the limestone, a shaft scattered with boulders and pebbles, potholes and minor cliffs. It had scoured the shaft smooth, burnishing the stone to a yellow luster.

Lenny bounded easily from boulder to boulder, springing down the slope to stand where rocks gave temporary purchase. "Lenny find better treasure!" he yipped. "Thecret treasure! Jewelth! Magic! Lenny show you!"

The others found the going more difficult. At times, the slope approached the vertical. They descended slowly, searching for handholds among the potholes and boulders.

Garni hammered a piton into the groove between a boulder and the streambed, and ran a rope through the piton's iron loop. Holding both ends of the rope, he backed cautiously down the slope. The others watched him.

He reached a flatter area where he could stand unsupported and called, "All right, who's next?"

Sidney spoke to Timaeus. "Are you sure you want to go down there?"

"Absolutely," he said, puffing on his pipe. "Adventure awaits us in the depths of Cytorax! Forward, my friends! *Fortuna favet fortibus!*"

"Lenny lead! Follow Lenny!" the lizardman yipped faintly from far down the shaft.

"Where is he taking us?" Sidney asked.

"To fame and fortune!" said Timaeus.

"More likely to an early grave," Nick muttered.

"I trust him implicitly," Timaeus huffed, and grabbed Garni's rope.

* * *

Drizhnakh, Garfok, and Spug were playing cards in front of the fire. They were on guard duty. No one took guard duty too seriously.

Drizhnakh and Garfok were both cheating. They both knew that they were both cheating. Spug didn't have a clue, of course.

They were playing Spatzle. For money. If they'd been playing anything else, Drizhnakh and Garfok might have played honestly. It wasn't too likely, of course, but they might have. Spatzle is played by orcish children. It is completely mindless—on the same level as Go Fish or Old Maid. There's no strategy. Both Drizhnakh and Garfok were bored with it. Which is why they had to spice the game up with some judicious cheating.

The problem was that Spazle was the only thing Spug would play. It was the only thing Spug *could* play. Spug was, as his orcish companions would have so charmingly put it, "a maroon." Not that your run-of-the-mill orc is exactly the world's leading intellectual light, but you get the idea.

As far as Drizhnakh and Garfok were concerned, cheating was the real game, anyway. It was a given that Spug would lose. The only question was whether Drizhnakh or Garfok would win. Skill at cardsharping, not skill at cards, was the requirement for victory.

Drizhnakh and Garfok were tired of Spatzle. For them, it had lost its charm. It was no longer pleasing. It had become otiose. As Garfok put it, "Dis is a dumb friggin' game, Spug." He threw down his cards.

Spug looked injured. "I likes it, Garfok," he said. "It's fun."

"I is had enough, ya maroon," riposted Garfok.

"Pick up da hand, Garfok," Drizhnakh said menacingly.

"Piss up yer aunt's leg! I says I's had it wiv dis game," said Garfok.

"Dat's cause you got a lousy hand, ya dipshit. Pick it up," Drizhnakh said.

"Yeah!" said Spug. "You is just got a lousy hand! You is just upset cause you is gonna lose!"

"Piss on you," replied Garfok.

Drizhnakh drew his sword and buried its sharp end in the table before Garfok. "Pick up da cards!" he yelled.

Garfok picked up his cards. "Tree of fangs," he said sullenly, throwing a card on the table.

Drizhnakh pulled a card out of his sleeve. Spug didn't notice. Garfok did. "Trump," Drizhnakh said. "Raise two copper."

Garfok sighed. Then he saw a flash of green by the door. He dropped his cards on the table, then tipped his chair back, keeping his balance by putting his knees under the table. He reached outside the door, grabbed Lenny by the neck, and pulled the lizardman into the room.

Lenny's legs windmilled as he tried to break free. "Hey!" said Garfok. "Look at dis! It's Lenny da Lizard."

Lenny went limp. "Lenny come to thay hello," he said hesitantly.

Drizhnakh smiled; his tusks made it a rather menacing smile. "It's da lizard kid," he said to Spug, "come ta visit." He laid his cards carefully on the table.

"Yeah," said Spug, nodding wisely. "An' just in time for lunch, too."

"I haven't had lizard in months an' months," said Drizhnakh thoughtfully.

"Say, kid," said Garfok, still holding Lenny by the neck. "Whatcha doin' down here anyway, huh?"

"Lenny going for thtroll," the lizardman said despairingly.

Drizhnakh poked the fire. "Where's dat roastin' skewer?" he asked Spug.

Spug started pawing through a pile of gear. "It's in here somewheres," he said.

"You got a load of tourists wiv you, kid?" Garfok asked, shaking the lizardman.

Lenny nodded.

"Dey is comin' down da shaft?"

Lenny hung motionless.

"Found dat skewer yet?" Garfok asked. Drizhnakh grunted and threw another log on the fire; he stared at Lenny and licked his chops.

Lenny shuddered. "Yeth," he said despairingly. "Five humanth. One dwarf."

"Youmans? Hey, Drizhnakh, sounds like mansflesh for lunch instead."

Spug nodded enthusiastically. "I like mansflesh," he confided.

"Tell ya what, buddy," Garfok said thoughtfully. "You go back to da tourists. Take 'em to Rog."

Lenny shook his head violently. "Not Rog," he said. "Lenny not go to Rog. Rog bad monthter. Kill Lenny."

Garfok sighed. "Listen to me, kiddo. Dese guys, da youmans an' such, dey fight Rog. You hang back. If Rog kills 'em, dat's fine wiv us. We'll letcha go home. If dey kills Rog, dat's good, too. Rog is a pain. And den, when dey're all wounded an' stuff from fightin' Rog, den we attack. And kills 'em."

Lenny considered a moment. "Rog hath big treasure. Gold. Jewelth," he said craftily.

"Dat's da beauty of it," Garfok said. "If dey kill Rog, we kill dem and get da loot."

"Share for Lenny?"

"Sure, kid. Sure. Dere'll be a share for you. Right, guys?" Garfok said.

"You bet," Drizhnakh said.

"Sure, Lenny," said Spug. "We give ya a share."

"Share for Lenny," Lenny said happily. "Gold. Jewelth. Magic!"

"Dat's right, kid," said Garfok, releasing the lizardman.

"Lenny go back. Take humanth to Rog."

"Dat's da ticket."

"Lenny thay good-bye," said Lenny and bounded from the room.

There was silence for a moment.

Drizhnakh collapsed against the table, shaking. "Ya got him good, Garfok," he gasped. Garfok grinned.

" 'Share for Lenny?' " Drizhnakh said. They both laughed.

Spug looked puzzled. "I don't gets it."

" 'Take humanth to Rog!' " Garfok said.

" 'Treasure for Lenny!' " Drizhnakh said, rolling on the floor.

"C'mon, guys," Spug said. "I don't gets it!"

Garfok grinned at him. "Does ya really think we is gonna give dat punk a share of da treasure?"

Spug thought that over. "Dat's mean," he said in a bewildered tone.

While Drizhnakh chortled on the floor, Garfok took the opportunity to switch his cards with Drizhnakh's.

Drizhnakh sat up. "We better tell da boss about dis," he said.

Sidney lost her grip on the rope, fell heavily down the slope, and slammed up against a boulder. She gasped for air.

Father Thwaite, who was crouching on a nearby ledge, gingerly made his way crabwise across the slope. "Are you all right?" he asked.

"My leg . . . ," she gasped.

He felt her leg. "It's not broken," he said, "but you'll have quite a bruise."

She stood up unsteadily. "I'll be okay," she said.

"I'll heal it when we get to the bottom."

"No, Father," she said.

"Why not?" he asked, in some surprise.

"I . . . I can't."

"I don't understand."

Sidney sighed. "I'm sorry, Father," she said. "I can't explain."

It was warm in Rog's cavern. He liked it that way. He liked his cavern very much. There was a pool to wade in. There was a comfy pile of gold to sleep on. And there were crocodiles in the pool for snacks.

Rog was having a snack right now, as matter of fact. He reached one paw into the pool and fished around. There was one! He grabbed the croc by the middle, lifted it out, and dropped it into his maw. The croc thrashed, and Rog chewed. It was crunchy. He swallowed.

He'd have a few more crocs, and then he'd go have a nice nap. Later on, maybe he'd go for a little walk through the caverns. Maybe he'd find an orc or two. It was a long time since he'd had an orc. Crocs were good, but it was always nice to vary your diet.

Rog was quite looking forward to his day.

From the base of the shaft, the rest of the party watched Kraki descend the last few feet. His foot slipped. He fell heavily onto the slope. He clutched his sword, and plummeted . . .

. . . into the pool at the base of the shaft. There was a splash. Garni raised his lantern high and peered into the water.

Lenny hopped into the circle of light.

"Where the hell have you been?" asked Sidney.

"Lenny thcout ahead! Lenny find big treasure!"

Kraki surfaced with a whoop. "Hoo!" he said. "Vater cold. Feels good." He slapped some water toward the party.

Timaeus studied the pool and shuddered. "Unhealthy," he muttered. Garni stepped back to avoid being splashed. Kraki backstroked across the pond.

"What's that?" said Nick, pointing at something floating in the water. It was barely visible in the lantern's dim light.

Lenny peered. "Ith crocth," he said.

It took Nick a moment to understand. *"Kraki!"* he yelled. "Get out of the water! Now!"

Kraki stopped backstroking and sat up, treading water. "Vhy?"

There was a thrashing noise, and the barbarian disappeared.

Timaeus cursed and began to chant, preparing a spell. Sidney drew her sword, then wondered what to do with it.

Kraki surfaced near them blowing. "Are you all right?" Garni shouted.

The barbarian laughed exuberantly. "Yah, yah," he said. "Look vhat I found." He held a crocodile by the snout, one jaw in each hand. The crocodile struggled to free itself, but Kraki was too strong. Kraki disappeared under the water again—then shot from it, to sit on the edge of the pool, still holding the croc.

"See my little friend?" he said, holding the crocodile toward the others. He opened and closed the jaws with his hands. "Vant a kiss?" he said, shoving the crocodile toward Father Thwaite. The cleric backed away. The crocodile's feet scrabbled, but it got nowhere.

"It's blind," said Garni. It was true; the crocodile's lids were sealed together. Its coloring was light in comparison to its surface-dwelling cousins.

"Many crocth in cavernth," said Lenny. "Thwimming bad."

"Throw it back," said Timaeus.

"Vhat? Not vant for dinner?"

"I don't think so, Kraki," said Sidney.

"Hokay," said the barbarian, and dropped the crocodile back into the pool. It swam away as fast as it could.

"About this treasure," said Nick.

"Big treasure, mathterth! Gold! Thilver! Lenny find good treasure thith time! Make up for trollth! Truth Lenny!" Lenny said, and bounded off.

They followed him down a brief passageway that opened into a large cavern. Bats fluttered overhead, moving like leaves whipped in a silent storm.

"I don't like this," Sidney said. "Where was he? What was he doing?"

"You fret too much, my dear," Timaeus said, pulling out his pipe and packing it. He brought his finger toward the bowl. Everyone else put their fingers in their ears.

Thunder sounded across the cave.

Timaeus puffed contentedly.

They came to a narrow crack, lined with geodes winking orange in the lantern light. Beyond the crack was darkness.

"Be very, very quiet!" said Lenny, holding a finger to his snout. "Follow Lenny." He led the way through the crack and into another cavern, as huge as the one before. They heard a splash off in the darkness. Lenny tiptoed across the uneven rock. The party followed, the lantern lighting their way.

Rog lifted another croc out of the water, then stopped. What was that noise? It sounded like a faint jingling. The croc thrashed in Rog's hand.

Lenny turned. "Thee?" he whispered. "Thee? Mathter like treasure?"

It was a veritable hill of gold. Well, maybe not a hill. More like a small mound. Actually, it was closer to a pile. Look, it was a lot of gold. Enough gold to set you up for life. Enough gold to make even a dragon's eyes gleam. A lot.

It wasn't just gold, either. There was the occasional flash of a jewel;

there were chalices, swords, suits of armor, and all sorts of other goodies poking out of the pile.

"Whoopee!" shouted Nick, diving headfirst into the pile. He flung coins into the air. "I'm rich! I'm rich!" he said. "I'm socially secure!"

Kraki smiled broadly. Sidney licked her lips. Garni took off his backpack and started fumbling through it. He pulled out a bag of hardtack, three small steel balls, a box of cocoa mix. He pulled out a rabbit's foot, a wooden stake, a mallet, and a box of iron nails.

"What are you looking for?" asked Nick.

"I've got a bunch of burlap sacks," said Garni. "We'll need them to get the treasure out. I know they're in here somewhere." He pulled out a compass, an astrolabe, and a heavy bound book. . . .

"I don't know," Timaeus said.

There was a loud noise. Rog heard it distinctly. It sounded like it came from . . . his pile of gold! His comfy pile of gold! Those darn orcs. They were always after his gold! And it had taken him so long to get a nice comfy pile, too. He'd teach those orcs a thing or two!

The croc still clutched in one hand, Rog ran toward his gold.

"Somehow, it seems too easy," said Timaeus.

Sidney turned white.

"What's the matter?" Timaeus said.

Sidney pointed.

Timaeus turned.

Twenty cubits away, there were two feet planted on the ground. The thing about these feet was that the body to which they were attached wasn't visible. Not that the body was invisible, exactly; it was just so huge that you couldn't see it all in the dim light of Garni's lantern. All you could see was a pair of huge, scaled, greenish feet, each with four toes, each toe sporting a claw the length of a man's arm.

Also visible, hanging about fifteen cubits off the ground, was a pale green crocodile, clutched in a huge, clawed hand.

"Run," suggested Sidney in a conversational tone.

"Vhat?" said Kraki and turned to see what Sidney was talking about.

"Run!" Sidney said more forcefully.

Nick craned around to look. Garni looked up from his backpack.

"RUN!" Sidney screamed.

"A felicitous suggestion," said Timaeus.

A giant, clawed hand felt over the pile of gold. Nick scurried out of its way just in time. They ran.

The hand found Lenny. It lifted him high in the air by one leg. "Mathterth! Mathterth! Thave Lenny! Pleathe thave Lenny!" he screamed.

Timaeus turned and hurled a fireball over his shoulder. It exploded somewhere near the creature's torso. There was a thunderous shout of anger. The creature dropped Lenny.

The monster pounded after them, the cavern shaking with each ten-cubit stride.

"Scatter!" Timaeus gasped. "Or it'll get us all!"

They scattered.

There was a boom, and something burned Rog. Ooh! That smarted. Now Rog was angry. Where was the one he had grabbed? Rog felt around for it. Rog would get them for this. Darn orcs.

Sidney and Nick made for the same hiding place—a niche at one end of the cavern. They squeezed in together, their backs to the cool stone. Nick put his arm around Sidney and nuzzled her neck.

"Cut that out," she hissed.

"Aw, c'mon, Sidney." He put a hand on her leg.

"Cut it out, you jerk," she whispered. "There's a monster out there."

"Yeah," said Nick. "We could die at any moment. Danger always adds an element of—"

"Do you remember what direction the cavern entrance is?"

"Mmm. Remember the time the town watch was looking for us? And . . ." Nick slid a hand around her back.

A dagger pricked his ribs.

"Oh, hell, Sidney," he said, drawing back.

"So where the hell were you last night, buster?" she said in a low voice.

"Uh—I thought we had an understanding—"

"Understanding? Understanding!" Sidney's voice was getting noticeably louder. "You shit! Our *understanding* was that—"

"Sssh!" said Nick.

There was silence for a moment.

"This is a hell of a time to pick a fight," said Nick.

"We're partners, Pratchitt," said Sidney. "That's *all* we are."

"But Sidney," Nick said, "what about—"

"That was then," said Sidney. "This is now. Now listen to me. We're not going to be able to beat that monster. Right?"

"No chance," said Nick.

"So if we want a part of that treasure, we've got to snatch it."

"Sure," said Nick.

"Let's go," said Sidney.

Suddenly, the space in the niche next to Nick was empty. "Sidney?" Nick whispered.

"Sidney?" he whispered a little louder, out into the vastness of the cavern. He couldn't see anything out there. It was as dark as the inside of a casket.

Cursing, he moved out into the darkness.

Kraki crouched against the uneven wall.

Kraki didn't care about treasure. Barbarians didn't worry about money. Glory, that was the thing. Great deeds to be sung in the long-hall, deeds that would resound in his name for all time to come. Killing a monster the size of a mountain, for instance. Preferably in single combat. With one arm tied behind your back. Blindfolded. With a hat pin.

Let's not, Kraki told himself, get carried away.

It was dark, as dark as dragon's blood. He couldn't even see himself. He had his sword. He had the strength of his right arm. The monster was out there.

He had no idea how to kill the thing. It was just too damn big. Without a good look at the monster, he had no way of knowing where its vulnerable spots might be. External organs are usually the best bet: eyes and genitals. The throat is good, too.

He felt the wall he crouched against. It was grainy, a little soft. There were a few cracks, a few holes. And it was soft enough that he might be able to carve a handhold with his knife if he needed to.

In the pitch darkness, Kraki began to climb. All of the monster's potential vulnerable spots were well off the ground. He had to gain some height.

It didn't look too good, Kraki had to admit. How could he fight a monster he couldn't see?

He kept on climbing. It never occurred to him to do anything else. Heroes fight monsters. Monsters fight heroes. It's just one of those things.

And I, Kraki told himself, am a hero. Yah, for sure.

Garni lay flat on his stomach. He was near a pool of water. His lamp had gone out in the confusion, though he'd hung on to his pack. His dwarven night vision let him see a few shadowy shapes, but he could make out very little. It was black, as black as an ogre's heart. He heard a splash from the pool; he hoped the crocs would leave him alone. But crocodiles were the least of his worries.

He wished he could see what was going on. He considered relighting his lantern, but decided against it. Doing so would only reveal his position to the creature out there.

He'd boasted to Nick about being prepared. Well, he might not be prepared to deal with monsters the size of mountains. But maybe there was something in his pack. . . .

He fumbled through it. Wood axe. Spare socks. Bedroll. Brandy. Nothing useful there. Oil. Salt. Wolfsbane.

Belladonna. Parchment.

Wait. Belladonna. No, not just belladonna. Essence of belladonna, thin crystalline needles extracted by some magical process from the root and leaves of the plant. Priests and chirurgeons used it as a local anaesthetic. The medicinal dose was one hundreth of a grain; a truly tiny amount.

Two grains would kill a man.

He hefted the packet. He must have—call it an ounce and a half. Something over six hundred grains.

Was that enough to kill the monster? It was damned big. Its body weight must be tremendous. Still . . . it was the only thing Garni could think of. And even if the dose weren't lethal, it might slow the monster down.

But how to get the monster to take the poison? He could dump the belladonna into a jar of pemmican. . . . But no. The monster wouldn't identify the jar as food.

I suppose, Garni thought, I could get it to eat me. He shuddered. For a moment, he contemplated capturing a crocodile and forcing it to eat the belladonna—but he was not about to wrestle blind crocs in the dark.

Could he get the poison into the monster without getting him to eat it? Wait . . . To use belladonna as a local anaesthetic, you dissolve it in alcohol and rub it into the skin. The alcohol penetrates. . . .

He picked up the bottle of brandy.

Rog was unhappy. He crisscrossed the cavern floor. Those darn orcs had disappeared.

Maybe they were huddling against the walls. Yeah, that's it! They must be huddling against the walls. Rog began to feel his way around the cavern, patting the walls with his fingertips.

Timaeus stood uncertainly in the entrance. It was dark, as dark as the seventh hell. He could see very little. Where had everyone gotten to? Any sensible person would make for the exit. Wouldn't they? That creature was unbeatable.

Wasn't it?

Perhaps not unbeatable, precisely. Just very tough. Very, very tough.

Wizards no more powerful than he had slain dragons, hadn't they? Admittedly, wizards far more powerful than he had also been eaten by dragons, but he didn't come on this expedition to shirk adventure.

Still, those claws . . . He shuddered.

Timaeus reached for his pipe, then stopped himself. Smoke would reveal his whereabouts. No pipeweed for now.

The monster was so big. And those scales! His fireball had bounced right off—doing a little collateral damage, perhaps, but nothing major. The monster was just so *big* . . .

Hmm.

What would happen if the thing tripped? At university, he'd learned that the velocity of a falling object is directly proportional to its weight. The creature was nothing if not heavy. It would fall *fast*—and hard.

Perhaps an entrapment spell on one foot . . .

Father Thwaite panted heavily. He crouched with his back to a sizable stalagmite. He could see nothing; the cavern was as dark as the sins of humanity.

What should he be doing? His companions were out there somewhere in the dark, no doubt worried, no doubt afraid. He would comfort them if he could, but he had no idea where they were or where he was, for that matter.

Was there anything he could do about the monster?

He prayed for spiritual guidance. He wished he had a drink.

The monster. Was it truly evil? Few creatures were. Its home had been invaded, and it had responded accordingly. Might it not be intelligent? Might it possess a soul? Could he, perhaps, reach it somehow, convince it that the little creatures scurrying about its feet could become its friends? Could he lead the creature into the path of righteousness and instruct it in the ways of the gods?

Even if it were not intelligent, perhaps he could calm it, gentle it as holy men are said to gentle the most ferocious of beasts.

Stop, he thought.

Yes, this is what he must do. He must go forth, unarmed and unafraid, to do battle for the spirit of the monster.

"Suicide," he groaned. The theology was ineluctable, but he didn't have to like it.

Father Thwaite closed his eyes and intoned his mantra. He rose and slowly walked forward across the chamber floor. He tried to gentle his thoughts, rid himself of emotion, and reach out with his mind to contact the mind of the monster.

It was hard to concentrate. Here he was, wandering out into the middle of an unlit cavern, trying to convert a fifty-foot monster ravening for human blood—that he couldn't even see. Thwaite wished he'd chosen a different god to follow. Dion had his good points—including a notable fondness for bibulation—but this predilection for martyrdom was not among them.

Ye gods, he needed a drink. Blind faith was always easier with a few stiff ones under the belt.

Garni sloshed the poisoned brandy. Now what?

Ideally, he wanted the monster to swallow the vial. Failing that, he'd have to splash the stuff onto its skin. The thing to do was hurl the brandy toward the creature's mouth; at worst, it would splash onto the face, and at best the creature would swallow.

How could he hurl the vial so high? The creature was big. . . .

He took out his eleven-foot pole and screwed it together. Maybe he could use the pole as a kind of sling . . .

Timaeus inhaled deeply and prepared himself. This would take all his skill. First, he'd need some kind of light spell, to see his target. Then, he'd need to get the monster to run. Finally, he'd need an entrapment spell—and he'd better put everything into it.

If this didn't work, they were probably dead.

At last. Kraki came to a ledge and pulled himself onto it. He was tired. His leg wound was throbbing. He needed a rest. He thought he was high enough to reach the monster's head, although it was hard to tell.

But how would he knew when it was nearby?

Bah. He could always bellow a challenge. No doubt it would come to a hero's call.

Nick knew Sidney was nearby because he could hear her breathe. "Found anything?" he whispered.

"No," she whispered back. "We should have come to the treasure by now."

"Let's—" Nick began, then broke off.

There was a . . . footstep. The ground shook slightly. The air moved.

Dalara and Dion, Nick thought. It must be standing right above us.

That's when the lights came on.

* * *

There was a flash and a bang, as of fireworks. That's what it was; streamers of white drifted slowly toward the cavern floor.

Aha, Timaeus thought, spotting the monster. There's the bugger. He cleared his throat. "NYA NYA! NYA NYA!" he shouted. "YOU CAN'T CATCH ME! NYA NYA! NYA NYA!"

Rog heard a bang. Then he heard one of the orcs yell something insulting. Or was it an orc? He bellowed and ran toward the yell.

Nick knew he was going to die as soon as the monster saw them. All it had to do was step on them.

It began to move away.

He fainted in relief.

Sidney looked about. "Of all the . . ." she muttered, and began dragging Nick toward the edge of the cavern. If Timaeus was about to start tossing spells around, she didn't want to be at ground zero.

Kraki sprang to his feet. He was startled for a moment, then realized the light must be more of the wizard's magic. The wizard yelled, and the monster began to run toward him.

What was the wizard planning? No time to wonder. Kraki was above the monster. It was not far away, and moving closer. Kraki drew his sword, screamed and leapt.

Aha! Light! Garni was ready. He swung the flask at the end of the pole. The monster opened its maw to bellow. Garni swept the flask back and let it fly.

It arced through space, directly toward the monster's mouth.

Timaeus shouted the Words of power. He felt the forces of magic work through him. He reached out . . .

Crimson lines of energy crackled across space and encircled one of the monster's giant limbs.

The foot stuck. Rog tripped. Slowly, slowly he began to fall.

Timaeus held motionless, pumping all his power into the spell.

Kraki's exquisitely timed leap *would* have landed him directly on the monster's head . . .

Only, the monster tripped.

Kraki made a grab for an ear as he fell past. He missed. He kept on screaming.

Garni's flask arced high—missed the stumbling monster—and fell.

Standing in the middle of the cavern, Father Thwaite peeled one eye open. His concentration had gone to hell. Where had all this light come from? Something hit him in the chest. It fell to his feet. He opened the other eye. It was a flask of some kind. It looked like brandy. Ah! That should do the trick. He unstoppered it and drank. Just what he needed. Although—there was a rather peculiar aftertaste.

With a splash, Kraki fell into the pool. He stopped screaming.

Rog was unhappy. He was falling over. This was turning out to be a bad day. Why did everyone always pick on him?

He hit the cavern floor. Everything shook.

Timaeus collapsed in exhaustion.

Everything was silent for a moment. Rog lay still. Garni lit his lantern.

Sidney limped up to the giant form. It was breathing, but—"It's unconscious," she reported. She stared at the monster. It had no eyes. "And there we were, creeping around in the dark like mice," she said disgustedly.

Garni let out his breath and turned to help Kraki out of the pool. "Vater cold," Kraki said. "Brr. Enough svimming for one day." The two walked toward the treasure, where Sidney and Thwaite joined them.

"Where are the others?" Thwaite asked.

"Nick's unconscious," Sidney said. "I left him over—"

Garni stared in horror at the open flask in Father Thwaite's hand. "Did you drink any of that?" he said urgently.

"Why, yes," said Thwaite.

Garni dived into Thwaite, knocking him over. The flask went flying. He tried to shove a finger down Thwaite's throat. Thwaite fought back.

"The dwarf's gone mad!" yelled Thwaite. "Help me!"

Sidney and Kraki exchanged glances. Kraki shrugged.

"That's poison!" Garni shouted.

Thwaite sat up with an alarmed expression on his face. "Oh, dear. Dear, me."

V.

A human would have found the chapel grim. To an orc, it was pretty normal. Guttering torches lit a garishly painted state of a multilimbed female deity with big fangs. She was clutching the severed limbs of several victims. The altar was a stone slab with a depression in the middle and blood runnels down the side. The walls of the chamber were soot-stained limestone. Orcs were prostrate on the stone floor, muttering prayers into the rock as Fragrit finished the sacrament.

Fragrit was a devout believer, yet he knew that whatever power this ceremony lent him did not come from the goddess Szanbu alone. Beneath the altar was an object which emitted a surprisingly strong magical field. The goddess' ceremony allowed him to tap some small part of the object's magic and use it himself. He shuddered to think what might happen if the spirit he was thus exploiting were ever to escape—and therefore prayed to Szanbu, Mistress of Madness, with fervor.

The screams of the sacrificial victim died away. Fragrit turned to his congregation. He raised the knife and beating heart over his head and said, "An' now, we is going to sing da Hymn of Propitiation, number twenty-seven in yer hymnals."

As Fragrit cleansed the knife and burned the heart in a brazier, strong orcish voices rang out with the time-honored words of the sacred song:

> "Oi, Miz Szanbu, please don't hang us,
> Or have us burned alive.
> Please don't whip us or filet us,
> Other victims we'll provide.

"Cries of fear, an' cries of anguish
Rise up to da heavens high;
Oi, Miz Szanbu, please don't eat us,
We'll bring more blood bye an' bye."

The ceremony over, Fragrit stationed himself by the exit and shook the hands of his parishioners as they filed out. "Nice ceremony, Padre," said one.

"Tanks, Dorog," said Fragrit. Others murmured their respects as they passed.

Drizhnakh, Garfok, and Spug bustled into the temple. "Oi!" said Drizhnakh. "Boss!" The worshippers stopped drifting out and waited to see what was up.

"Yes, Drizhnakh?" responded Fragrit.

"Well, yer worshipfulness," said Drizhnakh, "we caught dat Lenny da Lizard skulkin' around, and he says dere are a buncha youmans comin' our way. . . ."

Fragrit listened carefully to Drizhnakh's story. "Ah," he said. "Five youmans an' a dwarf. You done good, Drizhnakh." He turned to the congregation. "Awright, youse," he said. "Get yer weapons. Drizhnakh, Garfok—get Fifi."

Garfok looked at Fragrit, startled. "Not a chanst," he said.

"Whaddaya mean, not a chanst?" said Fragrit menacingly.

"I ain't gettin' Fifi," said Garfok. "No way. Unh uh. Get yourself some udder sucker."

"You is gettin' Fifi," said Fragrit, "unless you maybe wanta be da next sacrifice. Right, boys?"

Several of the other orcs muttered agreement. *They* didn't want to be the one to get Fifi, that was for sure.

Garfok looked with dismay from green orcish face to green orcish face. He swallowed. "Awright," he said faintly.

Timaeus lay prostrate on the rocks, unconscious—and naked. The others stared at him, more than a little puzzled. His lack of consciousness might be a side effect of the spell or the result of backlash—but his nakedness was harder to explain.

Sidney shook Timaeus's shoulder. "Magister!" she said. "Magister! Wake up!"

Timaeus groaned and flung one arm over his eyes. "Two lumps, Randolph," he said. "And a kipper or two, if you'd be so kind." He sat up suddenly and looked at his companions. "Oh," he said. "The monster . . . did I . . . ?"

"Yah," said Kraki. "Monster fall over. Knocked out. Good yob."

"Thank you," said Timaeus. He looked quite pleased with himself. Then, he realized the state of his dress—or lack thereof. He blushed and positioned his hands strategically. "Er . . . My clothes . . . What happened . . . ?"

Garni began looking through his pack. "Just a minute," he said. "I have a spare blanket. Somewhere." He hauled out a small club, a piece of flint, a silver spoon, a packet of needles.

"Lenny," said Nick to Sidney.

"Eh?" said Timaeus.

"He rolled you," said Nick bluntly.

Timaeus looked upset. "Nonsense," he said.

"Yah," said Kraki. "Vhere is the little bugger, anyvay?"

"Don't you think it's kind of suspicious that he's not around?" Nick asked Timaeus.

"Granted," said Timaeus, "but—"

"If you'd been found by a bunch of orcs, say, you'd be dead. Who else would take your clothes—and your purse, I bet—without offing you?" asked Sidney.

"My purse," said Timaeus somewhat dazed. "My . . . my pipe! Good lord, the conniving little devil has stolen my pipe!" He looked genuinely upset for the first time.

"Here's the blanket!" said Garni triumphantly from behind a pile of stuff. Timaeus draped himself in it.

"Douse dem torches," Fragrit ordered. The orcs obeyed. That left his lantern, with its closable door, as their only light. He surveyed his orcs; there were a good forty, all males with weapons. "Guys wiv swords an' such in da front row," he said. "Bows in da rear." They formed up.

Fifi stood in front of the orcs. All Fragrit could see, really, was her two hind legs and her massive, scaled rear. Atop her perched Garfok.

It was an uncomfortable perch. The huge lizard's spine was, well, spiny. Garfok shifted, trying to find a way to sit that didn't make his backside ache. He studied the reins in his hands.

In theory, it was simple. If he yanked on the left rein, Fifi's head would pull left, and she'd turn in that direction. If he yanked on the right rein, she'd turn right. There was a smaller rope tied to one of her spinal knobs; if he pulled on the rope, the hood covering Fifi's eyes would slip off. If he let the rope loose, the hood would drop back over her eyes.

There were only a few problems with this, Garfok knew. First, Fifi was a lot stronger than he was. If she wanted to turn left, all the yanking in the world wouldn't stop her. Second, the hood was supposed to drop in place if he let the rope go—but it didn't look any too secure to him. Third, he'd never ridden Fifi into battle before; training is all very fine, but there was no predicting what she'd do when spells started zipping past her and people started bellowing war cries. Fourth, Garfok was awfully visible to the enemy, perched as he was on top of the lizard.

Fifth, Fifi's neck was long and flexible enough that if she wanted to look back at Garfok—or at the orcs following her—she could do so pretty easily. The thought made Garfok distinctly uneasy.

Fragrit walked to Fifi's hooded head and scratched behind the spikes. "My widdle popsy," he crooned. "My widdle Fifi. Fifi wanna treat?" The massive, scaled tail wagged sluggishly. Fragrit held out a handful of unrefined sugar; Fifi sucked it up.

Garfok was tempted to pull the hood up.

"Awright!" shouted Fragrit. "Forward!"

Thwaite was either in a coma or a meditative trance; it was hard to tell which. He lay by the pile of gold, shivering violently.

"I vill carry priest," said Kraki patiently.

"Ye gods, man, do you realize what you're saying?" said Nick. "He must weigh a hundred and fifty pounds if he weighs an ounce. That's a hundred and fifty pounds of gold we won't be able to take out with us. *ONE HUNDRED AND FIFTY POUNDS OF GOLD!* Do you know how many pints of mead a hundred and fifty pounds of gold buys?"

"Are you saying we should dump him?" said Sidney.

"Tempting idea," said Nick. "I mean, he *has* sucked back enough poison to kill a dozen men."

"But the priests of Dion are able, so it is said, to detoxify any poison . . ." said Timaeus.

"Yeah, maybe. Okay, okay. But if he dies on us, we're going to feel awfully stupid."

Nick, Sidney, and Timaeus had loaded themselves with as much of the treasure as they could possibly carry. Kraki could carry a fair amount, even burdened by the priest, but that still left a heartbreakingly large pile of gold. "We've already got a king's ransom," said Sidney.

"And suppose we had to ransom a king," muttered Nick. "Then we wouldn't have anything left."

"Not much danger of that," said Garni. He had emptied his backpack and was sorting his equipment into two piles: objects to be abandoned to make room for treasure, and things he still wanted to carry. "Since there hasn't been a human king in two millennia."

"Are you done yet?" asked Nick.

"Yes," said Garni.

"You're throwing that much away?" said Nick, impressed.

"Eh? No, no. That's the necessary pile. I'm throwing away the other one."

"Gimme a break," Nick moaned. "Every ounce you can carry is worth a pound *argentum* . . ."

"Nick, lad," said Garni, "we'll never get back up that shaft without my mountaineering equipment. And any of these items—"

"Could save our lives. Garni, you're killing me."

"'Ve come back later," said Kraki. "Get rest of gold."

"No chance," said Nick. "There's no way we can beat that monster when it's awake."

"Hokay," said Kraki. "I kill now."

Nick thought about that. "No," he said finally. "The odds are, you'll wake it up. And if you do kill it, someone else will rip off the gold before we get back."

"Yah," said Kraki. "Also, no glory in killing sleeping monster."

"Speaking of which," said Timaeus, "I'd just as soon get going before it decides it's finished its nap." Garni nodded and began repacking his supplies.

"A little under two million," said Nick.

"Vhat?" said Kraki.

"I figured it out," Nick said. "At sixpence a pint, a hundred and fifty pounds of gold buys a little under two millions pints of mead."

Kraki patted Nick on the back. Nick stumbled under the impact. "Don't vorry," Kraki said. "Vith my share, I buy you all the mead you vant."

Fifi moved slowly, slowly down the corridor. Blindly, blindly, her head swung back and forth, back and forth. Members of her species were not fast; they didn't need to be.

There was a scurrying noise down the corridor. Fragrit held the lantern higher.

Lenny came running around a corner, peering back over his shoulder. He had what looked like a wizard's robes clutched in his arms.

Lenny turned, saw Fifi and the orcs, and stopped dead in his tracks. He was nonplussed.

"Look, guys," said Drizhnakh. "It's our pal Lenny."

"Lenny . . . Lenny come to find palth," the lizardman said nervously.

"Whatcha got dere, Lenny? C'mere," said Drizhnakh.

"Nothing," said Lenny, trying vainly to hide the robes behind his back.

"Lemme see dat," said Fragrit, snatching Lenny's burden. "Wizard's robes," he said. "Coupla daggers. Underwear. You steal da guy's underwear, Lenny?"

Lenny hung his head.

"A pouch wiv miscellaneous crap. Nice pipe," Fragrit said. "A purse!" He opened it. "Looks like a coupla quid." He pocketed the purse.

"So where is dese guys at, Lenny?" said Drizhnakh.

"Humanth beat up Rog," Lenny said.

"Dey did, did dey? Dey must be pretty tough. Good thing we got Fifi along," said Fragrit, patting her flank.

Lenny looked at the creature and shuddered.

"Dey'll head for da shaft wiv da treasure," Garfok said from atop his mount.

"Right!" said Fragrit. "We'll nab 'em dere."

The passageway that led from the cavern ended in a sharp right turn. Beyond the turn was a corridor that led past the pool, the shaft—and, at the moment, Fifi and the orcs.

"I'll scout ahead," Nick said, dumping his treasure. Silently, he moved into the passageway. He turned.

"Somefing's down da corridor," Garfok hissed.

Fragrit opened the lantern door. Nick froze in the light, startled. He turned back. . . .

Garfok pulled off Fifi's hood.

The lizard squinted in the light. Her eyes focused. She saw Nick.

With a crackle of energy, Nick Pratchitt turned to stone.

The adventurers watched Nick walk forward and turn. He was startled. He turned back to call to them. He turned to stone.

They were stunned.

"Nick!" shouted Sidney and ran toward him.

Timaeus grabbed her. "No, you fool!" he said urgently.

Sidney stood, gulped, and eyed the statue. She looked at Timaeus and nodded shakily.

Garni set down his backpack. Cursing under his breath, he pawed through it rapidly, tossing objects heedlessly, until he found the mirror.

* * *

"Da hood!" Fragrit said. Garfok dropped it in place.

They stood silently for a moment. Fragrit closed his lantern door.

"He's right in da entrance," Garfok said thoughtfully from atop Fifi. "I bet dey saw him when Fifi stoned him."

"Now what?" said Drizhnakh.

"Dey're warned," said Garfok. "Da thing ta do is attack while dey're confused."

"Only, if we get ahead of Fifi we can't use her. Cause she might turn *us* ta stone," said Fragrit.

"So's we either lose our best weapon," said Garfok, "or we sit here until dey figger out how ta beat us."

"Right," said Drizhnakh. "Fragrit, you is a friggin' military genius, ya know dat?"

"Shaddup, you two!" said Fragrit menacingly. "I is beginning ta think I know who is gonna be da next sacrifice."

They stood in the darkness, wondering what to do.

Garni tied the mirror to his eleven-foot pole and extended the pole down the passage. He juggled the mirror until he could see around the turn.

"Can't see a thing," he said. "It's dark down there."

"Here," Sidney said. She lit a torch and threw it toward the turn in the passage. Garni studied the mirror.

A torch rolled into the corridor. There was some kind of pole. And a shiny thing . . .

"Keep da hood in place!" Fragrit shouted.

Garfok was just about to pull the rope but stopped.

Drizhnakh looked at the packed orcish formation. "If dey use a fireball on us, we're goners," he told Fragrit. Fragrit glared.

"Awright!" Fragrit yelled, coming to a decision. "Garfok! Get Fifi movin'. You udder guys; move forward, behind Fifi. Bowmen! Nock yer weapons."

"Boy," said Drizhnakh caustically, "dis'll be a speedy charge." Slowly, slowly, the lizard moved forward.

"Oy," Garni said, peering into the mirror. "At least twenty orcs. All armed. And some creature I've never seen before, some kind of lizard. One of them is mounted on it."

Timaeus peered over Garni's shoulder at the mirror. "I believe it's a basilisk," he said. "They're quite rare. That would explain what happened to Nick."

"It would?" said Sidney.

Even without his pipe, Timaeus managed to give the impression of pontificating. "Yes. Their glance turns living creatures to stone. They're herbivorous, actually; quite an effective magical defensive sys—"

"They're coming this way!" Garni said.

Timaeus sighed. "My friends," he said, "I am sorry. My powers are exhausted, and in their absence, I fear we have little hope of victory. A basilisk is a fearsome foe indeed."

Kraki slapped him on the back. "Is hokay," he said. "You defeat big monster. No vonder nothing left."

"And yet," said Timaeus, "it is I who have led you to this evil hour, and I who must bear the responsibility for our failure."

Sidney looked at Nick's statue and sighed. "We could run," she said.

"Where?" said Garni.

Kraki flexed his muscles and drew his sword. "Is hokay," he said. "Ve kill many to serve us in undervorld. It vill be glorious."

Garni looked up. "It isn't over yet," he said. He pulled the pole in and untied the mirror.

Garni stood by the lip of the passageway. To see around the corner without risking himself, he held his mirror out with one hand. The others stood flat against the cavern wall.

Slowly, slowly, the basilisk turned the corner. Fifi's eyes were unhooded; she was going into battle. She brushed against Nick, who fell over with a clunk. She turned. The orcs trailed her.

Fifi trundled forward. On her long neck, her head was the first thing to come through the entrance and into the cavern. It swayed back and forth with every step. Fifi didn't notice the humans and the dwarf crouched along the cavern walls.

Fifi's head swung toward Garni. He grabbed it, turned it toward him . . .

And held the mirror before the basilisk's eyes. Fifi regarded herself dimly. She probably never realized what she was looking at.

Crackle. Fifi turned to stone.

Kraki roared and swung into the entranceway. He charged the orcs.

Clad only in a blanket, Timaeus stepped next to Fifi's statue and began to chant.

On her hands and knees, Sidney scrambled under Fifi's belly toward the orcs, a knife in her teeth.

Garni charged, waving a battle-axe.

"Fire!" yelled Fragrit. A swarm of arrows shot forward.

One bounced off Garni's helm. One hit Kraki's good leg. Unconcernedly, he pulled it out, shouted "YAH HAH!", and charged, flourishing his sword. Heads and limbs flew. He was always happiest when killing things.

Timaeus ducked behind Fifi to avoid the arrows, then stepped back out and began chanting again. Fragrit was chanting, too.

Sidney scrambled out between Fifi's front legs and buried her dagger in the throat of a surprised orc. She drew her sword and engaged two others.

Garni killed two orcs before the rest withdrew around him, unwilling to face his whirling axe. He stood with his back to the corridor wall. "Come here, greenie," he said to one. "Think you can kill me just by being ugly?"

Timaeus conjured a ball of flame in his hand and hurled it at the orcs . . .

It fizzled. He cursed.

A ray of blackness shot from Fragrit's pointing finger and enveloped Timaeus. The wizard fell.

Three orcs fought Sidney. She took a wound to her sword arm and dropped the weapon. One of the orcs clubbed her in the temple with a spear. She fell to her hands and knees.

Quickly, they tackled her and bound her arms and legs.

"Sidney!" yelled Garni. He tried to go to her, but the orcs moved in, and he was forced back to the wall.

Kraki fought all the way through the orcish horde, from one end to the other. He was covered in green gore and grinning maniacally. "Some fun, hah?" he asked an orc as he chopped him open from shoulder to breastbone. The orc did not reply.

Lenny was cowering in the rear.

"You!" yelled Kraki. "I kill you now, lizard pig!" The sentiment, however zoologically absurd, was at least heartfelt.

Lenny ran. Kraki ran after him.

"Get da bowmen up here," said Drizhnakh. They stood behind the orcs facing Garni and fired at the dwarf. An arrow hit Garni in the shoulder. His axework faltered. He spat at Drizhnakh.

The orcs moved in. He wounded one before they bashed him unconscious.

The orcs stood panting. Slowly, they realized the battle was over.

Fragrit hugged the head of the basilisk. "Fifi," he moaned. "Dey gots ya, Fifi."

Drizhnakh snorted and turned away. "Listen, youse," he said to the orcs. "Pick up da youmans and da dwarf. An' da treasure. We'll take it back to da temple. An' take da youman statue, too; it'll make a nice souvenir." He smiled and tugged on his tusks.

"Poor widdle Fifi," Fragrit said forlornly, petting the stone head.

"We better get out of here before dat guy wiv da sword comes back," said Dorog. "He's tough."

Timaeus was wrapped tight in the bonds of a glowing black net. He struggled but could not break Fragrit's spell. Three orcs picked him up like a sack of potatoes. "Release me at once!" shouted the wizard. "I am an Athelstani citizen!"

The orcs chortled.

Kraki stopped and leaned against the cool wall of the corridor. He couldn't keep up with the lizard, not with the wound in his leg. He panted.

He began to realize that he'd made a serious mistake. His friends were in danger back there. He hit his forehead with the heel of his hand. "Stupid, stupid," he told himself. He had to get back.

Only—which way was back? Where were they? Where was he, for that matter?

It was dark. He couldn't see anything. The stone was cool. The only sound was the slow drip of water somewhere in the middle distance.

VI.

"I sez sacrifice dem now," said Drizhnakh. "Dat way, we can have mansflesh for din-din."

"Yeah!" said Spug enthusiastically. "Mansflesh. Yum!"

"No way," said Fragrit. "Szanbu is already had a sacrifice today."

The three humans and the dwarf lay tumbled together in the odiferous cell where they'd been tossed. Filthy straw covered the stone floor. The orcs argued outside the barred window. Thwaite still shivered in the throes of belladonna poisoning.

"Garni?" asked Sidney.

"Yes?" the dwarf replied. His head hurt like the devil. He was seeing double.

"Are you all right?"

"I think I have a concussion," he said.

"And you, Magister?"

Timaeus cleared his throat. "I'm fine, save for a bruised ego," he said.

"We need to get them to open the door," said Sidney.

"Why?" asked Timaeus.

"So I can escape," said Sidney.

Timaeus wiggled, trying to find a more comfortable position in the straw. "And how are you going to manage that, my dear?" he said. "I'm out of magic. The two of you are wounded. Thwaite is poisoned. We're all tied up. Nick is a piece of garden statuary, and the gods only know where Kraki is."

Sidney chuckled. "Show a little faith," she said.

"Right," said Timaeus. He sighed, then yelled: "We have a recipe!"

There was silence from outside the door. "What da hell?" said Fragrit.

"We have a recipe," said Timaeus, "for mansflesh."

"What is you blabbin' about?" said Drizhnakh.

"We took it off some trolls," said Timaeus. "It really sounded quite good. If you must cook us, I would appreciate it if you'd take some care in the preparation."

"Shaddup in dere," said Fragrit.

"I mean, bad enough to be eaten by orcs. But if that is one's fate, one much prefers to go as a meal fit for kings, don't you think?"

"Shaddup," said Fragrit.

"How about some nice thigh steaks *au poivre?*" said Timaeus. "I have no idea whether human diaphragm will double for brisket, but my mother's cook had the most marvelous—"

The door slammed open. "Shaddup you," said Fragrit, driving a boot into Timaeus's aforementioned diaphragm.

A small black cat slipped out the open door. It limped on two legs.

Sidney, thought Garni. I had no idea.

The orc kicked Timaeus again. "Don't play with your dinner," gasped the wizard.

"Yah," Kraki said to himself. "This is basilisk." There was no mistaking the stony scales and the skinny neck, even in pitch darkness. "But vhere did they go from here?"

"*Mrowr?*" said Sidney inquisitively.

"Vhat's that?" said Kraki. Sidney came up and brushed against his legs. Kraki gave a start, then reached down and pet her. "Is kitty-cat," he said. "Pretty pussy." He stroked the length of her and scratched behind her ears. She purred. "How does pussy-cat get in caverns?" he asked.

"*Mrow,*" she responded and walked away from him. He followed a little, then stopped.

"Now vhat?"

"*Mrowr!*" Sidney said insistently. She came back to rub up against his legs again, then walked away in the same direction as previously.

"Pussycat vants Kraki to follow?" he asked.

"*Mrow,*" Sidney said, and walked a little farther away.

"Is crazy," Kraki said.

Sidney hissed, then meowed again. "*Mrowr!*"

Kraki sighed. "Hokay," he said. "Vith magic, anything is possible. And I got no better idea vhat to do."

"Orcs an' fellow believers," Fragrit intoned, "we is here today once again to propitiate Mistress Szanbu, Goddess of Madness, she whose curses roil da world, she who loves ta torture small, furry animals. Oi,

Szanbu, hear me now; we tanks you for our victory over da youmans."
Fragrit motioned toward a large, leather-bound chest that stood by the
altar. "We tanks you for da treasure dey was carryin', an' we promise dat a
goodly portion will be spent ta purchase further victims. Accept from us
dis sacrifice, in place of our own miserable lives. Let us live, so dat we may
bring you further sacrifices.

"Awright, fellas," he continued. "Let's have da cleric first." Garfok and
Dorog swung Father Thwaite's limp body up onto the altar and fixed the
manacles in place.

"I don't want to watch this," Garni said. Timaeus looked sick and made
no reply. He eyed Nick's statue, now occupying a niche to the right of the
altar. He prayed that somehow Kraki would find them.

Who is that?
Victims of belladonna poisoning do not enter a coma. Father Thwaite
was unconscious only because he was deep in a meditative trance. His
mind travelled the veins and byways of his body, helping his liver extract
the poison from his bloodstream, calming his rapidly beating heart when
the belladonna's stimulus threatened to make it burst. An untrained man
would have been dead many times over. Only Thwaite's powers stood
between him and death.

Still, his body shook with the poison. It stimulated his heart, his lungs,
his muscles; he twitched, his heart beat madly, he breathed in short gasps.
Were he not meditating, he would have been conscious: indeed, he would
have been preternaturally alert.

The voice in his mind broke his concentration, as being hauled around
the caverns by the barbarian had not, as the battle with the orcs had not,
as the stench of the cell had not.

No one belonged in his mind.
Who? he screamed silently. *What?*
A human, said the voice. *Beware, kinsman. You are in danger.*
Thwaite's eyes flew open. Above him stood an orc with a knife; and
beyond the orc, a wooden carving of Szanbu. Thwaite's own limbs were
manacled to an altar. He knew enough about the goddess to know a human sacrifice when he was one.

"Dion," gasped Thwaite, calling on his god, "aid me now!" It was an
expression of despair; he had no hope that anyone would answer.

And then, something happened that Thwaite had problems remembering later. Something very strange. Suddenly, he no longer felt the belladonna in his veins. Instead, he felt—good. Happy. Wonderful, in fact.

The orc was heating a sacrificial blade in a brazier. The blade glowed red. Well, maybe not wonderful, Thwaite thought.

But the feeling was familiar, somehow. He felt like—like he'd just had six pints of stout, he realized. But without the need to pee.

The orcish priest backed away, a look of horror on his tusked face. Thwaite didn't know it, but his entire body was englobed in brilliant, golden light.

Father Thwaite looked at the niche to the right of the altar. It held Nick Pratchitt, now a hunk of stone. Thwaite knew, somehow, that he must touch the statue's toe.

With a crack of thunder, Father Thwaite sat up from the altar, pulling the manacles right out of the rock. His muscles no longer twitched. However, his nose was red, and he was grinning happily.

"Boo," he said to Fragrit, who gulped, backed away some more, and fell off the stage and into the congregation.

In the distance there was thunder.

"Thunder?" said Kraki. "Vhy is there thunder in cavern?"

Sidney would have shrugged her shoulders if she'd had any. At least in this form, she could see in the dark. *"Mraow,"* she complained and led Kraki toward the orcish temple.

Thwaite touched the toe of Nick's statue.

Power thrilled through Thwaite's body. He could feel it pouring out of the altar, through him, and into the statue. The golden glow about Thwaite gradually diminished, and an equally golden glow spread across Nick Pratchitt. The orcs watched in awe.

Fragrit peered over the lip of the altar. In sudden fear, he realized the power he'd tapped for so long was free.

As suddenly as it had started, the power stopped flowing. Thwaite fell back on the altar. He felt wonderful. The room spun about him. He knew he should get up and do something, but it felt so much nicer just to sprawl there.

The statue looked down and opened its hands, the glow suffusing its form.

Sidney transformed. "Kraki," she said.

The barbarian whirled in the darkness. "Vhat?" he cried. "Sidney?"

"Yeah," she said. "We're almost there."

"Vhere?"

"The temple. Do you have an extra weapon?"

"Yah, a dagger. Here. Vhere did you come from?"

"Thanks. Never mind."

Standing still, Nick Pratchitt rose out of the niche and floated across the temple.

Nick touched Timaeus, then Garni. The bonds slipped from their bodies. Garfok and Dorog, who'd been holding the prisoners, were forced away as if by invisible hands.

Garni's wounds closed.

"My . . ." said Timaeus wonderingly, "my magic has been restored."

The tableau held for a long moment. Then, the golden glow about Nick Pratchitt disappeared. He fell heavily to the ground, unconscious and, to all appearances, a normal human being.

"Dey have defiled da temple!" screamed Fragrit. "Get 'em!" With a roar, the orcs boiled toward the altar.

Timaeus began to chant.

The temple door slammed open.

"Die, foul vights!" said Kraki. He charged in, waving his sword. Sidney, naked, kept close to him, holding a dagger. The orcs, threatened from both the front and rear of the temple, milled confusedly.

"Vights?" one orc said to another. "What does he mean, vights?"

"I think he means wights," said the other.

"But we isn't wights," said the first. "We is orcs."

"Beats me," said the second.

Kraki sliced both their heads off.

The orcs divided. Some charged Timaeus and Garni; others turned to face Kraki and Sidney.

"Duck!" yelled Timaeus. Sidney and Garni dropped prone.

"Vhat?" said Kraki. Sidney pulled him down.

"Duck?" said an orc. "What does he mean, duck?"

"I dunno," said another. "We is orcs, not—"

Timaeus's fireball exploded.

A handful of orcs survived, huddled at the side of the temple. All were scorched. Fragrit was dead, Garfok and Drizhnakh among the survivors.

"YAH HA!" yelled Kraki and waded into the orcs, whipping his sword back and forth. He was in his element. Orcish gore flew.

"Oi, Garfok," said Dorog. "Dat guy wiv da sword is gonna kill us all."

"Parley!" yelled Drizhnakh.

"YAH HA!" yelled Kraki again. He was happy. He was killing things.

"Parley! Parley!" the orcs yelled, scrambling to get out of Kraki's way.

Kraki paused, a little puzzled. "Come back," he yelled. "Fight like orcs, damn you!"

"Can we please surrender?" pled Drizhnakh. "Pretty please?"

"YAH HA!" shouted the barbarian, oblivious, as he killed three more orcs.

Drizhnakh had a brainstorm. He threw his sword against the temple wall with a clang. He walked up to Kraki, lay down, and exposed his throat. "Awright," he said. "G'wan. Kill me."

Kraki drew back his sword, then paused. "No fun," he complained. "Too easy. Get up and fight like orc."

"No," said Drizhnakh. "If ya wants ta kill me, it's gotta be like dis."

All the remaining orcs tossed their weapons away.

"Bah," said Kraki.

"Oh, let them go, Kraki," said Timaeus. "They're no threat."

Kraki pouted. "Hokay," he said reluctantly, hooking a thumb at the door. "Get lost."

The orcs scrambled out of the temple.

If the temple had looked grim before, it looked even grimmer now. Torches continued to gutter along the wall. Szanbu glared from behind the altar. Bits of orc lay hither and yon. Kraki sat down heavily on the dais. "Whew," he said and stretched out.

Nick rose groggily, Sidney supporting him. "Are you okay?" she asked.

"Yeah, I guess so." He noticed Sidney's state of undress. She was smeared with gore. "You've looked better, doll," he said.

Sidney looked at herself. "Uh, yeah," she said. "Garni! Do you have another blanket?"

"Aye," said the dwarf reluctantly. He was beginning to get a little tired of unpacking and repacking and unpacking . . .

Timaeus was trying to get sense out of Thwaite. Thwaite wasn't being terribly cooperative. He was singing bits and snatches of drinking songs. "What happened there on the altar?" Timaeus demanded.

"Hmm? Feel wonderful! Wonderful. And a hey down to the well, me lad, and a hey down to the well . . ."

"You glowed golden."

"Golden? Golden? Golden the ship was, oh oh oh . . ." Thwaite staggered away from Timaeus, beaming broadly.

Timaeus wondered somewhat irritably how the cleric had managed to find booze while poisoned, comatose, and bound to an altar.

* * *

Kraki sat up and wandered over to the altar. He grabbed the edge and pulled. It moved slightly. "Top comes off," he reported, and made to remove it.

"Wait!" shouted Garni.

Kraki looked down at the dwarf. "Vhat?" he demanded.

"It could be trapped," said Garni. "Leave the job to professionals."

Kraki scowled. "Bah," he said.

"I'll do it," said Nick. He motioned Kraki away; the barbarian stepped off the dais reluctantly.

Nick borrowed Sidney's ear trumpet and tapped over the altar, listening carefully. He frowned. "Magister," he said to Timaeus, "do you detect any magic within the altar?"

Timaeus raised his eyebrows, shrugged, and chanted briefly. There was a flash before his eyes. The wizard jumped back, blinking furiously. "My dear Nicholas," he said slowly, "that altar virtually exudes power. I've rarely encountered a magical field of such intensity."

Nick's eyes went wide. "We'd better be careful then," he said.

"Yust lift the damn top off," Kraki said impatiently.

Nick studied the altar for a moment, then looked at the statue of Szanbu. He took a coil of rope and tied it through the holes in the altar where the manacle pins had penetrated. He looped the rope through the brackets that held Szanbu's statue in place.

He motioned everyone away from the altar, moved as far away himself as the rope would let him, and pulled on the rope, using the brackets as a primitive pulley.

The rope strained. The altar top moved slightly. The brackets pulled free from the wall and Szanbu's statue crashed onto the floor.

Thwaite winced. Szanbu was far from his favorite goddess, but desecration was desecration.

Nick moved up to the altar and, crouching by its side, stuck a knife under the altar top. Carefully, covering his eyes, he pried the top up a crack.

Nothing happened.

He moved away from the altar and picked up the rope again. Standing as far away as possible, he pulled on the rope. The altar didn't budge. Kraki joined him and pulled too. The altar top slid off and hit the floor with a crash. It broke into several pieces.

Nothing else happened.

"Hoo boy," said Kraki sarcastically. "Big trap in that vone, for sure." He and Nick went forward to peer into the altar.

Nick gasped.

Lying in the altar was an exquisitely detailed, minutely rendered statue. The artistry alone was breathtaking. It was a life-sized depiction of a human male, wildly mustachioed, clad in pants and a leather harness, unarmed. His head was raised, as if he were looked upward; although he held himself proudly, his expression was one of trepidation.

But it was neither the artistry nor the subject of the statue that caught the eye. It was the material.

The statue shone richly, redly in the torchlight, shone with the unmistakable rosy tint of athenor.

Athenor: chiefest among the magical metals. Athenor: which cannot be termed pink, nor red, any more than gold can be called yellow. Athenor: from which the greatest, most legendary objects of power are formed. Athenor: ounce for ounce and grain for grain, far more valuable than gold.

Cautiously, Nick reached into the altar and rapped the statue. "Solid," he whispered. They were looking at a fortune; several fortunes; wealth beyond imagining.

"Who is it?" Garni asked.

Timaeus fingered his beard. "I don't know," he said. "But his garb is archaic. It must be immensely old."

Garni ran his hand along the statue and peered at it closely. "No tool marks," he said. "I can't imagine how it was cast."

"Let's get it out," said Nick.

Kraki reached in and pulled. The statue barely budged. "Must veigh a ton," he grunted.

They strung ropes under the statue and, pulling together, managed to haul it from the altar.

"How in blazes are we going to get this thing up the shaft?" asked Timaeus plaintively.

"Look," said Garni, "we'll worry about getting it out later. We still have other things to worry about. The chest, for one. And we still have wounded."

The others fell silent.

"Okay," said Nick. He walked to the chest by the altar and began to tap it.

"Not again," muttered Kraki.

"Right," said Father Thwaite, still dangerously red-faced but less obviously inebriated than before. "You're hurt the worst, Sidney, me lass . . ."

She shook her head, "I'm sorry, Father."

Garni took the priest by one arm. "She can't let you cure her," he said quietly.

"Why not?"

"She has . . . the taint of chaos."

"She's a sh-shapechanger?"

"It isn't widely known."

"You bet. People don't like shapechangers. Why doesn't she do something about it? Therianthropy can be cured."

"Yes, Father. But in her occupation, it comes in handy."

"Oh? What is she?"

"A cat. Who moves silently and sees in darkness. And can get places a human can't."

"A pussycat," said Thwaite. "That's nice. But . . . ," he furrowed his brow, "if she dies unsanctified—"

"That's her risk."

While they talked, Nick fiddled with the chest. He listened with the ear trumpet. He pressed all over the chest for buttons or moving panels. He tied a rope around it and tugged. He cut one of the leather straps that bound the chest, and began to work the strap free.

Kraki watched Nick with increasing impatience. "Bah!" he said finally. "Enough with this silliness. Vhen you go through a door in a tavern, do you check it for traps?"

"No," said Nick, "but—"

"It's yust a chest. Vaste of time. I show you how." He muscled Nick aside and yanked open the lid.

There was an explosion. Three steel darts shot forth and buried themselves in Kraki's chest. There was a faint hiss as a greenish gas spurted out the side. Smoke rose from the lid.

Kraki inhaled the gas.

"See?" he said hoarsely, bleeding from the dart wounds. "Is how varrior opens chest." He pounded his chest, coughed vigorously, and keeled over with a crash. Thwaite stumbled to the barbarian, pulling out his incense and aspergillum.

"Thoroughly unprofessional," Garni muttered, shaking his head.

Nick grinned bemusedly and peered inside the chest. "Looks like most of the treasure the orcs took off us," he said.

"More stuff to get up the shaft," Timaeus grumbled, wandering over to look. "My pipe!' he yelped happily, diving into the chest. He pulled out his pipe and wiped it with his blanket, then started pawing through the chest, looking for pipeweed.

VII.

Just dragging the statue to the base of the shaft was exhausting. They were all sweating, and Kraki, who'd borne the brunt of the labor, was panting heavily. The shaft itself was daunting. Their lantern lit only the first twenty cubits, but that was quite enough. They could see a five-foot cliff, thirty-degree slopes of smooth, water-worn rocks, and boulders blocking what would otherwise be the obvious path. They knew full well that the traverse became no easier at higher elevations.

"Can we set up some kind of pulley system?" Sidney asked Garni. The dwarf considered.

"I don't see how," he replied. "I only have about fifty feet of rope. To bear the weight of the statue, I'd have to quadruple it up—that only leaves a length of about ten feet. If we can find someplace to rest the statue every few feet while we move the pulley, we might be able to do it—but you remember what the shaft is like. Slanting places, cliffs, boulders . . ."

"Yeah." She turned to Timaeus. "How about magic?"

He puffed on his pipe. "Madam, we've been over this. The statue weighs close to a ton. The shaft is at least fifty feet high. The amount of energy I'd have to expend to lift a ton that far against the natural tendency of earthly objects to fall is simply prohibitive. Besides which, I am no polymage; my idiom is fire. Now, if you could find me a supply of magical energy to tap . . ." Timaeus took out his pipe and held it, staring into space. "Hmm."

"How about the statue itself? You said it holds a great deal of magical energy. . . ."

"Yes, bound in some way I cannot begin to fathom. But I have another idea."

* * *

"What the hell are they doing up there?" said Sidney impatiently. Timaeus and Kraki had disappeared up the shaft thirty minutes ago to prepare some spell the wizard had in mind. They'd left the rest of the party with the statue. Sidney eyed the pool suspiciously and worried about crocodiles. And about orcs. "What if those orcs come back?" she asked.

"Calm down," said Nick. "Everything'll be fine."

They stood by the base of the shaft. There was nothing to be heard but the occasional splash of a croc or squeak of a bat. And . . .

"Ssst! I hear something," Nick whispered. Walking on his toes, he moved out into the darkness.

There was the sound of a brief struggle.

"Well, well, well," Nick said. "What have we here?" He came back into the circle of light cast by the lantern, clutching Lenny by the neck.

"Lenny run away from bad orcth," Lenny said, studying possible escape routes. "Come to find friendth!"

Nick chuckled.

"What did I tell you, lizard?" Sidney said coldly.

Lenny said nothing. He looked forlorn.

"You betrayed us," she said.

"No! No! Lenny alwayth faithful. Bad orcth capture Lenny. Torture Lenny! Thay bad thingth. Make Lenny tell about friendth. Lenny want to help! Bad orcth make Lenny do bad thingth!"

"I told you that if you betrayed us, I'd hunt you down and kill you, lizard," Sidney said.

"No! No! Don't kill Lenny! Lenny alwayth faithful! Lenny found good treasures!" His legs windmilled desperately.

"I think he'd make a nice pair of boots," Nick said, studying the lizardman, still holding Lenny by the neck. Lenny whimpered.

"You can't just kill him out of hand," said Father Thwaite. He was sitting on the rocks, clutching his head. He was in the unhappy state between drunkenness and sobriety, when one is neither entirely sober nor free of the pains of hangover.

"Why not?" said Nick.

"He does have a soul," said Thwaite, "and he is no immediate danger to us."

"If we let him go, he'll just screw someone else," said Sidney.

"No! No! Lenny reform! Lenny thee light! Lenny join monathtery! Lenny thpend retht of life repenting thinth!" He began keening hymns, slightly off-key.

"Shut up, you," Nick said.

Garni cleared his throat. "I have a practical consideration to offer," he said.

"What's that?" asked Sidney.

"We need to get an awful lot of stuff up the shaft," said Garni. "He's an extra pair of arms and legs."

"True," said Nick, grinning. "Oh, all right. You live, Lenny, old pal."

"Lenny very, very grateful. Lenny love human friendth. Lenny do anything for humanth!"

"Stop grovelling!" snarled Sidney.

Timaeus was puffing. Kraki's torso was covered with a sheen of sweat. The pile of rocks was turning into a sizable hill.

They had scavenged the tabletop from the room where the trolls had been killed. Currently, it was standing between two outcroppings, a little way down the slope, holding the pile of rocks in place. "I hope this is enough," Kraki said. "Board is bulging." He was right. The inch-thick oak was visibly bending under the weight.

"I believe this will do," said Timaeus. He paused to think, filled his pipe, and—*Bang!*—lit it. Flames enveloped his head, then gradually dissipated.

"How does this vork, anyvay?" Kraki asked.

"It's quite an elegant spell, really," Timaeus said enthusiastically. "All we do is establish a magical similarity between these rocks and the statue. But we reverse the sign on the position vector. That way, the potential energy of the rocks lifts the statue! We don't have to invest much power ourselves, except to establish the identity."

"Hah?"

"Er . . . in layman's terms, eh? Ah, we make the boulders and the statue like two sides of a pulley, all right? Then, we release the boulders."

"They fall."

"That's right. And the statue rises."

"If you say so. Sounds like silliness to me."

"Don't worry, it'll work," Timaeus said. He turned to call down the shaft: "Fore!" he shouted.

A voice echoed back up. "What?"

Timaeus began to chant in a language Kraki didn't know. Timaeus waved his arms, chalked runes on the ground, and moved in a kind of dance. The smoke from his pipe formed patterns about his head.

"Now!" he shouted. Kraki yanked on the tabletop.

With a roar, the boulders hurtled down the shaft.

* * *

"What is keeping those bozos?" said Sidney.

Suddenly, the statue leapt upwards, as if yanked by a string.

The spell may have been elegant, but its effects were not. The statue flew up the shaft, bounding off obstructions, clanging off walls, and spinning violently. The racket was tremendous.

"Good thing it's made of athenor," muttered Garni. "Anything else would be mashed shapeless."

The noise of its passage died away. Then, there was another noise, like the roar of the sea.

"What's that?" asked Nick.

It got louder.

"I don't know," said Garni.

A rock nearly hit Thwaite. He dived for cover as it bounced down the corridor.

"Run!" yelled Sidney. They all ran for the cavern. A veritable avalanche thundered about them.

The statue narrowly missed Kraki as it flew up the shaft, spun past him, bounced off the ceiling, and ricocheted violently down the corridor. It clanged to a stop. The barbarian swore.

Timaeus smiled around his pipe and went to examine the statue. It was unharmed. Although the statue's expression had not changed, Timaeus got the distinct impression it was glaring at him. "Sorry, old bean," he muttered. He rather hoped they had no further adventures. His powers were just about exhausted once again.

Sidney panted as she pulled herself up the rope to the top of the shaft. "You could have killed us!" she yelled.

"I called a warning down the shaft," Timaeus said huffily.

" 'Fore?' " said Sidney. "You call that a warning?"

"Er . . . well, it did seem appropriate. Besides, I told you what I was going to do before Kraki and I climbed the shaft."

"You babbled something about rocks and kinetic energy! You didn't say you were going to start a landslide!"

"Sidney," Nick said, joining them, "cut it out, okay?"

"We could have been—"

"Look, it worked, all right? And nobody was hurt. You asked him to do the impossible, and he did it."

Sidney sighed. "Okay," she said. "I'm sorry. But, dammit, explain what you're going to do next time, all right?"

Timaeus puffed on his pipe with mild embarrassment.

* * *

Crouching in hiding, Garfok elbowed Drizhnakh in the ribs. "Did ya see dat?" he asked wonderingly.

"Yeah," said Drizhnakh. "Dat statue's gotta be worth a friggin' fortune."

"Yeah. Too bad we isn't strong enough ta ambush dem again."

"Uh huh," said Drizhnakh thoughtfully. "But I knows someone dat might be innerested. . . ."

"Pay Lenny now?" said Lenny.

"You're lucky we don't kill you, you little jerk," Garni said. "Get lost."

"Three pennieth an hour! You thaid tho!"

"If you're still here by the time I count ten, you're a dead lizard."

It was an exhausted troupe of adventurers that staggered into Gateway, pulling the massive statue of a man by its shoulders. The low stone buildings and dingy shops looked a lot like paradise. Or at least one of paradise's lesser suburbs.

"Hello, gents," said an orcish shopkeeper. "Had a good haul, huh?"

"What's it to you?" said Garni.

The shopkeeper wiped his hands on his apron. "Nuffing much," he said, " 'cept dat I gots da finest duty-free merchandise in dis whole burg."

"My good fellow," said Timaeus. "We are, as you see, overladen with recent acquisitions. Why should we wish to burden ourselves further?"

"Well, buddy, dere's a simple answer to dat. Ya see, da grand duke takes ten percent of anything you take trough customs."

"Ten percent? Gadzooks!"

Sidney nodded. "That's right," she said. "Standard tariff for treasure."

"An'," the orc continued, "each individual can take up ta a gallon of booze, two ounces of pipeweed, and tree quid of miscellaneous goods into da grand duchy duty free."

"I see," said Father Thwaite, eyeing the orc's floor-to-ceiling racks of bottled goods. Remembering his oath, he turned to Nick. "Perhaps you would be so good as to purchase me a bottle, lad," he said.

While the others loaded up on duty-free goodies, Timaeus conferred with Nick. "How are they going to take ten percent of the statue?" he worried. "It's worth the rest of our treasure several times over."

Nick smiled. "Leave it to me," he said. "It'll be a snap. I wonder if they've got a hardware store around here?" He wandered down the street.

Timaeus stared after him, then shrugged and went to look at the pipeweed. The variety was astonishing. "Quite a little racket," he mused, looking the store over.

Somewhere, Nick had found two mules and a cart, which certainly made hauling the statue easier. He sat in the cart, twitching the reins. Father Thwaite, already well lubricated, lay in the back on top of the tarp that covered the statue. Kraki sat with him. The three passed an open bottle of brandy back and forth; it was already a good third empty.

Timaeus puffed on his pipe and fretted. "I do wish Nick weren't drinking," he told Sidney.

"Why?" she said, somewhat surprised.

"I haven't the slightest idea how we're going to get the statue through customs. Nick says he has a plan—but if he's drunk . . ."

"Don't worry," Sidney said, smiling slightly. "He'll manage."

"Why do you suppose he painted it brown?"

"It was kind of obvious unpainted, wasn't it?"

"I tell you I got no papers, pig!" Kraki roared, shaking the official by his tunic.

"Kraki," said Nick, "you really ought to learn how to deal with bureaucrats. This is getting us nowhere."

"Hokay," said Kraki disgustedly, dropping the customs official and turning on his heel. "You talk to him."

"Sir," Nick said, "what is the procedure used when an individual from an ungoverned area enters the realm?"

The bureaucrat rubbed the back of his neck and swung his head back and forth, checking to make sure nothing was broken. "He's issued papers of transit, unless there's reason to believe he's an undesirable, in which case he's turned away at the border."

"So shouldn't you issue him letters of transit?"

The bureaucrat sighed. "It's highly irregular," he said. "Anyone who goes into the Caverns of Cytorax is supposed to have papers already."

Nick flipped a large gold coin in the air and caught it. The bureaucrat's eyes followed the sovereign hungrily; it was as much as he was paid in a week.

"I'll bet you're saying it'd be illegal for you to issue Kraki papers."

"Well, no, actually I do have that authority. . . ."

"Huh," said Nick, flipping the coin again. "I guess it's not my lucky day. You win that bet." He flipped the coin to the bureaucrat, who neatly caught and pocketed it, looking around to make sure no one else was watching.

* * *

Customs was a long, low room with a half-dozen tables. They brought the cart and their equipment up to one table and began dumping the treasure onto it. A customs official stood by; his eyes bugged as he saw the quantity of gold they unloaded. Other officials were busy checking travellers at other tables; Gateway had apparently been doing a brisk business in duty-free items this morning.

The official made a quick division of the treasure, expertly appraising some of the jeweled weapons and chalices and taking a rough ten percent for the crown. Then, he pointed to the cart.

"What's in there?" he asked. The tarp covered the statue.

"A, ah, religious reliquary," said Timaeus nervously. "Of little intrinsic worth. Artistic value only."

"Let me see," said the official, twitching back the tarp. The brown-painted statue did not look particularly impressive. He took out a pocketknife and scraped a small area free of paint.

His jaw dropped. "Guh," he said expressively.

Smoothly, Nick took one of his arms. "Keep your cool, my friend," he said. "What's your name?"

"Corcoran Evanish," the official said. "Why?"

"Well, Mr. Evanish," said Nick, "you've just become a rich man."

"What?" said the official.

"That statue, as you must realize, is worth considerably more than the rest of our treasure put together."

"I wouldn't doubt it," Evanish said fervently.

"I believe you'd normally confiscate the item, auction it to the highest bidder, and forward ninety percent of the auction price to us."

"Yes," said the bureaucrat. "That would be the indicated procedure."

"But you know how things are. The highest bidder would be some crony of the grand duke's. We'd be lucky to realize a few percent of the statue's actual value."

Evanish harrumphed. "That's no concern of mine," he said, "and I certainly have no doubts about the integrity—"

Nick interrupted him. "So," he said, "you see, we have a mutuality of interest."

"I beg your pardon?"

"We desire to get this statue through customs in order to realize the full value of our discovery. You can help us do so. We are prepared to be extremely generous in token of our gratitude for your assistance."

"Are you proposing a bribe?"

"No, no, certainly not. Nothing of the kind. Think of it as a gratuity, an expediter's fee, a little . . . lagniappe."

Evanish licked his lips and looked cautiously around the room. The brown-painted statue had attracted no particular attention. "Ah—there is my job to consider," he said.

"Ah, but a man of sufficient means need hardly labor at this dreary occupation. May I offer you—a full pound of gold? In archaic coin, no doubt of even greater value to antiquarians."

Evanish pursed his lips. "Not here," he murmured. "We're searched at the end of the shift. I will require one hundred pounds *argentum,* to be deposited in the Royal Bank of Dwarfheim. I will supply you with an account number."

Nick choked. "One hundred . . ."

"Ninety. And don't think about backing out. I have your names, and I'll turn you in if the money isn't deposited within three days."

Nick did a rapid calculation. "Seventy-five quid," he said.

"Eighty."

"Done."

This time, all six rode in the mule cart. The brandy flowed like water. The cart was more than a little cramped. The two mules were clearly unhappy, but no one much cared.

Nick was reading Kraki's papers. "Hey, Kraki," he said. "Says here you're a dwarf."

"VHAT?" said the eighteen-stone, six-foot eight-inch barbarian.

Garni chuckled. "Sure," he said. "You entered the grand duchy from the Caverns of Cytorax, which, by international law, are dwarven. You must be a dwarf."

Kraki shook his head. "I vill never understand civilization," he said. "Who's got the brandy?"

Part II.

ANOTHER DAY

I.

The sky was azure overhead. The fields were tan with stubble. Birds wheeled, gleaning discarded bits from the recently completed harvest. It was quiet, or nearly so. There was bird song; the susurrus of the wind; the clink of harness; the low, muttered conversation of ten thousand men. It was a good day to die.

There's no such thing as a good day to die. Why do all these heroic cretins sound the same?

There was something on the hill, a point of darkness. Then, there were a thousand. Suddenly, I was alert; it was the advance guard of the enemy army. I could see the standard now, a crimson rag and a green, grimacing, tusked orcish face.

Great. In fifteen minutes, it's going to be like a meat grinder here. Why don't we run like the dickens?

Drums sounded and a hundred voices bawled orders. And there was another standard, and another, and another—

The crest line was dark with the enemy.

Gah. I bet if we work fast, we can find a horse and . . .

"My liege," said a voice from my right. "You must not go."

"Aye, I must. The Royal Horseguard is our only reserve. Should their charge falter, our cause is lost. I must lead them."

No, no, bad idea. *Bad* idea. Listen . . .

The general said, "My lord, if we lose this battle, something may yet be salvaged. The wizards of the White Council hold out yet. But you are the land; your health is our health. We cannot afford your loss . . ."

Good advice. Listen to this guy.

"None may call me coward," I said. "Where my soldiers go, so go I."

Oh shit.

He sighed and held a horn out to me. "If you must go, at least fortify yourself beforehand."

"What is that?" I asked.

"Strong spirits," he said.

Good idea. If we're going to get ourselves killed, at least . . .

"No," I told him. "I will need all my wits about me."

Who *is* this jackass?

"Then I will send for tea," he said.

The smell of my mother's kitchen as she baked. I sat on a stool and drank the tea, waiting for the cookies to be done. . . .

No! No! I called my batman to me, and called for my horse . . .

She pulled out the baking sheet, and there they lay, bubbling a little yet in the heat, roughly circular blobs of dough—they smelled wonderful.

Dion take it! Listen to me, you fool . . .

I bit into one. It burned my tongue a little, but the taste of the raisins and

Men dying . . .

Cinnamon . . .

Nick sat up. The blanket was on the floor. Someone was pounding on the door. Something about cookies . . .

"I say!" said the door. "Is anyone about?"

"Just a goddamn minute," shouted Nick. He pulled on his pants and stumbled over to open the door to his flat.

The man in the hallway was slight of build. He wore a waistcoat, hose, and a ruffled shirt; his pale blond hair was drawn back in a ponytail. He raised a monocle to his right eye and studied Nick's bare chest and sleep-fogged face without approval. "How do you do," he said. "I am Wentworth Secundus Jorgesen, *Magister Alchimiae.*"

"Already got one," said Nick, and tried to shut the door.

Wentworth stuck one elegantly shod foot in the jamb. "Ahem," he said. "Perhaps I should explain my presence."

"Perhaps you should get lost," said Nick.

"I conducted a simple magical scan of the city this morning," Wentworth said, leaning on the door. "I do it frequently, to recalibrate my equipment. I use the powerful magical loci of the city to orient things, you see."

Nick stopped pushing. Garni wandered up, wearing nothing but underwear. His beard was mashed flat against his face on one side, and his hair was a mess.

"What did you find?" asked Nick.

"An extremely strong magical field is emanating from your flat," said Wentworth.

Nick and Garni exchanged glances. They both began to push on the door.

"Damn it!" shouted Wentworth, as his foot was squeezed against the jamb. "I just want to know what's—OW!"

"Go away," said Garni.

There was silence for a moment.

"Look," said Wentworth. "Let my foot out. Please?"

"Okay," said Nick. He let up the pressure. Wentworth snatched his foot away. Nick slammed the door shut and put his back to it. Garni worked the lock.

"I'm willing to pay for the information," said the door plaintively.

"Sorry," said Garni. "Go away."

"You're a mess," said Nick.

"What?" said the door.

"Not you," said Nick. "The dwarf. Get lost."

Nick and Garni waited. After a while they heard footsteps. Garni went to the window and looked out, squinting in the bright morning light.

"What do you see?" asked Nick.

"He's leaving," said Garni. "But he looks kind of . . ."

"What?"

"Determined."

"Hell."

"It occurs to me, young Pratchitt, that we have a problem. If our friend can detect the statue—"

"So can every other third-rate wizzo in the city of Urf Durfal." Nick went to the thundermug and pissed into it.

"Right you are," said the dwarf. "What are we going to do about it?"

"Beats me," said Nick, buttoning his fly. "We'd better tell the others, though."

Garni crouched in the middle of the room and pried up a floorboard. Beneath the floorboards of their basement flat were timbers, supported at the edge of the building by the foundation; and below them, about three feet of crawl space. Lying on the dirt was the brown-painted statue. It still looked like it was waiting for something unpleasant to happen.

Garni let the board fall back. "Still there," he grunted. "I think one of us should stay while the other goes to the inn. To make sure nobody nabs it while we're gone."

Nick went to the basin, poured out a little water stored in a jug, and splashed his face. He began to develop lather from a bar of soap with a brush. "Good idea," he said. "I'll go."

"You just want breakfast," Garni grumbled, moving back to make his bed.

Nick stropped the straight razor. "Yup," he said cheerfully.

It felt nice in the gutter. Thwaite had no desire to move. The sun was warm on his skin. His mind hung somewhere about three cubits up and a bit to the right of his head. The world whirled about in a familiar manner.

"We'd been on campaign for monthsh," said Vic. He lay in the gutter, too, a few feet from Father Thwaite. Vic was old, toothless, white haired, his face and hands weatherbeaten and worn. "Sho when we found that the villa's pantry wash shtocked with pickled quailsh eggs, crottled greepsh, and caviar, we were pretty excited, as you might imagine."

Thwaite had trouble believing that Vic had ever been a soldier. The oldster had lived on the streets of Urf Durfal for as long as Thwaite had known him. He had, as far as anyone knew, always been white haired, shrunken, and more than a little senile.

"When was this, Vic?" Thwaite asked.

Vic raised his head a little and seemed to regret the motion. The two of them had imbibed a truly impressive quantity of alcohol in the last twenty-four hours. "During the reign of Shtantiush," he said. "Haven't you been lishtening?"

"Yes, yes, Vic. Stantius the Third?"

"That'sh right, heh heh," Vic cackled. "How old do you think I am, anyway?"

Thwaite contemplated this while Vic continued with his interminable story. Stantius III had ruled close to two millennia ago. No one was that old. Thwaite smiled woozily and took another slug of his Château d'Alfar '08. It was good wine, one of the finest white Linfalians on the market, a *premier cru* of the elvish appellation—not the usual beverage of your gutter-dwelling wino.

The wine was all that was left of his fortune. He'd been rich, twenty-four hours ago. That was how long it had taken him to blow his share of the treasure. A fair portion had gone on the booze he, Vic, and half the neighborhood had downed over the night; but the bulk had gone to better cause. Many a poor family would wake up this morning with a coin or two that had none the night before. Many a starveling cat napped contentedly, the remnants of a fish head in its stomach. Two urchins now had apprenticeships with respectable artisans. And the temple had funds enough to sponsor at least four feasts.

All, of course, in humble obedience to Thwaite's ecclesiastical instructions. He had precisely sixpence left.

A boot shoved him in the ribs. "I might have known I'd find you here," said a voice. "Drunk in the gutter."

Thwaite dimly made out a face. "Good morning, Sidney," he said.

"Come on," she said. "We've got to get to Kraki's inn."

"All right," said Thwaite. He rose, stumbled a few paces, and fell to his knees.

"Going, Geoffrey?" said Vic.

"I'm afraid so, Vic," mumbled Thwaite, trying to get on his feet again.

"There wash shomething you shaid lasht night," said Vic, sitting up on one elbow. "Shomething about . . ."

Sidney helped Thwaite up and steadied him on his feet. "What?

"Shomething about . . ."

They began to walk off, Thwaite quite unsteadily, Sidney half holding him up.

"About a shtatue!" said Vic, triumphant at remembering.

"What?" demanded Sidney, turning. "Father! You know you're not supposed to—"

"A shtatue. What wash it you shaid?" said Vic.

"I'm sorry, Sidney," said Thwaite, not particularly repentently. "I must have been—"

"Drunk," she said. "That's not much of an excuse, Father, given that you're drunk almost all the time."

"You have to tell me about the shtatue!" said Vic, clawing at Thwaite's robes from his position in the gutter.

"Forget it," said Sidney, shoving him away with her boot.

"It'sh important," Vic said.

"What could be important to a bum in the gutter?" she said. She flipped him a ha'penny coin. "Shut up and forget about it." She frog-marched Thwaite away, giving him what for.

"Shtatue," Vic muttered to himself, sitting on the slate curb. He shook his head, trying to clear it. My memory ishn't what it ushed to be, that'sh the problem, he thought. Why, I remember when . . . Remember when . . . Well, anyway, my memory ishn't what is ushed to be.

There was a shtatue once, a shtatue. And I was . . . Wait! Vic looked up and blinked. There, in the center of the fountain, was a statue. No, that'sh not it, he thought. It was only Roderick II, the father of the current grand duke, caught in heroic bronze (as well as, it should be said, Roderick's charger, Valiant, a horse every bit as notable as the grand duke). The statue had been there for decades, gradually turning green and gaining a thick coat of bird droppings.

A pigeon stood on the cobblestones in front of Vic. It turned its head aside and studied Vic out of one eye. Vic pulled a crust out of his pocket and extended it to the bird. The pigeon hesitated, then made a grab for it.

"Unh uh," said Vic. "Shay pleashe."

The pigeon studied him. Vic waggled his fingers and said a Word.

"Shay pleashe," he repeated.

"Please?" said the pigeon.

Vic gave it the crust.

"Thanks, mac," said the pigeon, pecking at the bread.

Corcoran Evanish blinked. The maître d' was a cyclops. Evanish hadn't expected a nonhuman, but the creature looked suitably impressive in formal attire. Corcoran felt quite out of place. The foyer was elaborately decorated, the walls covered with murals, the ceiling adorned with plaster friezes.

The cyclops studied the man's drab velveteen cloak and worn shoon. "May I help you, sir," he said, his tone clearly intimating that the only help likely to be forthcoming was a foot to the seat of the pants to assist Evanish out the door.

"Yes," said Evanish hesitantly. "I'm here to see Ross Montiel."

The cyclops raised one eyebrow. This was only natural, as he had but one. "Yes, sir," he said dubiously. "Follow me, if you will, sir." He led the way into the restaurant beyond.

It was of unusual construction, built of large sheets of glass held together with black-painted cast-iron frames. The impact was light, airy, perhaps dangerously insubstantial. The novel architecture was permitted by a recently discovered alchemical process for the manufacture of flawless sheets of glass.

The morning sun shone brightly through the glass roof; from the floor rose plants, gaudy flowers, whole trees shading tables. Lizardmen bounded about the floor, clad in black coats, bearing platters of food and dirty dishes.

"Hi, Corky," said Montiel in a high-pitched, piping voice as he looked up from his menu. He sprang to his feet—all three-foot six of him—and said, "Sit down, sit down." The elf smiled in the usual goofy elfin fashion; despite himself, Evanish smiled back.

Montiel had always been a cipher to Evanish; his mannerisms were typically elven—sweet, merry, a little twee. Yet he had become one of the biggest crime lords in Urf Durfal, intimately involved in prostitution, smash-and-grab operations, fencing, and the numbers. Evanish found it difficult to reconcile the image of sweetness that the elvenkind seemed determined to maintain with Montiel's vicious reputation. How the creature himself managed to live with the conflict was beyond Evanish's comprehension.

They sat. Corcoran studied the menu. "How are ya?" piped Montiel.

"Fine, fine," said Corcoran, buried in the folder. "Customs duty isn't the most challenging job in the world."

"Oh, but you're good at it," said Montiel enthusiastically, waving over a lizardman. "And how's the missus?"

Corcoran peered over the menu in some surprise. "I'm not married," he said.

"Oh, sorry," said Montiel vaguely. "Why don't you stop by Madame Laura's sometime? Tell them I sent you."

Corcoran colored. "Er, I'll keep it in mind," he said.

"Yeth, thir?" said the waiter.

"I'll have the oat bran with assorted fruits," piped Montiel. "And some of your yummy herbal tea."

"Yeth, thir," said the waiter, scribbling on a pad. "And you, thir?"

"Ah, two eggs. Over easy. And a rasher of bacon, please," said Corcoran.

"Tea?" asked the lizard.

"Please." The lizard bounded away.

Montiel peered at Evanish with wounded eyes. "Oh, Corky," he said sadly. "Your diet is going to be the death of you."

"What?" said Corcoran with some embarrassment.

Montiel shook his head. He stood on the table, and leaned over to poke Corcoran's stomach. "You need to get some fiber in there," he said. "You're eating nothing but fat. Fat fat fat."

Corcoran rubbed his stomach. "I'm not fat," he said.

"No, but you will be," said Montiel, retaking his seat. "Look at the typical middle-aged human. Overweight, gouty, ruddy jowls. Years of poor diet."

"Well . . ." said Corcoran, but Montiel was not to be interrupted.

"Animal flesh is poison!" he squeaked. "Do you know how they raise pigs in this country?"

Corcoran had a fair idea, but preferred not to think about it.

"There's a practice knows as 'pigs following cows,' " piped the elf. "Cows aren't very efficient about turning feed into flesh. There's still a lot of nutritional value in their dung."

Corcoran began to turn green. "Please," he said.

"So they feed it to the pigs, which are much more efficient. Pigs can not only survive on the stuff, but thrive."

Corcoran swallowed and rubbed his eyes. The food arrived. The bacon was still sizzling.

Montiel stabbed in the direction of the bacon with his spoon. "Bullshit," he squeaked. "That's what you're eating." He began to spoon up his oat bran.

Corcoran pushed his bacon around with his fork. "I have some information that may be of value to you," he said.

Montiel swallowed a mouthful of peaches and said, "Uh huh?"

"A . . . highly magical object of considerable value was taken out of the caverns yesterday."

"Oh, yeah?" said Montiel, his attention firmly on Corcoran. "How much value?"

Corcoran cleared his throat and took a swallow of tea. "Immense value," he said. "I couldn't begin to estimate."

"What do you want for the information?"

Corcoran considered. "Five pounds *argentum*," he said.

"Does anyone else have this information?"

"Other than the party which found the item? I don't believe so."

"Okeydokey." They settled on four pounds ten.

Kraki stumbled into the taproom. He went to the bar, leaned over, grabbed a glass, and filled it with porter. He drained the glass, filled it again, and sat heavily down at a table. He leaned back in the chair. It creaked under his weight.

The innkeeper approached. He was walleyed. Both eyes seemed to do their best not to focus on Kraki. The man crouched a little and wiped his hands repeatedly on his apron. "Excuse me, honorable," he said in a quaver, ready to run if necessary.

"Yah," said Kraki and took a gulp of the beer.

"Please, sor," said the innkeeper miserably. "I hate to bring it up, really I do, but it's been weeks and weeks, and this inn were not too profitable, you know, my wife and I—"

"Stop vhining," said Kraki, looking at the innkeeper for the first time.

The man cringed. "Sorry, sorry, forget I said a thing," he said and began to scuttle away. He still bore bruises from the last time he'd mentioned Kraki's tab.

Kraki nabbed the innkeeper by one arm. "Vhat is it?" Kraki said, shaking the man.

"It . . ." said the innkeeper. Then, he drew a deep breath. "It were your bill, sor."

Kraki hurled the innkeeper to the floor.

"Bah!" he shouted in disgust. "This is vhat civilization is all about. Money money money!" He hurled a purse at the innkeeper. It hit the man in the head and raised a lump. "Here," he said. "Have your damn money."

The innkeeper grabbed the purse and, blubbering, crawled for the kitchen. He noticed that the purse was rather heavy. He stopped, opened it, and peered within.

It was filled with gold coins. He gaped. Slowly, he poured the contents on the floor and began to count.

It was a bloody fortune. It would buy the tavern several times over. He gulped and looked at Kraki, who was getting more beer from the bar.

The innkeeper swallowed and put the gold back in the purse.

He went to Kraki and patted the barbarian on the back. "Thank you, sor," he said. "Thank you." He leaned closer and said, "You can stay as long as you bloody like." Then, he scuttled away.

Kraki shrugged, watching the man go. He would never figure out why these people did what they did. He drained his glass.

II.

The foreign minister and the ambassador from the County Palatine of Ishkabibble were gabbling about something, but Grand Duke Mortimer paid them no attention. He frowned at his plate and peeled the egg away with his silver fork. He peered at the mushroom thus revealed through the magnifying glass he kept on his watch fob. It was a simple mushroom omelet, prepared with the dreadfully plebeian *Agaricus campestris*—but the crown of the mushroom, he could see, had receded noticeably from the stem. He pursed his lips. How vulgar, he thought. This was a sign of age. The mushroom must have been picked several days previously. As such, it was perfectly suitable for use in a sauce or soup, but no longer quite delicate enough for direct consumption, as in an omelet. There was no excuse for this, Mortimer thought; before the chef sliced the mushroom, he must have been able to see the dark gills of the *campestris,* themselves a clear signal of age. I will have to have a chat with the *chef de cuisine,* he thought.

He turned to the Baroness Veronee, who seemed uninterested in her own omelet. "I do wish you'd join me this morning," he said. The baroness was ravishing in a high-collared red velvet dress, which set off her pale skin most wonderfully, as did the black lace veil that covered but did not hide her aquiline features. "I have a most unusual *Amanita,* " he said. "Grown from spores imported from Far Moothlay. I had difficulty establishing it at first, but it seems to do very well on horse dung." To the joy of Urf Durfal's criminal class, the Grand Duke of Athelstan's only abiding interest was mycology, the study of mushrooms and other fungi. The dungeons beneath Castle Durf were now largely given over to his studies, packed full with dung, humus, and pale fungal growth. Whenever the grand duke needed room for a new variety, another dozen criminals were pardoned.

"It does sound wonderful, Morty," said the baroness, resting one crimson-nailed hand on his arm and hiding a yawn with the other, "but I've been up all night at the most *ennuyeux* ball. I really must retire shortly."

Sir Ethelred Ethelbert, the current foreign minister, sighed heavily and pinched the bridge of his nose. *"If* you please, my liege," he said, "the situation in Ishkabibble is most grave."

"Sorry, sorry," said the grand duke, a little guilty that he hadn't been paying attention. "What exactly is the problem?" he said.

The ambassador threw up his hands and began to eat his omelet, which had grown cold while he waited.

Sir Ethelred smiled grimly and spoke through his teeth. "The Great Evil Empire," he said, enunciating carefully, "is on the move. After centuries of quiescence, it has once again invaded human lands."

"Yes, yes," said Mortimer, taking off his glasses and polishing them with his handkerchief, "but what has that got to do with us?"

"The County Ishkabibble is fighting valiantly against a combined force of orcs and trolls," said Sir Ethelred. "The capital city of Ish is under siege."

"We will fall," said the ambassador through his omelet. "And soon."

"Unless," said Sir Ethelred, "help is forthcoming from other human realms."

"You frighten me," said Baroness Veronee, placing her right hand above her left breast. The grand duke watched both hand and breast avidly. "Surely we are in no danger here."

The foreign minister shook his greasy locks. "No immediate danger, I assure you, my lady. Nonetheless, should the forces of darkness go unchecked . . ."

"What have our military men to say?" said Mortimer.

Major Yohn looked up, a stricken expression on his face. He commanded the Fifth Frontier Warders, recently returned from the suppression of the Meep banditti. He was thoroughly enjoying his time at court: he'd spent close to two years in the field, sleeping in mud and picking fleas out of his hair, and Urf Durfal was heaven by comparison. There was superb food, wine, women . . . his only real problem was keeping his battle-hardened men from getting out of hand. Carousing was one thing, but they'd nearly destroyed a tavern three days ago.

Yohn was no courtier. He was a potter's son. He'd joined the army because he'd been taken in by all that guff about visiting exotic places and rising rapidly through the ranks. The idea of talking directly to the grand duke filled him with dismay.

He was thankful, therefore, when General Carruthers spoke up. Car-

ruthers commanded the Ducal Guard. The Guard was permanently stationed at Castle Durf; the only action it had seen any time in the last three
decades was against the citizens of the city, who rioted from time to time,
usually around Carnival.

"Hah!" said Carruthers, and snorted through his mustache. "Orcs and
scum. Send us to Ish, my liege! We'll put the blighters down in no time."

Yohn rolled his eyes. The force besieging Ish was the largest army anyone had seen in centuries. The average age of the Ducal Guard was thirty-
five. Most of them had a hard time squeezing into their breastplates. Mem-
bership in the Guard was a sinecure for successful bourgeoisie and petty
nobles. Faced with anything but unarmed rabble, they'd probably turn tail
and flee.

"Good, good," said Mortimer. "What about the others?"

Sir Ethelred closed his eyes briefly. "What others, Your Grace?"

"Hamsterburg, Alcala, Stralhelm—you know."

"Ishkabibble is appealing for aid to all of the human lands, Your Grace.
And to the elves and white orcs as well."

The ambassador sighed heavily but did not speak.

"War." The Baroness shuddered and took a sip of red wine.

Mortimer watched her red lips part and licked his own. He shook his
head. "Let the closer lands bear the burden," he said.

"Your Grace," said Sir Ethelred, somewhat distressed. "I must advise—"

"No," said Mortimer petulantly. "Enough of this. If there's a grand
alliance or something . . . But for now . . ."

Yohn mulled this over and took a sip of the grand duke's superb Alcalan
red. Mortimer kept a good cellar. Gods knew, Yohn had no desire to see
action again any time soon. But any idiot could see that Sir Ethelred was
right. Yohn toyed with the idea of resigning his commission and heading
for Ish himself.

A page boy charged into the room. Two guards intercepted him. He ran
headlong into the breastplate of one. "Sorry," he gasped, rubbing his head.
"Message for the minister." The guards let him through, and he went to
Sir Ethelred. Ethelred took a piece of paper from the boy, put on pince-
nez, and peered at the message.

"Most extraordinary," muttered Sir Ethelred.

"What is it?" said the grand duke testily.

Sir Ethelred peered at him over the glasses. "My liege, the Sceptre of
Stantius is glowing."

"What?" asked Baroness Veronee in a low voice.

Sir Ethelred looked at her. "Just came over the news crystal," he said.

He cleared his voice and read. " 'Oyez, oyez, oyez. Chief Herald, Free City Hamsterburg. Let it be known throughout the human lands that the Sceptre of Stantius, symbol of the True King of Mankind, glows once again, foretelling the imminent accession of a new king. More to follow. Thirty.' "

"Thirty?" asked Mortimer. "What's that?"

"It means, 'the end,' " explained a minor counsellor.

"If they mean 'the end,' " complained Mortimer, "why don't they just say . . . My dear! But we've just finished breakfast."

"I am sorry, Morty," said Baroness Veronee, rising to leave, "but I must go."

While they argued, Sir Ethelred and the Ishkabibblian ambassador conferred. Yohn eavesdropped. "What does this mean?" asked the ambassador.

"Gods only know," muttered Ethelred, rereading the message. "There hasn't been a king in two thousand years. Since Stantius the Third. Deuce of a time for this."

"No," said the Ishkabibblian ambassador with dawning hope. "The timing may be excellent."

Thwaite's head and forearms were splayed on the rudely hewn wood table. He was snoring.

Nick had one arm around the serving wench, a grin on his ferretlike face. "Got any hotcakes?" he asked.

She giggled and bobbed her head. Sidney rolled her eyes.

The innkeeper wiped his hands on his apron. "And you, honorable?" he asked Timaeus.

"I say," said Timaeus. "Didn't I note a kettle of greeps on the fire?"

"Yes, sor," said the innkeeper. "Freshly crottled."

"Excellent. Three fried eggs and a side of greeps, if you will."

"Yuck," said Nick.

"Some kind of fish, aren't they?" said Sidney.

"Oh, no, ma'am," said the innkeeper. "That's not true. When I were a lad . . ."

GREEP STEW

"When I were a lad, I lived in the mountains of Far Moothlay. Me ma had died in childbirth, and we lived—me da, and me seven brothers—in a little croft down by the river. I were the eldest, and so I bore the brunt of things. It were I me da made go and fetch the water on the coldest days, and it were I he made keep t'others in line. Wintertime was cruel, most cruel.

The wind whipped off the mountaintops and fair froze our croft through and through, the moss in the chinks between the building stones not enow to hold back the draft. Me da spent half the day cutting logs to keep the fire burning, and were it not for the wee greepies we ne'er would have made it through to spring.

"For lying in our rude straw bed, the greepies crowded round, their poor white-haired bodies chill in the cold. And between the eight of us and the many, many greeps, we stayed warm through the bitter night.

"And when the last of the yams were gone and the pottage running low, we'd take a little one round the back, and butcher it. It were not my favorite task, but it were needed, and so I took care to strike straight and firm to spare the greepie from pain.

"And then, it were haggis time. Aye, well I remember the cold winter nights and the haggis o' greep a-roasting on the flame. Oh, we ate the flesh as well, aye we did, but we were not rich folk, and did not discard the entrails. I know it be not high cuisine, but the liver and lights we chopped and mixed wi' the last of our oats, and boiled it to a pudding. And we stuffed it with the rude seasonings, plants that grew about our croft, into the stomach of the poor little creature, and let it turn over our wood fire.

"And then at last the spring would come, and the little stream by our croft would run strong. Then would I go up in the mountains with all our greeps, up to the gray stone peaks and the brilliant meadows. The heather would come a-blooming, and the ewe greeps would drop their greeplets. Aye, gladsome was it to watch the young greepies, a-bounding with the joy of spring through the flowers of the moor.

"And though I have made my home in the city nigh these twenty years, and though me da lie long in his shallow grave, still I remember the wee white greeps frolicking in the cool mountain air; and still I remember the peppery taste of haggis o' greep, that king among all puddings."

"I'll skip it," said Sidney. The innkeeper turned to Kraki.

Kraki's eyes were glazed, and he was harrying one massive black tooth with an equally black and massive thumbnail. He took his hand out of his mouth and said, "I have fried liver."

Timaeus began to tamp his pipe. "Now," he said, "to business. I asked around at my club—"

"Wait a minute," said Sidney. "I thought we agreed not to mention the statue."

Timaeus paused, pipe in the air. "I merely inquired as to the name of a discreet dealer in antiquities and rare *objets,*" he said. "Besides which, the members of the Millennium are gentlemen all. I have no fear of indiscretion."

"Yeah, yeah," said Sidney. "Fine. Unfortunately, our comatose friend hasn't been so good." Thwaite gave a snore.

"What's he been up to?" asked Nick.

"The usual," said Sidney. "He got drunk last night, gave away his treasure, and—well, I don't know what he said, but I found him in the gutter with some geezer called Vic, who wanted to know more about a statue."

"Typical Father Thwaite," said Nick. "Hey, sugar, is that all you're bringing me? Ham and eggs? No perfumed notes? A lock of your hair?" The serving wench giggled so hard that the myriad dishes she'd managed to pile onto her arms, hands, and chest threatened to fall.

"You owrtn'ta make me laugh, sir," she said, piling dishes on the table.

Timaeus, bored with this byplay, brought his forefinger to his pipe.

"I only do it to see your glorious smile," said Nick.

There was a thunderous explosion. A flash lit the room. The wench shrieked and dived under a nearby table. Kraki's liver went flying across the room.

Timaeus puffed happily. Sidney sighed.

"Is . . . is it all right, gentles?" came a tremulous voice from beneath the table.

"Yes, yes," said Timaeus testily. Nick clearly wanted to say something but was having trouble containing his laughter.

The wench crawled out from under the table. Woebegone, she fetched Kraki's liver and dusted the sawdust off. "I'm awfully sorry, sir," she said, and plopped it before him, then fled toward the kitchen.

"I say," yelled Timaeus after her, aghast. "You can't expect him to eat—"

Kraki picked the liver up in his hands and gave it a hefty bite. "Ha?" he said through a mouthful.

"Never mind, never mind," said Timaeus. He puffed for a moment while everyone else ate. "Who is this Vic fellow, anyway?" he asked Nick.

"Hmm? Oh, don't worry about him. He's an old guy, lives on the street around Five Corners parish. Been there for years. Mumbles a lot, tells stories to the kids. Senile as hell. Everyone'll just figure he's telling another of his stories."

"It's not Vic I'm worried about," said Sidney. "It's—if he told Vic, who knows who else he told?"

"Well," said Nick, "if you want something to worry about, worry about this: an alchemist showed up at our apartment this morning. Got us out of bed. He said he'd detected strong magic coming from our place and wanted to know what was up. I got rid of him, but Garni stayed to hold down the fort."

Timaeus dabbed at his beard with a napkin. "I expected the magical community to start noticing eventually," he said. "However, I had hoped it wouldn't be quite so soon. This reinforces my belief that we must find a buyer as soon as we can. Which brings me back to Jasper." He har-rumphed, and picked up a forkful of greeps.

There was a silence for a moment, save for the clinking of cutlery.

"Who?" said Nick.

"Eh? Jasper, Jasper de something something. Dealer in antiquities and rare *objets*. He has a shop on Jambon Street, so I'm told," said Timaeus.

"We don't exactly have papers proving we own the statue," said Sidney. "You sure this guy'll deal with us?"

"We can but try. I was assured as to the gentleman's discretion."

"I'd feel happier talking to a fence."

"We've been over this ground, madam. The item is so precious that a dealer in stolen goods would be hard-pressed to obtain even a fraction of its true value." Timaeus pushed aside his plate, which was polished, and took up his pipe again. "Relax," he said.

"All right," said Sidney. "But I'm coming with you. And everyone else had better go visit Garni. We don't want someone nabbing the statue while we're out."

"Don't vorry," said Kraki. "Anybody take, I kill." He burped loudly.

The coach of Baroness Veronee pulled directly into the coach house adjoining the main part of her mansion, obviating the need to exit into the painfully bright daylight. The mansion was modest as baronial residences go, a small sandstone town house, decorated in the dark style that had been popular during the reign of the current grand duke's father. Veronee's official residence was off in Barony Filbert, a decaying old pile of stones that had been in the family for centuries. She hadn't been back to Filbert in years; she much preferred the social whirl of life in the capital. More-over, there was little scope for espionage in the dank hills and gloomy orchards of her barony.

Rupert, the butler, met her in the parlor. The drapes were, as always, tightly drawn. "An exhausting night," she said. "Is my bed prepared?"

"Yes, my lady," said the butler. "However, we have . . . visitors." He spoke as if their presence pained him.

"Visitors?"

"Yes, my lady. Orcish visitors."

"Where are they, Rupert?"

"In the pantry, my lady. I thought it best to restrict them to the servants' quarters." He led the way.

Baroness Veronee surveyed the wreckage with dismay. Orcs in my pantry, she thought. They were worse than roaches, ants, mice, and raccoons combined.

There was flour and sugar all over the floor. Unable to read any of the labels, the orcs had opened everything in the pantry to make sure they weren't passing up some rare delicacy. One was chewing on a huge smoked ham he'd cut loose from the rack overhead, his tusks ripping away massive chunks, which he masticated messily. Another was peering into an empty bottle of cooking wine, apparently hoping to find a last drop or two within. The third had a jar of honey between his legs. His right hand was stuck in the jar.

"Good morning," said the baroness.

They jumped. "Oi, miss!" said one. "Nice grub ya got here!"

"Where's Cook?" said the baroness to Rupert.

"I don't know, my lady."

"Better go console her."

"My lady," he said hesitantly, "do you think it advisable that I leave you alone with these . . ."

She gave a low, throaty chuckle.

"Yes, yes, of course," said Rupert and left hurriedly.

"Now, then, my green-skinned friends," said the baroness. "Why are you here?"

They looked at each other. "Well, miss, word is dat you is innerested in things dat goes on in da caverns."

"Important events, yes."

"Well . . . do ya mind if we siddown?"

She inclined her head and led them into the kitchen. The one with the jar of honey was still trying to get his hand out. She stayed on her feet.

"Thanks, ma'am. An . . . dere's also da li'ul matter of payment."

"Indeed? And will you pay me for the mess you've made of my pantry?"

The orc with the jar of honey tried to hide it behind his chair.

The first orc was not abashed. "We isn't gonna tell ya nuffing if we don't get paid."

"How do I know that what you've got to tell me is worth money?"

The orc's face fell. He conferred briefly with the others.

"Awright. It's about a statue."

"Yes?"

"A statue made out of dat red metal."

"Copper?"

"No, no, dat magic stuff."

She raised an eyebrow. "Athenor?"

"Yup. Solid, an' dat's a fact."

"Two pounds," she said.

"Ten quid," said Garfok.

There were seven cellars beneath the town house of Veronee. There had been two when she bought it—a wine cellar and one for roots. Only the baroness and her servants knew about the others, for the simple reason that the earth mage who had built them was dead. The baroness had seen to that.

The house above was for show. She held dinner parties there; from time to time, she put up a guest. But she never slept there. Her workrooms, her living quarters, and her livestock were kept below.

She stripped off her veil and her red velvet dress and donned a simple cotton shift. By the light of a single candle, she surveyed her study. Wood and metal held back the sandy walls. The bookcases stood a good foot from the soil, lest they be destroyed by contact with wet earth and insects. One whole wall was given to her menagerie: small animals in cages. There were cats, dogs, rats, pigeons; she paid small boys to trap them for her. The cost was negligible.

In the country, she used farm animals, but in the city, she made do with available resources. From time to time, she needed greater power; then, she had one of her servants buy a horse and lead it here through the tunnels that connected her domain with the outer world.

For the most powerful spells, only sapient beings would do. It was usually possible to lure a derelict with promises of food and money.

Her masters would want to know about the Sceptre of Stantius immediately. And there was also the peculiar matter of this athenor statue to report.

She went to a cage. The droopy-eared dog within sprang to its feet upon her approach. Its tail began to wag. The wagging rose to a frenzy. The dog gave tiny leaps as she opened the lock. She picked it up and removed it from the cage. "Nice doggie woggie," she said.

As she carried it to the table, it licked her face and tried to get down. "Arfy warfums," she said.

She put it on the table and rolled it onto its back. It yipped playfully and tried to get to its feet, but she held it in place. She spoke a Word, and another.

She spoke softly, but her Words resounded in the chamber.

The dog looked at her with trusting brown eyes as she raised the knife.

She struck. And she raised the pumping neck to her mouth. Blood spurted over her face and her shift. She swallowed hungrily.

The life force gave her power. She shaped it with her spell. And when the Right Honorable the Baroness Veronee, *Magistra Necromantiae,* spoke again, her words were heard far across the world, on the plain of Arst-Kara-Morn.

Corcoran Evanish stood in the street outside an imposing structure whose pillars were demons carved in stone. His meeting had gone well. Evanish was now another five pounds richer; and a powerful demonologist now knew about the statue.

Corcoran Evanish studied his list. He crossed the demonologist's name off. There were twenty-three names to go. He pursed his lips, put the list away, and strode off down the street.

III.

The plate-glass window was lettered in gold leaf: JASPER DE MOBRAY, KGF, it said, and below that, "DEALER IN ANTIQUITIES * RARE OBJETS * DIVERS ENCHANTMENTS. " To the bottom right was a carefully painted sigil—a boar's head and the motto *"Adiuvo Te."*

"What's KGF?" asked Sidney.

"Knight of the Golden Fleece," said Timaeus. "One of Athelstan's more modest honors." His tone was mildly disapproving.

"Where does the name come from?" she said.

Timaeus cleared his throat. "The primary qualification is the contribution of large quantities of gold to the ducal fiscus."

"In other words," Sidney said, "the grand duke fleeces you of your gold . . ."

Timaeus grinned around his pipe. "And then he knights you," he said. "Precisely."

Sidney chuckled, and they entered. One expected shops on Jambon Street to be orderly and elegant; commercial rents in the district were far from low. Nonetheless, the place was a positive jumble, more reminiscent of a junk-yard than an art gallery.

An entire wall was given over to shelves bearing potions and dusty alembics. Stuffed creatures of various sorts hung from the ceiling: there were alligators, giant crayfish, several boars, a basilisk's head, and the eight-legged body of a truly gigantic spider. In one corner were piled at least a hundred swords, several of which glowed. A sign above them said, UNTESTED MAGICAL SWORDS—£10 EACH, £100 THE DOZEN. One wall bore the stuffed head of a unicorn. There was a locked glass case filled with rings and assorted jewelry. There were carved ivory statues. There were carefully painted metal figurines. Considerable floor space was given over to furniture: bookstands, armoires, secretaries, and cases. Another whole section contained weaponry of every conceivable type: knives, swords, axes, mauls, morningstars, war hammers, pole arms with blades of a plenitude of shapes and styles, and more exotic weapons Timaeus failed to recognize. There were innumerable religious relics—statues, icons, aspergers, prayer mats, and sacrificial stones. And the books—the books could fill a library.

It was to the bookshelves that Timaeus went. He studied spines and pulled down a volume, one bound in some black, shiny substance he could not identify. It caught his eye because it bore no title.

He opened it at random. A mist rose from the page and began to form into a purplish tentacle, complete with suckers. Timaeus stared at the volume, unaware.

The book closed with a snap. "No, no, sir, you don't want that one," said a voice. "I should say not, heh." The voice emanated from a point of green light that hung right above Timaeus's shoulder. "Very dangerous volume," said the light, "full of unusual and heterodox concepts." The light zipped over to another volume, which came down from the shelves, apparently on its own, and thrust itself into Timaeus's hands. "Now here's something better suited to the man of adventure, which I perceive you to be."

"Thank you," said Timaeus, somewhat bemused. He studied the cover, which proclaimed the contents *Shrood's Bestiary, Being an Universal and Compleat Cyclopoedia of the Fauna, Monsters, and Mythological Creatures of the Known World, Both Factual and Legendary, Newly Revised in Light of Recent Discoveries.*

"And you, miss," said the green light, zipping across the room to Sidney. "I perceive that you, too, are an adventurer. Perhaps you would be interested in one of our many magical swords? We are having an especial offering this week, ten pounds for untested weapons. All are guaranteed to be magical, but we have not tested further; you may be purchasing a weapon of truly legendary power or, conversely, one with a simple blade-sharpening enchantment. I'll thank you to return the brooch in your front-left trousers pocket to the display on table three."

Blushing, Sidney did so.

The light paused in midair and rose slowly toward the ceiling. "But I sense . . . I sense that these goods do not meet with your approval. I sense . . . I sense marital discord in the flat above. Damnation." There was a thump from overhead and the muted sound of shouting voices.

The light abruptly dropped about two feet. "Let's try that again," it

said. "Hmmph. Perhaps you're in the market for somewhat more sophisti-
cated goods." It zipped across the room.

"Sir Jasper," said Sidney.

"No, no, don't tell me," the light said. "Adventurers both, eh? How
about seven-league boots? Almost new, only used by an amateur giant
killer on alternate Tuesdays. No?" It zipped to another table. "How about
this," it said, and a bundle of yarrow sticks rose aloft. "Damsel-in-distress
locator. Very useful for the questing knight. No?" The sticks tumbled back
to the table.

The light zipped to a display case, which opened. A ring rose from it.
"How about this? Just got it in. Reputedly, it turns color when in the
presence of a god or goddess—very useful, what with all these damned
deities wandering around incognito and exacting horrible punishments on
those who treat them discourteously."

Timaeus snorted and looked the bookshelf over further. He pulled down
a heavy tome, entitled *An History of the Hamsterian Empire.*

"Damn," said the light, and zipped back to Sidney, hanging about two
feet in front of her forehead. "Let me see . . ."

"Actually, we're not here—" Sidney began.

"No, no," interrupted the light petulantly. "I need the practice. Let me
see. You're upset with your partner . . . Oh, really? Hmm. Oh, my dear!
I am so sorry."

"Look," said Sidney loudly. "Stop it. Stop fumbling around in my
mind."

The light backed off. "Oh, dear, oh, dear," it said. "This is most rude of
me. I hadn't intended to go quite so deep."

Timaeus looked up briefly, then returned to his book. Its prose style was
quite archaic. He flipped through it, studying the color plates, chewing on
his pipe stem.

"It'd be a lot faster for me just to explain," said Sidney.

"Yes, yes, of course," said the light, somewhat abashed. "Please go
ahead."

"Okay," said Sidney. "We have this statue. It's of a full-size human
male. It's made of athenor."

The light made a fast circle around the room and stopped before her
again.

"Athenor?" it said.

"Yes," she replied.

"Solid?"

"Yes."

"How much does it weigh?"

"We haven't weighed it," Sidney said, "but it's damned heavy."

"It would be."

There was a sudden choking sound from Timaeus. His pipe hit the floor. The light zipped over to the wizard. "What's this?" it said, hovering over Timaeus's shoulder.

Timaeus looked up and slammed the volume shut. "Nothing, nothing," he muttered. "How much do you want for this?"

"Three pounds ten," said the light. As Timaeus fumbled for change, it went back to Sidney.

"Who's the artist?" it said.

"Don't know."

"Hmm. Do you know who is depicted?"

"No."

"Is it enchanted?"

Timaeus cleared his throat. "It puts out quite a magical field," he said, "but it doesn't respond to any of the standard tests. If it has a function, we haven't been able to divine it."

"Mmm," said the light, "that may be a problem. I suspect the statue is worth more for its metal value than for either its artistry or magical function. But if it was created for some magical purpose, dissipating the mana so that it may be melted down may be difficult. Can you supply a provenance?"

Timaeus and Sidney exchanged glances. "I'm afraid not," said Timaeus.

"I don't deal in stolen goods . . ." said the light. "Ah, so that's it, eh? Evaded customs, what?"

Sidney swallowed. Timaeus moved toward her. "Nonsense," he blustered.

The light cackled. "Don't worry, old man," it said. "Not the first adventurer to cheat old Mort of his due. Nor the last, I should think." It cackled again. "And I could tell you a story or two of my own adventuring days . . . but they are long behind me." The light whizzed around the room again.

"Now then," it said. "We do have a few problems selling this object. *Imprimis,* artist, subject, and provenance are unknown. *Secundus,* it's highly magical, and no one knows why. *Tertius,* it's a damned lot of athenor to put on the market at once—if we melt it down and sell the metal in ingot form, the local market for the metal will certainly crash.

"And *quartus,* I *could* buy the thing myself, but it would take more of my fortune than I care to commit. So I must either find a buyer and simply take a cut as a go-between, or find investors to share part of the risk.

"So here's my offer. Sight unseen, I'm willing to pay ten thousand pounds *argentum,* subject only to the proviso that the object must prove to be as you have described it—the life-size statue of a human male, cast of pure athenor. If you are willing to provide additional information, to let me test the object, and to give me a few weeks to line up investors, I may be able to offer a considerably greater sum."

Timaeus's yearly income was two hundred pounds. He considered the amount exiguous, but many a petty nobleman or *haut bourgeois* survived on considerably less. He choked again and grabbed for his pipe as it fell.

Smoothly, Sidney said, "Well, it is a little less than we'd hoped to get. But it's a reasonable offer."

"Ten th-thousand . . ." stuttered Timaeus. Sidney glared at him.

"We'll have to confer with the other members of our group," Sidney said hurriedly. "And we'll think about your other offer, too." She hustled Timaeus outside as fast as she could.

"You idiot," she said as soon as they were beyond the door. "You nearly blew that." She walked him briskly down the street.

With shaking hands, Timaeus packed his pipe. "Ye gods," he said. "That's enough to buy my father's demesne several times over."

"How do you think I feel?" she said. "Until the caverns, I'd never seen more than ten pounds in a single place. But only an idiot accepts a first offer."

Timaeus bristled. "These mercantile considerations," he said airily, waving one hand, "are beneath one of noble blood."

Sidney snorted. "Okay, okay," she said. "Let me do the bargaining, all right?" She leaned away from Timaeus as he lit his pipe.

Thunder filled the street. Passersby dived for cover. A horse reared and whinnied, overturning a cart. Sidney and Timaeus marched on innocently.

Timaeus puffed deeply. "Perhaps I'd better, madam," he said softly. "And you'd better look at this." He opened his newly purchased book to a color plate.

They stopped, and Sidney studied the painting. It depicted a man in his thirties wearing archaic military dress and a prominent mustache. He had a rather silly grin on his face. The legend underneath the portrait said, "Stantius III of the White Council, last human king, captured by the forces of darkness at the Battle of Durfalus, 3708 of the Modern Era."

It was the man depicted by the statue. There was no mistaking the mustache.

Sir Jasper de Mobray, KGF, whizzed about his shop, polishing things invisibly and absentmindedly. He judged that he'd hooked them. A minor nobleman and a thief; ten thousand quid was so far beyond their experience as to be staggering. Oh, they'd bargain a bit, but they'd bite.

On the other hand—there was many a slip 'twixt cup and lip. It was hard to hide an object as valuable as the one they described. They might elicit an offer from someone else. Or someone else might steal it.

That could not be allowed. Under no circumstances could he permit the statue to fall into the wrong hands.

It depicted Stantius III. He was certain. Timaeus's reaction upon viewing the color plate had been unmistakable.

And the Sceptre of Stantius was glowing, in far-off Hamsterburg.

Sir Jasper was unsure of the import but certain there was a connection. Once, he had been an adventurer himself. He had stories to tell, that he did; one didn't become a nearly invisible, flying wizard of the mental arts, an adept of the Cult of the Green Flame, and a Fullbright of the Loyal and Fraternal Sodality of the Boar by accident.

He had a sixth sense about these things. And he knew that the forces of darkness were on the march. He had a vague feeling that the statue of Stantius was considerably more valuable than its metal content implied. He had the feeling that it could move nations.

A small spark split off from the green light that was Sir Jasper.

"Damon!" said Sir Jasper.

"Yeah?" said the spark.

"Go to the Grand Boar. Tell him—the hunt is on."

"Yeah, yeah. Whatever."

"Get going, you!"

"All right, all right, you don't have to get testy." The spark zipped through the plate-glass window.

Kraki stood in the doorway of Nick and Garni's flat, the body of Father Thwaite slung over one shoulder, his free hand poised to knock. Nick had asked the barbarian to go to the flat with Thwaite to make sure Garni was all right. "I'll meet you later," Nick had said.

There wasn't, Kraki noted, much point in knocking. There wasn't any door to knock *on*. Whoever had broken in had not been a skilled locksmith. He'd simply smashed the door open. Kraki approved.

"Hallo?" he said. "Garni Dwarf?" He walked into the room and deposited Father Thwaite on a pile of rubble.

The apartment was a shambles. Whoever had searched it had broken the furniture up by slamming it into the walls. Huge clumps of plaster lay on the floor; sections of wall were down to the lath. Clothing and bedding were strewn about. Straw from the ripped-up mattresses was everywhere.

The thundermug had been smashed; its smelly contents puddled in one corner.

Garni's equipment was hither and yon, most of it broken. Garni was nowhere to be seen.

"Fine thing," muttered Kraki to himself. He wandered over to the center of the floor and pushed aside some rubble. Nick and Garni had said they had a secret compartment in the floor. Kraki didn't really know where, but . . . Yes, the cracks around those floorboards looked a little prominent. He pried them up with his fingernails.

The statue was still there, peering up uncertainly.

Kraki put the floorboards back.

"Bad guys come," he said to himself. "Take dwarf as hostage. Search for statue. Don't find."

He surveyed the room.

"Not very good searchers," he muttered. "Vhy not look under floorboards?" He shrugged.

He looked around the room. There were only two ways in—the exterior door and a window. He pulled the remnants of a bedstead to one end of the room, a position that gave him a clear view of both apertures. He drew his sword, sat down, and laid the sword across his knees. And waited.

Father Thwaite rustled. A moment later, he sat up, rubbing his eyes. He surveyed the room. "Good lord," he said. "What happened here?"

Kraki sighed.

IV.

"**H**ey," wheezed Vic. "Give an old man a peach?"

The fruit vendor glared at him and continued to pile apples onto the table.

Vic stood in the shade of the fruit stand awning and contemplated the statue of Roderick II. Old Mad Roddy looksh good on horsheback, he thought. It was a brilliant summer morning, already hot, the square redolent of dried horse dung and the smells of fresh food. The women of the neighborhood went from stall to stall, stocking up on produce, fresh-killed chickens, the occasional piece of meat.

A matron wearing a loose-fitting dress and sensible shoes flounced up. "Good morning, Jeremy," she said. She had a serving boy in tow, with a small wooden wagon.

"Morning, ma'am," the vendor replied. "What'll it be today?"

She looked over the display. "Are those peaches fresh?"

"Aye, yes, ma'am," he said. "Just in today. Heard about the Sceptre of Stantius?"

"I'll take three dozen," she said. The serving boy began to load them onto his wagon. "In Hamsterburg? What about it?"

Vic coughed directly into the apple display. Neither seemed to notice.

"It's glowing," said the vendor. "News is all over town. They say there's going to be a king again."

Vic placed both hands on the apple table and put his back into the cough. He gave a tremendous, racking wheeze.

The matron laughed scornfully. "Some people will believe any . . . What is that man doing?"

Vic noticed their attention. He redoubled his efforts. He wheezed,

hacked, and choked. He wheezed some more. Spittle flew into the apples.
The matron was appalled.

"Shorry," gasped Vic. "Just my conshumption acting up." He coughed
again.

"Martin," said the matron in a faint voice. "Put those peaches back."
She walked rapidly away, giving Vic an uneasy glance. Somewhat embarrassed, the servant boy began to take the peaches out of the wagon and put
them back on the table.

The vendor cursed, thrust three peaches at Vic, and said, "Get the hell
out of here."

Vic cackled and grabbed them. He wandered out into the square, the
sun warm on his back. He gummed the overripe fruit toothlessly. He tore
off bits of skin and tossed them to the pigeon. "How do you like that?" he
asked the bird.

The pigeon pecked at the peach skin. "It's okay," it said.

Glowing, eh? Vic thought. He stared up at Roderick again. I remember
a shtatue. Long ago, sho long ago. There was a shtatue that disappeared.
And then . . .

He scowled. I ushed to be able to remember these things, he lamented.
Lived beyond my time, that'sh the problem. Hanging on too long. He
wandered in a circle around the statue, gumming his peaches, juice running down his chin, trying to remember . . .

And then it came to him. He almost swallowed a peach stone and
doubled over, coughing. Shtantiush! he thought in triumph, hawking spittle into the street. It'sh Shtantiush!

Someone kicked Garni in the ribs. There was a high-pitched giggle.

His eyes still closed, he shook his head. It felt fragile. This was the
second time he'd been knocked unconscious in a single week. Much more
of this, and I'm in for irreparable brain damage, he thought.

"I know you're awake, dork," said a high-pitched voice. Someone
kicked Garni in the ribs again.

He peeled open one eye. The foot that had kicked him was small. It was
shod in a green cloth boot with a curly toe. The foot belonged to an elf.
Garni had never seen the elf before. "Goodness gwacious," said Garni
nastily. "It's a fearsome elfy-welfy." He sat up.

The room was small—little more than a cubicle. It was bare of furniture. Garni sat on the pine-plank flooring. There was a single, tiny window
at the back of the room.

The elf sneered. "Gosh, Garni, old boy," he piped. "Guess you're in for
a rough time."

In addition to the elf, the room contained two mountains. At least, that's what they looked like: they were human, but they were narrow at the top and wider farther down. They had the false-fat look of goons everywhere: their stomachs and torsos were huge—with solid muscle, not with fat. Garni didn't recognize the elf, but these guys had snatched him from the apartment. They were grinning.

Outside the room, there was hubbub. It sounded like a market—people talking, something clanging, the clop of horses. Garni could smell water and old, undisturbed dust.

"Where's the statue, dork?" said the elf.

Garni perked up. That meant they hadn't found it. "What statue?" he said.

That was a mistake. One goon picked him up, twisted an arm painfully, and threw him to the other goon. Goon number two slugged Garni in the stomach several times. Hard.

Garni fell to the floor and retched. He wished he had a war axe.

The elf giggled.

"Permit me to introduce myself," said Garni to the pine boards.

"We already know who you are, dork," chirped the elf.

"And who the hell are you?"

"I think maybe I'll ask the questions. Where's the statue, dork?"

"Gawrsh," said Garni. "The widdle elfy-welfy is twying to act tough. Ain't he cute?"

Goon number one picked him up again. Garni's abdomen was starting to become rather tender. "Cute," he gasped into the goon's face.

"Duh, boss?" said goon number one.

"Yeah?"

"I don't think he's gonna talk, boss."

"Probly not," sang Montiel. "But I like watching dorks crawl."

"Okay," said the goon. Both thugs played kick the can with Garni's ribs for a while.

"That's enough," said the elf after several minutes. Garni lay on the floor, blood running into his beard. The elf sounded disappointed. "All for nothing, dork," he said to Garni. "You're a hostage, anyway. Your friends will give up the statue, I bet—after we start sending 'em pieces of dork."

Garni tried to think of something witty, but his brain wasn't working too well just then.

"You guard the room, Fred," said the elf as he minced out the door.

All of a sudden, the room was empty. "I hate pointy ears," said Garni to the air.

* * *

The Grand Boar was in full dress. His face was completely masked by a boar's head, tusks curving skyward, glass eyes staring glassily, bristles bristling impressively. His eyes peered out through the boar's mouth. He wore the robes of office and dark green cummerbund that befitted his rank. He was sweating heavily.

"Jasper, old man, delighted to see you," he said, despite the fact that all he saw was a greenish glow. He offered the forefinger and pinky of his right hand in the ritual Boar handshake. He felt something grab them and perform the shake.

"Manfred, it's been a while, hasn't it? And how is your darling Amelia?"

"Growing up too quickly for my taste," said the Grand Boar, shaking his tusks. "Things have changed since I was a boy, I must say."

"The way of the world, old thing. The way of the world. Have some sherry?"

"Don't mind if I do." They wandered over to the side-board. A carafe of pale brown liquid rose and poured two drinks. Both glasses rose into the air; one pressed itself into the Grand Boar's hand.

The room was filling up with others, many wearing boar masks, though most far less elaborate than Manfred's. They greeted one another with glad cries, gave the ritual handshake, and talked of the latest news and the jokes in current circulation.

The room itself was luxuriously appointed, with overstuffed armchairs, footrests, and heavy oaken tables piled high with books. At the back of the room was an elevated stage, and behind it, the coat of arms of the order: a boar's head, and the motto of the Loyal and Fraternal Sodality of the Boar, *Adiuvo Te*—"I Aid Thee."

The Grand Boar laboriously climbed the short stairway to the stage and walked to the lectern. The three Fullbrights of the Urf Durfal chapter sat on the couch behind him. They were Jasper de Mobray, KGF and *Magister Mentis;* Wentworth Secundus Jorgensen, *Magister Alchimiae;* and Morglop Morstern, cyclops, and a *landsknecht* of renown.

The Grand Boar cleared his throat. Silence grew as the members of the order noted his presence at the lectern and seated themselves. The herald put a horn to his lips and blew. The last vestiges of conversation died away at the sound.

"The hunter's horn sounds," said the Grand Boar.

"And we prepare," responded several dozen voices.

"Ahem," said the Grand Boar. "I called this meeting in response to an urgent summons from Brother Jasper. I thank you for responding so promptly. Actually, I don't have the slightest idea what's up. Jasper?"

"Wait a minute," said an argumentative voice from the audience. It belonged to a dour-looking dwarf in the back. "What about the reading of the minutes?"

"Oh, bother," said the Grand Boar. "I'll entertain a motion to dispense with the reading of the minutes."

"So moved," said a bored-looking woman in black leather garb, wearing an eyepatch.

"Second," said several voices.

"Is there any dissent?"

The dwarf said, "Yes!" in a firm voice.

The Grand Boar sighed. "All right, all right," he said. "All in favor, say aye."

There were scattered ayes.

"What are we voting on?" asked a puzzled voice.

Testily, the Grand Boar said, "All right, we'll do that again. All in favor of dispensing with the reading of the minutes, say aye."

There was a chorus of firm ayes.

"All opposed?"

The dwarf was the only one who said "Nay."

"That's that, then," said the Grand Boar. "Jasper?"

The green glow moved from the couch to the front of the stage.

"Wait a minute," said the dwarf.

"Yes, Brother Horst?" said the Grand Boar irritably.

"Whatever the Fullbright has to say is new business."

"So?"

"Old business comes first," said the dwarf in a satisfied tone.

There were groans from the audience.

"Really, Horst," said the Grand Boar. "Things would go so much faster if—"

The dwarf shook his head determinedly. "Rules is rules," he said.

"Bloody hell," the Grand Boar muttered under his breath.

"Knew we should have blackballed the blighter," said a voice in the audience.

"Move to dispense with the old business and move straight to the new business!" said the woman in black.

"Second!"

"Right!" said the Grand Boar. "All in favor?"

Lots of ayes.

"Opposed."

"Nay," said the dwarf.

Everyone glared at him.

"Finished, are we?" demanded the Grand Boar. The dwarf folded his arms and jutted his beard.

"Well, then. Jasper, if you please—"

"You're supposed to open the floor," said the dwarf.

"Someone sit on him, please," said the Grand Boar.

There was a scuffle at the back of the room. The dwarf shouted something incomprehensible as several members sat on him.

"Sure you don't want to be Grand Boar?" Manfred whispered to Wentworth. "I'd resign in an instant."

"Not a chance," Wentworth whispered back.

"Thank you, Brother Manfred," Jasper said loudly. The Grand Boar seated himself. "As you may have heard," said the point of green light, "the Sceptre of Stantius, a relic of the long-lost human empire kept in the safekeeping of the Lord Mayor of Hamsterburg, is reported to be glowing."

"Aye," said a white-beard from the rear of the room. "And legend has it that this foretells the accession of a new true king of the human realms."

There was a skeptical buzz.

"Be that as it may," said Jasper. "This morning, I was visited by two adventurers, one Timaeus d'Asperge, a fire mage, and his associate, Sidney Stollitt. Neither is a member of our society.

"They reported to me that they had acquired a life-size statue of a human male, cast in solid athenor."

My words and Good lords rose from the assemblage.

"They did not tell me, but through my magical powers I divined, that the statue depicts Stantius the Third, the last human king, the last to hold the Sceptre of Empire, now known as the Sceptre of Stantius. They also reported that the statue emanates strong magical power, the source and purpose of which they do not know . . ."

There was a stir from the couch.

"Yes, Brother Wentworth?" said Jasper. That worthy rose and came to the lectern.

"There may be a connection," he said. "This morning, I did a magical scan of the city, a simple alchemical process I use to calibrate my equipment. I noted a strong source of magical energy that I had never previously detected. Extraordinarily strong, Brother Jasper; only the magical protections about the grand duke's castle register more strongly at the present time."

"Hmm."

"I traced the emanations to a flat in the Five Corners parish—an unlikely area to find such powerful magic, you'll agree." There were murmurs of assent; Five Corners might not be the worst slum in Urf Durfal, but it was not far from it. "The inhabitants of the flat, a human male and a dwarf, refused to permit me entry or to provide any explanation. Their landlady told me that their names were Garni ben Grimi and Nick Pratchitt."

"Yes?"

"Further inquiries revealed that Pratchitt is a partner in Stollitt and Pratchitt, a firm that does guard work, assembles expeditions into the caverns, and, per rumor, dabbles in theft and the sale of smuggled goods."

"The selfsame Stollitt who visited me this morn?"

"I do believe so."

"Then the powerful object you detected may also be this statue."

"It would seem so."

"If the object is as powerful as you indicate—"

"It must be of world-shaking import."

There was silence in the room.

"I venture to suggest," said Jasper, "that there is some connection between the appearance of this statue and the reports from Hamsterburg. Precisely what this connection may be, and what this may mean for the free peoples of the globe, I cannot say. I believe it important that we obtain this statue for further study."

The cyclops spoke from the couch in a deep, grating voice. "Ish is at war with Easterlings," he said. "Is connection? Do trolls move to prevent human king?"

There was silence as the Boars considered this.

"What do you ask of us?" the Grand Boar said to Jasper.

"I have opened negotiations with d'Asperge and Stollitt toward the purchase of the statue," said the green light. "They're well aware of the mere monetary value of that much athenor. . . . I may need to call upon the Sodality's financial resources to close the deal."

"Would you care to phrase that as a motion?" said the Grand Boar.

"Er . . . I'm not up on the niceties of the rules of order," Jasper said sheepishly.

A man clad in forest green spoke: "I move that Brother Jasper de Mobray, a Fullbright of our assemblage, be permitted access to all the treasure and wealth of the Urf Durfal chapter of this order for the purpose of purchasing the athenor statue of Stantius the Third, subject to an accounting of all expenditures." There were several seconds.

"Any opposed?" said the Grand Boar.

There were sounds of struggle from the back of the room. Horst the dwarf rose to his feet and managed to shout, "Nay," before several others dragged him back down.

"Carried by acclamation," said the Grand Boar.

"Also," said Morglop.

"What's that?" asked Jasper.

"This statue, it must not go to ones who would misuse it. We must protect it."

"Good idea," said Jasper. "Will you take on that task?"

"If you wish," said the cyclops, resting one hand on the hilt of his broadsword.

"I'll go too," said Wentworth.

"Good fella," said the cyclops and slapped Wentworth, not the beefiest of men, on the back. The impact propelled him off the stage and into the first row.

"Many sorrows," said the cyclops, peering over the edge of the stage.

V.

Timaeus and Sidney stood in the shattered doorway. "Boy," said Sidney, "Nick is messy, but this is ridiculous."

"Dwarf is gone," said Kraki, rising, his sword in his hands.

"Beg pardon?" said Timaeus. He and Sidney came into the room and looked at the chunks of plaster and smashed furniture with bemusement.

Father Thwaite stood up a little unsteadily. "The place was like this when we got here," he said. "Kraki believes that someone came, searched for the statue, failed to find it, and snatched Garni as a sort of consolation prize."

"The statue's still here?" said Timaeus.

"Yah," said Kraki, stamping on the floorboard. "Is here."

"This is most upsetting," said Timaeus. "Sidney, perhaps we ought to sell the statue before—"

Timaeus broke off. There were footsteps and giggles from down the corridor. "Hold that thought, doll," said Nick Pratchitt's voice, "just let me get my keys. . . ."

Nick stood in the doorway, the servant girl from the inn under one arm, keys in the other hand. Openmouthed, he surveyed the wreckage. "Holy maloney," he said.

"Good morning, Mr. Pratchitt," said Sidney icily. "Perhaps you would introduce us to your companion."

"Ohmigawrsh," said the wench, looking at the rubble.

Nick cleared his throat. "I—ah, hadn't expected you all back so soon," he said.

"Clearly," said Timaeus, enjoying himself. "Garni's gone, you know."

"Huh?" said Nick.

"Bad guys snatch," said Kraki. "But statue still here."

"Nickie?" said the wench. "Are we stayin' here? Cause I gotta be back at the inn by—"

" 'Nickie'?" said Sidney in a dangerous tone, advancing toward Nick Pratchitt.

At that instant, the window shattered with a shocking clash. A multilimbed, ochre body tumbled into the room. It righted itself on batlike wings and thrust a sword toward Kraki, the closest figure in the room.

The barbarian ducked, raised his own sword, and faced off against the demon.

There was a clap of thunder, the noise of a teleporting body displacing the air. In the center of the room, another demon floated, this one a shark-toothed furry little creature. It darted toward Sidney, snarling.

She drew her own blade and backed toward the door.

The wench screamed and scrabbled back down the hall, tripping over debris. Yet a third demon, yellow eyes glaring from within a cloud of dark smoke, appeared, right behind Nick.

"Watch out, Nick," yelled Timaeus. Nick spun and backed into the room drawing his own blade, a simple dagger.

Father Thwaite searched desperately through the rubble. He needed brandy . . . brandy . . . He knew Nick had some, and it must be somewhere in all this stuff.

Caught between two demons, Nick and Sidney fought back-to-back. The toothy creature darted for Sidney's leg, but she struck it a glancing blow, and it backed off, bleeding a yellow fluid. The smoky demon gave a disconcerting, hollow laugh, and spat a line of flame toward Nick. He dodged. "I told you to go back to the apartment!" screamed Sidney. "To protect Garni and the statue . . . And look what you—"

Nick spat at his opponent, hoping that the demon's use of flame meant it was fire-aligned and that water would harm it.

His spittle did no apparent damage. "I sent Kraki and Father Thwaite," he said defensively. "Anyway, I—"

Timaeus released his spell. A dart of flame shot across the room and through the body of the smoky demon. The dart passed through the smoke, leaving a hole—but smoke expanded to fill the hole again. Flames shot through the doorway to start a fire in the stairwell. The demon repeated its strange, bass laugh.

"You jerk!" yelled Sidney, dodging her demon again. It bit her in the shoulder. She stabbed at it gingerly with her sword, trying not to injure herself. "The point is, what the hell were you doing?"

Father Thwaite was chanting now, shouting some prayer across the room.

Nick's demon was closing, moving slowly across the space between them; Nick swiped at it with his dagger, but the weapon had no effect on the discorporate creature. "What's it to you?" shouted Nick angrily. "You've made it clear that—"

"We're sitting on trouble," said Sidney, "and you're crawling into some tart's skirts. OW!"

Father Thwaite sprinkled brandy over the toothy demon, brandy that glowed with blue light. The demon screamed and dissolved into nothingness. Some of the brandy entered Sidney's wound, stinging terribly.

Thwaite flung the rest of the brandy toward the smoky demon. It disappeared with a snap.

The last of the demons climbed out the window into daylight, Kraki thrusting after it with his sword, a long, ragged tear in its wing.

For a moment, there was peace in the room.

"I'm tired of your constant carping," shouted Nick, turning to face Sidney, his dagger in his hand. "All I get from you is—"

"Carping! Is that what you—" Sidney yelled.

"Someone had better do something about that fire," said Timaeus. The stairwell was still burning. Sidney and Nick continued to yell at each other.

"Hokay," said Kraki, walked into the hall, unbuttoned his fly, and urinated onto the flames.

"Yes!" shouted Nick. "Carping! 'I don't like this, I don't like that.' I remember when you used to think that we—"

"Ahem," said Timaeus.

"You're the one that screwed it up, Nicholas Pratchitt!" yelled Sidney. "I was quite content to be your partner and not your—"

"Good day, goodwife," said Timaeus loudly.

Nick looked at the wizard. Timaeus pointed toward the doorway.

A plump, middle-aged woman stood there. "Mrs. Coopersmith," Nick groaned. It was his landlady.

She entered the room and looked around. She grew grim. "I knew I should never have rented to a dwarf and a single man," she said. "More of your wild parties, I suppose."

"What? Mrs. Coopersmith! This isn't our fault. We—"

She turned to him and shook her finger. "I don't care whether it's your fault or not, young man! I want you out! Now!" she shrieked.

"But Mrs. Coopersmith, the lease says—"

"The lease doesn't say anything about smashing the walls! And fires in the hall! And huge men urinating in the stairwell!"

Kraki came into the room and gave her a sheepish grin.

"Disgusting is what it is," she said. "There's an outhouse out back, you know."

"We're paid up through the end of the month," Nick said defensively. It was true. He and Garni had paid her from their share of the treasure.

"I want you out!"

Nick sighed heavily. "We can't," he said. "Not now."

"Out!" she yelled.

"Mrs. Coopersmith," said Sidney, "Nick has a legal lease. You want him out, you've got to buy him out."

Mrs. Coopersmith wiped her hands on her apron and scowled. "We'll see about that," she said with determination and flounced away.

Thwaite bound up Sidney's wound. "Where did those things come from?" Timaeus wondered, fumbling through his pouch for some pipeweed.

Nick frowned. "First someone snatches Garni, then demons show up," he said. "I get the feeling that too many people know about this statue. Maybe we should move it. . . ."

"Where?" said Sidney. "How are we going to get it out of the neighborhood without attracting attention?"

"Don't worry," said Kraki. "I am here. I protect statue."

"Of course, of course, thank you, Kraki," said Timaeus, packing his pipe. "Perhaps we should simply accept de Mobray's offer. It does seem as if the statue is becoming too hot a potato for us to handle, and . . . Hello? Can we help you?"

Someone stood in the doorway. He (she? it?) wore a brown monk's robe that fell to the floor. The robe's cowl was deep, so deep no hint of a face could be seen. The cowl turned, scanning the room. Silently, the figure held out an envelope.

"What do you want?" said Sidney.

The figure wafted the envelope back and forth.

"Say something," Sidney said.

Thee was a faint, dry whisper, like a distant wind. "Something," it sighed.

"Everyone's a comedian," Sidney snarled and grabbed the note. She sniffed. The envelope was perfumed and tied with a ribbon. It was addressed to Magister Timaeus d'Asperge, No. 12, Cobblers Lane, Apt. 1.

"For you," she said, handing the letter to Timaeus. The wizard raised an eyebrow and opened it.

It was written in a delicate hand on expensive rag paper. The ink was the color of dried blood. Timaeus scanned a few lines, then read the whole letter aloud:

To Magister Timaeus d'Asperge:
My dear boy! I cannot tell you how thrilled I was to hear of your daring escapade in the Caverns of Cytorax. When first we met, I thought you rather unprepossessing, I am ashamed to admit. I should have known that there was more to you than met the eye. After all, a scion of the House d'Asperge must of necessity be destined for greatness! Athelstan needs more young men of your fortitude and enterprise.

Timaeus preened. Sidney snorted.

Per report, you acquired a certain remarkable piece of statuary in the course of your expedition. An individual whom I have the honor of representing is interested in acquiring this item. In fact, he was quite forceful in expressing his eagerness to me. He has authorized me to make an offer of £20,000 *argentum* for its delivery.

Timaeus stuttered over "twenty th-thousand."

The offer strikes me as more than generous, and I trust that it will meet with your approval. In the spirit of friendship, however, let me say that my principal is not a gentleman who brooks refusal. When frustrated, he has a tendency to become quite petulant. To speak of such things is painful, yet I believe it is my duty to say that, should this offer be refused, we may be compelled to take more forceful steps toward the object's acquisition.
Under the circumstances, I believe it best to preserve a certain air of mystery. Hence, I will say only that
I remain, your faithful and loving friend,

. . . And there it broke off. There was no signature, only a drop of dried blood at bottom right.
"Twenty thousand pounds is a lot of money," said Nick.
"I don't like the tone," said Thwaite. "And I don't like that." He pointed to the robed apparition. The cowl turned to face the priest, but the figure had no other reaction.
"The note is obviously not from Garni's kidnappers," said Sidney. "Or they'd mention him."

"Yah," said Kraki. "If ve sell statue, kidnappers be upset."

"I would dearly like to be rid of the damned thing," said Timaeus. "I say we accept."

Thwaite moved faster than Sidney would have believed possible for a middle-aged wino with a hangover. He darted to the doorway and threw back the creature's cowl.

Where the figure's head should have been, a bleached skull grinned. It turned atop a bony spine and studied each of the room's occupants in turn. Skeletal fingers reached up and flipped the cowl back in place.

"Do you want to deal with that?" Thwaite hissed.

There was silence for a moment.

"I'll deal with anyone whose silver clinks," said Nick.

Timaeus eyed Nick skeptically. "Under the circumstances," Timaeus said, addressing the cowled figure, "I believe we must refuse the offer."

The cowl faced him and nodded once. The figure glided away.

The cowled lich glided down Cobblers Lane. It was annoyed. It was terribly annoyed. This idiot idea of wandering about the city had been the damnable baroness's notion. "The entire population will flee in terror," it had told her. "Skeletons just don't walk the streets of this city, not in broad daylight."

"You'll wear a robe," she had said, "with a cowl."

"Oh, fine," the lich had whispered. "A robe with a cowl. Dandy. And suppose some religious nut wants to confess to me, eh?"

"You'll handle it," she had said impatiently.

"I'll handle it," it had said. "No doubt I shall. I don't see *you* volunteering to gad about in the daytime."

"I've had a bad night," she had said, "and I don't want any back talk."

"I'll stick out like a sore thumb."

"You'll do as you're damned well told."

It gave a soundless sigh and hesitated in front of an alley opening. It looked up the street to make sure it wasn't observed.

But it *was* observed. A peasant in an oxcart was gawping at it. The oxcart was filled with dead fish and was moving slowly down the street.

Damnation, thought the lich. It put its back to the nearest building and tried to act nonchalant. It didn't feel in the least nonchalant. No one goes around in full robes on a hot summer day, it thought to itself bitterly. Not even the devoutest of monks. Damn the bitch.

The oxcart moved down the street, slowly, slowly. The damned peasant's head swivelled, his eyes tracking the lich as his oxcart moved, his mouth agape. It's a wonder flies don't crawl down the damned man's throat, the lich thought.

Finally, the peasant turned the corner. With relief, the lich glided into the shadows of the alley. From here, hidden by shadows, it had a good view of the door to number twelve. It waited to see what the humans would do.

Really, it told itself, I wish they had accepted the offer. It's going to be so much more work this way.

It sighed again. The baroness was a harsh mistress, it told itself. She made her servants work their fingers to the bone.

Literally. It chuckled dryly.

VI.

Kraki had a broom. He was sweeping energetically. Plaster dust flew about the room.

"Cut it out," said Nick.

"Ve clean up, yes?" said Kraki.

"Why bother?" said Nick. "I have a suspicion I'm going to be moving soon, no matter what we do." Kraki shrugged and dropped the broom.

Timaeus lit his pipe. The explosion knocked more plaster loose from the walls. After the flames died down, he said, "And now what shall we do?"

"You said you wanted to sell," said Sidney.

"On reflection," said Timaeus, "I deem that inadvisable. We can expect a ransom note for Garni to show up sooner or later. I suspect it will demand the statue. Would you rather have the money or the dwarf?"

"Now you mention it—" said Nick.

Father Thwaite stared at him. "Garni ben Grimi is *your* friend," he said pointedly.

"All right, all right," said Nick. "But look . . . tracking people down is something Sid and I do all the time. We ought to be able to find Garni and spring him."

"Oh yeah?" said Sidney. "We don't have much in the way of clues."

"I want to start with Jorgesen," said Nick.

"Who?"

"Wentworth something Jorgesen, the alchemist who showed up at the apartment this morning," said Nick. "It's the only name we've got to work with. If he isn't involved—and I bet he is, somehow—then maybe he'll help us. And it looks like we'll need help, if demons and stuff keep on showing up and trying to grab the statue."

"A reasonable supposition," said Timaeus. "I, for one, want to find out more about this statue."

"What do you mean?" asked Sidney.

"My dear, are you aware of the magical properties of athenor?"

"Huh? I know they make rings and stuff out of it."

"Athenor is one of the few metals that can hold mana, the essence of magic. Consequently, it is used in the creation of magic rings, amphorae for the imprisonment of djinn, magical arms and armor, pentacles for demonologists . . . the list is endless. A ton of the stuff is an *inconceivable* quality. There must be *some* record of the statue's creation, some hint of its purpose. At the university, I can—"

"Okay, sure," said Sidney impatiently. "But here we sit on top of the damn thing, and you want to run off and do research? I say we get Garni back, sell the statue, and—"

"Jasper said it himself," said Timaeus, puffing deeply. "If we can supply a provenance and some idea of the object's intended function, we can command a considerably greater price."

"Look," said Sidney, "we're going to have to send people off looking for Garni, right? And some are going to have to stay here to protect the statue. Judging by the fact that Garni's been snatched and we've been attacked by demons, all in the space of a couple of hours, whoever stays here is going to have plenty of things to worry about. I don't like the idea of splitting our strength further. And you're our only wizard . . ."

"Thwaite can stay," said Timaeus with irritation. "He handled the demons quite well, I thought."

"Thank you," said Father Thwaite in surprise.

Timaeus waved a hand in acknowledgment. "And who other than I could do the research? Shall we sent Kraki?"

"Yah, I go," said Kraki.

"He'd probably burn down the library," muttered Sidney. "I don't like it, but—go. Get back here as quickly as you can."

"You going to come with me?" asked Nick.

"N-no," said Sidney, "I don't think so. You've got about the same skills and contacts as I—why don't you take Kraki for muscle?"

"Good," said Kraki, flexing his pectorals. "Ve kill people until they tell us vhere dwarf is, yah?"

"Something like that," said Nick with a grimace. "Come on."

The lich was doing its best not to think.

It was bored. Mortally bored. Bored beyond human comprehension. Bored as only the millennia-dead can be bored.

It must be hot, it thought, then suppressed the thought. Empty the mind, that was the trick. Empty the mind, let time pass without notice.

Bored.

It *thought* the day was hot. But it had no way of knowing for sure. The sun was bright. The sidewalk shimmered. But the lich had no body to feel warm or cold.

Bored.

A fly landed on its robes. A flicker of interest passed through the lich, then died. The fly walked into the cowl and around on the lich's skull. The lich felt no disgust, no squeamishness. It had no stomach with which to feel disquiet.

Noon was approaching. The lich felt no hunger.

Bored.

An attractive woman walked by. The lich felt no attraction.

Bored.

Nick and Kraki left the building across the street. At last, thought the lich. It waited until they turned the corner. Then, it began to follow.

The cowled robe glided down the street. Small children gaped. The religious bowed their heads in respect. Some of the more magically sensitive felt a chill and made a gesture of warding.

I *do* stick out like a sore thumb, thought the lich in mortification. Damn damn damn the bitch.

It worried that Nick and Kraki would spot it. It hung back. It could feel the life force burbling through their bodies, the fragile taste of life in the distance. It allowed itself, briefly, to feel a desire to crush that life, to drain it to fuel its own half-living existence—then followed, followed its life sense, followed with no need to keep its prey in line of sight.

It glided on.

Garni was getting hot. The room was stifling.

He studied the room's only window. It was pretty small. On the other hand, he was pretty small, too. He just might be able to squeeze through it.

He leapt up, grabbed with both hands, and pulled himself onto the sill. He peered through the window.

There was a river down there. It passed underneath the building . . . Aha! He must be on the Calabriot Bridge. It was one of four over the River Jones, six if you counted the two bridges to Nob Island. Of the four, it was the only one with buildings along both edges. There were shops all up and down the bridge, mostly goldsmiths and jewellers.

The door opened suddenly. One of the goons stood there—Fred, the elf had called him. "Hey!" said Fred. "Get away from there!" He ran into the room and pulled Garni away from the window.

"I'm not going to jump," Garni said. Fred put him down heavily.

"Sure you ain't," said Fred. "I ain't gonna let ya. Chow time." He went back to the door and fetched a bowl of stew.

It looked unappetizing, but Garni ate anyway. Gods only knew when he would get another meal. Fred, Garni reflected, was obviously not too bright. Dwarves are heavier than water. Jumping from the window would have been suicide.

"Dja year about the scepter?" said Fred, watching the dwarf eat.

"The what?" said Garni.

"The scepter thing. In Hamsterburg. They say it's glowing or something."

"So?" said Garni.

"Means there's gonna be a new king. Or something."

Garni stared at the goon suspiciously. "So what's that to me?" he said.

Fred colored. "I dunno," he said defensively. "Just tryna make conversation. Sheez."

"Okay, okay," said Garni. "I'm done."

Fred took the bowl and left the room, muttering to himself. He locked the door behind him.

Garni went back to the window and stared down at the river. A new king. Garni scowled into his beard. His grandfather had been the dwarven king. But upon his death, the gods had chosen another, not of Garni's line. That's the way it happened, the mantle of kingship descended on someone's shoulders, someone chosen by the gods. It could be anyone.

But Garni's family had been forced to leave Dwarfheim. There was nothing personal in the deportation order; it was just good political practice. You didn't want to leave potential malcontents lying around.

A barge passed under the bridge. Garni wondered if he could leap into the barge—but it was to his right, not directly beneath the window. Too bad.

The elves had a king, too. So did the cyclopes. So did all the free peoples, except for the humans. Garni had always wondered about that.

They'd had one, long ago. And if the goon was to be trusted, they'd have one again soon.

Garni wondered what that might mean.

The sign overhead said YARROW'S ALCHEMICAL EMPORIUM—MORE POTIONS FOR THE PENCE! Nick pushed the door open. A bell tinkled.

"Be with you in a minute, Nick," said Mike Yarrow. He turned to an old woman with a head scarf. "These leeches will suck those bad humors right out, Mrs. Anver," he said. "Just put the little bastards right on the boil and let them leech away."

"Oh, thankee, Master Yarrow," she said bobbing her head. "Thankee kindly." Clutching her package tightly, she hobbled out the door.

Kraki wandered the shop and stared at shelves full of vials, bottles, alembics, paper packages, and tubes. He picked up a small bottle and stared into it. A gnarled homunculus hung in a brownish liquid. Kraki wondered what it was but was unable to read the label. He shook the bottle, but the homunculus remained motionless.

"Sold any elixirs of youth lately, Mike?" asked Nick Pratchitt.

Yarrow laughed. "Nothing like that," he said. "Business is pretty slow."

"Too bad," said Nick. Mike Yarrow was a self-taught alchemist; he had neither the money nor the connections to gain a place at the university, nor the brilliance to win a scholarship. Without a degree, his clientele was restricted to the poor and the miserly. Business was always pretty slow.

"I'm trying to find an alchemist," Nick said.

Yarrow raised an eyebrow. "You've come to the right place."

"No, a different alchemist."

Kraki leaned on the counter. It creaked dangerously. "Ve looking for this guy, Ventvorth something."

"Wentworth Jorgesen. Master alchemist," said Nick.

"Oh, sure," said Yarrow. "He's got a shop on Fen Street. Good reputation, pretty swank clientele. Comes from County Meep originally. I'm told he used to be an adventurer."

"Do you know where he lives?" asked Nick.

"Afraid not," said Yarrow. "He probably has a villa someplace."

Nick gave a whistle. "He's rich, huh??"

"I guess so," shrugged Yarrow. "He's one of the better-known wizards in the city."

"Well, I guess the shop is a place to start. You have the address?"

"Sure, got it right here." Yarrow pulled out an address book.

The bell on the door tinkled again.

"Yes, sir?" said Mike Yarrow. "How can I help you?"

The lich picked up a straight razor from the counter. It leaned over and opened Yarrow's throat.

The alchemist fell back against a shelf. Bottles crashed to the floor. His hands scrabbled. Blood pumped out onto the counter.

The lich spoke a Word. It tapped Yarrow's ebbing life force and used it to fuel the spell. A shame, really, the lich thought. It bore the man no animus. And killing innocents was a messy business. Dangerous. The authorities tended to get upset. Unfortunately, it knew no spell to compel the living to tell the truth. The dead, now—that was a different matter.

It spoke another Word. The corpse behind the counter rustled.

"Do you hear me?" whispered the lich.

A sepulchral voice responded. "Yes."

"What did your last customer want?" whispered the lich.

"Leeches," said the corpse tonelessly.

What? "What did they want leeches for?"

"For her husband's boils," said the corpse.

The lich gave a silent sigh. Truth spells have their drawbacks, it thought.

"You were visited a few minutes ago by two men," it whispered. "Were you not?"

"Yes."

"What were their names?"

"Nick Pratchitt and—I don't know the other."

Good. "They wanted leeches?"

"No."

"What did they want?"

"The address of an alchemist."

"Were you not an alchemist?"

"Yes."

The lich was beginning to get irritated. "Whose address did they want?"

"Wentworth Jorgesen."

"And the address?"

"Seventy-six Fen Street."

Excellent.

With the last of Mike Yarrow's life force, the lich shaped another spell and reported to its mistress.

VII.

Wentworth Secundus Jorgesen locked the door to his shop and put up a 'Closed' sign.

"Ready?" asked Jasper.

"Righto," said Wentworth. He opened a door and led Jasper and the cyclops up a flight of stairs.

"Really," said Jasper, shedding a dim green light on the wallpaper, "I'm looking forward to this. I haven't done anything adventurous in, oh, ages."

They came to the roof. Most of it was sloping orange tile, but there was a small landing area. "Taxi!" shouted Wentworth.

"We not walk?" asked Morglop, a little uneasily.

Off in the distance, a black spot moved among the clouds. There was no response to Wentworth's shout.

"Why waste the time? Hoy!" yelled Wentworth. "I say! Taxi!" He waved his arms wildly. The black spot moved on, oblivious. "Damn," muttered the alchemist.

There was another moving spot, this one a little larger and lower, barely clearing the minaret of a nearby temple. Morglop sighed, then put two fingers in his mouth and gave a loud whistle.

The flying carpet swooped down and landed on the roof.

"Hah-doh," said the driver. It was a small, monkeylike being with wings. It wore a turban. "Where be going, sahib?"

The Boars got onto the carpet and sat down. Morglop looked distinctly unhappy.

"Cobblers Lane, between Jameson and Thwart. Chop-chop."

"Two shillingi," said the creature, holding out a paw.

"One shilling sixpence," said Wentworth briskly.

The creature bowed its head meekly. "Honest afreet mek honest bargain," it whined. "Small one at home ver' hungry. Two shillingi."

"What cheek," said Wentworth. "You creatures don't have children, and Cobblers Lane is a zone six destination. The fare is one shilling sixpence, and you'll be paid when we get there. Cobblers Lane, and yarely now, or I'll have you up before the licensing board."

The creature chattered in rage as the carpet swooped away. Morglop closed his eye.

The lich stood in the basement of Wentworth's Fen Street shop. It was dark, gloomy, the only illumination a thin line of brilliant sunshine, shining through a crack in the metal doors that lay flat in the sidewalk above. A stair led to those doors; they were opened only during the morning, when deliveries were made to Wentworth's shop.

About the lich lay bundles and bales, shelves stocked with bottles and packages. And with it stood twenty-four zombies, in varying states of decay. One was Mike Yarrow's corpse. No point in wasting a perfectly good deader, the lich thought to itself.

It was irritated. It was beginning to develop a headache. Why are humans always so unreasonable? it thought. £20,000 was a substantial sum of money. And the baroness was not a woman to cross lightly.

It sighed a soundless sigh. It's going to be so much more work this way, it thought. For a moment, it longed to be in its grave. For just a decade or two. A little rest, that's what it needed. A little rest.

Aha, it thought. It sensed Nick and Kraki's life force approaching. They were drawing nearer.

It gestured. The zombies readied their weapons.

"Damn," said Nick. The door to the shop was locked and the sign said 'Closed'.

"Look," said Kraki, pointing up as a shadow passed over them. It was a flying carpet. There were a number of figures on it. Nick recognized Wentworth by his monocle and long, blond hair.

"Hey!" he shouted. "Wentworth! *Hey!*" There was no response.

"Now vhat?" said Kraki.

"Taxi!" shouted Nick.

A carpet swept to the street and came to a halt a dozen cubits away. Nick and Kraki ran for it. "Follow that carpet!" yelled Nick to the afreet. He and Kraki tumbled to the weave as the carpet yanked into the sky.

"Ah, now, sahib," said the afreet. "This be costing you."

"Ten shillings if we catch them," Nick promised the creature. "Two if we fail."

"Ver' good, sahib, ver' good! We catch for sure," said the afreet delightedly, bobbing its turban.

The carpet sailed through the azure sky, bright sun warm on their necks, a stiff breeze blowing past. Slowly, they closed on the carpet ahead.

"Ahoy!" shouted Nick. "Ahoy the carpet!" He waved.

The lich swept the steel door back and sprang to the sidewalk.

Its prey swooped into the sky on a flying carpet.

The zombies halted, still in the cellar dimness.

For a long, long moment, the lich stared skyward. Finally, it got a grip on itself. Frustration, it thought savagely; after five thousand years, you'd think you'd learn to deal with frustration.

"I say," said a voice from behind. "What's all this?"

The lich turned. The speaker was a stout man in formal dress, carrying a walking stick.

"What's it to you, meat puppet?" the lich whispered harshly.

The man turned red. "Now see here," it said. "Merely because you're a man of the cloth, you can't expect—"

The lich threw back its cowl. Its skull grinned in the daylight.

The stout man's eyes bugged, then turned up in his head. He tumbled to the sidewalk, his walking stick rolling into the gutter.

The lich reentered the basement and pulled the steel door closed. It felt faintly better.

Definitely a headache, it thought. The pain was worse than ever. It wondered why these ailments of the flesh still plagued it.

"My word," said Jasper. "Look behind us."

Wentworth turned and peered at the carpet following them. "Gadzooks!" he said. "I believe that's Pratchitt. Who's the muscle boy?"

"Don't know," said Jasper.

Morglop emitted a faint moan. He was lying flat on the carpet, his hands clutching desperately at the fringe.

"How'd they know we planned to spy on them?" asked Jasper.

"Bloody mysterious," said Wentworth, "but we've got to lose them. Afreet! We must lose that carpet."

"No, sahib, is not possible."

"Don't give me that, you monkey!"

It shook its turban sadly. "Reckless flying bad. License be yank. Against regulation."

"One pound *argentum* if we lose them, you pirate."

"Now sahib be talking!" said the afreet. Suddenly, the carpet yanked into a sharp turn. Morglop moaned a little louder.

Wentworth's carpet turned suddenly and increased speed. "Follow them!" ordered Nick.

"Aye, sahib, aye," said the afreet, and their carpet turned, too. Nick and Kraki leaned into the turn and clutched at the carpet edge.

"Vhat is problem?" grumbled Kraki. "Ve yust vant to talk to them."

Nick was tight-lipped. "Evil flees where no man pursueth," he said.

"Vhat?"

"I wasn't sure Wentworth was involved, but he is. Otherwise, why would he run from us?"

"Yah," said Kraki. "Maybe is demon summoner?"

"Maybe," said Nick grimly.

The carpet swooped and turned sharply, dogging its prey.

"They're still following," said Jasper.

"This calls for strong measures," said Wentworth, pulling a flask from inside his tunic. "Driver, loop back over them."

The afreet looked at him. "One shillingi."

With a curse, Wentworth tossed the creature a coin.

The carpet went into an immediate inside loop. For a long moment, the city was below their heads. Morglop moaned again. "Bravo," said Jasper.

Wentworth dropped the flask. It tumbled toward their foe. . . .

Nick and Kraki looked up as the Boars' carpet flew overhead.

A flask tumbled toward them. "Evade!" shouted Nick.

Their carpet darted right. The flask exploded with a *whump!*

Kraki stood up. "Bastards!" he shouted, waving his fist. "Cowards!"

The carpet turned sharply, and he almost fell over the side. Nick grabbed him and pulled him back.

"Be careful," Nick said.

Kraki drew his sword with a snick. "Fly under them," he told the afreet.

The afreet glanced at the sword worriedly. "I try, sahib," it said.

They swerved after the Boars' carpet. The Boars tried to lose their pursuers. Their carpet swivelled around the minaret of a temple and climbed sharply toward a cloud.

Suddenly, thick white fog hung around them. It was cool in the cloud.

They broke out of the mist. The other carpet was above and to the left.

"Hah!" said the afreet. "In blind spot."

* * *

"Where are they?" said Wentworth. He and Jasper scanned the sky.

"We lose," said the afreet confidently.

A sword came stabbing up through the carpet. It missed Morglop's thigh by inches. It disappeared and stabbed up again, in a different place.

"My carpet!" wailed the afreet. Chattering in rage, it zoomed into a climb.

Everyone clutched the fibers desperately. Morglop's green skin couldn't turn white, but it was definitely turning pastel.

The carpet zigged and zagged, almost tossing them off with each swerve. It dived directly toward a temple dome and veered aside at the last instant.

Doggedly, Nick and Kraki followed. "Bad thing," said the afreet. "You pay if this carpet be damage." Nick nodded.

The enemy carpet dived straight at a dome. Their own afreet anticipated the enemy's last-minute swerve, turning before the other carpet did. Unfortunately, they turned left, while the enemy carpet turned right.

When they rounded the dome, they saw the Boars flying off toward the east. The enemy had gained distance in the trip around the dome. Nick and Kraki followed grimly. The enemy carpet began to climb. The speeds of both carpets dropped as they gained altitude.

"Uh oh," said the afreet.

"What's the matter?" said Nick.

"Heading for Morning Temple."

"Vhat's that?" asked Kraki.

Wentworth turned white. "No," he said. "Not there."

The afreet glared at him. "You want I lose?"

"Yes, but—"

"Get flat on carpet. Minimize wind resistance."

"Ahem," said Jasper. "Sorry, brothers, but I believe it best that I meet you at Cobblers Lane. . . ."

The point of green light flitted away from the carpet and headed north.

"Coward," muttered Morglop.

"You'd do the same, if you could fly," said Wentworth.

The cyclops peeled his eye open to see where they were heading. He shut it again with a shudder.

The Boars' carpet broke into a sudden dive. It gained speed rapidly as it headed toward a vast temple complex. White-domed buildings stretched for nearly a mile by the River Jones, with manicured gardens among them. A wall kept out the rest of the city.

"I follow?" said the afreet hesitantly.

"No," said Nick after a long pause. "Too risky." Their carpet broke away.

"Vhat is problem?" asked Kraki.

"Watch," said Nick.

The Boars' carpet was a mile up when it passed over the wall of Morning Temple. It started to plummet.

"The whole temple's a null-magic zone," said Nick. "The Sons of the Morning think magic is wrong. Unnatural. They won't use it."

Kraki watched, speechless. Only the momentum of the Boars' carpet kept it sailing over the temple. It flapped in the breeze as it fell in a parabola.

"If they don't clear the far wall, they're dead," said Nick.

They fell.

Wentworth pulled a flask from one of his many pockets and took a sip. They fell.

Morglop opened his eye and, mesmerized, could not shut it again. He stared grimly at oncoming death.

They fell.

The wall approached. The afreet keened a prayer.

They fell.

The wall was growing larger. Morglop made a choking noise.

They fell.

They were going to hit. Wentworth began to turn transparent at the edges.

They cleared the wall.

The magic came back.

The carpet snapped rigid. They slammed into its surface as it pulled upward. At the bottom of its arc, it scraped the ground, but then they were aloft again.

"Grab me!" yelled Wentworth. Morglop took his arm.

The alchemist fluttered in the breeze like a flag. Only Morglop's grip kept Wentworth from flying into the sky.

"What is it?" said the cyclops, surprised.

"I took a potion of weightlessness," said Wentworth, somewhat shamefaced. "I didn't think we were going to make it."

"Nice of you to offer me sip," said Morglop, more than a little nastily.

"I only had the one dose," said Wentworth defensively. "There wasn't time."

"Yah, sure." Morglop suddenly noticed that the buildings below looked awfully tiny. He gripped Wentworth tight enough to make the alchemist squeak and closed his own eye equally tight.

"They make it?" said Kraki.

"Think so," said Nick after a moment.

"Where take sahib?" said the afreet.

"Tell you what," said Nick slowly. "What say we ransack Wentworth's shop? Since he's gone and all."

The barbarian grinned. "Sounds like fun," he said.

"Back to Fen Street," said Nicholas Pratchitt.

The lich stood in the basement, staring motionless at the ray of light that shone between the steel doors. I need a drink, it thought. Or a smoke. Or a hallucinogenic drug. Or anything. It really didn't matter.

Of course, it thought, I couldn't do anything with a drink. Except wet my robe.

If it didn't capture the humans, the baroness would use its skull for an ashtray.

Perhaps I ought to make a break for the city limits, it thought. No, that was a stupid idea. The baroness would track it down. And outside the city, it was so much harder to find victims.

The zombies stood around, motionless. They're no help, thought the lich, they're brainless. Well, actually, not brainless. Their brains were rotting into mush, but they did have brains of a sort. What I mean is, thought the lich, they don't have any intelligence. They make me sick.

Well, not sick, exactly. It didn't have anything to feel sick *with*. They made it feel as if it wished it *could* feel sick.

Or something like that.

All I have left to look forward to, thought the lich, is a bleak future of unremitting labor in the cause of villainy.

Work, work, work.

It makes me sick, it thought.

Well, not *sick,* it thought.

It wished it had thought these things through before it rose from the dead.

It wondered where Pratchitt was. It wondered what the hell it was supposed to do.

* * *

The carpet deposited Nick and Kraki on the roof of Wentworth's shop.

"I said two shillings if we didn't catch them," said Nick. "But here's five."

"Thank you, sahib," said the afreet, kissing Nick's hand. "Thank you, oh, thank you." It kissed his hand some more.

"Yeah, yeah, sure," Nick said, withdrawing his hand and wiping it on his pants. The carpet zoomed away.

"Door is locked," reported Kraki.

"I'll open it," said Nick. He pulled a leather case from his coat pocket. Inside were his lock-picking tools.

Kraki looked at them, grunted, and tore the door off its hinges. "Come on," he said, bounding down the stairs.

Footsteps sounded in the shop above. The lich looked up at the floorboards speculatively.

It went to the interior stairway and floated up the steps. It opened the overhead hatch.

"Hmm," said Nick, looking about the shop. "Quite a supply of healing draught." He pocketed several small bottles.

"Bah," said Kraki. "Vhat are ve looking for?"

"Anything suspicious," said Nick. He sniffed. Was that the smell of rotten meat?

"I think ve find it then," said Kraki.

"What?" said Nick. He turned.

A hatch in the wooden floor was open. The lich was rising up the stairs, its cowl thrown back. Behind it, zombies followed.

"Mike!" said Nick, recognizing Yarrow's reanimated corpse.

Kraki drew his sword with a *scritch* of steel.

Nick backed toward the stairs to the roof, but the lich sped past him to block escape.

Kraki advanced on the zombies. "Yah hah!" he shouted. He whapped off Yarrow's head. It tumbled to the floor.

"You killed Mike," Nick accused the lich, drawing his own blade.

"Do surrender, won't you?" whispered the lich. "I have the most splitting headache."

Kraki chopped another zombie through the waist. It fell into two halves. Yarrow, headless, put his pig-sticker through Kraki's shoulder. Kraki twirled, and chopped Yarrow in half, too.

"Bah," he spat in disgust as he watched both halves squirm. "How can you kill the dead?" He retreated, keeping his sword moving to ward off attack while he considered the problem.

"No dice," said Nick to the lich. "Don't suppose you'd consider surrendering to us?"

The lich made no reply, but gestured ritually and spoke a Word.

Nick thrust his épee into the brown robe. The blade bent into a curve as it grated against bone.

Kraki waded forward, slicing the arms off the zombie facing him. He'd decided to chop them up into bite-size pieces. They couldn't do much harm that way.

Nick's blade was useless, a thrusting weapon against a creature with no flesh to thrust into. He threw the épee away and grabbed for the lich's arm, intending to break it. When he touched the lich, he realized he'd made a mistake. Suddenly, he was weak—too weak to stand. He fell awkwardly to the floor.

Nick could feel weakness spreading from his limbs toward his vital organs, feel life slipping away as the lich drained life force from his frame . . .

But apparently the lich wanted him debilitated, not dead. The creature moved away from Nick, and strode toward Kraki's back.

"Watch out!" yelled Nick.

Kraki whirled and sliced into the brown robe.

The lich's ribs shattered. Its skull went flying.

A zombie arm grabbed Kraki's ankles and tripped the barbarian. He fell and hit his head on the counter. While he was more or less defenseless, three zombies jumped him. Kraki rolled around on the floor, ripping at rotting flesh, but more zombies joined in.

One zombie went and picked up the lich's skull. It carried the skull to Kraki and touched it to the barbarian. Kraki went limp.

"Idiots," whispered the lich harshly. "Look at me! I've fallen all to pieces." The zombies combed the room, searching for fragments of lich.

Nick and Kraki watched, weak as kittens, as zombies tied them up. "Can I give my friend a healing draught for his shoulder wound?" asked Nick.

"No," whispered the skull petulantly. "Don't you fools know when to give up?"

The zombies shouldered the two humans. They filed down the stairs and into the basement.

As his eyes adjusted to the darkness and his nose to the stench, Nick marvelled. He had never known these tunnels existed beneath the city.

"Foul unearthly vights," muttered Kraki sleepily. "I vill destroy you all." He wrestled weakly with his bonds.

The living, reflected the skull, are a royal pain in the neck. Well, not in the neck, perhaps, since it didn't seem to have one right now. A pain in the coronal suture or maybe in the lower part of the parietal bone. Its headache was worse than ever—which was quite distressing, considering that all it had left to ache was its head.

"There," said Wentworth. "Land there."

The carpet swept down to the flat slate roof of number eleven, Cobblers Lane. Morglop staggered off and collapsed.

A point of green light was already hovering over the chimney pot. "There you are," said Jasper. "Glad to see you made it."

"No thanks to you," muttered Morglop.

The upper stories of the building, like those of many in Urf Durfal, protruded out over the street. Property taxes were based on a building's lot size; this was a way of gaining extra room without paying higher taxes. The slate flags that covered the roof sloped gently toward the edge of the building, but the shape of the building itself hid the Boars from viewers in the street. Conversely, by peering over the gutter, they could watch people going in and out of the building across Cobblers Lane—number twelve, Nick and Garni's building.

"One pound, sahib," said the afreet, holding out a paw.

Wentworth, still weightless, was hanging by one arm from the chimney. "Oh, bother," he said. "I don't have that much cash on me."

The afreet chattered its anger. "Sahib promise! Say one pound if lose pursuit! This one lose bad persons! One pound!"

"I'll have to write you a check. Morglop, give me a hand, will you?"

"What?"

"Just hold on to me, will you? I need both hands."

While Morglop kept Wentworth from blowing away, the alchemist found a bottle of ink, a slip of paper, and a quill. He trimmed the quill with a penknife. He put the bottle of ink on the chimney—and it blew away.

"Oh, bloody hell," said Wentworth. "The ink's weightless too."

Not to be denied its payment, the afreet pursued the tumbling bottle and retrieved it. "How can this be?" asked Morglop. "You drank potion. Ink bottle not drink potion."

"It's magic, you twit," said Wentworth irritably. "That's part of the enchantment. Covers ancillary items. Otherwise, to be truly weightless you'd have to strip buck naked. Not the sort of sorcery a gentleman would practice, eh?"

He dipped his quill in the ink and began to write the check. After a few strokes, his pen went dry.

He examined the tip of the quill and tried again. It went dry again.

"I'll be damned," he said. "The ink won't draw because it's weightless —nothing to push it down the quill. I'm sorry, my good, er, entity," he told the afreet, "but I'll have to ask you to come to my office to pick up your money."

The afreet bared its teeth. "Is cheat! Is fraud! Carpet badly damage! Sahib be bad man!"

Wentworth rolled his eyes. "Oh, really," he said. "Here's my card. Just come to the office any time tomorrow, there's a good creature, and I'll pay you the pound."

The afreet stared uncomprehendingly at the piece of pasteboard. It hopped up and down on the carpet with its bandy and rather hairy little legs. "Pay now! Pay now!" it screamed.

"Better pay," advised Jasper, hanging out over the edge of the roof. "People in the street are beginning to stare."

Wentworth had a total of nine weightless shillings and four pence. Jasper had three shillings eightpence. Morglop had four shillings sixpence ha'penny.

They dumped all this loose change into the afreet's outstretched paws. The creature's lip's moved as it counted the money, snatching after one or another of Wentworth's coins as the wind threatened to blow them away.

"I'm afraid that will have to do," said Wentworth in an injured tone.

The afreet glared at them, then took off, muttering to itself.

There was a sausage vendor in the street, Jasper noticed. The sausages smelt wonderful. "I say," he said. "What are we going to do for lunch? We're flat broke, now."

Morglop, who was feeling rather peckish, scowled.

VIII.

Being carried by zombies was not, Nick thought, particularly comfortable. One of his bearers had no remaining flesh to speak of; its shoulder bone stuck painfully into Nick's back. And the smell of rotting flesh was something awful.

The tunnel led to a chamber where torches flickered. Nick craned to see where they were going.

A woman waited for them. She wore a flared, black dress—an expensive one, Nick judged—and a veil that obscured her features. The orcs that stood next to her wore rusty armor and had large, ugly tusks. Given a choice, Nick thought, he'd rather look at the woman.

They stood together next to an unlighted pit. Nick had a feeling he was going into the pit. He hoped there wasn't anything nasty down there. Snakes, say.

"Hello, gorgeous," said Nick. "Hell of a way to pick up men."

The orcs chortled and elbowed each other. "Oi, Garfok," said one. "It's da big guy."

"You," said Kraki weakly. "I should have killed you in caverns."

Nick glanced at Kraki. "Friends of yours?" he asked.

"Hah? Ve have met, yes. These are orcs who turned you to stone."

"What happened to you?" the Baroness Veronee asked the skull.

"Don't ask," it whispered.

"Take it to the house," she ordered one of the zombies, meaning the lich. "And its bones, too. I'll fix you up later."

"As you wish," the lich whispered despondently. Some of the zombies departed.

"What am I going to do with you fellows?" she asked Nick and Kraki.

"Several possibilities spring to mind," said Nick.

The veil hid her smile. "You'd enjoy it less than you think," she said in a throaty voice.

"We can have din-din," suggested Drizhnakh.

She glanced at the orcs. "Oh, no," she said. "They're far more valuable as hostages."

"We doesn't have ta kill them," said Garfok. "We can just whack off a coupla arms. Da big one looks like he's got a lotta meat on him."

The stench of the zombies was strong in Nick's nostrils. "How can you guys think of food with all this rotting flesh around?" he said.

"Don't bother me," said Drizhnakh. "How 'bout you, Spug?"

"I likes it," said Spug. "Makes me think of my mum's home cookin'."

Even the baroness looked faintly disturbed at that. "Throw them in the crypt," she said briskly.

Nick groaned inwardly. He'd been right. The orcs swung him up—then he plummeted down . . . and smashed into damp stone. Experimentally, he struggled with his bonds. Nothing seemed to be broken. Kraki landed with a thud nearby.

"Kraki," Nick gasped. "You okay?"

"No," said the barbarian. "Am very depressed."

By the dim light of the torches they saw a veiled face peer into the hole. "By the way," said the woman, "in the unlikely event that you should escape, please tell your companions that I shall not rest until the statue is restored to its rightful owner."

"Who's that?" gasped Nick, still starved of air.

She gave a low chuckle. "Well may you ask," she said. "In the meantime, please rest assured that you will again see the light of day—at least, if your friends act reasonably."

"I vill kill you," said Kraki.

"That would be difficult," she said. "You won't die of thirst or starvation. You'll find plenty of sewage and a more than adequate supply of live prey." Somewhere, a rat squeaked. "See?" she said. "Ta, now."

Rats, thought Nick with relief. It's only rats.

The orcs gave a disturbing, rattling laugh as they pulled the massive stone slab over the opening. It grated as it shut out the last vestiges of torchlight.

Nick and Kraki lay in darkness.

"Why do I get talked into these things?" said Nick. "Instead of spending the afternoon in bed, I'm lying in a sewer with orcs standing guard."

"Don't vorry," said Kraki. "Soon, a maiden escaping from an evil prince to whom her father has promised her in marriage vill flee through the sewers and stumble upon us. Smitten vith my charms, she vill free us both."

"What?" said Nick.

"Or else," Kraki said, "a vizard, seeking to hire me to kill another vizard who has been his enemy for a thousand years, vill summon us to his vizard's tower by magic and free us from these bonds."

"I see," said Nick, struggling with the rope around his wrists. "What makes you so confident?" A rat scampered over his body.

"Is inevitable," said Kraki philosophically. "Happens in all the best sagas. First, you get thrown in pit. Then, you become king. Or something. You take the bad vith the good. Don't vorry, Nickie. I am hero. Heroes don't die in sewers."

"Thanks, Kraki," Nick said. "I feel much better now."

Timaeus strode purposefully across the Common, puffing on his pipe. It was a pleasure to be back in familiar surroundings, amid the Imperial architecture and carefully tended greenery of the university. It hadn't been long since he'd left, but somehow the place already seemed a little foreign.

Halfway across the green, he noticed that the sky ahead was filled not only with gathering clouds, but with a pillar of smoke. He frowned and redoubled his pace toward Scalency Hall, where the Department of Fire had its offices.

The pillar of smoke was rising from a window on the side of the building. Doctor Renfrew, in the blue-tinted ermine and preshrunk silks of the Department of Water, stood outside, amid a crowd of gawking undergrads. He was directing three water elementals, dousing the surrounding grounds and nearby buildings to prevent sparks from carrying the fire. Scalency Hall itself, built wholly of granite without supporting timbers, was virtually indestructible, at least to fire—a necessary condition, given the number of literally hot-tempered academic disputes that arose among the faculty whose offices it contained.

"Good afternoon, sir," Timaeus addressed Renfrew. "What is happening?"

Renfrew eyed, then ignored Timaeus. He shouted Words of power at his elementals; clearly, keeping the playful undines about their tasks was occupying his full attention.

"Old Calidos has combusted at last," said an undergraduate gleefully. "No test of the convolutions today!"

"Good heavens," said Timaeus, and broke into a run through the line of spray about the hall.

"Wait!" yelled the undergraduate. "Come back. You could be killed—"

Timaeus muttered Words of power as he ran, puffing between syllables. He was damnably out of shape. He *could* be killed; but it was not likely. Fire was his element, after all.

The door to the hall—a slab of slate on brass hinges, wood being far too ephemeral for the tastes of fire mages—was noticeably hot to his touch.

As he entered the foyer, Timaeus could feel his heat-resistance spell kick in; the air in the foyer felt almost cool. As he sprinted up the steps, he could feel the heat beginning to rise again.

Timaeus paused at the door to Magister Ardentine's office. The adjunct professor of thermal philosophy was busy stuffing books and papers into a heavy leather bag.

"How is he?" Timaeus panted.

Ardentine looked up nearsightedly. "Terminal burnout," he said. "Shame, really."

"We knew it was coming," said Timaeus.

"Certainly," said Ardentine irritably. "What's the temperature?"

Timaeus peered at the thermometer at the back of Ardentine's office. The professor was too nearsighted to see it. "Halfway between water and paper," he said. It was marked off with the boiling, melting, or burning temperatures of various materials.

"Bother," said Ardentine, redoubling his efforts to save his books before the temperature in the office rose too high. "I'm going to lose some of these. Lend a hand, won't you . . . ?"

But Timaeus was gone.

Calidos's office was like a blacksmith's forge. The air shimmered, the metal chair in which the elderly mage sat glowed red. Calidos himself was a dancing flame, human form still discernible. He looked white, shrunken, even older than Timaeus remembered.

"Doctor Calidos," Timaeus sputtered. "You mustn't . . ."

"Ah, d'Asperge," said Calidos in some surprise.

"Sir," said Timaeus in distress, "you must be aware that—"

"I'm in terminal burnout, yes indeed," said Calidos almost happily. "And it does these old bones good to feel warm at last."

Timaeus gulped unhappily. This was the fate of all too many a fire mage. Repeated manipulation of the element increased one's own similarity to fire. When Timaeus had taken courses with Calidos, the old man had left scorch marks on exam papers. He'd heated his own chambers nearly to the boiling point of water, but even so complained about the cold. Undergrads, lacking strong heat-resistance spells, dreaded meetings with Calidos; few were willing to accept him as their don. Timaeus had done so, partly from bravado and partly from a genuine desire to learn as much of his discipline as he might; Calidos's mind might no longer be as sharp as it had been in his youth, but he was still highly respected, widely acknowledged as one of the giants of his field.

"Why is no one here to control this?" demanded Timaeus.

"This is the fourth time this semester," Calidos said. "The signs have been gathering for weeks. My time has simply come, my boy. I choose to go as gracefully as I may. Come, 'tis not so bad; I go to immortality, of a sort."

"As a salamander," grunted Timaeus, "not in the Lady's bosom—"

"Pshaw," said Calidos. "Infantile religious maunderings. Far better to rise to the sphere of flame, to burn incandescently for all time—"

"But without a mind," said Timaeus sadly. "Elementals have no—"

"And do the gods promise immortality in the same mind? The philosophers believe in a duality of mind and body, while the religions add spirit, creating a trinity of self. The spirit may survive death, but the body clearly does not. Spirit and body are separable; hence, one may conclude, spirit and mind are separable also."

The heat was rising further, and Calidos's voice was becoming fainter. It was hard to make out his form now, he was glowing so brightly.

"Doctor," said Timaeus. "Do not go. I need—"

"You're a fine mage," said Calidos faintly. "You do not need my aid. A bit hasty and hot-tempered, perhaps, but this is characteristic of our discipline, those aspects being similar to fire. I—"

"Doctor Calidos!" shouted Timaeus. "I am not speaking generally, but in specifics. Please hang on; I need help researching—"

"Farewell, lad," whispered Calidos, now so bright that Timaeus was forced to avert his eyes. "Good of you to come and say good-bye to an old man."

And suddenly, the glow began to fade, like fireworks in a dark sky, quickly diminishing from white to red to orange, a collapsing ball of flame. "My true name," came a faint whisper, "is . . ."

But it will not be repeated here, lest it be misused by the unscrupulous.

Timaeus was astonished. Knowledge of Calidos's name would allow him to summon the elemental Calidos had become from its place in the Sphere of Flame. And the elemental formed from the spirit of a master mage would be powerful indeed.

He would have to use this power sparingly. So powerful a salamander would be difficult to control; it would be foolish to risk its wrath.

The sphere was gone now. The chair had melted down to slag, and the granite walls still emitted a somber glow. Timaeus realized he was expending power to maintain his heat-resistance spell; no point in that now. He withdrew from the room and sadly descended the stairs.

No time for mourning, he chided himself. What to do now?

"I done good, huh, Ross? Huh?" said Fred the goon.

Fred stood six foot six and weighed more than twenty stone. He filled a substantial portion of the tiny maid's bedroom. Unfortunately, Fred wasn't alone in the room. There were three other goons, all of approximately equal stature. There were also two elves—Montiel and a subordinate—and a rather weedy human water mage. Judging by the wizard's odor, his enthusiasm for the substance he manipulated magically seemed not to encompass actually immersing himself in it, at least, not on any regular basis.

The seven of them stood cheek by jowl. They'd had problems getting the door closed. The day was hot, and the room was stifling. The water mage's bathing habits did nothing to improve the atmosphere.

"Gee, Fred," chirped Montiel. "I just don't know what to say."

"That good, huh, boss?" Fred beamed.

Montiel scrambled over one of the goons and made his way to the room's single window. He peered out. Below was a courtyard, bordered by the block's other buildings. Montiel shook his head sadly. "It's my fault, Fred," he piped.

A look of uncertainty passed across Fred's face. "Huh?" he said.

"I should have known better than to trust an important job like this to a *complete imbecile!*" Montiel shrieked. The elf hopped up and down on the tiny bed.

"But, boss," said Fred unhappily. "You said I should rent a room."

"A room, not a closet! And I told you I wanted a room across the street!"

"Well, gosh, boss. We're in number eleven, right across the street from Sidney Stollitt . . . just like you said!"

The elf threw up his hands. "Explain it to him, Billy," he said to one of the other goons.

Billy threw a hand across Fred's shoulder. "Duh, look, here, Freddie," he said. "The window don't look out on the street. It looks out the back. How we gonna keep an eye on the building across the street if we can't see it? Huh?"

Fred's face scrunched up, as if he were about to cry. "Gosh, I'm sorry, guys," he said. "I'm awful sorry."

"And it's in somebody's house, too," said Montiel. "How're we gonna keep it a secret if the people in the house see us come and go all the time?"

Fred buried his head on Billy's shoulder in shame.

There was a knock on the door. Billy and the third goon drew swords, nearly decapitating each other. Ross pointed at Fred.

"Yeah?" said Fred hesitantly.

"Uh . . . will your friends be staying to dinner?" said a timorous female voice. "I mean, my husband doesn't even know we have a boarder, and—"

"Hell with this," piped Ross. "Billy, take 'er."

Billy opened the door. As soon as he turned the knob, he staggered into the hallway, propelled by the pressure of the others in the room. He tripped over a blond woman, smashed through the railing which ran the length of the hall, and fell down the stairs.

The woman shrank back and put both hands to her mouth.

Montiel sighed. "Your turn, Georgie," he said.

The third goon walked out the door, casually tossed the woman to the floor, and stood over her, his sword at her throat.

Montiel smiled and walked out the door himself. "Oh, Georgie," he said in a sorrowful chirp, "you know how I hate brutality." The goon grinned and stared directly into the woman's frightened eyes.

"Hiya!" said Ross Montiel. "My name is Ross. What's yours?"

"El . . . Elma," whispered the woman, eyes wide.

"Elma! That's a nice name," said the elf. He motioned to George, who sheathed his sword. "Gosh, I just know we're going to be friends." Montiel held out a tiny elfin hand.

She swallowed and looked at George uncertainly.

"C'mon," said Montiel. "Shake!"

She grabbed his hand and gave it a tentative shake. She sat up and shuffled on her bottom until her back was against the hallway wall. She stared at Montiel.

"That's better," said Montiel. "I'm glad we're going to be pals, 'cause we're going to be staying over. Just for a little while."

"How . . . how long?"

"Is that any question to ask friends who've come to stay? C'mon, Elma, you'll make me think you're unfriendly. If you're unfriendly, I'll have to give you to George to play with."

The goon stared at Elma and licked his lips.

"So let's keep this on an elevated plane, okay? Do what you're told and, who knows, you might even live. How 'bout that?" Montiel said brightly.

"Please," she whimpered. "Please, Mr. Elf. We're simply folk, we don't mean anybody any harm—"

"Oh, Ross, Ross, Elma, call me Ross," said Montiel. "Mr. Elf sounds so, I don't know, formal. Now, don't worry about a thing. We promise to treat your house just like it was our own. Right, boys?"

"Right, boss," said a chorus.

"And we absolutely promise not to steal anything we can't physically carry. Georgie, toss her in the cellar."

"Do I get ta play with her first?"

"No, no," said Ross. "Only if she's a bad girl."

The goon pouted.

"Now, Fred," said Ross, putting a tiny hand on the huge man's shoulder. He had to go onto tiptoes to reach. "I'm going to give you a second chance. I need a note delivered . . ."

The lich glided through the catacombs. It waggled its neckbones; they felt reasonably secure. The baroness seemed to have done a good job sticking it back together again.

Once, it told itself, I was the terror of the Cordonian Plain. Strong men blanched at my name. The skulls of children decorated my parapet.

It mulled over the past for a moment. And now, it thought scathingly, I'm to be the baroness's messenger boy. Again.

Any urchin in the city would be more than happy to deliver her missives in exchange for a copper or two. But no. It had to be it.

It sighed.

Bitch, it thought. It wondered whether this headache was permanent. Just what I need, it thought, a migraine for the next millennium.

IX.

Sidney stared out the window. Her shoulder wound was smarting. It looked like it might rain.

Thwaite sat by the hearth, munching on a sausage he'd bought from a vendor down the street.

"Do you ever get the feeling that we don't know what's going on?" said Sidney.

"*Mmphm?*" said Thwaite through a mouthful of meat.

"It's been too long," she said. "Nick and Kraki should have reported back by now."

"*Mmrphl.*"

Sidney watched as a goon left the house across the street, and grew alert as he came directly to their own building. She drew her sword and walked quickly but quietly across the room to the door. She stood next to the door, flat against the wall.

Thwaite watched her, became alarmed, and dived behind what was left of Nick's bed, the remnants of his sausage flying.

The goon appeared in the broken doorway. His lips moved. ("Ross said to knock.") He tried to knock on the door, but it wasn't there. He looked puzzled.

Sidney sprang into the doorway and put her sword to the man's Adam's apple.

"Who are you?" she hissed.

His eyes were saucers. Ross hadn't said anything about girls with swords. "I . . . I'm Fred," he said. "Pleased to meetcha." He held out a hand, which Sidney made no move to take.

Thwaite peered up from behind the bed. He eyed his sausage, now on the floor, rather sadly.

"What do you want?" said Sidney.

"I got a message for you," said the goon. "From R—from somebody." He reached into his pocket.

Sidney's sword scraped his chin. It drew blood. The goon froze. "Move slowly," she said.

Moving glacially, he took a folded piece of parchment from his pocket.

"Out of the way, mortal," hissed a voice from behind the goon. Sidney peered around Fred. A brown-robed figure with a deep cowl stood there.

Fred scanned his eyes as far to the right as they could possibly go without turning his head.

"Begone, fiend!" shouted Thwaite, springing from behind the bed. He made the sign of the god and his hands began to glow with white light.

"Oh, do save your energy," whispered the lich wearily. "I'm only the postman today." Two skeletal fingers extended past Fred, holding an envelope.

Fred saw the bones. He gulped loudly. Sidney's sword bobbed with his Adam's apple.

"Fine," snarled Sidney, stepping back but keeping her sword aloft. "Just leave your ransom notes on the floor. They are ransom notes, aren't they?"

The lich merely let its envelope go. It drifted lazily into the room and toward the floor. Fred dropped his note and stepped back. He whirled, stared at the cowled figure, and fled, whimpering to himself. The lich stood in the doorway, impassive.

"That it?" said Sidney.

"I'm to take a response," whispered the lich.

"Tell them," said Thwaite, "the answer is no."

"Don't you think we ought to read these first?" said Sidney.

"No," said Thwaite. "I will not traffic with undead."

"Is that your response?" whispered the lich.

"For now," said Sidney. "Get out of here."

Wordlessly, the lich glided away. Sidney went to pick up the letters.

"I'm going to check on the statue," Father Thwaite said, and began to pry up the floorboards.

Fred's letter was a folded piece of parchment. Sidney unfolded it and began to read.

> Priss:
>
> Golly, Priss. It's real tough having to do this kind of stuff. I mean, I remember when you used to be smaller than me. You were so cute. You thought I was pretty neat, too. I still remember that time you nearly pulled my ear off . . .

Anyway, it's funny how things work out. But, look, we need to make a deal. I got something you want, and you got something I'd really like to have. So hey! Why don't we trade? One dork for one statue. The dork's slightly used, but I guess he has kind of a sentimental value for you guys. And you know I think blood is really icky, but, golly, we might have to whack off a few bits to close the deal. Know what I mean?

Listen, drop me a line by sundown. Or, well, you know. If you want to talk, just wave from the window and someone'll come.

Sorry about this. No hard feelings, huh, sugar?

There wasn't any signature. "Montiel," Sidney said. "Ross Montiel's got Garni." She didn't know whether to be relieved or upset. God knew, the dippy elf was capable of anything. But at least he was a known quantity.

That skeleton guy, now, that was another thing. Its letter was much like the one it had delivered before. The letter was written, apparently in blood, on expensive paper; the envelope was perfumed. Sidney opened it.

To Master Timaeus d'Asperge:

My dear Timaeus, I write you again, but this time in trepidation rather than admiration. I wish for you the greatest of worldly successes; yet I fear that your stubborn resistance may instead bring you low. Please heed my warnings, dear boy! You do not know what forces you deny.

Rejecting my monetary offer was unwise. I have been reluctantly compelled to take stronger steps to acquire the statue. Specifically, I have taken two of your companions captive—a thief known as Nicholas and a large and terrifyingly well-endowed barbarian.

Dear child, please be advised of the seriousness of this matter! The principal I represent *will* acquire the object in question; preferably in peaceful wise, but, if necessary, over the prostrate bodies of you and your companions. To speak of such things is distasteful, but the facts must be faced; please accept my assurances that all concerned would far prefer a less sanguinary resolution.

Should this offer, too, be spurned, the next step in our negotiation is clear. As much as it would distress me to do so, I would be compelled by your refusal to treat your friends harshly. Please be assured that there will be no tasteless brutality; I am quite skilled in these matters, and should I be called upon to exercise my skills, your comrades will endure memorable and exquisite agonies.

You have until day's end to accept.
I remain, sir, your loving and devoted friend,

And again, there was no signature; only a drop of blood at lower right. "Where the hell is Timaeus?" she muttered. "Just my luck, someone snatches him too." She turned to survey the room. "Father?" she said.

No one was there.

The floorboards hiding the statue had been pried from the floor and laid aside. Quickly, Sidney went to the hole in the floor and peered inside.

The statue was gone.

Thwaite was gone.

Where there had once been only dirt and timbers, a tunnel led off into the earth.

"Father?" she called forlornly down the tunnel.

"I don't like the look of their visitors," said Wentworth. He held onto the gutter. Every once in a while, the breeze threatened to blow him out over the street. He had to clutch the gutter to remain hidden on the roof.

"Odd group," agreed Jasper. "That thug returned to the house below us, you know."

"Did he?" said Wentworth. "Hmm. I wonder who's down there."

A large drop of rain hit Morglop on the head. The cyclops looked up. "Damn," he said. "Should have oiled sword."

"What should we do?" asked Jasper.

"Wait," said Wentworth. "We've seen no immediate threat to the statue."

"Going to get wet," complained Morglop, looking upward.

X.

It was a gray noon in the city of Urf Durfal, capital of the realm of Athelstan. Atop the great volcanic pipe called Miller's Seat perched the many towers of Castle Durf. Within, His Grace the Grand Duke Mortimer was sitting down to lunch: a magnificent specimen of *Lycoperdon giganteum,* stuffed with *bitoks de porc* in a delicate paprika cream sauce. The grand duke eyed the stuffed puffball mushroom with anticipation.

In the courtyard of the castle, Major Yohn drilled the Fifth Frontier. He drilled them daily—but not, any longer, at dawn. The last time he'd roused his men that early, two thirds had been staggeringly drunk.

General Carruthers, watching from the battlements, made snide comments about the low-born soldiers below.

Across the city, workmen downed their tools and called for buckets of ale to chase their bread and cheese. Housewives took a break from scrubbing kitchen floorboards or boiling the wash or plucking chickens or darning clothes, and heated up a bit of tea. The shops on Jambon Street continued a brisk trade, tradesmen sneaking a sausage or an apple from under the counter.

Barges passed up and down the river. Farmers who had brought produce to market this morning eyed their stock, hoping they'd be rid of it by nightfall. Wizards, by and large a late-rising group, yawned, stretched, and called for their servants. Cats prowled the alleys looking for mice, and urchins lifted purses. Remarkably, no one was actually murdering anyone else at the stroke of noon, although three burglaries and an assault were in progress.

Thunder sounded. It began to rain.

In the markets, vendors put up awnings to protect their wares. Shoppers scuttled for cover. The town watch decided this was a good time to forget

about patrolling and visit the pub. Thieves cursed and headed for door-
ways. Cats crouched miserably in whatever shelter they could find.

The grand duke took a bite of his repast. His look of delight turned
instantly to pain. The chef had not taken kindly to criticism of this morning's omelet and, in revenge, had over-peppered the *bitoks.*

In an alley off Cobblers Lane, the lich examined its robe. The soaking
cloth draped itself revealingly over the lich's naked bones. It didn't mind
the wet, but worried about the uselessness of its disguise.

In number twelve, a woman wearing black peered into a subterranean
tunnel, wishing these things happened to someone else.

And down in the catacombs, two men lay bound in darkness, oblivious
of the weather.

Kraki was chanting sagas to himself. He'd gotten to a long genealogical
section—some hero was reciting his lineage for the edification of a foe:

> ". . . Sired he Gostorn,   gap-toothéd one;
> Gostorn the mighty   eater of mince,
> Apples ate also   apricots too,
> Mighty pie eater   eater of pies . . ."

It passed the time, Nick supposed. He spent his own time trying to work
his way out of his bonds. The knots were not particularly well tied. It was
hard, Nick thought, to tie good knots when your fingers were half rotted
away.

The stone slab grated aside. Dim torchlight glinted into the crypt. Even
this faint glow was enough to make Nick squint.

"Oi," said an orcish voice. "Either of you bums play Spatzle?"

"Vhat?" said Kraki.

"Spatzle?" said Nick, grinning. "I think I've heard of it. Isn't that the
one you play with a stripped deck?"

"You hasn't never played?"

"Sorry," said Nick. "I'm not much of a card player. But I wouldn't
mind learning."

"Bah," muttered Kraki. "Such games are for children and vomen."

"He says he's willin' to learn," said Garfok over his shoulder.

"Come on, guys," said Spug. "Let me owe ya."

"No chanst," said Drizhnakh. "You is broke. You is lost all yer dough."

"Oi!" said Garfok to Nick. "Gotny money?"

Nick thought quickly. He had about ten shillings on him. "Kraki!" he
whispered. "How much money have you got?"

"Don't know," said the barbarian. "Most of treasure."

"You're carrying most of your share?" asked Nick incredulously.

"Yah. I leave in inn, it get stolen."

He was probably right, Nick reflected. "Yes," he called up to the orcs. "I've got a few pounds."

"I says we let 'im in," said Garfok.

"Not much point in playin' wiv ourselves," said Drizhnakh. Cheating Spug was profitable; with him out of the game, it was more than a little pointless.

"Not da big guy, though," said Spug. "He's mean."

"Right," nodded Drizhnakh. "Don't wanna let *him* loose."

"Jake by me," said Garfok, then turned to call down to Nick. "You is in."

After a momentary scuffle, the orcs extended a short ladder into the crypt. Garfok climbed down to collect Nick. Kraki struggled wildly with his bonds. He cursed. "If I can yust get loose," he muttered.

"Never mind that," whispered Nick urgently. "Give me your purse!" He rolled over so he was back-to-back with Kraki.

The barbarian pressed his purse into Nick's bound hands. "Vhat you going to do?" he said.

Nick grinned in the darkness. "We'll see."

Garfok grabbed Nick, flung him over one shoulder, and started back up the ladder. As he reached the top, Drizhnakh took Nick, stood him up, and cut the ropes tying his hands.

"What about my legs?" said Nick.

"You isn't going anywheres," said Drizhnakh.

"Here," said Garfok. "Siddown." He pointed at a spot by a wooden crate the orcs were using as a card table.

Nick sat down. He smiled at the orcs. "Okay," he said. "Why don't you tell me how this game is played?"

"Right," said Drizhnakh, sitting down and picking up the deck. "Dere is four suits—fangs, ears, axes, and greeps." He dealt four cards in illustration.

"Greeps?"

"Greeps."

"What are greeps?"

"Don't get him started!" warned Garfok.

Mrs. Coopersmith strode determinedly down Cobblers Lane, flanked by six tough-looking men. One carried a sock full of sand. Another carried a rough-cut stick of lumber.

Wentworth peered at the men from the roof of number eleven, hanging on to the chimney by one hand and screwing his monocle into an eye with the other. "I say," he said. "What do you suppose they're after?"

Morglop only grunted.

"I sense . . . ," began Jasper. "I sense . . . a discontented sausage merchant with a surplus of product. Damnation, Jorgesen, why did you have to give that afreet all our silver? I'm half starved. *And* half drowned."

"Never mind that," snapped Wentworth. "What is that woman doing with those thugs?"

Mrs. Coopersmith barged through the doorless doorway. Several mean-looking men barged in after her. "This is it," she said. "I want them out today."

Sidney backed toward one wall and drew a sword. The man with the stick of lumber faced her. "Let's 'ave none of that, missy," he said. "Let's make this a peaceful eviction, eh?" Two of the other goons flanked him. The rest of the men started grabbing objects, carrying them down the hall, and dumping them in the street.

"Stop it!" yelled Sidney. "You bitch. We got rights!"

"You don't got no right to tear the place up!" the landlady shouted back. "You're out! If you don't like it, you can bitch to the grand bloody duke!"

"Good lord," said a familiar voice from the hole in the floorboards. "What's going on here, Sidney?"

She glanced toward it, then did a double take. "Father!" she said. "Where the hell have you been?"

Thwaite clambered out of the hole. "The statue's gone," he said.

"I can see that. Where were you?"

"Eh? I scouted down the tunnel a bit . . ."

"Find anything?"

"No. It goes on for quite a distance."

Satisfied that Sidney wasn't going to turn violent, the goons continued carrying objects from the room and dumping them in the street. One of them grabbed a bundle of Garni's miscellaneous stuff—eleven-foot pole, several steel cylinders, a heavy book. "Hey!" yelled Sidney. "Put that back!" She grabbed the book and wrestled with the goon.

"My son," said Thwaite to another thug. "Do you feel comfortable with what you're doing? Do you feel justified in the eyes of the gods in tossing a fellow mortal into the street?"

"Sorry, padre," said the thug, bowing his head in respect. "There's ther sacred rights of property ter consider. And besides, I gots ter earn a living."

* * *

Bedding, bits of straw, and an amazing variety of possessions began flying into the street.

Morglop was instantly alert. "They after statue!" he shouted. He leapt over the edge of the roof, fell three stories, and absorbed the impact with a crouch.

"Have you noticed," said Wentworth conversationally, "that brainlessness seems to be a uniform characteristic of swordsmen?" He picked up a piece of slate to give himself some weight, dragged himself to the edge of the building, and drifted toward the street, pulled by the slate. As soon as he had a direct line of sight, he hurled a flask through the basement window of number twelve. The force of the throw pushed him back into the parlor window of number eleven as he drifted past. Montiel, who was peering through the window, drew back as the floating wizard's body pressed against the glass.

The flask exploded in the basement flat. Flames splashed about the apartment. Several of Mrs. Coopersmith's crew hit the floor. None was more than slightly injured. A fire began to grow in one corner of the room.

"Now look what you've done!" Mrs. Coopersmith screamed at Sidney. She beat at the fire with a blanket.

Morglop lumbered down the hall. The goon with the stick of wood blocked his way. "What the bloody hell do you—" shouted the goon.

Morglop bellowed, "Surrender or die!" He swept his sword back.

The goon dropped the stick and ran.

A point of green light flew through the broken window and into the apartment. A green ray shot from Jasper and struck a goon. The thug's eyes rolled up in his head. He tumbled to the floor.

Morglop strode through the doorway, waving his sword. The goon with the sock of sand stood by the wall and tried to kibosh the cyclops. Morglop stepped aside; the sock whistled past; Morglop sliced the goon through the pancreas.

"Jasper!" Sidney said, recognizing the green glow and jumping to the conclusion that the dealer in antiquities was attempting to steal the statue himself. "Bastard!" She backed toward Thwaite and the hole. "Let's get out of here, Father," she said.

"I concur," said the cleric. They dived into the hole.

"Hey, boss," said George. "A buncha wizzos is attacking the apartment."

"Oh, phooey," said Montiel. "I can see that, George. Micah," he said to his elven subordinate. "Get back to headquarters as fast as you can and get reinforcements."

Micah took off out the back door and ran, zigzagging past the out-houses.

Ross turned back to his goons. "Okay, guys!" he said. "Time to earn your pay." George, Fred, and Billy ran out the front door and down the stoop, swords in hand. "You too, pal," said Montiel to the water mage. He shoved the odiferous fellow outside and locked the door after him.

The water mage stood uncertainly in the rain, then followed the goons unhappily. Montiel watched from the parlor window.

Morglop killed two of Mrs. Coopersmith's men. The rest fell to their knees. "We surrender!" yelled one.

"I got a wife an' three kids," yelled another.

The landlady picked up Garni's umbrella and used it to beat the cyclops about the head and shoulders. "Now, miss," said the cyclops, fending blows off with his sword and forearm.

"Ruffian!" she shrieked. "Brigand! Murderer! I'll have the watch on you! Get out of my building!"

She chased him around the apartment. The thugs, still on their knees, watched bemused.

Wentworth pulled himself in through the door and, hanging in midair, screwed his monocle into an eye. "Gadzooks," he muttered. A fire burned merrily in one corner. Trash and bits of plaster were all over the place. There was a large hole in the floor.

Jasper zipped up to the alchemist. "They were apparently evicting Pratchitt," he said. "Don't seem to know anything about the statue."

"Fine," spat Wentworth. "Dandy. I hate swordsmen, truly I do."

George, Bill, and Fred charged into the room. George stabbed Wentworth in passing. He yanked his sword back to remove it from the floating alchemist.

Wentworth stayed on the sword. Weightless, he wafted back and forth as George shook the sword, trying to get Wentworth off. His eyes glazing, Wentworth grabbed the blade and pushed himself off the point.

Astounded, George studied his sword for several moments before re-turning to the fray.

Morglop engaged Bill and Fred. Either one he could probably have killed instantly, but together they were reasonably well matched against him. Swords rang and sparks flew.

Since no one was paying them any attention, Mrs. Coopersmith's evic-tion crew took the opportunity to escape out the broken window.

Wentworth's weightless blood drifted in globules about the room. On the verge of unconsciousness, he pulled out a healing draught and gulped it greedily. He floated, semiconscious, as the potion began to do its work.

Jasper shouted a Word. A ray of green light struck George. George froze.

The water mage peered in through the basement window. He, too, spoke a Word. Blue energy began to glow about his hands.

At the back of the room, the fire raged merrily.

Mrs. Coopersmith battered Morglop from behind with her umbrella. "You try my patience, woman!" yelled Morglop. He reached behind and yanked the umbrella from her grasp. While he was off-balance, Billy struck him a glancing blow.

Jasper spoke another Word. Under Jasper's mental control, George attacked Billy from behind.

The water mage released the blue glow about his hands. A sphere of water smashed across the room, tumbling Morglop and the three goons to the floor.

The fire hissed out. The room filled with the smell of wet charcoal.

"Trouble at the flat," gasped Micah. Montiel's lieutenants crowded round.

Soon, messengers spread out across the city, carrying Montiel's summons to the underworld.

Sounds like a battle zone, thought the lich. Explosions, bolts of energy, and the clash of weapons sounded from down the street. It peered around the corner to see a brilliant green flash shine from the window of number twelve.

It pulled back into the alley. A bedraggled cat peered out from under a heap of trash. "Puss, puss, puss, puss," the lich whispered. "Here pretty pussy." It held out its sleeve, taking care to hide its bones, trying to give the impression that it was holding a treat.

Hesitantly, the scrawny cat came forward. The lich grabbed it and broke its neck. The lich felt the life force flow through its frame. It spoke a Word. The spell seized the cat's expiring spirit and placed a compulsion on it. The spirit flew out of the alley and across the city, toward the town house of Baroness Veronee, carrying the lich's message.

She would come, it reflected, daytime or no. And she'd come with all her resources.

* * *

Corcoran Evanish stood in the shelter of a doorway, out of the pouring rain. He studied his list. He crossed off the fifteenth name. Eight more to go. He patted his burgeoning purse with satisfaction.

His work was well done:

In a lonesome garret, a wizard clad in red spoke to her familiar. "Come, my pet," she said. "Solid athenor; think of it."

In a filthy inn, a huge, bearded man drained his tankard and spat out the lees. "Awright, gents," he said. "There's a job we can do that'll make us all rich."

Down by the harbor, the captain of an elvish ship spoke to his crew. "And after we have it, it's away and downriver for us," he said.

In a study in Old Town, the ambassador from Hamsterburg spoke to his spymaster. "There may be a connection with the sceptre," he said, "which, as you know, is the embodiment of our claim to rightful rule of the human lands."

A dozen groups plotted, and the battle raged.

Major Yohn prowled the battlements of Castle Durf. He was restless. It was too early to start carousing, his men were fine, nothing much was going on at the castle.

The view from Castle Durf was spectacular. It was an eminently defensible spot, a volcanic pipe that loomed over the city. Cliffs fell away on three sides to the city below; the only approach was a long, low ridge leading to the castle. From the battlements, it was possible to see the entire city and a good portion of the region. The rain reduced visibility, but the gray skies and wet streets lent a certain somber grandeur to the town.

Yohn passed a member of the Ducal Guard. The man's mail was rusted in spots. Yohn scowled.

"What's that?" said Yohn. Out over the city there were flashes of light. A brief explosion revealed people flitting around on a carpet.

The guardsman yawned, scratched himself, and looked. "Beats me," he said.

"Give me your spyglass," said Yohn. The guard shrugged and handed it to him. Yohn peered through it.

Ye gods. Looked like a battle over there. "Five Corners Parish, isn't it?" Yohn said.

"Huh?" said the guardsman. "Yeah, sure. Guess so."

It was obviously no riot. Rioters wouldn't have access to that much magic. Yohn handed back the spyglass and hurried away. If he knew his men, most of them were sleeping, preparing for the night's revels. He'd better get them organized, send out some scouts, find out what was going on. They might be sent into action at a moment's notice.

Nick raked in the coins. He grinned from ear to ear. Spug stared, round-eyed and gape-tusked.

"You is sure you hasn't played dis game before?" said Garfok.

"Oi, Garfok," said Drizhnakh disgusted. "He's a bloody cardsharper, ain't it as plain as da boil on yer face?"

"Another round, boys?" said Nick. He squeezed the deck with his right hand. The cards shot across a cubit of space to be caught in the left hand. He performed three quick poker cuts with his left hand alone.

"I is down to da last copper," said Garfok, fumbling the coin.

"Tell you what," said Nick. "I'll advance you a shilling for every question you answer."

"What?" said Garfok suspiciously.

"It's not like I'm asking you to let me go or anything," Nick explained. "I know you're too sharp for that. No, I realize I can't win my way to freedom."

"Dat's for sure," said Drizhnakh. "Da baroness would moider us if we let ya loose."

"She's a baroness, huh?" said Nick. "That's interesting. For instance," he said to Garfok, "I'd give you a shilling of silver if you'd tell me her name. Now, what could be the harm in that? I'm not going anywhere, after all."

The orcs glanced at each other, then moved away. They conversed in low voices.

"It's a shilling each," said Garfok.

"Sorry?" said Nick.

"We'll go fer it," said Garfok, "but we decides how many questions you gets ta ask, and we gets one shilling, each of da tree of us, fer every question."

Nick raised an eyebrow. "You're a hard . . . er . . . orc, Garfok, but it's a deal."

He shoved three piles of silver across the floor.

"Veronee," said Drizhnakh. "Da Baroness Veronee."

XI.

A toothpick nearly embedded itself in Timaeus's eye. He ducked behind the door. When he peered back into the room, a wild-haired face stuck up from behind the gaming table. It was wearing an archaic Imperial helmet. "Damnation!" it shouted. "Arbalests are bloody worthless."

A dark-skinned man stood up on the right. "They're siege machines," he said. "What do you expect at a field battle?"

"No," muttered the man in the helmet. "It's the damned rubber bands. Musn't wind them so tight."

The two leaned over the table. Rank upon serried rank of metal soldiers stood on little hills of sand. There were infantry, cavalry, a dragon or two elevated above the fray on sticks. Stands of orcs stood slavering, their officer's whips measuring out command radii. The arbalests were on a ridge to the rear. The man in the helmet turned a tiny crank on one of the siege machines and laid a toothpick against the rubber bow string.

"Professor Macpherson?" said Timaeus.

The man in the helmet stared briefly at the intruder. "Yes? My office hours are ten to . . . d'Asperge, isn't it?"

"Yes, sir," said Timaeus.

"A year may not seem long in the geologic scale of things," said Macpherson scathingly, "but it's too long to wait for a term paper. Your failure stands."

Timaeus blushed. Damn, but the man had a memory. "I haven't come about that," he said. "I need your help."

The dark-skinned man studied the table. "I do believe the II Cobatrix can see my hill trolls," he said. He produced another stand of minatures, and placed them on the table.

"Gadzooks!" said Macpherson. "Well placed. I shall have to commit the reserve." He pushed several stands of soldiers about the table with a sort of miniature rake.

"It's about Stantius," said Timaeus.

Macpherson snapped to attention. *"Ave!"* he shouted. *"Ave* Stantius!"

The dark-skinned man bellowed, *"Ash nazg thrakataluk!"*

"None of your damnable orcish gibberish!" yelled Macpherson. "The Imperium shall prevail. The vexillation from the V Victrix attacks the Severed Hand–Standard orcs, over here. I make it a seventeen to twenty-four assault."

The dark-skinned man studied the table. "Looks right," he said. There was the clatter of dice. Macpherson frowned and removed several figures from the table—two Imperials and six orcs. He laid them to the side. The dark-skinned man picked up one of the figures and studied it idly.

"I'm sorry to intrude," said Timaeus, "but it is rather important. You see, I've acquired this statue—"

"I say, Macpherson, old man," said the dark-skinned man. "You've got the uniform of the V Victrix wrong."

"What?" said Macpherson. "Devil I do!"

"Look here," said the dark-skinned man. "The coat buttons are blue."

"Yes, that's right," said Macpherson.

"Yet the Edict of 2837 specifies buttons 'dyed in the color of the Cataphringians'—a sort of muddy ochre," said the dark-skinned man.

"A statue of Stantius the Third—" said Timaeus.

"Nonsense!" said Macpherson. "Nobody knows quite *what* color is 'the Cataphringian,' and I have a monograph somewhere about that maintains it was, in fact, identical with the Imperial purple. But that's all irrelevant, as the V Victrix was, by order of the Emperor Sculpine, entitled to adorn its buttons with the crest of the Blessed Bode—predominantly cobalt blue in color."

"Entirely cast in athenor," said Timaeus.

"But Sculpine antedates the Edict of 2837," said the dark-skinned man. "Surely the V Victrix would have adopted the new standard uniform."

"Surely not!" said Macpherson. "Does one abandon a mark of distinction, merely because some general order—?"

"Absurd! Would one dare to defy an Imperial edict . . . ?" said the dark-skinned man.

"I was wondering what you could tell me about Stantius's capture, and if you might know anything about—" said Timaeus.

"Fool!" shouted Macpherson. "What do you know, anyway? The Early Successor States is your period! I'm the authority here, and if I say the buttons were blue, then they're damned well blue!"

"Are not!"

"Are so!"

"Are not!"

Timaeus sighed.

A steady stream of mud-brown water flowed into the tunnel opening. Beyond was a weed-covered lot, perhaps two acres in extent. Not far away, tenements rose. On the far side of the lot stood a shanty town—lean-tos and shacks made of scrap wood and pieces of trash.

"Where are we?" Sidney said.

Father Thwaite pulled himself out of the tunnel, depositing a layer of mud on his robes in the process. He looked around.

"We're about three blocks from Roderick Square," he said.

Sidney clambered up beside him, likewise smearing herself with mud. The heavy rain began to wash it off, simultaneously drenching her.

"I don't suppose the statue is hidden in the underbrush," she said.

"Not a bad hiding place," said Thwaite. "People wouldn't expect to find a valuable object in a place like this."

Sidney knelt and examined the soil around the tunnel. "I'm no tracker," she said, "but the statue is awfully heavy. I don't see any wagon tracks or the kind of path you'd expect if several people carried it. It's like it was spirited through the air when it got here."

Thwaite shrugged. "Not impossible," he said. "Demons could do it."

Sidney nodded slowly. "Yes. But could demons have dug that tunnel?"

"Maybe, Sidney; demons come in a fantastic variety of shapes. Look, if we're going to chat, can we get under cover?"

"I'm going to look around," said Sidney.

Thwaite headed for the cluster of shacks. He bent over and scuttled under a lean-to.

There was a snore; Vic was lying on a pile of straw. "Vic," said Thwaite softly.

The old man woke up with a snort. "Geoffrey," he said. "What are you doing here?"

"I might ask the same of you."

"I shleep here a lot," said Vic.

"Oh." There was silence. The rain drummed on the canvas overhead. The lean-to was in a spot with good drainage, but a rivulet of water ran down Thwaite's back. He realized he was pressed up against the canvas, and water was leaking through. He leaned away.

The old man rested on one elbow and eyed Thwaite keenly. "Sho what're you up to today?" he inquired.

"Nothing much," said Thwaite vaguely, looking at the rain.

"Sho where'd you find thish shtatue, anyway?"

Thwaite sneaked a guilty glance at Vic. "Sorry, Vic," he said. "I'm not supposed to talk about that."

Vic's mouth tightened. "Play it your way, then," he said, rolled over, and made as if to go back to sleep.

With some startlement, Thwaite noticed that a pigeon was standing in the shelter of the lean-to, close to one end. It eyed him beadily.

Thwaite stared out into the rain.

Sidney was glad it was warm. She was drenched; if it had been cold, she'd have been miserable.

She searched the lot carefully. She walked clear across it, moved to the right a few cubits, and traversed the lot again. She was determined to search every square foot. The statue could be hidden anywhere, buried in underbrush.

But it wasn't.

She did discover a mound of dirt about six cubits from the tunnel. It was vaguely humanoid in shape, as if someone had made a snowman from dirt. The rain was gradually pounding it into mud.

Sidney stared at it, sighed, and then attacked it with her hands. It was just possible that the statue was hidden inside. She got dirt under her fingernails. She got mud all over her clothing, her face, and her hair. It took her a few minutes to convince herself that the statue wasn't there.

It wasn't.

She went to look for Thwaite among the shacks and lean-tos. "Father?" she called.

"Here, Sidney," he replied. She found him by the sound of his voice. He was with some old guy—the same geezer he'd been with in the gutter this morning.

Vic gave up pretense of sleep and sat up.

"You," she said to him.

He stared at her with the bright-eyed gaze of senility. "Hello?" he quavered.

"We met this morning," Sidney said, bending over and moving into the lean-to. She hunkered down by the cleric.

"Thish morning?" the old man's brow furrowed. "Let'sh shee . . ." His voice trailed off, and he muttered inaudibly to himself.

"He's gone," said Thwaite. "It comes and goes. What happened to you? You're a mess."

"Never mind," said Sidney with some embarrassment. She swiped futilely at her face, dirtying it further. "It's not here."

"Did you expect it to be?"

"Not really. You know, I'm getting tired of being pushed around."

"Hmm?"

"No statue; everyone a hostage; Nick and Garni's flat trashed by jerk wizards. And I've just been sitting around waiting for things to happen."

"Well, Nick and Kraki tried to do something—"

"And just wound up in a closet somewhere. The hell with it." She stood up in the rain determinedly. "Let's go get Garni."

"How the devil do you propose we do that?"

"Come on."

Vic continued to mutter to himself.

The guard at the gate looked Sidney up and down. She was dripping wet, her hair was plastered to her head, her pants were covered with burrs, and there were smears of mud across face and shirt. "If you're here for a job interview," he said, "the answer's no."

"Very funny, jocko," she snarled. "I want to see Madame Laura."

The guard laughed in her face. "But she doesn't want to see you," he said.

Sidney slugged him, hard, in the stomach. He bent over. She knocked him on the back of the head with the pommel of her dagger. He fell to the brick paving.

She walked briskly through the gate and toward the door.

Thwaite went briefly to the guardhouse door. "Sorry," he said, and blessed the guard, who was sitting up, groaning.

Sidney took a key from her pocket, unlocked the heavy wooden door, and flung it open. She strode into the foyer.

All motion in the room stopped. Everyone stared at her.

A nobleman of middle years, clad only in a leather harness, was on his hands and knees on the rug. A bit was in his mouth. A flame-haired, soft-skinned lovely rode on his back, holding the reins. A look of horror passed across the nobleman's face.

One of the chief officers of the town watch lay on a couch, his coat off and his shirt unbuttoned to the navel, a glass of whiskey on the table beside him. A dark-haired girl who could hardly have been older than sixteen sat next to him, legs drawn beneath her, one hand inside his shirt.

On the long staircase with its patterned rug stood a dark-skinned woman wearing the helm of a Ducal Guard and not much else. Sidney headed for the stairway.

Thwaite trailed her, goggling at the girls and the sumptuous furnishings. The room was lit with small fire elementals, trapped in globes affixed to the walls. That was expensive and, should a globe be broken, quite dangerous.

"Hey!" said the woman wearing the helm, standing with hands on hips halfway up the staircase. "Where the hell do you think you're going? And you're getting mud on the carpet."

"Out of my way," said Sidney. The woman moved to block her. Sidney faked right, then left, and the woman scrambled to keep in front.

"You can't come in here," she said.

"Actually," said Sidney, "that's why people visit this place."

"What?"

"N-never mind. Get out of my way, bitch, or I'll get more than mud on you."

Thwaite peered over Sidney's shoulder from down the stairs. "Try not to actually kill anyone," he pleaded.

Sidney pulled her sword. The woman's eyes went wide, and she backed up the stairs. Sidney pursued. The woman halted, took a breath, and screamed loudly.

Sidney grabbed her and pushed her over the bannister. The woman caught the edge of the stairs and dropped, unharmed, to the floor below. She glared at Sidney. "Have you considered a career on the stage?" Sidney asked, trotting up the stairs to the landing, Thwaite close behind her.

Several hall doors opened. A dwarf wearing nothing but trousers and carrying an axe came into the hall. His chest was amazingly hairy. Two human women peered over his shoulders.

A thin man, naked as a jaybird, rushed out. He stared at Sidney and her sword, and transformed into a hawk. He fluttered past her, toward the main door.

At the end of the hall, a door smashed open. Madame Laura strode forth. "What is the meaning of this!" she shouted.

Madame Laura was a stout woman whose age, beneath copious makeup, was difficult to discern. Her nails were close to six inches long, each painted a slightly different shade of red. Her dress had more frills and ruffles than you can shake a stick at. She eyed Sidney's mud-smeared form severely and reached back through the door for a loaded crossbow.

" 'Lo, Mom," said Sidney.

Thwaite stared from Madame Laura to Sidney and back, agape.

They sat in comfortable armchairs in Madame Laura's office. Laura sat behind the desk and wafted a lady's fan. The windows were open a crack, to let in the air but not the rain; but the room was still rather warm.

Thwaite and Sidney wore robes. Servants had taken their clothes away to be cleaned. The silk evening gown Thwaite wore, decorated with needlepoint dragons and fish, was worth a small fortune—and heavily perfumed.

"My dear," Laura remonstrated, "I do wish you'd chosen a less dramatic entrance. The Baron of Montrance was beside himself. And Magister Prescott, fearing discovery, apparently transformed into a bird and flew the coop—without, I might add, paying for services rendered."

"Sorry," said Sidney shortly. "I . . . I need your help."

Laura sighed and eyed the ceiling medallion. "Of course you do, my dear," she said. "We could start with a manicure. And your hairstyle is too, too outré. Now, I have in mind the most eligible young man—"

"Mother! Stop it."

Laura looked her daughter over and sighed. "Of course," she said gently. "Of course you need my help. I don't hear from you for two and a half years, except when Ross complains that you refuse to use him to fence your goods. Really, Prissy, you do go out of your way to alienate people who'd be happy to help. . . ."

Sidney stood up abruptly. "This was a mistake," she said. "Where's my sword?"

"Priscilla," said Laura. "Sit down. I've got your clothes and you're not going anywhere until I find out what's wrong."

Sidney sat down and glared at her mother.

"What is it, dear?" said Laura.

Sidney sighed. "Ross has kidnapped a friend of mine," she said. "I'm going to rescue him. I need to know where he's being kept."

Laura pushed herself back from the desk. "Darling!" she said, appalled. "Ross owns half this place, dear, you know that—I . . ."

"The elf says he'll start chopping pieces off by nightfall."

Laura shook her head repeatedly. "What in the world have you done to drive him to such extremes?" she asked.

Sidney looked out the window. "It's a long story," she said. "Basically, he wants a statue we took out of the caverns. Everyone and his brother wants it, too."

"I'll call Ross in," said Laura with decision. "We'll talk this out. I'm sure—"

"Mom! You don't understand. I don't have the statue."

"Oh, my," Laura said. "Oh, my. That does put a different complexion on things. Who does?"

"How the hell should I know?" Sidney snarled.

"Don't get all high and mighty with me, young lady!" shouted Laura, waving her fingernails. "You disappear for close to three years, show up asking for help, and you're just as impossible as—"

"Oh, come on."

Laura gave an irritated sigh, opened the desk drawer, took out a flask, and downed a slug of something. Thwaite eyed the flask and licked his lips. Laura noticed. "Oh, my good sir," she said. "I am most dreadfully sorry. I have been shirking my hostly duties." She rang a bell. "Can I get you something? And you, Priscilla."

"I wish you'd stop calling me that."

"It's your name, isn't it?"

"My friends call me Sid," Sidney said defensively.

Laura shuddered delicately. A boy of about eight flung the door open and charged in. "Hi, Laura!" he said.

"Monty, we need something from the bar. What would you like, Father?"

"Er . . . your house whiskey will do fine," he said.

Madame Laura hid a smile. "Nonsense," she said. "Monty, fetch a snifter for Father Thwaite, and tell Frederico to give us four fingers of that single malt the baron brought last week, he'll know the one. Scilla?"

"Tea," Sidney said.

"And a pot of tea," Laura said with distaste.

"Okay, Laur'," said the boy. "Can I keep a frog in my room? Mom says—"

"What your mother says goes," said Laura. "But tell Cook to give you a mason jar, and you may keep it in the wine cellar, if you promise to feed it every day."

"Gee! Thanks, Laura." The boy disappeared. The door slammed shut behind him.

"Now, then," said Laura. She waited expectantly.

Sidney knew what was next. She gritted her teeth and resigned herself to the inevitable. "I'm sorry, Mother," she said, as gracefully as she could. "Look, I know it's probably half my fault, but every time I see you . . ."

Laura waved a crimson-nailed hand carelessly. "Never mind, my dear, never mind. Ross will have my derriere in a sling if he learns I've helped you pry your friend loose, you know."

"I'm not planning on telling him."

"You did barge in here in a rather—"

"Look, I doubt anyone down there recognized me."

"In your state? Quite possibly." Laura sighed. "All right then. You are my daughter, and it is my *devoir* to aid you. Can you supply particulars?"

"Thanks," said Sidney. "Okay. The guy is a dwarf. Garni ben Grimi. He was taken from a flat in Five Corners. Number twelve, Cobblers Lane. At about eight o'clock this morning, some goons nabbed him. They searched the flat for the statue, which was there, actually—but were too stupid to find it, even though they smashed the place up pretty badly."

"I have spoken to Ross about his tendency to employ the less than capable."

"Yeah. Anyway, that's about it."

"No other leads?"

"Not right now."

"This is not much to go on. However, I will provide you with a list of those of Ross's safe houses I know about. Obviously, he may have ones I don't know about. However . . . hmm." Laura leaned back, and tapped one ruby fingernail against her chin. "I recall that he has a shop on the Calabriot Bridge. A goldsmith's, used as a front and also to launder funds. He has several rooms in the back. Knowing Ross's sense of humor, I would venture to guess that he's got the dwarf there."

"What? Why?"

"Makes disposal easy. Just drop the creature off . . . dwarves are heavier than water, you know. And it's a good way to torture the poor lamb, too. Just hold him over the river . . ."

"I get the picture. Do you have the address?"

"Yes, of course. I will ask you to memorize the list before you depart, as I do not want it widely circulated."

"Thanks, Mom," said Sidney.

"There is one other thing."

"What?"

"Why do you never write or come to call? We've had our differences, but, really, Priscilla, two whole years . . ."

"Okay, okay."

"It's not that I ask much from you. You've gone your own way, and although I shudder to think of the life you must lead—"

"Mom!"

"Still, it doesn't seem like a great imposition to ask you to stop by occasionally—more than once a decade would be nice—"

"All right, already! Mother, you're driving me nuts."

The door smashed open. Monty staggered in, carrying a tray.

"Here we are," said Laura.

They rode Madame Laura's carriage through the streets with the blinds tightly drawn.

"Priscilla?" said Thwaite.

"Don't you start in," said Sidney.

"I was just wondering . . ."

"That's my real . . . I mean, that's the name she lumbered me with."

"Ah," said Thwaite. "May I inquire . . . ?"

"What is it?" Sidney said irritably, holding the blind aside and peering into the rain.

"Does your mother also bear the taint?"

"What? Oh, you mean, is she therianthropic?"

"Yes," said Thwaite.

"Yes," said Sidney. "It's inheritable."

"As are most diseases of the blood," said Thwaite. "I do wish you'd consent to let me—"

"No," said Sidney.

For a moment, there was only the clop of the horses' hooves and the patter of raindrops. Then, Thwaite chuckled. "I assume her alternate form is the same as yours," he said.

"Yes," said Sidney, puzzled.

"Appropriate," said Thwaite.

"What do you mean?"

"That she should run a cathouse," said Thwaite.

"We're pinned down," said Wentworth.

Morglop stood up, brought his crossbow to his shoulder, aimed through the basement window, and fired. The bolt went through the stomach of one of Montiel's men. Morglop ducked back down. A dart of flame shot through the window and splashed against the far wall. Plaster fell from the ceiling at the impact.

While Morglop cranked the crossbow to ready another shot, Jasper looked out the window himself, trusting to his partial invisibility for protection. Through pouring rain, he saw demonic forms flitting overhead; occasionally, they'd make a foray to the street below or drop rocks on unwary combatants.

"Where did all these blasted fools come from?" muttered Wentworth. He was drooping noticeably toward the floor as his potion of weightlessness wore off.

"Oh dear," said Jasper.

"What?" said Morglop, risking a peek himself. Down the street, a massed formation of zombies, perhaps forty in all, marched toward the flat. They were still half a block away.

"Zombies," said Wentworth. "Demons. Thugs. Where did they all *come* from?"

"I would guess," Jasper said, "that they're after the statue."

"Haven't seen action like this since Ishkabibble Front," said Morglop. He snapped another bolt through the window. A demon flew past with the arrow in its forelimb, chittering in rage.

"You'd think even those idiots in Castle Durf would notice something was up," said Jasper. "If this gets any worse, the whole parish will be in ruins."

"I believe that it's time to initiate a strategic withdrawal," said Wentworth.

"You mean, run?" said Morglop.

"Er, well, yes."

"Good idea," said Morglop.

"What do you propose?" asked Jasper. There was an orange flash through the window. When they looked out, a tentacular demon was eating zombies and screeching merrily.

"That tunnel," said Wentworth. "The statue must have been taken down the tunnel. With luck, it's a safe way out."

"Tunnel?" said Morglop uneasily.

"Don't tell me you're claustrophobic, too," said Jasper.

"No, of course not," said Morglop defensively. "I *like* midwinter holidays."

Wentworth eyed the cyclops suspiciously.

XII.

Feeling exposed and wet, Sidney crouched on the rooftop. The rain-laden breeze blew past her. The bridge hung out over the river; there was no shelter up here to cut the wind.

To the left and below her was the street that ran the length of the bridge. She crouched atop one of the buildings that lined it. Even in the rain, there was some traffic—a nobleman's carriage travelling to the suburbs on the far side of the River Jones, a scurrying jeweller returning to work, jacket held overhead to provide some meager shelter.

She peered into the street and tried to read the sign over the shop immediately below her. Montiel's front was Samuel Berber, Goldsmithy. She wasn't having much luck; letters frequently looked distorted through a cat's eyes, and she was reading the sign from an odd angle. She *thought* she had the right building.

She padded up the sloping roof to the peak and down the other side, to look at the river. Below her was a window, and another below it. Both were shut. She could leap to the sill of the upper window—but she doubted she could leap back, at least as long as the window was shut. The sill was quite narrow.

While she contemplated it, a head stuck out from the window below, the one on the bottom floor. It peered down at the river. The head looked as if it might be dwarven.

"*Meow?*" said Sidney.

Garni looked up. "Sidney?" he said in a low voice. "Is that you?"

"*Mrowr!*" Sidney transformed and clutched at the roofing tiles. In human form, she suddenly realized just how far down it was to the river. And she had no faith in her clumsy body's ability to retain its purchase on the rain-slick tiles.

"Garni?" she called softly.

"Yes!" said the dwarf, craning for a glimpse of her.

"Are you okay?" asked Sidney.

"All things considered," said Garni. "I'm still in one piece, at any event. I've been hoping a boat would go under the bridge below my window, so I could jump."

"Forget that," said Sidney. "That's suicide."

"I wasn't thrilled by the idea," said Garni. "Can you bring a rope?"

Sidney considered. As a cat, she couldn't carry much—but if she got Thwaite to tie a rope to her, perhaps she could manage. "I'll try," she said. "Back in a while."

Thwaite glanced up and down River Road. The cobbled street curved along the River Jones, one side lined with expensive houses, the other with the rocky wall that had been built to contain the river. At intervals, small piers extended into the water; this was not a dock area, but people came here to fish, and the wealthy inhabitants of the houses along the road kept pleasure boats. No one was watching.

To Thwaite's left, the Calabriot Bridge extended out over the river. Thwaite hiked up his robe and, cradling Sidney and the rope in one arm, climbed up onto the railing that ran along the river. He teetered atop the railing, then stood upright and stabilized himself by leaning against the side of the first building on the bridge.

He couldn't quite reach the building's rain gutter.

Sidney stood on his hands and stared at the roof. A loop of the rope was around her neck; the rest, tied in a coil. She was to drag it along the rooftops behind her. But she didn't trust her ability to leap from Father Thwaite's hands to the rain gutter, not with the rope to load her down.

Thwaite almost toppled from the railing, then leaned against the building again. He pulled Sidney back down to his chest. "Too far?" he said.

"Mrow," she said, looked at him, and pawed at the loop around her neck. She grabbed the rope with a claw and shook her head, trying to drag it off.

Thwaite got the idea and removed the loop. *"Mowr!"* Sidney said urgently.

He tucked the rope between his legs and lifted her up again. She leapt lightly to the roof.

She peered back down at him. He took the rope and tossed it up to the roof with her. *"Rowr,"* she said, thanking him.

Gingerly, Thwaite stepped back into the street. An urchin was watching him with wide eyes.

"And who might you be, my child?" said Father Thwaite.

The grimy girl eyed him suspiciously, then ran off down the street.

The cleric sighed and went back to the shelter of a doorway.

Sidney nuzzled the loop and tried to get it over her head. Not having hands had its drawbacks. If she transformed, she could easily manipulate the rope; but the loop was too small to fit around a human neck.

She hooked a claw into the rope and dragged the loop onto her head. Then, she couldn't get her claw out of the fibers. Her paw dragged the loop to the side. It fell back onto the roof. She gave a small meow of frustration.

She tried again. This time, she got it. The loop slipped down around her neck.

She trotted off, pulling the rope. It was heavy sailor's cable; Thwaite had gotten it at a pier a few blocks downriver. It was a good half-inch thick and twelve cubits long; it must weight close to a stone, probably more than she herself did in cat form.

It was hard work, dragging the rope.

She was two-thirds of the way down the bridge to Garni's building when something odd happened. Suddenly, the rope didn't seem so heavy. She stopped and turned around.

The coil had come undone. The main part of the rope was three cubits behind her, in a loose clump; she was unravelling it as she moved.

Thwaite had purposefully tied the coil with a loose knot. The idea had been that she could undo it with teeth and claws when she got to Garni. But this way, she'd be forced to drag the rope in a long line. It might get hung up on some obstruction along the way.

She decided to transform and retie the coil. Then, she realized that she couldn't get the loop off her head. It had tightened under the strain.

This was bad news. But it left her no alternative. She started forward again. The coil gradually unwound as she pulled the rope along.

She wished it weren't quite so wet. She walked forward ten feet, twenty . . .

Suddenly, Sidney was yanked off her paws. She tumbled down the rain-slick roofing tiles, toward the edge of the roof and the river below. It was a long fall to the water, down there . . . and she couldn't swim. And she was weighted down by rope—

Her claws skittered over the tiles. The rope around her neck was pulling her down, down . . . she felt her speed gathering—

A claw hooked under a tile. The claw was almost yanked out of her paw —but it held. She came to a halt.

She lay on the tile in sodden fur for a long moment, panting. She peered down the slope.

The rope ran directly down the slope from her, over the edge of the building. She puzzled over that; before she had been yanked off her paws, the rope had run behind her, along the roof. Gradually, she realized what had happened. The rope behind her had slipped down the slope of the roof. The loose end had plunged over the edge, pulling the rest of the rope with it. The rope had continued to slide—until it yanked her off her paws. If she hadn't caught that tile, the rope would have pulled her into the river.

How was she going to get the rope to Garni now?

She scrabbled her way back up the sloping roof. Then, leaning away from the edge, she paced carefully forward.

For a while, the rope followed smoothly, running along the edge of the building. Then it got hung up on the edge of a tile. She moved forward, and the rope began to pull up over the obstruction and onto the roof—until something suddenly gave. The section of rope she'd dragged onto the roof plummeted back over the edge, and she was nearly yanked off her paws again.

At least she was prepared this time—and she wasn't yanked as hard. She kept her footing.

Sidney hoped no one in the building below would look out his window and see the rope dangling. He might be tempted to lean out and pull on it. . . .

She came to Garni's building at last.

Now what? She had planned to transform and, in human form, tie the rope around a nearby chimney. But with the loop over her head, there was no way to transform without killing herself—and it was now too tight to be removed.

If she could get down to Garni, he could remove the loop. But once down there, she couldn't get back up; there was no way she could jump two stories, even as a cat.

It was a conundrum. Up here, she couldn't get the rope off; down there, she couldn't tie the rope to the chimney. What was she going to do?

She meowed.

A moment later, Garni stuck his head from the window. "What took you so long?" he said in a low voice.

She flicked an ear. *"Mrowr."*

"This is the rope?" he said, and grabbed it.

She hissed violently and backed away. If Garni tried to climb now—

"Not ready yet?" Garni asked.

"Mrow!" she said.

"Okay," he said. "Meow when ready."

She sat back on soggy haunches. Her fur was wet through and through and wasn't getting any dryer. She'd gotten this far, and she wasn't going to give up now. But how was she to tie the rope?

She studied the chimney. Perhaps if she just wrapped the rope around it three or four times, that would do . . . yes, that sounded plausible.

She ran around the chimney four times, pulling the rope after her. She tried to keep it tight against the bricks. Then, she studied her work. It looked reasonably sturdy. Faint heart never won fair lady, she thought to herself, then realized how ridiculous that sounded. *"Mrowrorw!"* she said, as loudly as she could.

Garni grabbed the rope and, using it to steady himself, stood on the windowsill. He began to climb. Sidney could see the rope go taut.

The chimney was not in direct line with the window. The rope held against a tile for a moment—and then the tile broke off. Garni swung at the end of the rope along the side of the building. Sidney heard him grunt. She envisioned the dwarf scraping along the stucco, losing his grasp and falling. . . .

But the rope continued to swing gently back and forth, like a pendulum. *"Mrow?"* said Sidney.

"I'm okay," the dwarf gasped. He climbed gingerly.

Sidney was suddenly yanked forward by the loop around her neck. The rope had slipped around the chimney an inch or two. Garni gave a yelp as he dropped an equal distance. Sidney felt a momentary panic. The loop was tighter than ever.

Uncomfortably tight.

"Sidney?" said Garni.

"Mrow!" she said, hoping he'd hear urgency in the sound. He began to climb again.

The rope slipped again. It slipped a third time. Desperate, she hooked claws under the tiles and held on, hoping that the little resistance she could add would stop the rope from giving.

It helped, but she could feel the loop tightening . . . tightening. . . . Breath rasped in her throat.

Garni pulled himself over the gutter and onto the roof. Sidney was choking.

He came to her. She clawed desperately at the loop. She could barely breathe. He sized up the situation quickly. While Sidney choked, he worried at the loop and the knot that held it. . . .

The loop loosened. Sidney panted for air. She stood up wearily, and rubbed up against the dwarf.

"Thanks, Sid," Garni said, and stroked her wet fur.

On hands and knees, he followed her across the sloping, rain-slick tile.

The grand duke stood on the battlements of Castle Durf. "I see what you mean," he said, lowering the looking glass.

Flying creatures whirled in the skies over Five Corners parish. Several buildings had collapsed. At least one building was in flames. There was a flash of green and then a red line that hung in the sky for a second or two.

"Still," said Mortimer petulantly. "I hardly see why you needed to drag me away from my studies. If there's unrest in the city, put it down. Eh?"

"My men stand ready, Your Grace," said Major Yohn.

"What? You puppy," said General Carruthers contemptuously. "Your Grace, I hardly think a passel of backwoods bandit fighters are what we need here. My men will make short work of whatever's out there."

"Fine, fine," muttered the Grand Duke. He itched to get back to his mushrooms. "See to it."

Carruthers smiled nastily at Yohn, then turned and strode off.

Carruthers would probably make a botch of things, Yohn reflected. He'd better restrict his men to the castle. He expected a summons to arms before the night was out.

Nick's legs were stiff. It was uncomfortable, sitting on the floor with ankles bound. He scooted forward and pulled in the coins.

Garfok's ears were drooping. Drizhnakh looked upset. Spug was grinning tusk to tusk.

"Dis is a dumb friggin' game," said Garfok.

"You is just pissed cause you is losin'," said Spug.

"So is you, ya maroon!" said Garfok.

"Ya got anything better ta do?" said Drizhnakh. There was no response, save the crackling of the torch.

"Another round?" said Nick.

"Yeah, sure," said Garfok resignedly.

"Good," said Nick. "What can you tell me about the statue?"

Garfok and Drizhnakh exchanged glances. "What statue?" Drizhnakh said.

"Come on, boys," said Nick. "You know about the statue. The one we took out of your temple. The one the baroness said she wanted. That statue. What do you know about it?"

"Nuffing," muttered Garfok.

"Now, now," said Nick. "No answer, no pay. No pay, no play."

"Okay, okay," said Drizhnakh. "But we doesn't know much. A long time ago, see, our granfaders' granfaders used ta live in the Orclands. But dere was dis big brouhaha. Da Dark Lord got pissed at dem or somethin'. So dey split, wiv dis statue thing."

"Dat's what Gramma said, anyhow," said Garfok. "I din't know it was in da temple, though."

"Fragrit din't never tell nobody nuffing," said Spug.

"Dat's right." Drizhnakh nodded.

"Thanks, boys," said Nick. He shoved three stacks of silver coins across the table.

Timaeus studied the gaming table as the others argued. He was no judge of military matters, but it appeared as if the II Cobatrix was badly out-flanked. And there did seem to be a great many orcs. He wondered how Macpherson planned to pull this battle off.

Macpherson and the dark-skinned man were pouring over an incunabulum and bickering.

"Vellantius says the dress was *standardized,* doesn't that imply that previous distinctions were eliminated? And . . ."

"Yet, in the same paragraph, he refers to the elephant head emblazoned on the shields of the Ceterinae auxilia. This indicates a degree of variation from the accepted standard. . . ."

Timaeus puffed on his pipe and wandered about the table. Macpherson, or more probably his graduate students, had done a fine job painting the figures. He had to squint to make out some of the finer details in the gray light. He picked up an orc.

"Leave that be," snapped Macpherson. "Positions are important, and you'll never set it back in precisely the same place."

"Oh, let the poor lad alone," said the dark-skinned man. "It's not that vital." They began to argue once again.

Timaeus studied the table. The historians had built little hills of sand and had stuck bits of painted lichen here and there to represent trees. A ribbon of blue indicated a river, in the center of which stood an island.

Nob Island, Timaeus slowly realized. The River Jones. And that steep-sided hill must be—"Miller's Seat," he said. But where was Castle Durf? And the city of Urf Durfal?

The dark-skinned man looked over. "That's right," he said. "Topography look familiar, eh?"

"Yes," said Timaeus. "I assume this is how it looked in Imperial days?"

"As near as we can tell," said Macpherson. "Durfalus, later Urf Durfal, was little more than a market village."

"And this battle?" asked Timaeus.

"The Battle of Durfalus," said Macpherson. "3708. Where Stantius the Third was captured by the orcish forces."

Timaeus pondered this for a moment. "And the V Victrix was on this ridge? Here?" he said.

"Quite so," said Macpherson. "I've maneuvered them into approximately the same position. And—"

"What happened to V Victrix?"

"Destroyed," said the dark-skinned man, "to the last soldier. They died defending Stantius, and the Dung-beetle Clan trolls hauled away the bodies as provender."

"Hmm," said Timaeus. "In that case, why don't you do some digging?"

"Pardon?" said Macpherson.

"Where is this?" said Timaeus, pointing to the ridge. "Collin Hill, somewhere, isn't it? Looks like—mm, Market and Sylvan streets. If they all fell there, you should be able to find the bones, armor, weapons. Perhaps even a button or two."

Macpherson's eyes lit up. "An excellent notion!" he said enthusiastically. "I've been meaning to bring out my Intro Ancients class on a field trip. Just the thing, set the undergrads to digging ditches. That's about all their intellectual attainments render them suitable for, in any event."

" 'Twould certainly solve the argument," said the dark-skinned man. "Mind if I tag along?"

"Afraid I'll plant blue buttons if you don't?" said Macpherson nastily.

"I wouldn't put it past you," said the dark-skinned man.

"Good heavens, look at the time," said Macpherson. "I've got a seminar with my graduate students in fifteen minutes . . . we'll have to continue the game another time."

"Oh, bother," said Timaeus. "Look, I have a few questions you may be able to answer. Do you mind if I—"

"Come along," said Macpherson shortly, pulling on a pair of boots and a canvas jacket. "Ask on the way." And he strode quickly out the door, Timaeus nearly trotting to keep up.

"Stantius," said Timaeus. "What happened to him after he was captured?"

"No one really knows," said Macpherson, bounding down the stairs. "Except Arst-Kara-Morn, of course. They took him back to the Orclands."

"And then?"

Macpherson threw open the door to the hall and dashed out into the rain. "Devil should I know?" he said. "Ask the Dark Lord."

"Why was he the last emperor?" said Timaeus, puffing to keep up. He hated the rain. Water and fire mages don't mix too well.

"Damned good question," said Macpherson. "The mantle of imperium never descended on another."

"How is that possible?" asked Timaeus.

Macpherson shrugged, scattering raindrops from his canvas jacket. "Perhaps Stantius isn't dead. Perhaps Arst-Kara-Morn performed some great magic to prevent it. Perhaps the gods got tired of humanity, and decided they'd not bother selecting our next king." He paused briefly to let Timaeus catch up, then squelched onward, diagonally across the Common. "We do have some sketchy evidence that a great ritual magic was to be performed on the plain of Arst-Kara-Morn after Stantius's arrival. What happened then, it is impossible to know. Humanity, of course, was in the throes of a dark age, and the orcs were nearly as badly off; some great civil war broke out. Arst-Kara-Morn took centuries to recover, and it's only now that they've launched another great war of conquest."

"Is that what it truly is?" said Timaeus, disturbed. "You think this thing at Ish is . . ."

Macpherson splashed through a puddle, wetting Timaeus to the knee. "Damned right," he said. "Just the beginning."

"Do you know anything about a statue?" said Timaeus.

"What statue?"

"A life-size statue of Stantius."

Macpherson ran up the steps to Cranford Hall. Gargoyles peered down from the soffit. "All over the empire during his reign," he said.

"Cast entirely of athenor," said Timaeus.

Macpherson halted, blinked, and peered at Timaeus. "Impossible," he scoffed. "No one would be so profligate with the metal. Why, its magical uses alone—"

"I know about that," said Timaeus. "But I've, ah, heard a rumor about such a statue, and I was wondering whether there's any historical record."

"No," said Macpherson, shaking his head. "I've never run across any such mention." He peered more closely at Timaeus. "If you should run across such a thing, I should be extremely interested in examining it."

Morglop was quite relieved when the end of the tunnel came in view. Several sections of the tunnel were already on the verge of collapse; once, a cave-in had begun around them, and they'd had to run to avoid burial.

Morglop pulled himself over the tunnel's lip. Wentworth, recently restored to his accustomed weight, followed. It was drizzling. Jasper flitted around Morglop and into the rain.

"Where are we?" said Wentworth.

"Just a mo," said Jasper. He flew straight up for a few dozen cubits and surveyed the city. He zipped back down to the other Boars. "Near Roddy Square," he said.

Morglop studied the ground around the tunnel. He noticed the impressions made by a pair of boots. He began to follow the tracks. They led to one edge of the lot, then walked along it. They turned, and walked back. On the third iteration, Morglop realized that whoever had worn these boots had been searching the lot, perhaps for the statue.

He came back to the others, who were examining a pile of dirt. Someone or something had been digging at it. "Someone here before," Morglop said. "Search for statue. Not find. I am puzzled; no wagon, no heavy prints. How they take statue from tunnel?" He shrugged.

"Recognize that?" said Wentworth, nodding at the mound of dirt.

"I believe so," said Jasper. "It looks like what's left of an earth elemental when the summoned force dissipates. So we're looking for an earth mage, eh?"

"So it would seem."

"Now what?" said Morglop.

"Tracking the statute from here looks pretty futile," said Wentworth. "Let's go back to my shop, and I'll conduct a magical scan. With luck, I should be able to pinpoint the statue's current location."

"Okay," said Morglop. "Get cleaned up. Have tea."

"That sounds pleasant," said Jasper.

XIII.

Ross Montiel stood in the top floor of number eleven with his pet water mage. George's body lay in the street. Ross peered at it sadly. "Golly," he said. "Micah is sure taking his time."

The water mage was close to tears. "Duh-duh-demons," he blubbered. A winged form flitted past the windows.

"I can see that," said Ross.

"And zuh-zombies!"

"Right, right," said Ross.

There was a creaking sound from the roof. Ross looked up uneasily.

There was a sharp crack, then a rumble. Plaster fell about them. Ross and the water mage ran for the stairs.

The roof ripped off the building. Above them, peering in, was a giant demonic form, something with compound eyes and tentacles. It emitted a peculiar high-pitched giggle. A tentacle grabbed the water mage, who was too terrified to attempt a spell. He screamed. The demon giggled again and inserted the mage in a massive, toothless maw. It gummed the wizard to death.

"Oh, phooey," said Ross as he skipped down the stairs. It was hard to find magicians who worked cheap. "Who's running these darn demons, anyhow?" he muttered.

Someone was banging on the cellar door. "Let me out!" yelled Elma.

"Shut up!" shrieked Ross. Where was Micah, anyhow?

Ross considered running across the street to number twelve. He went to the parlor window. A phalanx of zombies marched down the street, heading for a bunch of dockyard toughs.

Ross recognized the dockers. It was the Death Spuds, a petty waterfront gang. He'd fought a gang war with them once. He was happy to see them die.

Where was Micah, anyhow?

Up ahead, odd shapes flitted among the clouds. Carruthers, who was rather nearsighted, failed to see them. There was the occasional flash and boom of a spell.

"Righto," said the general. Behind him was a century of the Ducal Guard, a hundred middle-aged men on horses. "We'll sweep the blighters before us, what?"

"I say," said one of his men. "This'll be fun, eh? Haven't seen action since last Carnival."

"A hundred men charging on horseback ought to give the scum what-for, eh, lads?" said the master sergeant. There were chuckles.

"Right, then," said the general. "On my mark, charge!"

With yells and laughter, the horsemen thundered down Thwart.

Three of Micah's thugs broke from hiding. They darted down Thwart Street into the doorway of the next building. Micah watched them go.

A demon swooped. It had three rotating wings, an arrangement Micah had never seen before. It grabbed one of the goons in its claws and began to lift.

"Now!" piped Micah. Crossbows twanged about him. Several bolts hit the demon. The demon was startled enough to drop the goon. The goon fell twenty feet and broke his neck on the cobblestones.

The other two made it to the safety of the doorway.

Micah sighed. There were too many demons and random blasts of magic out there. The only reasonably safe way for his men to get to Montiel was by working down the street from building to building. The buildings provided a modicum of shelter from demonic attack and haphazard explosions. Unfortunately, Micah was losing too many men. It wasn't just the demons, either. There seemed to be at least a dozen opposing groups out there—zombies, elves, dockyard toughs . . . Half the city was out after the statue.

"Better get the next group ready," said Micah to a hulking thug.

"A lot of the boys are deserting," said the thug.

"Of all the disloyal twerps," said Micah.

"Aw, come on," said the thug. "These guys signed up to kneecap debtors and make an easy quid. Monsters from the nether hells ain't in the job description."

Another group of thugs dashed for the far doorway. They made it.

"Ross is in danger," shrilled Micah. "He needs us."

The thug dug a finger into his ear and drilled for earwax. He didn't want to respond to that statement. In his opinion, a boss who got himself into this much trouble didn't much deserve to stay boss.

But no one was asking his opinion.

The elven sailors huddled in the ruins of an apartment building. "Gosh, Cap'n," said one. "This was supposed to be easy money."

"Yeah," said another. "Grab a statue and run."

"Sorry, guys," said the captain. "Looks like a lot of other bozos heard about this statue thing, too."

The baroness's headquarters was in a sewer. The scent left something to be desired, but it was well hidden, and the catacombs gave her scouts ready access to the whole parish.

The lich plodded up to her, dragging a dead elf. The baroness grabbed the body and inspected it. She spoke a Word; she spoke several. She did not need to kill an animal to fuel this spell. Enough people were dying up above; she tapped the energy of their deaths.

She completed the spell. A zombie elf lurched to its feet and back down the corridor to join the rest of her forces.

"Where is the statue?" the baroness demanded.

"It's a madhouse out there," whispered the lich. "I count at least six contending forces."

"Damn those orcs," muttered Veronee. "They said they were selling me an exclusive."

"And," whispered the lich sarcastically, "an orc's word is his bond."

"Spare me," snarled Veronee. "When will you have it?"

"Hard to say," the lich whispered. "We're half a block from number twelve. It shan't be long."

A fireball exploded in the rubble.

As the flames dissipated, the form of a paunchy, red-haired young man in a maroon greatcoat appeared. He held an elaborately carved meer-schaum pipe and stared about the rubble that had once been number 12, Cobblers Lane.

"Good heavens," said Timaeus. A sudden whistle increased in volume and intensity. He threw himself flat on the ground and rolled behind a cast-iron bedstead.

A flash of green exploded in the street. Cobblestones, thrown from the roadbed, flew in all directions, shattering windows. In its place, the explosion left a thorntree, standing two stories high. Its branches moved restlessly, searching for prey.

The thump and thunder of other spells could be heard. So could shouting voices and the screams of the dying.

On his hands and knees, Timaeus scrambled about what was left of the flat. He'd teleported because his trip to the university had taken far longer than he had expected; too long.

He hoped Sidney wouldn't be too upset.

"Sidney?" he called. "Nick? Father Thwaite?"

Awestruck, the elves held their fire. A hundred men thundered past on horseback. A hundred men in mail. A hundred men with lance and sword. Horseshoes struck sparks from the cobblestones. At the van floated the flag of Athelstan.

They certainly looked impressive.

Then they met the zombies.

The big advantage a man on horse has over a foe on foot is mass. When a cavalryman charges you with lance extended, a ton is hurtling at you at twenty miles an hour. All of that kinetic energy is concentrated at the point of the lance. That lance can penetrate any mail.

A horseman's advantage is also his Achilles' heel. Picture cavalry charging pikes. The pikes are longer than the lances. Guess whose point penetrates whose mail?

A massed pike formation can defeat a cavalry charge every time if—and this is an important if—the formation holds. For a cavalry charge is a fearsome sight. Many a pikeman has turned and fled when faced with the reality of a ton of flesh and steel hurtling down his throat.

Unfortunately for the Ducal Guard, zombies have no imagination. Being dead already, they have no fear of death.

General Carruthers was supremely confident of the Ducal Guard's ability to sweep all opposition before it. He kept his confidence right up to the instant that he ran his mount into the zombies' pikes. The horse screamed, fell on its back (flinging Carruthers ten feet into the curb), and broke its leg. It continued to scream as the rest of the hundred piled into it, horses falling, men dying on pikes or trampled underfoot.

The irresistible force met the immovable object. The immovable object won.

Zombies with swords and axes moved out to dispatch the wounded. Soon, there'd be a whole bunch of new zombies. Necromancers have something of an unfair advantage that way.

Limping in clanking armor, scared out of his wits, General Carruthers fled down the street.

There wasn't anybody here, Timaeus realized.

In the distance, there was the clash of arms, the sounds of screams, and a tremendous clatter. More spells rocked the air. I've got to get out of here, Timaeus thought. Cobblers Lane was an unhealthy place to be.

He hoped that the rubble did not contain the bodies of his companions. If it did, he'd never find them.

Where would they have gone?

No way to know. But Kraki's inn sounded like a good bet. Timaeus began to prepare another fireball teleport.

A second fireball flashed in the ruins across the street. Montiel opened the door a crack. Incredibly, there didn't seem to be anyone in the street right now. He darted out and into the rubble of number twelve.

It didn't take him long to find the tunnel below the floorboards. He ventured down it a short length but couldn't go any farther. A few cubits in, it had collapsed.

He stood in the tunnel for a long moment. Spells boomed and crashed in the distance. "I've been taken," muttered the elf. Obviously, the statue was gone.

Corky Evanish had said no one else knew about the thing. Corky Evanish had been lying through his teeth. Corky Evanish had some questions to answer, Ross decided. If the customs official answered them with alacrity, Ross might even let him live. For an hour. Or two. The elf smiled to himself in anticipation.

Ross clambered up the side of the hole and pulled himself onto the rubble. "Uh oh," he said. A bunch of guys in rags were waiting for him.

"Hi fellas!" said the elf. "You've just become a bunch of rich . . . dead guys." They were dead, all right. Some of them were weeks dead. They gave off quite a pong.

"It is awfully hard," Ross reflected, "to bribe zombies."

Ross was getting a little frightened, but he hid it well. The zombies hustled him into the sewers. Ross used the sewers to dispose of corpses. He was beginning to suspect that he might wind up a corpse himself.

"Who are you?" said the veiled woman to Montiel in a melodious but somehow threatening voice.

"Hiya doll," said the elf, trying to get a glimpse of her legs. "Montiel, Ross Montiel. But you can call me sugar."

She gave a low chuckle. "The dead have no epithets," she said. She motioned to the lich. Montiel died quickly.

"My apologies," she told the corpse. She spoke the spell that would allow her to interrogate the spirit of Ross Montiel. "Where is the statue?" she asked.

"Beats the hell out of me," said the sepulchral but somehow still shrill elven voice.

Veronee grimaced. Her zombies had already sifted through the ruins. The elf had been her last hope for information. She was tired and testy. She'd been up all day for nothing.

"I await your orders," the lich whispered.

The gods only knew where the damn thing was, Veronee thought. Someone had nabbed it, that much was clear. Judging by the mess up top, half the city was trying to find it.

"Back to the house," she told the lich.

"What about the zombies?" it whispered.

"Let them fight on," she said. The zombies were of no account. It was easier to let them be cut to pieces than to try to find some place to keep them until needed.

It was time, reflected the baroness, to give Morty a visit. The grand duke might be a fool, but Sir Ethelred, the foreign minister, ran a fairly effective intelligence network. The statue might be anywhere in the city; if anyone could find it, Sir Ethelred could. All Morty had to do was give the orders. He'd be happy to give her the statue as a present, Veronee thought; more than happy, if she were to give him the reward he desired. The thought was distasteful—but, Veronee thought, *exitus acta probat,* after all.

As long, she thought, as she managed to keep the truth of the matter from Sir Ethelred.

"Catastrophe," blubbered General Carruthers. "Foul sorcery and knavish tricks."

"What exactly—" said Sir Ethelred, peering over his pince-nez.

"Demons!" shouted the general. "Necromancy! Undead! The whole parish in chaos! Mobilize the army! Send out word across the realm! The grand duke must flee to his—"

"Thank you," said Sir Ethelred testily. "You may go."

Carruthers looked from the foreign minister to Major Yohn and back again. The general knew when he was being snubbed.

He gritted his teeth. He hadn't exactly returned in triumph. Blushing in shame, he strode from the library.

Major Yohn turned to Sir Ethelred, his leather chair creaking. "It's hard to believe that a simple magic object found by some adventurers could cause this much chaos," he said.

Sir Ethelred shrugged. "Per rumor," he said, "it's an object of fantastic value, as well as of magical power. Something that seems almost calculated to arouse greed among our less virtuous citizens."

"What would you have me do?" Yohn said.

"The most important thing," said Sir Ethelred, "is simply to restore order. It's a rather formidable undertaking, to be sure, but—"

"I believe it is feasible," said Yohn matter-of-factly.

"Good," said Sir Ethelred. "I shall leave it in your hands."

"A pity Carruthers was—"

"Carruthers is a fool," said Sir Ethelred shortly. He curled a greasy lock around one forefinger.

"The grand duke seems to trust—"

"You leave Mortimer to me," said Sir Ethelred. "How long do you expect you'll take?"

Major Yohn stood. "I shall report when I have a better notion," he said. "Farewell."

"And godspeed," said Sir Ethelred, rising and shaking the young soldier's hand.

Timaeus stood at the bar of the Inn of the Villein Impaled. "What's your pleasure?" said the wench.

He eyed her plump bodice, then thought better of it. "Ah—pint of bitter," he said. "In a clean glass, mind." He didn't think much of the inn's standards of hygiene. "And would you have any pipeweed?"

"Aye, sir," said the wench, and went to fetch him his drink and smoke.

He was beginning to get worried. His friends weren't here. He'd been up to Kraki's room, but there was no sign of recent occupancy. Timaeus frowned, shrugged, then settled in at a table by the window. He'd just have to wait for someone to show up.

He peered through the window into Roderick Square. Old Mad Roddy still posed atop his charger. Timaeus drank a silent toast to Valiant, Roderick's horse, who, per legend, had considerably more brains than his rider.

A wizened derelict came to the table. "Buy a drink for an old man?" he wheezed.

Timaeus was about to give him the brush-off when he noticed a pigeon on the man's shoulder. "Where'd you get the bird?" he asked.

"Heh," said Vic craftily. "Buy me a drink, and I'll tell you the tale."

So Timaeus did, and Vic began to spin him some yarn about a shipwreck and a cursed bird. Timaeus fed the pigeon pretzels and had some more beer.

XIV.

The sign on Wentworth's door said "Closed." Sidney glanced through the window. There didn't seem to be anyone inside the shop.

The only other pedestrian in the street, a fop with a rapier, ran through the rain in a futile attempt to protect his silk blouse. Though no eyes were on her, Sidney didn't pause as she passed Wentworth's storefront. She merely strolled past the shop and around the corner.

Garni and Father Thwaite were waiting for her, huddled against the side of the building.

"It's closed," Sidney reported. "I didn't see anyone inside."

Father Thwaite was unhappy with this development. "Are you certain it's necessary to break in?" he said. "It seems rather rude—not to mention illegal."

"Look, Father," said Sidney. "Last thing we knew, Nick and Kraki were headed here. Then they disappear, and some guy who's been on a strict diet for five or six centuries shows up with a ransom note. Maybe Jorgesen has nothing to do with it. But I wouldn't bet on it. Rude or not, I'm busting in."

Thwaite sighed.

"What if Jorgesen shows up while we're ransacking the place?" asked Garni.

They stood in silence for a moment. "We'll worry about that when it happens," Sidney said. "I just wish we were better armed." She had only her sword; the others had no weapons at all.

Through the gray light and pouring wet, they walked back to Fen Street. Garni and Thwaite stood in front of the door and argued about nothing in particular while Sidney worked on the lock. A lone carriage came down the street, its horse morose in the rain, its driver buried deep in his cloak.

Garni and Thwaite moved to shield Sidney from the driver's eyes as she worked.

The lock came open. They hustled inside. Sidney locked and closed the door behind them.

Father Thwaite took a sniff and immediately began to chant a prayer. He threw his arms wide; silver light appeared, encircling Garni and Sidney as well as Thwaite.

Instantly, Sidney drew her sword.

"What is it, Father?" Garni demanded, reaching for a battle-axe that wasn't there.

Thwaite shook his head and continued to chant.

Sidney circled warily, looking for danger. "Gods," she said. "What a smell."

"What is it?" said Garni.

Sidney rounded the counter. "Rotten meat," she said. "That's what it is."

Garni peered over her shoulder. The floor of the shop was covered with dismembered bodies in an advanced state of decay. "Gah," he said. "They've been here a long time."

Thwaite stopped chanting. The silver light dissipated. "Sorry," he said. "I smelled zombies, so I . . ."

"No need to apologize, Father," said Sidney. "You didn't know they were dead."

"Zombies are dead," said Thwaite. "You mean . . . dysfunctional, I suppose."

"Whatever," said Sidney irritably. She blinked; she recognized one of the corpses. "Mike Yarrow!" she said. "Hell." She stood over the body for a moment. "He looks fairly fresh."

There was the sound of a key in the lock.

Sidney dived behind the counter. Garni rolled under a worktable. Father Thwaite darted up the stairs to the roof.

". . . nice cup of tea . . . my word, what a pong," said Wentworth as he entered the shop.

Morglop sniffed. "Undead!" he grated. He hurled Wentworth to the floor, whipped out his sword, vaulted to stand atop the counter, and peered about alertly. Then, he noticed the mess on the floor and relaxed.

Wentworth picked himself off the shop floor. He was irritated. "My dear cyclops," he said. "It is not considered courteous to play skittles with the person of your host. . . ." He caught sight of the dismembered bodies. "Oh dear," he said. "And the cleaning woman doesn't come till Tuesday."

Garni lay against a wall. A severed hand in an advanced state of decay rested less than a foot from his nostrils. Garni's nose twitched. He hoped the newcomers would leave soon. Either that or find him. He could feel bile rising in his throat.

Jasper flitted into the shop. The point of green light circled the room. "Wentworth, old chum," he said, "I know your potions contain somewhat exotic ingredients, but really. Eye of newt and toe of frog is all very well, but rotting human flesh . . . Hullo. What's that?"

"What's what?" said Wentworth, gloomily searching through his pockets for his handkerchief. The smell was really quite revolting.

"I sense . . ." said Jasper. "Ah, Miss Stollitt. What a pleasure to meet you again. Do introduce us to your two companions."

With some relief, Garni rolled out from under the worktable. Shuddering, he pushed the dismembered hand away with his boot. Sidney and Thwaite reluctantly joined him.

Wentworth stared at the trio, handkerchief to nose, in undisguised astonishment. "Jasper," he said, "will you please tell me what in creation is going on?"

The smell of zombie wasn't nearly so bad in the back room, at least with the door firmly closed. Sidney, Thwaite, and Garni sat on stools at a scarred and battered old oaken table.

Morglop leaned over Sidney. His single eye was golden, huge in his face; a scar slashed his right cheek from top to bottom. In one ear, he wore a feathered earring. His mail was polished but well-worn, a few broken links visible. His triceps bulged. He wore a sword, a pommelled dagger, and throwing stars. He looked dangerous. "Crumpet?" he growled, scowling and holding out a plate.

"We'll never talk," said Sidney defiantly. She clenched her fists and sat bolt upright on the plain wooden stool.

Jasper's green point of light hung over another stool. "But my dear," he said, "all I ask is that you explain—"

"You can kill a free woman," said Sidney fiercely, "but you cannot break her." Her jaw was set.

Wentworth, who had been bustling in the background, appeared with a steaming pot and a platter bearing teacups. "Tea?" he said brightly.

"Do your worst," snarled Garni. He folded his arms across his chest and jutted his beard. Thwaite, pale, nodded agreement.

"The last we saw your friend Pratchitt," said Jasper, "he and a rather muscular fellow were pursuing us by carpet over the skies of this city—for no discernible reason, as far as we could tell."

Sidney made a rude noise. "I don't know what you've done with Nick and Kraki, and I don't know what you're going to do with us. But remember this, villain—"

"Really," said Jasper. "This is all quite unnecessary."

Since no one had responded to Wentworth's offer, the alchemist poured cups for Jasper, Morglop, and himself. Jasper's teacup rose from the table and tilted back in midair. There was a slurping sound. The tea level dropped noticeably. Wentworth turned to Garni. "One sugar or two?" he asked.

"I will not break bread with my enemies," Garni growled.

"It isn't bread," Wentworth pointed out. "It's tea. And I rather hope you *don't* break the china."

"What makes you think we enemies?" asked Morglop, popping a whole crumpet into his mouth. His mail jangled as he sat at the table and pulled over the jam.

Sidney snorted. "First, you offer to buy our statue. When we don't immediately agree, you kidnap two of our group, threaten to kill them unless we give you the statue—and, when that fails, assault Nick's flat and try to snatch the statue by main force. This doesn't count as friendly behavior where I come from."

"You don't have the statue?" asked Jasper urgently.

Sidney glared at him. "Bring on your tortures," she said. "We'll never tell."

"Well," said Wentworth wearily. "Really. You break into my shop, spread dead people all over my floor, smash up my merchandise, and refuse my tea. Breaking and entering is one thing, but deliberate rudeness is quite—"

"What?" said Garni.

"I mean to say," said Wentworth, "after all. It's only a bloody spot of tea. I'm drinking out of the same pot, am I not? There should be no cause to suspect poison."

"No, no," said Garni. "What was that about dead people?"

"And damned odoriferous they are, too," said Wentworth. "I haven't the foggiest idea how I'm to get rid of them. I can't just set them out with the trash; people will look askance."

"Wait, wait," said Father Thwaite. "You mean the zombies aren't yours?"

"Mine?" said Wentworth. "What the devil do I want with zombies? Cuthbert knows, finding capable salesmen is difficult enough, but I suspect that animated corpses would rather put off my clientele. . . ."

"They aren't ours, either," said Sidney slowly.

"No?" said Wentworth. "Then whose are they?"

"Precisely," said Jasper with satisfaction.

They all stared at him. Or rather, in his general direction.

"What do you know about it?" Garni demanded.

"Less than you," said Jasper. "However, consider. There was a fight here between a group of zombies and . . . an unknown. The statue has disappeared."

"You don't have it?" said Sidney.

"Would that I did," said Jasper. "The whole purpose of watching your apartment was not to snatch the statue at an opportune moment—I do have certain respect for the notion of property rights, my dear, and I can raise sufficient capital to purchase it from you should you desire to sell— rather, it was to ensure that the item did not fall into the wrong hands."

"Like whose?" said Sidney skeptically.

"Do you know what your statue is?" asked Jasper.

"Do you?" said Garni.

"Er . . . well, no, not entirely. But . . . I suspect it is important. That is, not merely of value for its metal content, but important on a far higher plane."

"Hah?" said Sidney.

"You know about the Sceptre of Stantius?"

"It's glowing, right? And there's some silly story about a new king . . ."

"Precisely. And your statue depicts Stantius."

"So?"

"So? Consider! How much magical energy does the statue contain? There *must* be a connection between it and the sceptre—and, possibly, with the war in Ishkabibble. Suppose the legend of the king's return is true; would not—ah—certain parties take considerable pains to forestall the legend's fulfillment?"

"If you were just watching the apartment," said Thwaite, "why did you attack us?"

"We didn't," said Jasper.

"No?" said Sidney. "You didn't? Muscle boy here didn't come charging into our flat waving his sword?" She pointed at Morglop with her thumb. "Friend Jorgesen didn't try to blow up the building with explosive flasks?"

Wentworth cleared his throat. "No," he said. "Rather, certain members of our party ascertained that the statue was in imminent danger of capture by the forces of darkness."

"What?" said Sidney.

"Therefore, we acted to prevent it from falling into the hands of the lords of evil."

"I beg your pardon?" said Thwaite.

"You were under attack when we arrived, as you may recall," Wentworth said. He took a sip of tea.

"No, we weren't," said Sidney.

"Yes, we were," Thwaite reminded her. "We were being evicted."

"Mrs. Coopersmith?" said Sidney unbelievingly. "You thought Mrs. Coopersmith was a servant of chaos?"

Morglop swallowed and looked at the ceiling.

"I said that a member of our party came to this conclusion," Wentworth said scathingly. "I didn't say that this individual was even remotely justified in so deciding."

Morglop cleared his throat but said nothing. Everyone stared at him.

"Why am I beginning to believe this?" complained Sidney.

Garni grinned.

"One of the principles of my order," said Father Thwaite, "is: never ascribe to malice what is adequately explained by incompetence."

"A wise rule," said Jasper.

"Everyone else attack too," said Morglop defensively. "Human thugs, demons . . ."

Wentworth snorted. Morglop hurriedly took another crumpet.

"Let me get this straight," said Sidney. "You didn't attack us to get the statue."

"Correct," said Jasper. "Actually, I had hoped you still retained possession."

"No." Sidney sighed.

"The statue doesn't show up on a magical scan," Wentworth said to Jasper.

"Damnation," said the green light. "What does that mean?"

Wentworth shrugged and took a sip of tea. "It's either out of the city or someone's masking it."

"Masking it?" said Garni.

"Hiding its magical emanations," said Wentworth.

"Is that possible?" Garni asked.

"Certainly," Wentworth said. "It's not an easy thing to do. It would take a fairly powerful mage. But it's by no means impossible. It's merely a variant on a simple invisibility spell."

"Okay," said Sidney. "Look here. Nick and Kraki have, we think, been kidnapped by a necromancer. At least, what delivered their ransom note was a skeleton in a robe. If—and I'm only saying if—those zombies aren't yours, then I buy your story. But why are you so concerned about the statue falling into the wrong hands?"

"Yeah," said Garni. "Who are you guys?"

"Jasper de Mobray, *Magister Mentis* and KGF, at your service, sir," said Jasper. The green light dipped, giving the impression of a bow.

"No, I mean you lot," said Garni.

"Am Morglop," said Morglop.

"We're Boars," said Wentworth.

Garni looked at him as if he were mad. "Of course you are," he said soothingly. "I'm a gazelle myself."

Morglop chuckled.

"Members of the Loyal and Fraternal Sodality of the Boar," said Wentworth with irritation. "An ancient order of chivalrous souls devoted to righting wrongs and fighting evil."

Sidney snorted. "A club where overgrown adolescents go to suck back booze and tell each other lies about adventures they never had."

"Now Sidney," said Thwaite reproachfully. "The Boars distribute free capons to the poor every Mathewan's Feast, and—"

"One of our many charitable endeavors," said Jasper.

There was silence for a moment. "First," said Sidney, "I get hooked up with a aristo firebug with delusions of competence. Then, I get involved with a bunch of overage boy scouts."

"You can always go home to mum," suggested Thwaite.

"It's beginning to look more attractive," muttered Sidney.

"Well," said Wentworth, "let's see what we can find out about those zombies." He rubbed his hands with anticipation, pushed his chair back, rose, and dumped several ounces of crumb on the carpet. A marmalade cat materialized and began to do its part for household cleanliness.

They stood in the front room. One hand holding a scented handkerchief to his nose, Wentworth carefully opened an ivory box with the other. Within, there lay a dragon's tooth.

"This is a rather rare item," he said, his voice slightly muffled by the handkerchief. *"Avagrrine!"* he shouted.

Vibrating slightly, the dragon's tooth rose into the air and hung at about chest height. It turned black and swung to point at the door to the cellar.

"Black," said Wentworth, "for necromancy. Not that this is any surprise, to be sure. And it is indicating that a source of necromantic magic either came from or exited through the cellar door. Or possibly both."

Morglop opened the door and peered into the dark cellar. "Need light," he said.

Wentworth took a lantern from its hook by the cellar door. He put his handkerchief into his pocket and, breathing through his mouth, withdrew a small flask from inside his coat. He opened it and poured a single drop onto the lantern's wick. The wick flamed.

Wentworth led the way into the cellar, holding the lantern high, the dragon's tooth floating before him. "Aha," he said. "That tunnel was not here before." The tooth pointed directly toward a roughly dug hole in the side of the cellar wall.

"Not tunnel again," muttered Morglop.

"Hunh," said Sidney. "Okay. Let's go take a look."

"Can you give us some weapons?" Garni asked Wentworth.

"Of course," the alchemist said.

Cards were scattered across the wooden box. In the flickering torchlight, Garfok and Drizhnakh looked hangdog in defeat. "And where is her headquarters?" asked Nick.

Garfok looked at Drizhnakh. Drizhnakh shrugged resignedly. "She gots a place on Collin Hill," said Garfok. Nick skated each orc a shilling, picked up the deck, and began to shuffle.

"Oi!" said Spug suddenly. "Wait a minute. I gots an idear."

"Oi, Drizhnakh," said Garfok. "Ya hears dat? Spug gots an idear." They both chortled.

"No, really," insisted Spug as Nick began to slap down cards. "Look. Dis guy's got alla da dough, right?"

"Dat's right," said Garfok soothingly.

"So we is lettin' him ask questions so's we gets a stake, right?"

"Right you is, Spug!" said Garfok. "Dat is real good. Ya got it right da first time, even."

"Okay," said Spug. "Why'nt we just take da dough? We gots swords an stuff, right? Huh, guys?"

Nick stopped dealing. He looked at the orcs nervously. Drizhnakh's jaw dropped. A dazed look appeared in Garfok's eyes.

"Oi!" shouted Drizhnakh. He sprung to his feet. *"Arrrrgh!"* He ran to the chamber's uneven, rocky wall. He banged his head against the stone. *"Arrrrgh!"* he said. He banged his head again. Soon, he was building up a good rhythm: Thud thud thud thud.

Spug whimpered. "I's sorry, guys," he said. "Gosh, I's sorry I's so dumb. But how come—"

"You is right," said Garfok.

"Huh?" said Spug.

"You isn't wrong," said Garfok. "You is right."

"I is?"

"Yup."

There was a moment of silence, broken only by the thud of Drizhnakh's head against stone. Then, Spug leapt for joy. "Hah!" he shouted. "I is right! I is right!"

There was a thunk. The wooden box jerked two feet across the floor, cards flying off it and into the air. A quarrel protruded from the box's side. "Freeze," said a voice.

The orcs froze. Drizhnakh stopped banging his head on the wall and peered dizzily at the speaker.

Sidney Stollitt stood in the passageway, a crossbow in either hand. One was still loaded.

"Oi," said Garfok. "If we rush her . . ."

Two figures appeared flanking her: a dwarf with a great axe and a cyclops with a sword. A point of green light flew past them and into the chamber.

"I'd advise against any precipitate action," said Jasper.

Garfok gnashed his tusks.

While Sidney covered the orcs, Garni moved forward to disarm them. "Where's Kraki?" the dwarf asked Nick.

"In there," said Nick, nodding toward the crypt.

Morglop and Garni heaved the slab aside. Sidney peered down into the crypt. Kraki, bound and bleeding, peered up at her uncertainly. He frowned. "Don't worry," Sidney called. "We'll have you out of there in a jiffy."

"Ah . . ." Kraki said.

Nick handed Sidney the ladder. She lowered it into the crypt, then descended. Dagger in hand, she approached Kraki's form.

"Stop!" bellowed the barbarian. Sidney halted. Suddenly alert, she peered around the crypt, looking for danger. "What is it?" she hissed.

"I vill not be rescued by a voman," Kraki said.

"What?" said Sidney unbelievingly.

"Vhat you mean, vhat? I can yust hear the bards sing about this vone. 'And the damsel rescued the hero in distress, hey tiddly tiddly a-tiddly wink-oh.' No vay."

"Cut it out," said Sidney with some irritation. She knelt by Kraki. The barbarian rolled away as fast as he could, until he hit the wall of the crypt.

"You vant to humiliate me?" he demanded. "Stay avay, or . . ."

"Or what?" said Sidney nastily.

"Mother of Tsich," he said. "I'd be laughingstock of Northland. Kraki, son of Kronar, rescued by a girl. Vhat if my father heard about it?"

"Fine," said Sidney. "Stay here. See if I care." She turned and climbed the ladder again.

"Hokay by me," said Kraki from the crypt. "If vord get out, I never marry. No Northland voman be my vife. Folkmoot bar me from speaking. Companions shun me. Some hero, me."

At the top of the ladder, Sidney rolled her eyes. "You do it, okay?" she said to Garni. The dwarf grinned and took her dagger.

In the front room of Wentworth's shop, the three orcs cleaned up the dismembered zombies under Morglop's monocular glare. The others were with Nick and Kraki in the back. Still weak as kittens, Nick and Kraki sat at the oaken table and fortified themselves with tea and brandy.

". . . so the orcs agreed," said Nick. "I asked them who our captor was."

Everyone leaned forward.

"They said it was the Baroness Veronee."

There was a shocked silence.

"There must be some mistake," said Wentworth. "The baroness is a well-respected courtier, an intimate of the grand duke himself. . . ." His voice trailed away.

"Hmm," said Jasper. "You're saying she's a necromancer?"

"According to our green-skinned friends," said Nick.

"I say," said Jasper to Wentworth, "who do we have at court?"

"Mmm," said the alchemist. "How about Sir Ethelred?"

"He's a Boar?" said Thwaite with interest.

"No," said Wentworth, "but his secretary is."

"Who's Ethelred?" asked Garni.

"The current foreign minister," said Wentworth. "His portfolio includes espionage; and I believe, therefore, the baroness's activities fall under his purview."

"Fine," said Sidney. "Warn the court. But we'd better do something about her ourselves."

"I quite agree," said Jasper. "She has the statue, I expect."

"How do you figure?" said Garni.

"I reason as follows," said Jasper. "I don't have it. You don't have it. Someone dug a tunnel to snatch it out. Veronee apparently has access to a network of catacombs and tunnels beneath the city, as evidenced by your capture and the zombies in Wentworth's shop. Ergo, it seems likely she is the one who stole it. *Quod erat demonstrandum.*"

"Sounds good," said Garni.

"Damon!" said Jasper. "A message for the Grand Boar!"

A small green light separated from Jasper. "No dice," said Damon.

"What? I need to send a message—"

"It's after quitting time," said Damon nastily.

There was a hostile silence for a moment. "You have a dangerous amount of gall, my young friend," said Jasper. "You exist at my sufferance, you know."

"You gonna snuff me?" said Damon. "Gonna be pretty hard to send a message if you do."

Jasper was speechless for a moment. "Right," he said in an annoyed tone. "Time and a half."

Damon considered this briefly. "Okay, Jazz," he said. "You got a deal."

Some time later, the Grand Boar surveyed the crowd. "Jasper has called the Sodality to arms. Who will answer?" he shouted through his tusks.

"I!" shouted a voice. "And I!" "And I!"

"Forget it," said a dwarven voice.

The hunter's horn sounded. They headed for the door.

XV.

The grand duke was engaged in a tricky bit of work. He took the scissors and carefully cut at the base of a *Lactarius piperatus*. The blue-gilled bolete was precisely the right size for harvesting; but harvesting it presented dangers. In common with other mushrooms of the genus *Lactarius,* it oozes a milk when cut, like the stem of the common dandelion. Unlike that of other *Lactarii,* the milk of *piperatus* is extraordinarily acidic. It is inadvisable to take the fungus with the bare hands. Unless the acid is washed off immediately, it begins to eat into the skin.

Some scholars have gone so far as to classify *piperatus* as poisonous. The classification has its merits: if one eats a crown of the mushroom raw, one experiences severe gastrointestinal pain. Some might even find the experience fatal. Yet the same would be true if one were to eat a raw chili pepper.

This, in fact, was Mortimer's discovery, one of which he was inordinately proud: *piperatus,* when properly prepared, is delicious. Even with the milk pressed from the crown, the mushroom is extremely hot; but this merely makes it an ideal spice for addition to dishes intended to be fiery. Mortimer's kitchen used *piperatus* exclusively when strong spices were called for.

Mortimer's mining lantern shone on his mushrooms as he worked. He lay atop a mound of composted dung mixed with humus, goggles protecting his eyes from any spray of milk. A man-at-arms entered the chamber. "Your Grace?" the soldier said.

"Yes?" said Mortimer, without looking up. He was involved in his work.

"Your Grace, the Baroness Veronee requests an audience."

It took a moment for this to penetrate Mortimer's concentration. He rolled to his side and stared at the soldier through his goggles. "She does?" he said.

"Yes, Your Grace."

"She's here?"

"Aye."

Mortimer stood up. He held the scissors in one hand and a blue-gilled fungus in the other. He was clad in dung-smeared overalls and rubber waders. Goggles made him appear rather froglike. Why would the baroness have come on such short notice? Could he dare to hope . . . ?

"Have the kitchen prepare us a nice big *Fistulina hepatica.* With fried onions," he told the soldier. He suddenly realized that he was in no shape to receive anyone. "And tell Reginald to draw me a bath."

As he hurried through the dungeons toward his bath, he wondered what might go well with the *Fistulina.* Perhaps the Château d'Alfar '06. No, too light; an earthier wine was needed, a full-bodied red. Perhaps the St. Tammanie. Or the Sang du Démon. Yes, definitely the Démon. That would do nicely.

Veronee tapped her foot impatiently. She stared at the tapestry. Some clod in plate mail was standing over a dead griffin, holding the beast's severed head in one hand. He was grinning—the clod, not the griffin. "Heroes," the baroness sneered to herself.

She'd been waiting a good half hour. She was somewhat peeved. Had her hold on Mortimer begun to fade? There'd been a time when he would have seen her instantly.

"Please follow me, my lady," said a manservant. The baroness turned away from the tapestry and followed him. He led the way down a corridor and into Mortimer's private chambers.

Mortimer was waiting for her in his salon. He lounged in an over-stuffed armchair, wearing a silk dressing gown with a gorgeously rendered red dragon on the front. He held a briar rather awkwardly in one hand. His silk-slippered feet were up on a footrest carved in the shape of an heraldic lion. Veronee had to smile; her fears were groundless. Mortimer was obviously trying to look dashing. He was succeeding, unfortunately, in looking like a nearsighted fungus fancier in a bathrobe. Which was only fair, since that's what he was.

"My dear lady," Mortimer said, rising and waving his unlit pipe. "How pleasant to see you." He motioned the guards to get out, and they, with a grin, complied. "May I offer you a glass of wine? The Sang du Démon '89, quite a good year."

"Of course, Morty," said the baroness.

The grand duke poured two glasses of wine, handed one to the baroness, and posed—one slipper atop the head of the lion footrest, his right arm draped across his knee and holding his glass. The intention was to appear debonair; the result was to appear awkward.

"Oh, Mortimer," said Veronee throatily, placing one hand on his arm. His wineglass shook. "I need your assistance in the most dreadful way."

The grand duke swallowed hard. "Gah," he said in surprise. She'd come to him for help? Most unlike her. "Yes, umm, of course, yes. How can I help you, hmm?"

Veronee pulled out a lace handkerchief, dabbed at her eyes, and twisted it between lacquered fingernails. "Your Grace," she said and gave a sob, "I am ruined."

"My honor!" said the grand duke, standing upright. "What has happened?"

"The fundament of my family's fortune," she said despairingly, "has been filched."

"Your fortress in Filbert has been pilfered?" said the duke, shocked.

"Nay, nay," sobbed the baroness. "Our fortune is not founded in our Filbert fortress. Rather, it flows from a figure."

"A figure?" said the grand duke, puzzled.

"A statue," explained the baroness, "full-scale, depicting a man in archaic harness. It has magical properties, bringing wealth and well-being to its owner. And now it is gone!" She broke down and heaved sobs into her handkerchief.

"Now, now," said the grand duke. "Now, now. Fear not, dear lady." He patted her arm somewhat cautiously.

Veronee threw herself into the grand duke's arms. His wineglass hit the floor with a crash. He nearly tumbled over the footrest. "My lord," she sobbed, burying her face in his dressing gown. "I know you will help me!"

Unable to believe his good fortune, the grand duke stroked her hair. "What can I do?" he asked.

She looked up at him. "Oh, Morty," she cooed, "can your men not find my statue?"

"Eh?"

"If a reward is posted; if the guard searches diligently . . ."

"Oh, yes. I suppose. We'll have the herald make an announcement immediately. Sir Ethelred can coordinate the search."

She covered his faces with kisses. "Oh, Morty! I shall be forever grateful."

Idiot, he thought. He'd given away the farm. Here he had her at his power, and he'd simply granted her request. Surely he could have extracted some minor dalliance in exchange for aid? He cursed his tutors.

Neither romantic badinage nor haggling had been part of their curriculum. Tutors, he reflected, never taught you anything important.

Mortimer cleared his throat. It was in his mind to suggest that a little advance gratitude would not be amiss, but he could not find the words.

She tucked her head into his reedy chest. "Mortimer?" she asked softly. "May I tell you something?"

"Of course," he said.

"I . . . I have always found you attractive."

The grand duke's Adam's apple bobbed like a yo-yo. "Yes?" he squeaked.

"Do you think . . . I mean . . . are you expecting anyone soon?"

"No," he moaned.

Somehow, they began to move toward the bedroom door.

The Baroness Veronee doubted he'd make much of a bed partner. On the other hand, she felt hungry. Yes, she thought, she could definitely use a . . . bite.

Sir Ethelred Ethelbert was in the library. He perched unsteadily on a ladder, a book in one hand. He gaped down at Jameson, his secretary.

"Are you sure?" said Sir Ethelred. "Baroness Veronee? A necromancer? And a spy for Arst-Kara-Morn?"

"The information is from my Sodality connections," said Jameson. "I do not believe they would make such an accusation baselessly."

The foreign minister replaced his book on the shelf. Slowly, he descended the ladder. "If we act on this information and it proves false, it will mean my head," he said.

"Yes, sir," said Jameson.

"On the other hand," said Sir Ethelred, "if I can make it stick, I can probably get Mortimer to see reason about the Ishkabibble crisis. The baroness has been one of the primary obstacles. . . ."

"Sir, ah . . . the grand duke is with the baroness now."

"Now? Where?"

"In his private chambers."

"In his private chambers?" Sir Ethelred looked distinctly uneasy. He shook his greasy locks. "Delightful. I shall rush in, find him *in flagrante,* and inform him that the lady with whom he is *delicto* is a spy. I'm sure he'll appreciate the stern vigilance of our guardians of public order."

"Sir," said Jameson uneasily, "he could be in danger at this very moment."

Sir Ethelred sighed. "It's taking a terrible risk," he told Jameson. "Young men are supposed to take the risks. We old fogies are supposed to stay in our studies and pull the strings. Ah, well; *miseria fortes viros probat,* eh?"

Mortimer sprawled on the big four-poster bed. The curtains to the bed were drawn. He snored gently. Two small wounds were visible on his neck. Poor pathetic twit, thought the baroness; he'd never even gotten his pajamas off.

Veronee wiped the blood from her chin. They were always suggestible in this state. "When you awake," she said to the grand duke's slumbering form, "you shall do as I say. You will remember nothing of this conversation—"

There was a pounding at the door. There were shouting voices. She distinguished the voice of that meddling minister, Sir Ethelred something. "My liege!" it shouted. "You are in dire peril!"

She sat bolt upright. They knew she was in here, of course. She had entered Castle Durf openly and requested an audience with Mortimer. If they were saying he was in danger . . . her cover must be broken.

There was the sound of an axe chunking into the door.

That clinched it. Interrupting the grand duke was one thing. Breaking down his door was quite another, especially when he was engaged in an amour with a noblewoman. Either they knew what she was, or a coup d'état was in progress. She doubted the latter.

How had they found out? No time to worry about it now. There was just time to finish the poor bastard. She leaned over Mortimer and drank deeply. The life rattled from his body.

Naked, she ran to the French windows and threw them open. There was a bolt of lightning. She started.

For by the flashing light, she saw the ghost of Mad Roderick, atop his charger Valiant.

For an instant, she was sure her sins had caught up with her. Mortimer's ancestor was about to wreak his revenge.

Then she realized that she was seeing no ghost.

It was a statue.

A bronze statue.

A statue identical to the one in Roderick Square.

How odd, she thought. Did Morty have a replica made for his terrace?

Axes chunked repeatedly into the heavy wooden door. It wouldn't hold much longer.

She noticed that the statue had pigeon droppings on its shoulders. She examined it more closely.

It *was* the one from Roddy Square.

If it wasn't in Roddy Square, then what was?

The door splintered.

The Baroness Veronee transformed into a bat and launched herself into the night.

Eighteen Boars had answered the summons. Garfok counted them. In all, Garfok thought, the three orcs were surrounded by twenty-six heavily armed people of various races, all armed to the teeth, most with powerful magic items, many with intrinsic magical abilities. And every single one of them disliked orcs. Garfok had resigned himself to the prospect of a shallow grave in Wentworth's cellar.

". . . taking a party this size and this well armed through the streets of the city is inviting trouble. Ergo, we need you to lead us through the catacombs to Veronee's mansion," said Jasper.

"No chanst," said Drizhnakh.

"Unh uh," said Garfok.

"Does ya think we is stupid or somefing?" said Spug.

"You vant to live, or vhat?" said Kraki.

"Oi, sure we wants ta live," said Drizhnakh.

"Then you take us to house of baroness," said Kraki.

"Dat don't sound like da way to ensure my future survival, if ya follow me," said Garfok.

"Look at it this vay," said Kraki. "If you take us to baroness, maybe she kill you. If you don't, for sure *I* kill you."

"It ain't dat easy," said Drizhnakh. "Da problem wit' da baroness is dis: if she wants ta rip out yer eyeballs wit' red-hot tweezers, a little thing like da fact dat you're dead ain't gonna stop her."

"Perhaps I can suggest an alternative," said Father Thwaite.

"Huh?"

"Burial in consecrated ground would prevent the use of your body or spirit. . . ."

"So yer offer is dat you'll bury us in a churchyard after ya kill us, so's da baroness can't turn us into zombies? Dat's real generous, I gotta say."

"We're wasting time," said Jasper. "Look here, I admit that there is a certain danger that the baroness will wreak revenge upon you should you aid us. However, the odds are that you would survive the experience."

"Sez you."

"We're offering you your freedom. . . ."

"Da freedom to be a dead guy."

"Surely a sufficient cash payment would overcome your reservations."

Garfok grinned delightedly. "Now yer talkin'," he said.

While Jasper haggled and Morglop kept his eye on the captives, the others began to prepare.

"Two healing draughts per person," announced Wentworth.

Garni nudged Sidney. "Take them," he said.

"We'll be okay," she said. "We've got Father Thwaite."

"They cost a good pound *argentum* on the open market," he said. "You never know when one might come in handy."

"Oh, all right," she said.

Wentworth handed Garni a lacquered box containing three red gems.

"What's this for?" said Garni.

"They're—rather like congealed fireballs," said Wentworth. "Throw them and they explode."

"Ah . . . same radius as a fireball?"

"Quite. Do be careful with them."

"You bet."

"Don't test that in here!" yelled a woman in black.

"Why not?" asked an elf who was pointing a rod toward a window.

"If it backfires, it could wipe us out," she said. "And you don't know how many charges it has, anyway."

Wentworth showed Sidney his cache of small weapons. She found room for six throwing stars and a brace of daggers under her belt.

"I beg your pardon," said Father Thwaite, tugging at Wentworth's sleeve. "Would you have any brandy?"

Wentworth frowned. "Fortifying yourself before a battle may sound like a sensible notion *a priori,*" he said, "but I've found that the effects are more deleterious than beneficial."

Thwaite sighed. "Nonetheless . . ."

Wentworth shrugged and found the cleric a flask.

The alchemist moved around the shop, pulling down vials, flasks, and powders. He handed them out hither and yon. A good portion of his inventory was going into the pockets and packs of the assemblage.

This was, Sidney thought with satisfaction, perhaps the best armed group of adventurers she'd ever seen. The baroness would never know what hit her.

"Look at dese dips," whispered Garfok to Drizhnakh. "Dey actually think dey've got a chance."

Drizhnakh gave a hollow laugh. "When does we make a break for it?"

XVI.

This, thought the Baroness Veronee, is no fun.

She dodged crazily through the sky. It was raining fiercely. Her fur was wet through and through. Lightning crashed from time to time; she prayed none found her.

Below her, she saw her destination: Roderick Square. Grand Duke Roddy posed as always, sword aloft. Valiant had three feet on the ground. That meant something or other, Veronee thought; died in battle or didn't die in battle or something of the kind. Two feet aloft meant something else.

She fluttered around the monument. She tried to land on the sword blade; she grabbed for it with her legs, expecting to swing to a halt and hang facedown—the usual perch for a bat.

She almost broke her neck. There wasn't any sword.

She flew to the edge of the square and hung from the rafters of the Inn of the Villein Impaled. It sure *looked* like a sword was there.

She wanted to examine that statue more closely. Specifically, she wanted to touch it, to see if it felt like a man on horseback—or more like the life-size statue of a human male.

Unfortunately, bats have no hands. To feel the statue, she'd need to return to human form.

Equally unfortunately, her clothes were now in a pile by Mortimer's bed. Veronee suspected that a naked woman climbing up Mad Roddy's statue would elicit a certain amount of interest. Not that there were many people in the square just at present.

She caught a whiff of smoke. Pipeweed, she thought. She peered through the inn's small and rather dirty window. There were two men sitting at a table. One was a geezer, passed out on the table. The other was a large, red-haired young man, smoking a pipe—Timaeus d'Asperge, she thought in some surprise.

Hmm. Could she possibly have misjudged him? Could he have been clever enough to disguise the statue as Mad Roddy? Or was his presence here mere coincidence?

There was, she decided, only one way to find out.

She fluttered to the statue and transformed. She climbed it and felt the figure.

There was no doubt about it. This statue was not what it appeared to be. It merely looked like Mad Roddy. It *felt* like the life-size statue of a human male.

Someone must have replaced Roderick's statue and, for want of anything better to do with it, decided to play a practical joke on Mortimer.

Who might have done the deed?

"Hey, sugar," came a voice. "Don't you know 'bout Odd Rod? You wan' sa'sfaction, you lookin' in the wrong place."

She looked down. A drunk had accosted her. She leapt to the cobblestones.

"Aroint thee," she said contemptuously. The drunk leered and grabbed for a buttock.

She clouted him on the side of the head with her fist. Momentarily, the drunk looked surprised; then, his eyes flickered and he keeled over, unconscious. She caught him and lowered his body to the street.

"So when was this?" asked Timaeus, taking the pipe from his mouth—but his drinking mate had passed out at the table.

And no wonder, Timaeus thought blearily. One of the advantages of being *Igniti* was an ability to handle considerable quantities of firewater, but there was a limit to anyone's capacity. Both he and the oldster had imbibed a truly alarming volume of liquor in the course of the afternoon.

Timaeus was beginning to worry about Sidney and the others but could think of no better place to look for them; of course, in his current state of inebriation, he couldn't think much at all.

He leaned back in his chair and puffed on his pipe contemplatively. He looked out the rain-smeared window. He felt warm and comfortable. He felt vaguely guilty that he wasn't searching more strenuously; but where to look?

Outside, a naked and rather attractive woman walked by. Timaeus blinked twice.

The door to the inn swung open. "Innkeeper!" the woman called. "I plead your assistance." Given her state of deshabille, thought Timaeus, she sounded quite commanding. With a shock, he recognized her. It was the Baroness Veronee. "Extraordinary," he muttered and rose from the table.

The innkeeper's wife was wrapping a shawl about the baroness. The innkeeper shouted orders to his serving maids. One wench brought her a stoup of mulled wine, another a broiled chicken. The innkeeper guided her to a seat.

Timaeus cleared his throat and approached. "My lady," he said.

The baroness looked up and leapt to her feet. The shawl slipped, displaying an alarming amount of cleavage. "Darling Timaeus!" she cried. "How wonderful to find a gentleman in this dark hour."

Timaeus's breast puffed a little at being so described. "Can I be of any assistance?" he asked.

She extended a hand for him to kiss. "Chivalry is not dead," she murmured. After he'd done the honors, she continued: "Yes, my dear. Can I possibly impose on you to escort me home? These streets are not safe for a woman alone, as I have, to my cost, discovered this evening."

"Of course, Baroness," said Timaeus. "I should be delighted."

Moments later, he was swaying through the streets, stumbling over the cobblestones, rain battering at his greatcoat. He wondered what he'd gotten himself into this time—and how he'd ever find his friends.

"You are most kind to help me," said the baroness, "but I feel I should warn you."

"Sorry?" said Timaeus. Between the alcohol in his veins and the rain-slick cobblestones underfoot, he was having a hard time concentrating on conversation.

"My life is in danger."

"What? Surely not! A woman in your position, a member of the grand duke's court . . . ?"

"Precisely." Veronee sighed as they hurried through the rainy dark. "I am a victim of conspiracy."

"My lady!" said Timaeus. "I had no idea." He was somewhat skeptical; it was hard to imagine the court of Mushroom Morty as a hotbed of intrigue.

They hurried on in silence for several minutes. At last, Veronee spoke again. "I perceive that you have seen through my fabrication," she said in a low voice. "Pray forgive me. It is not court intrigue that I fear. Rather, I have—enemies."

She increased her speed. Timaeus had almost to trot to keep up. He cleared his throat.

"Before I say more," said Veronee, looking at a tenement as they passed —anywhere but at Timaeus—"I must know your allegiance."

"Sorry?" said Timaeus, bewildered.

She halted suddenly and stopped him with a hand on his arm. She peered at his face, her own face drawn. "Who is your liege?" she asked intensely.

"What? Why, the grand duke, I suppose—through the proctor of Durfalus University, of course. . . ."

"You have no other?" she asked, staring intently into his eyes.

Timaeus was taken aback. "Hmm, well, technically my father . . ."

She sighed, and her shoulders slumped. "I shall have to trust you," she said softly. She turned and walked forward again, this time more slowly.

"Athelstan may seem a dull enough place," she said, "but it has strategic value. It dominates the valley of the River Jones, and in Durfalus University it possesses one of the great magical colleges of the human lands. It attracts a certain amount of attention from the espionage bureaux of the surrounding regions."

Timaeus was startled. "Are you saying you're a spy? For Alcala? Or Hamsterburg?"

She gave a throaty laugh. "Would that it were anything so simple," she said. "No, my friend, I work for . . . other masters. Surely you know of the war in Ish."

Timaeus nodded.

"Petty human squabbles are mere embroidery on the fabric of the eternal war between Arst-Kara-Morn and the free peoples."

"Yes, of course," said Timaeus. "But that struggle is fought out over centuries, not . . ."

"Nonetheless," said Veronee, "each of the combatants has its own collectors of information."

"And you?"

"I am a servant of the Council," she said.

A thrill passed through Timaeus. The White Council? Could it possibly be more than legend? The wisest mages of all the world, joined to fight the eternal battle against the eastern foe? Heroic legends and boyhood daydreams fused within him.

"It hardly need be said," said Veronee, "that our cause has its opponents."

"My lady," said Timaeus thickly, "I shall do whatever I can to aid you."

Romantic sap, thought the baroness. Caught up in the baroness's tale, Timaeus had hardly noticed when they began to climb Collin Hill. And here was her town house.

* * *

"I would appreciate it if you would stay for the night," said the baroness. "Under the circumstances, I believe it would be reassuring to have a man about the house."

"Of course," said Timaeus.

"This is Rupert," said Veronee, waving at the butler. "He will get you anything you need. You'll forgive me for a few moments? I have some things to attend to." While Timaeus examined the bookshelves, she motioned to Rupert and headed to the door from the room. "Has Cook begun supper?" she asked.

"Yes, my lady," Rupert said. "But I believe a guest can be accommodated."

"Good," said the baroness. When they were out of the room, she closed the door behind them. "Forget supper," she said in low tones. "Prepare to flee."

"My lady?" said the butler, raising an eyebrow.

"I have killed the grand duke," she said. "I believe the palace has a fair idea that I am responsible."

Rupert blanched. "Yes, my lady," he said faintly. "I shall prepare the carriage at once."

"Good."

"Shall I tell Cook?"

"Mmm? Ah . . . no." Cook, unlike Rupert, had no value except as a servant. Moreover, she knew too much. Best that she burn with the house.

"I understand, my lady," said Rupert. "Will that be all?"

"Better see if Timaeus wants something," said Veronee. "Slip something in his drink to make him . . . suggestible."

"Very good, my lady," said Rupert.

Veronee descended into her cellars.

"Go to the crypt," she told the lich. "Tell those fool orcs to leave their prisoners and—"

"I've been," whispered the lich.

"Pardon?"

"I went to check on those idiots," the lich hissed. "Capturing the thief and the barbarian was a pain in the neck. Or the upper thoracic region, at any event. I wanted to make sure they hadn't escaped."

"And?"

"They had."

"Who had what?"

"The crypt was open and the orcs were gone," the lich whispered.

Veronee blinked. "Any sign of a struggle?"

"No obvious bloodstains."

"Damn," said Veronee. "Well, no matter. I know where the statue is. We're going to obtain it and flee."

"Flee?"

"To Arst-Kara-Morn."

The lich shuddered. Well, it would make a change. "What about your mission here?" it hissed.

"I've been compromised," said Veronee. "We have several spells to prepare. I need fresh zombies to lift the statue into the coach. I need demonic horses to pull us faster than pursuit can follow. And I need to burn down the house."

"Burn it?"

"Too much evidence to destroy any other way," she said, waving at the cellar that surrounded them.

"How do you propose to do that?" asked the lich.

Veronee smiled tightly. "I have a . . . cooperative . . . fire mage upstairs," she said.

"Ah," said the lich. That ought to do the trick. Fire mages tended to explode at death in any event. A properly handled sacrifice ought to work wonders.

"Come," said the baroness. "Let us begin."

There were four kittens in the cage. They mewled piteously as the baroness unlocked the door. She picked one up and held it to her cheek. "Puss, puss, puss," she said. The tiny cat rubbed its head against her cheek and purred throbbingly.

The Fifth Frontier Warders were three hundred strong. They'd left the few horses they had at home; cavalry is good for scouting and cowing unarmed crowds, but horses are vulnerable to spells. In a magic-heavy urban combat zone, infantry's the thing.

Major Yohn surveyed his troops. They were in a loose tortoise, overlapping shields, spears forward. He fretted about magic. With magic, a wizard can deliver a great deal of energy at a single place and time, to devastating effect. Consequently, dispersal is sensible whenever magic is expected.

But infantry is most effective en masse. Infantry delivers its energy at the point of its spears and the edge of its swords. The more spears and swords per cubit of frontage, the more damage it can do. Concentration of force at the point of the enemy's weakness is the essence of its strategy.

It was a conundrum for which there was no single solution, Yohn knew. Each situation had its optimum response, its own best combination of concentration and dispersal. His lieutenants had been for a dispersed approach, house to house fighting across the parish. That, Yohn knew, would lead to casualties. Too, it might drag on for days. The quicker he could restore order, the higher he would rise in the estimation of the court.

And Yohn was sick of being known as some backwoods bandit hunter. Suppress unrest in full view of Castle Durf, and his star would rise.

A massed formation was required. So he made the best compromise he could. The wards were out.

At each corner of the formation, and at several places in between, minor adepts raised standards. Each standard was a regimental icon, many times bloodied; each had been raised in many battles, in many lands. Each was rich with tradition, honor, and, more important, mana. The traditions, the antiquity, invested them with power.

They were the poles across which the Fifth Frontier strung its spell.

For the Fifth Frontier had no great wizard, no collegiate *magister,* no major adept. It had only a few minor talents, a few traditional wards; and the voices of three hundred men.

In unison, they chanted the Words, the Words of power. Other than the adepts, no man had any inkling of the meaning of the Words. No single man contributed a tenth, a hundredth of the energy a single trained mage could have brought to bear; for few of them had the slightest magical comprehension.

But there were three hundred of them. Together, they forged a spell of considerable power.

Yohn prayed it would be enough.

He was in luck. The rumor of the statue was spreading across the city still; but those at the center of the maelstrom had already learned that the statue was gone. Yohn did not have to contend with the Boars, Ross Montiel's disciplined goons, Veronee's zombies, or demons; they were gone. Only a dozen or so other groups remained, each after an object of fantastic value. An elven ship's crew, now fighting only for survival; a shadow mage, skulking through the alleys and sending out shadows of daggers to destroy those in his path; dockyard toughs, down to a disciplined core, holding number twelve at the moment and sifting desperately through the rubble in search of something no longer there; twenty disciplined Hamsterian soldiers, in civilian garb, bearing forged papers, out to collect an item that would bolster the lord mayor's dubious claim to the rule of all humanity; a gnomish artificer with small but deadly clockwork dragons to do his fighting, hoping to obtain a lifetime supply of athenor to fuel his devices, . . . and others. Many others.

But none, any longer, with the magical prowess to break the wards of the Fifth Frontier.

The Fifth Frontier marched down Thwart. The opposition melted before them. Here, quite evidently, were the grand duke's men, out to restore order to a parish that was now largely ruins.

Oh, they took casualties. The Hamsterian soldiers stood their ground and fought, convinced that the Athelstani had discovered their mission and would show no mercy. They died to the last man, taking a good dozen of Yohn's men with them. And several of Yohn's officers died with mysterious stab wounds in their backs. But the shadow mage gave up when he realized he could not hope to rout so large a force.

There were fools who loosed a quarrel before they realized what they faced. There were those who panicked and fought when they might have surrendered. But within two hours, Yohn controlled Five Corners.

XVII.

From the kitchen at the rear of Veronee's town house ran a simple wooden stair down to an innocuous root cellar. There, Cook stored potatoes, root vegetables, and the dried mushrooms the grand duke insisted on giving Veronee from time to time. A door from the root cellar led to a disused wine cellar. The wine cellar held dusty wine racks and a few bottles of wine; Veronee drank very little and kept only meagre stock to meet the needs of her occasional guests. The previous owner of the town house had been a lover of wine; he had died accidentally in a particularly ghastly way —coincidentally, shortly before Veronee bought the place. Or not so coincidentally, actually.

At one corner of the root cellar, a trapdoor lay under a pile of enormous dried mushrooms (a subspecies of *Lycoperdon giganteum,* a full four feet across at the crown). Under the trapdoor was a spiral stair.

The stair ran down a circular shaft that a cooperative earth mage had dug through the sand underlying Veronee's house. The mage, too, had expired of unnatural causes at an early age, a fact the baroness found propitious, as she had no desire for others to learn of her subterranean secrets.

At the foot of the stair was Veronee's workroom. It was a large chamber, lit by tapers affixed to the earthen walls. The floor was a wooden platform suspended over the earth on blocks of stone. About the walls were bookshelves, several inches inward from the earth itself, avoiding direct contact with the soil. Worktables and chairs were scattered about the room. Cages stacked against one wall held small animals for Veronee's use.

Two doors led from the workroom: one to the room where Veronee kept her records, and the other to a smaller chamber containing prison cells.

The baroness had reason to hold people occasionally, usually prior to involving them in her magical preparations.

The prison chamber had another door; it led to the catacombs themselves. This served a dual purpose: as a bolthole through which Veronee might flee if the authorities should descend unannounced, and as a means for her servants to visit the city surreptitiously. The prison chamber also contained a small stair, leading to what Veronee called her morgue: little more than a pit, it was used to store corpses until needed.

From the records room, a short stair ran to Veronee's bedroom. Veronee forewent the traditional coffin in favor of a comfortable feather bed; a pillow filled with earth sufficed to provide contact with the soil in which she had been buried, one of the unhappy requirements of her current . . . incarnation.

Veronee stood in her workroom. A corpse, fairly fresh, lay on the table before her. In her hand was a kitten. She raised a knife high and plunged it down. She spoke Words of power.

She tossed the dead kitten over her shoulder and completed her spell. The corpse rose from the worktable and stumbled over to join five other zombies in front of a bookshelf.

The lich entered the room, dry bones piled like firewood in its brown-robed arms. It tumbled the bones onto Veronee's table. "That's the lot," it whispered.

"What?" said Veronee. "Only seven?"

"I haven't had time to fetch more bodies," whispered the lich irritably. "We used up most of the morgue in the fight at Five Corners."

"Very well," said Veronee. "It will have to do." She went to the cages. A large rat stared at her malevolently. She preferred more tractable animals but had exhausted her supply of kittens and puppies. Rats were smart; they weren't trusting.

She reached into the cage. The rat struck at her hand, but she was too fast. She grabbed it by the neck. It struggled fiercely.

She spoke a Word and went to the worktable. She picked up her knife and spoke again. The bones rustled.

Halfway through her spell, a pounding noise came from her prison chamber. She was so startled that she almost lost her concentration. Determinedly, she focused on the spell. She spoke faster; gradually, control returned. The pounding noise continued as she completed the spell.

The lich moved toward the prison chamber to take a look. When Veronee finished, she ran to join it.

At the far end of the chamber, a heavy door barred the way to the catacombs. An axe blade protruded through the door. The blade pulled out, readying for another swing.

"I believe we have company," whispered the lich.

Her mind awhirl, Veronee slammed and bolted the door between the workroom and the prison chamber. Who was out there? Sir Ethelred was, no doubt, dispatching men to arrest her even now; but soldiers would come through the streets. Would they not?

She whirled on the zombies. "Kill anything that comes through that door," she said, pointing to the door she'd locked. They moved to form a semicircle around it.

"Come on," she snapped to the lich. Both of them ran for the spiral stair.

If the attackers weren't men from the palace, who could they be? No one else knew about the catacombs . . .

Except those damned orcs.

They skittered upward, the lich's foot bones clanging hollowly on the metal stairs. "Those orcs," Veronee gasped. "They've betrayed me."

"Ah," whispered the lich. They came to the root cellar. "But to whom?"

"To Pratchitt and the barbarian, fool," she snarled.

"Shall I close the trapdoor?"

"No," Veronee said. "I have to think." Pratchitt and the others must be attacking below. The zombies would hold them off for a while. But how would she get the statue into her carriage without zombies to lift it?

Timaeus, thought the baroness. An excellent idea. What a pleasure it would be to use the fool against his friends.

"Those zombies won't hold them long," the lich whispered.

"Very well," said Veronee. "Get Cook."

"Ah," said the lich. It shrugged and climbed the wooden stairs to the kitchen.

While she waited, Veronee cursed herself for her stupidity. The orcs were both stupid and greedy: cleverness could outwit them and gold could buy them. She had been foolish to leave them unattended.

Still, she thought, if I ever encounter Garfok and Drizhnakh again, they will wish they were dead. Then, after a while, they'll wish they *weren't* dead.

Veronee chuckled to herself and readied her silver knife.

Bony fingers opened the door to the kitchen. A tiny, gray-haired woman looked up tiredly. "Bitch wants you," whispered the lich.

Cook stood up and sighed. She trudged to the cellar door, muttering something. She climbed laboriously down the stairs, clutching the wooden bannister for dear life. Resignedly, the lich followed after.

"Thank you, dear," said the baroness when Cook reached the cellar floor. The old woman bobbed in a perfunctory curtsey. *"Amatagung!"* Veronee shouted.

Cook looked up with a puzzled expression. With a flourish, the baroness sliced into her own palm, drawing a line of blood. She stepped sideways and began a slow dance.

Cook, terrified, backed directly into the lich's arms. Its bony fingers grabbed her and held her tightly.

The baroness's chanting came to a climax. With a single stroke of her knife, perfectly timed with the steps of her dance, she cut Cook's throat. The baroness knelt with the woman on the cold stone floor, sucking greedily at the throat. After a moment, she stepped back, wiped her mouth, sighed with satiety, and finished severing the head, chanting Words of power.

Finished with her spell, she held Cook's head before her. Blood dripped from the stump of the neck. Cook's eyes moved, looking sluggishly about the room.

"Good," whispered Veronee. Quickly, she moved to the spiral stair and tossed the head down the shaft.

"Come," she said to the lich.

Timaeus tottered around the parlor. The room was spinning. He was beginning to regret having asked Rupert for a whiskey. He'd been drinking all afternoon; the whiskey was proving to be the final straw.

He tried to focus on the title of a book. He was pulling it off the shelf when the door flung open and the baroness Veronee hurried into the room. "Timaeus!" she cried. "They are here!"

Timaeus looked up. "Who?" he asked thickly.

"The servants of darkness!" she cried, taking his hand. "They attack from below. Come, we must flee." She tugged him toward the door.

"But my lady," said Rupert, entering the study. "We cannot hope to outdistance them; they have magical steeds."

"Then all is lost," Veronee said and threw herself into an armchair, weeping. Timaeus stared at her, aghast. Before he could comfort her, Rupert spoke.

"I will stay," said Rupert bravely. "Perhaps by sacrificing my miserable life, I can hope to buy you some scant seconds."

Timaeus's mind was moving fuzzily, but he had a fair idea what was expected of him under the circumstances. Noblesse oblige, and all that.

"Nay, faithful servant," he said unsteadily, "attend your mistress. I shall stay and serve what use I may."

Veronee rose and flung herself into his arms. "Oh, bravest Tim," she said, and kissed him soundly. "I will remember you always." She took his hand and tugged him toward the door. "Come," she said. "They will attack through the cellar, from the catacombs."

"What?" said Timaeus.

"You must face them there."

"I shall do what I may," said Timaeus. He was beginning to wonder how he'd gotten himself into this one.

Veronee led him through the kitchen and down into a root cellar. She pointed to the spiral stair. "There is where they will come."

"Righto," said Timaeus, reaching for his pipe.

"Then . . . farewell, dearest Tim," she said, kissed him once more, and scurried out the door.

Garni plunged the axe into the door again.

Morglop stood with Kraki, right behind the dwarf. Their weapons were out. They were ready to charge through the door.

Wentworth crouched beside the door, an explosive flask in his hands.

Wizards stood in a semicircle behind Morglop and Kraki, readying spells. "They won't know what hit 'em," said one Boar to another.

Sidney was at the rear with several Boars, guarding the orcs. The last thing anyone needed was to worry about a stab in the back from their green-skinned "allies."

"It's going," grunted Garni. On his next swing, the door splintered.

Spells poured through the opening. The prison chamber resounded with green flashes, red explosions, a burst of yellow light. Arrows shot through the door. Fighting men poured in, swords and axes ready. . . .

"Is empty," said Kraki with frustration, dancing about the room. He looked distinctly upset.

Morglop prowled the room, double-checking to make sure that no danger lurked. A spell had melted the bars of one of the prison cells into surreal shapes. Char marks could be seen on the walls.

"Boy, we sure showed them," said one Boar to another. Morglop snorted.

"We've lost the element of surprise," said Wentworth, surveying the room through his monocle.

"Yes," said Morglop. Bashing down doors with axes was not the way to sneak up on someone.

Morglop went to the door on the far wall, the one that led to Veronee's work chamber. He tested the knob. The door was locked. He waved to Garni. "Another door," he said.

"Right," said the dwarf, hefting his axe.

"Hell vith this!" yelled Kraki. He hurtled toward the door, shoulder first, sword in his trailing hand. Morglop stepped out of the barbarian's way. Kraki impacted the door. It burst off its hinges and slammed onto the floor of the room beyond.

Kraki fell to hands and knees on top of the door. He looked up. Seven zombies were about to kill him. He raised his sword and parried desperately.

The others scrambled toward the door. No one was in position; Kraki had acted too abruptly.

Wentworth turned a dangerous color of red. "After him!" he screamed at Morglop.

"I can't," said the cyclops. He hovered by the door, trying to wedge his way through, but the zombies kept Kraki hemmed in against the opening.

Several wizards gathered behind Morglop, wondering whether to chance a spell. The doorway gave them a narrow line of sight into the room beyond, but Kraki was dodging wildly as he struggled with the zombies. A spell might as easily hit him as an enemy.

The barbarian was already wounded in two places. He was a superb swordsman, but seven opponents were more than he could handle.

"Do something!" shrieked Wentworth.

"Care to be more specific?" snorted Morglop.

A beam of black light shot through the door, inches from Morglop's eye. He reared back in surprise.

The beam struck one of the waiting wizards. The man's face wrinkled and his hair turned white. He clutched his chest, stumbled, and fell prone.

Morglop stared past the zombies. A severed human head hung behind them, floating in midair. Blood dripped from its neck. Its eyes focussed on the cyclops. A black beam shot. . . .

Morglop darted to the side. The black beam struck the door frame; the wood instantly rotted and turned to dust.

"Everyone out of doorway," Morglop shouted. The order was unnecessary. Everyone was already scrambling away from the opening and to the sides of the room.

Kraki, no fool, backed through the door, parrying wildly. "Morglop!" he yelled. "Vhen they follow, fight from side of door." Then, he ducked out of the head's line of sight, ready for the first zombie to come through the door.

But they didn't come.

Kraki sneaked a peek. The head stayed in the workroom. The zombies were completely motionless. Veronee's order had been very explicit: "Kill anything that comes through that door." Only one thing had come through the door, and Kraki had left again. Patiently, they waited for something else to kill.

Father Thwaite was crouching over the wizard that the black beam had struck. "What's wrong with him?" Morglop asked.

"He's dead," said Thwaite.

"Dead?" echoed Wentworth. "How did he die?"

Thwaite looked at the alchemist. "Of old age."

Wentworth raised an eyebrow, then shrugged. After all, they were dealing with necromancy.

"We're pinned down," said Sidney.

"That," said Wentworth, polishing his monocle, "is about the size of it."

"How about a fireball?" asked a young Boar in a chain mail byrnie. Morglop rolled his eye.

"These cellars are too small," Jasper answered testily. "A fireball would fry us to cinders."

"Oh," said the Boar.

They sat or stood in silence for a moment. "Now what?" asked Wentworth.

"Why dontcha give up while da givin' is good?" suggested Garfok. "Before da baroness gets here."

"Shut up," Sidney said, poking the orc with her blade.

"Gosh," said an elf maiden finally. She wore a green cap with a point that flopped over one eye, green leggings, and curly-toed shoes. She had a bow over her back. There were little cozies over her arrow points. "I can get that mean monster!"

Everyone stared at her. Elves, thought Jasper. He knew it was uncivilized of him to harbor prejudice for an allied species, but he hated elves. They were so damned . . . cute.

"You can, eh?" Wentworth said.

"Sure, mister!" she said brightly. She knelt against the wall, right by the edge of the door, and nocked her bow. While the others watched, she pulled the bowstring back to her ear, leaned into the door opening, and let fly. She leaned back out of the doorway.

A black beam shot through the door and splashed harmlessly against the far wall.

The elf maid nocked another arrow, leaned into the doorway again, and let fly again. She hesitated, then stood up, square in the middle of the doorway.

Nothing happened to her.

She stuck her tongue out at the zombies, then turned to Jasper. "See?" she said brightly. "Told ya."

Warily, Jasper flitted into the doorway. Beyond the still-motionless zombies, the severed head swivelled and bobbed wildly, one arrow protruding from each eye.

"Good work," Jasper said grudgingly. The elf maiden giggled.

Morglop stepped into the doorway. The zombies stood in a rough semicircle about the opening. They were as motionless as the corpses they were. The cyclops stepped through the door.

Instantly, the corpses raised their weapons and closed on him.

He stepped back over the lintel.

The corpses halted as instantly as they had moved.

"Strange," said Morglop. "Why don't they attack?"

Father Thwaite peered through the doorway. "Zombies have no volition," he said. "They merely follow orders. They were probably ordered to attack anything that comes through the door. You're on the other side of the door."

"Good," said Morglop. "So why not throw rocks at them until they die?"

"That would work," said Father Thwaite. "But this may be somewhat quicker." He pulled out a flask of brandy, hesitated, took a hefty swig, then began to chant. Within moments, a blue glow had imbued the flask. He took an aspergillum from his robe, poured the brandy into it, and, standing on tiptoes, leaned through the door to sprinkle brandy on the zombies.

With the first sprinkle of brandy, one zombie fell to its knees. With a second, it fell lifeless to the stone floor. Soon, the zombies were nothing but sprawled corpses.

The group drifted into the workroom. The statue wasn't here. The severed head kept on bumping into Kraki blindly. He brushed it away. "Up stairway?" he suggested.

Morglop peered up the spiral stair. He shrugged. "Wentworth," he said, "let's get organized."

Timaeus sniffed suspiciously at a mushroom and put it aside.

He peered down the spiral stairs. It filled the shaft, meaning he had no way of knowing what was down there. He lit his pipe (*bang!*), and settled back on a sack of potatoes to wait for the foe.

Sounds of combat floated up the stairs. Timaeus frowned and listened closely. After a while, the noise stopped.

Some minutes later, a footstep clanged on the metal stairway. Timaeus couldn't see who his foe was, but someone was coming up the stairs. He cleared his throat and said a Word.

A ball of flames appeared in his right hand. He tossed it negligently down the stairway.

It bounced down along the spiral.

There was an explosion.

Flames gushed back up the shaft, enveloping Timaeus.

His greatcoat began to burn. "Shoddy workmanship," he muttered, batting at it with his hands. He got the fire out. His clothing smoking, he peered down the stairway.

"That should hold them," he said, and sucked on his pipe contentedly.

A small ball of flame rolled under Morglop's feet and into the room. He wondered what it was.

Garni knew. Instantly, he dived over the stairway bannister, putting the metal of the stair between himself and the fireball.

Sidney dived under a worktable.

Morglop noticed their reactions and dived for the floor himself. Like most of the Boars, he was an instant too late.

The small ball of flames became a *big* ball of flames. There was a loud noise.

After a while, the smoke cleared enough for Garni to see the room. Several of the Boars were down, Wentworth among them. Jasper flitted about the room, but he moved more slowly than usual.

"Cleric!" Garni said weakly.

Father Thwaite was ministering to someone else. He paused long enough to look at Garni, and say, "Use your healing draught."

Wentworth awoke to find Sidney holding a flask to his lips. He sputtered, then drank deeply. "Necromancy," said Sidney bitterly. "You said there was necromancy. You never said anything about fire magic."

Wentworth sat up and wiped his mouth with a sleeve. "Didn't sense any," he said. He pulled out his dragon's tooth and threw it into the air. It hung motionless for a moment, then turned black and pointed at the severed head, still floating aimlessly around the room, arrows poking from its eyes.

"Yes, yes, I know that already," snapped Wentworth, rising gingerly to his feet.

The tooth swivelled, hesitated, then pointed to a zombie corpse.

"Right," said Wentworth, disgusted. "I know about that too. *And* the other zombies," he said with irritation, as the tooth began to point to another.

The tooth pointed directly at him and turned yellow. "Yes, I know I'm an alchemist, thank you very much," muttered Wentworth. "Fire magic. All right? How about fire magic?"

The tooth swung about, as if uncertain. Then, it darted to the stairwell and pointed straight up.

"There!" said Wentworth triumphantly. "See?"

Sidney stared at him as if he were mad. "Gosh, Mr. Wizard," she said, lapsing into elvish tones. "I'm so impressed. There's a fire mage up there, I bet! Thanks for warning us, Mr. Wizard, sir."

Wentworth turned crimson. He opened the ivory box in which the dragon tooth's was normally stored, walked over, held the box open around the tooth, and snapped it shut.

"That," Morglop said to the Boar in the chain mail byrnie, "is why you don't use fireballs."

Kraki conferred with Morglop. Jasper flew over to join them. "How ve get up stairs?" Kraki asked.

Morglop studied the staircase. "Run?" he suggested.

This sounded like suicide, even to Kraki. He shrugged. "Hokay," he said.

"Wait a sec, will you, lads?" said Jasper. "Why don't I run a recce, eh?"

"Vhat?" said Kraki. Without waiting for an answer, Jasper began to fly up the staircase in a tight green helix.

"He means, he'll go and take a look," explained Morglop.

As he flew up the stairs, Jasper mustered his concentration. He whispered Words, readying a spell. He was hoping to take his foe by surprise.

He shot out of the stairwell and into another earthen chamber, this one lit by a single torch. A man in a greatcoat sat on a sack of potatoes, his mouth open in surprise. Smoke curled over his head.

Jasper shouted the final Word of his spell. Green light enveloped his foe. Jasper plunged deep into his enemy's mind, seizing control of the man's body. . . .

Timaeus slumped over onto the potato sack. His eyes were glazed. His pipe hit a mushroom. He drooled onto the burlap.

Jasper flitted around the fire mage, studying him. Why in heaven was Timaeus here? And why had he thrown that fireball?

Gingerly, Jasper began to feel through Timaeus's mind. To his surprise,

Jasper found a compulsion, a desire to help a woman in distress. . . . The spell was crude, short term, easy to break. A magician of some other branch of the art must have imposed it on Timaeus. Jasper released the fire mage. "I say, d'Asperge, old boy," he said. "What's all this about, then, eh?"

Timaeus blinked and sat up groggily. "J . . . de Mobray?" he said unbelievingly.

"Spot on."

Timaeus reached for his pipe. It wasn't in its accustomed pocket. He noticed it on the mushroom and reached for it. "What happened?" he said. "I remember a green light . . . then I blacked out."

"I'm the green light, of course," said Jasper. "What the devil do you mean by fireballing me?"

Timaeus stared at the point of green light. "Fireballing you?" he said in some confusion.

"And," said Jasper, "your friends Sidney Stollitt, Nick Pratchitt, Garni, that Kraki fellow . . ."

Timaeus puffed fiercely on his pipe. "Forces of evil," he muttered disgustedly. " 'Farewell, dearest Tim!' " He scowled.

"Beg pardon?" said Jasper.

Timaeus's ears were an interesting pink. "Er . . . is everybody all right?" he asked.

Jasper sighed. "No fatalities, I believe," he said.

"Thank Dion," said Timaeus.

They had found the parlor. The injured were draped in couches and chairs. Father Thwaite had found Veronee's modest cellar, and several were sipping sherry.

Wentworth stood in the center of the room looking harried. "No statue?" he said unbelievingly. "None at all? Not even a bust? A lawn ornament? A toy soldier, for Cuthbert's sake?"

"We've been all over the joint," said Sidney. "The baroness doesn't have Stantius. Or if she does, it isn't here."

Wentworth turned to Kraki. "Nothing?" he said despairingly.

"Nothing," said Kraki.

"Unh uh," said the elf maiden.

"Zilch," said Garni.

There was silence for a moment.

Wentworth gave a little hop of frustration. He hurled his monocle to the floor. It cracked. He turned to Jasper. "This was your idea," he yelled.

"Me?" said Jasper in an injured tone. "Me? Hmm, ah, well. That is to say. It was my idea, wasn't it?"

"No point in recriminations," said Sidney tiredly. "The question is: now what?"

"Vhere is orcs?" said Kraki.

Sidney sat up straight. "Oh, hell," she said. "I haven't seen them since the fireball."

Drizhnakh, Garfok, and Spug hustled down the catacomb.

"Har har," giggled Spug. "We sure showed dem dumb youmans, huh, guys?"

"We was lucky," said Garfok petulantly. "Dey got smeared, and wasn't payin' too much attention. Dat's all."

"Well, anyway," said Spug, "we gots free. Right guys? We is okay now."

"You maroon," sneered Drizhnakh. "We is in da sewers of a city populated by hostile youmans, every one of dem scared shitless of orcs and as likely ta gut you as say hello. We got no money, no chanst of gettin' any, and no place to go."

Spug sucked on his tusks sadly. "Well," he said, "at least we is free."

"Free ta starve," muttered Garfok.

"Unh uh," said Spug, cheering up. "Remember what da baroness said? Dere's plenny of sewage ta drink an' rats ta eat down here. Remember guys?"

"Dat's right," said Garfok, a little happier. "It ain't so bad, Drizhnakh."

"Oi," said Drizhnakh. Perhaps Garfok was right, he thought. Drizhnakh was rather partial to rat.

XVIII.

A peasheful evening, Vic thought. He liked warm, summer storms. At least, he liked them when he had shelter. He stood, dry under the eaves of the Inn of the Villein Impaled, a bottle of wine in one hand. His pigeon nestled in the eaves, its head under one wing. Vic took a pull on his flask.

The air smelled fresh, as it rarely did amid the flatulence of the city. The rain washed it clean. Puddles pooled on the cobblestone street.

A lazhy evening, Vic thought. A day well done. He raised his bottle of wine to Roddy and took another swig. A day well done becaushe . . . becaushe . . . now what did I do today? Shomething important. I remember that. Shomething . . .

Lightning flashed. The downpour redoubled. Vic studied the chaotic intersection of ripples in the fountain around Valiant's hooves. A carriage, two trotters in its harness, rumbled into the square. Vic peered at it with interest.

Rupert brought the carriage to a halt. Lightning flashed, revealing the statue of Roderick. Rupert hiked up the collar of his cloak; a trickle of water escaped down his back.

The baroness, snug within the carriage, twitched back a curtain and peered into the rain.

"Now what?" whispered the lich.

The baroness smiled. "Rupert," she called sweetly, "can I see you for a moment?"

Cursing, the butler got down from his perch and stepped into a puddle. He muttered a brief oath, opened the carriage door, and climbed inside. "Yes, my lady?" he said, crouching in the carriage interior.

"Amatagung!" said the baroness. The lich grabbed Rupert's arms.

"Wait a minute," said Rupert.

The baroness grinned and spoke another Word.

"What about my back wages?" Rupert said desperately.

"What would you do with them in hell?" whispered the lich.

"Would it help to say I'm sorry about nabbing the silver?" said Rupert.

The baroness drew her knife. "Chin up," whispered the lich.

Rupert knew this was not intended as consolation. Doggedly, he wedged his chin into his collar.

The lich stuck a bony finger under Rupert's chin and lifted.

Straining, Rupert tried to keep his head down. The lich was too strong. Rupert realized he was a dead man. Defiantly, he lifted his head and stared proudly into Veronee's eyes.

She sliced his throat open. Blood flowed.

"I endeavor," mouthed Rupert's lips as the life departed his body, "to give satisfaction." Neither Veronee nor the lich noticed.

Veronee drank deeply of Rupert's blood. Strength coursed through her limbs.

"And it's so hard to find good servants these days," the lich whispered. Veronee ignored it. She opened the carriage door and stared at the statue. She'd have to wade through the fountain. Her boots would be ruined.

The spell would not last long; she was burning Rupert's life energy at a considerable rate. But while the magic lasted, she ought to be able to lift a ton or two of athenor. She shrugged, stepped into the puddle, and waded toward the statue. The water was cold. She climbed up Roddy's pedestal and gripped the statue's knees.

She lifted.

She pulled.

She strained.

The statue wouldn't budge.

She felt the force of her spell ebbing.

This was inexplicable. She could heft an elephant as if it were a three-month babe. Why couldn't she lift the statue? Was there another magician about?

The only other person in the square was an ancient codger, standing under the eaves of the Inn of the Villein Impaled with a bottle of wine in one hand. He held the bottle to his mouth, sucked back a swallow, and gave Veronee a toothless grin.

The old man was clearly no danger. However, Veronee thought, he might do to power another spell. She stalked over to him. "How would you like tuppence?" she said soothingly. There was a pigeon in the rafters of the inn, she noted.

"Tuppenshe?" Vic said. "Sure," he said, holding out his palm.

The baroness gave him a ha'penny. "I need you in my carriage," she said. "You'll get the rest there."

Vic didn't move. "Forget it," he said.

She turned. "What?"

"I shaid, forget it," he said. "You won't get . . . won't get . . ." What was it so important that she not get?

Veronee stared at him. Her eyes narrowed. She pointed at the old man and spoke a single Word. It resounded across the square like the crack of thunder.

A beam of brilliant black light shot toward Vic. Rain sizzled in its wake.

Vic raised a hand. The beam struck his palm. It dissipated into the rain in a spray of a thousand colors.

Vic smiled. "Shtill got it," he congratulated himself.

Veronee gasped and backed toward her carriage.

"What was that all about?" the pigeon asked Vic.

The Boars had begun to drift away. The fight was evidently over, and it was getting on toward dinner time. "Hope you find it, Jazz," said the woman with the eye patch. Jasper winced at the familiarity. Since he was largely invisible, she didn't notice. She looked down the stoop of Veronee's house and into the rain. "Oh, well," she said, and ran down the stoop and up the street.

"Maybe the baroness had the statue when she left," suggested the Boar in the byrnie. He didn't look inclined to leave, so Jasper shut the door.

"I don't think so," said Timaeus wearily. "She left in a coach. A statue as heavy as ours would have weighed it down. I would have noticed that."

"She never had it at all," said Wentworth with finality. "We jumped to the conclusion that she had it on rather inadequate evidence."

Jasper cleared his throat guiltily but said nothing.

"Vhat about dinner?" said Kraki.

"Wait," said Sidney. "Okay, if she never had it, someone else does. We don't know who."

"Very helpful," snapped Wentworth.

"We know they took it down the tunnel," said Father Thwaite.

"Correct," said Wentworth. "To the vacant lot. Where it disappeared into thin air."

"Could be," said Sidney. "Could magic do that?"

Morglop chuckled. "Take a look at Jasper," he said.

They all did. The point of green light shifted back and forth with mild embarrassment. "Yes, well," said Jasper. He had, he supposed, disappeared into thin air. About twenty years previously. In a manner of speaking.

"We've been all over that lot," said Sidney, "looking for evidence. But we didn't find anything."

"What about the dragon's tooth?" said Garni.

Wentworth stared at the dwarf for a long moment. "Ah," he said at last. "Not a bad idea."

A carriage careened through the streets of Urf Durfal, a carriage pulled by demon horses. Their necks were flayed open, their flanks streaked with blood; they hauled the carriage with unearthly speed. A glow of sinister light streamed forth from around the carriage doors.

Inside, bone gripped flesh.

The carriage hit a pothole. The lich and Veronee were thrown across the compartment. They fetched up against the door, then tumbled to the floor.

The lich dug its thumb bones into Veronee's neck. She gasped out a Word.

The undead horses hurtled onward through the streets.

Veronee brought up her hands and wrenched the lich's fingers away. It stabbed for her eyes and missed.

If the lich survived, it would bring the story of her failure to Arst-Kara-Morn.

Hence, she had no alternative but to destroy it.

Ergo, to preserve its own existence, it must destroy her.

They thundered out the Eastern Gate and down the Alcalan Pike. The pike was, if anything, less well paved than the city streets. Veronee was flung against the luggage rack, then to the back of the seat. Gasping for breath, she spoke another Word.

The lich scrambled toward her across the carpet.

The carriage hurtled into the night. Within, two creatures, neither now human, battled on.

It was drizzling steadily. The breeze stirred rain-laden weeds. The earth of the vacant lot was soggy beneath their boots. They were down to a dozen: Timaeus's friends, the three Fullbrights, and three other Boars.

A frightened face peered at them from the shantytown. The vagabonds, beggars, and dispossessed peasants who camped out here did not expect visitors, not this late, not in the rain. Visitors meant hoodlums out to bash in a few heads and steal the shanty dwellers' meagre possessions.

Sidney's light cotton clothing was soaked through. She glanced at

Timaeus; he looked, if it were possible, even more uncomfortable and bedraggled than she.

"Now what?" asked Nick.

They stood in a loose circle around the remains of the collapsed tunnel. Mud-laden water drizzled down into the opening; soon, it would disappear entirely.

Wentworth removed the dragon's tooth from its ivory box. *"Avagrrine!"* he said.

The tooth rose from his palm. It hung in midair. It swivelled uncertainly, as if searching. . . .

It steadied. It pointed away from the tunnel. Garni held his lantern higher to get a better look. The tooth was brown.

"Earth magic," pronounced Wentworth.

"Makes sense," Timaeus grunted.

"Undoubtedly," said Wentworth. He spoke another Word. The tooth moved forward. The party followed.

They came to a mound of dirt. Earlier in the day, it had been roughly human in shape. Now, it was nothing more than a vague pile.

The dragon's tooth turned sky blue. "Air magic," said Wentworth.

The tooth pointed upward at an angle and began to climb into the rainy sky. "Jasper!" said Wentworth. "Follow it, will you, old boy?"

"Of course, of course," said the point of green light. It flitted after the tooth.

"We must be dealing with two wizards," Wentworth explained. "An earth mage and an air mage. Once they got it out of the tunnels, the air mage took over and summoned an air elemental to carry the statue."

The party followed on the ground below Jasper, craning to watch him. The tooth was no longer visible, but Jasper shone brightly enough to be seen.

"I say," Jasper called back. "It's flashing blue and silver!"

"An illusionist, too?" said Wentworth. This was getting out of hand.

"To cloak it in invisibility," suggested Timaeus, "so that no one would gawp at a huge statue sailing overhead."

"I suppose," said Wentworth.

They came to the edge of the lot and stepped into the street. Jasper sailed over a building. Everyone ran, splashing through puddles, to get around the building before Jasper disappeared across the next street.

"Red!" called Jasper.

"Fire magic?" said Timaeus.

"Yes," said Wentworth uncertainly. They scurried on another hundred feet.

"Purple!" shouted Jasper.

"What?" said Wentworth.

"Purple," Jasper repeated. "Violet, lilac, mauve. Are you deaf?"

"What's purple?" Garni asked.

"Deuced if I know," muttered Wentworth. They followed Jasper, craning.

"Orange!" said Jasper. He skirted a small temple. They followed.

"Yellow!" said Jasper.

"Alchemy?" said Wentworth in a puzzled tone. He was getting a glazed look in his eyes.

"Gold!" said Jasper. He went over another building. This time, they had to run around the block. He was already disappearing over the next block, and they had to run around it, too.

"Pink!" Jasper called faintly.

"We are dealing," gasped Wentworth, "with a magical conspiracy of mammoth proportions. There must be dozens of wizards—dozens!"

They dashed into Roderick Square and halted. Timaeus held his sides and panted. He wasn't used to this much exertion.

The tooth was slanting downward now. It headed directly toward the statue. It flared silver again, then sailed on past Mad Roddy (and Valiant, of course), across the square, to the Inn of the Villein Impaled.

It came to rest a foot off the ground, pointing directly toward the recumbent form of . . .

Vic peeled open an eye. It was dry under the eaves. Just right for a nap. He was surrounded by a motley group of wizards, fighting men, and thieves. "Shpare a copper for old man?" he wheezed, sitting up. "Oh, evening, Geoffrey."

The tooth flickered from one color to another. As Wentworth watched, agape, the colors flickered faster and faster, until there was nothing left but a white blur.

Vic focused on the dragon's tooth. "Ah," he said, and rubbed an eye.

"Damn thing must be defective," said Wentworth. He grabbed the tooth, held it by his ear, and shook it experimentally.

Vic chortled. He stood up and held out a hand. "Give it to me," he said.

"Old man," Wentworth said, "we don't have—"

"Give it to him," Timaeus said faintly.

Wentworth dropped the tooth into Vic's palm. Vic pointed it to Wentworth. It flared yellow. "Alchemy," Vic said. He pointed the tooth at Timaeus. It turned red. "Fire," Vic said. He pointed the tooth at the pigeon, who stood under the eaves, watching the proceedings beadily. The tooth flared green. "Nature magic," Vic said.

"What do you mean?" said the pigeon.

They looked at it, startled.

Vic walked across the square, holding the tooth. The others trailed him. He splashed through the puddle around the statue, and touched the tooth to Valiant. The tooth turned silver. Vic turned back to Wentworth. "Illusion," Vic said. He spoke a Word.

Stantius stood in the rain. He was still painted brown. Rain rolled down the paint.

"Shee?" Vic said, handing the tooth back to Wentworth. "It worksh."

Wentworth choked. "You are a mage?" he asked the old man.

Vic cackled. "You bet your ash, shonny," he said. Wentworth looked pained.

"Why did you steal the statue?" Sidney demanded.

"But . . ." Wentworth said, "there had to have been a dozen magicians. . . ."

"Or," Timaeus said, "one polymage."

"That's absurd," Jasper said. "There hasn't been a full-fledged polymage for centur—"

They were all silent for a long moment. Vic was the focus of all eyes. The only noise was the patter of rain.

Vic shifted uneasily from one foot to another. "Sure I'm a mage," he said. "Bet your ash." He cackled.

Jasper flitted about the statue in an erratic way. "Extraordinary," he said.

"What's that?" said Sidney.

"A spirit is bound into this object," he said.

"What?" said Father Thwaite. "A human spirit?"

"Perhaps," said Jasper. "The spirit of a sapient, surely. I've only encountered this once before—I had a sword, once, with a spirit and mind of its own. Unusual form of magic."

"What is it thinking?" said Timaeus.

"Sorry?" said Jasper. "Oh, nothing as far as I can tell. That is, a mind, if present, is not active. Spirit and mind are separable, you know."

"Yes," said Timaeus, "I know."

"Ve find statue," Kraki pointed out. "Now, ve have dinner, hokay? Old man tell us story over food."

Vic's eyes acquired a glazed look. He mumbled and began to wander off.

"Vic!" said Father Thwaite urgently. "Vic!" He took the old man's arm. Vic looked up. His eyes cleared. "Oh, Geoffrey," he said. "Evening."

"Vic," said Thwaite. "You have to do something about the statue."

"Shtatue? Shtatue? That'sh right. Now . . . ?"

Thwaite pointed at the statue. "You have to hide it again," he said.

Vic peered at the statue. A look of comprehension passed across his face. He spoke a Word.

Stantius became Roderick (and Valiant) once more.

"Food now?" said Kraki.

Vic looked at the barbarian. "Sure," he said. "My treat."

"Sure, Vic," said Father Thwaite soothingly. "Your treat." He began to steer the old man gently toward the inn.

"No," said Vic. "We'll go to my club."

Timaeus raised a skeptical eyebrow. Vic's shirt was multiply patched and threadbare. His pants had holes at the knees. He wore leggings made of rags. "Your club?" Timaeus said.

"Sure," said Vic. "The Cloud."

Timaeus almost swallowed his pipe. The Cloud Club was the most prestigious gentlemen's society in all of Athelstan. Its members looked down on members of the Millennium, Timaeus's own club, as Millennials looked down on peasants. "The Cloud," he said severely, "does not admit urine-stained vagabonds."

Vic cackled. He spoke a Word. He spoke several.

There was a stiff breeze. It scattered rain.

There was a questioning noise on the wind.

Vic spoke again.

The air elemental bore them aloft, into the sky. There was nothing between them and a fall, no carpet, no magical steed.

Morglop moaned and closed his eye tight.

Sidney grinned manically as they plunged through the night sky.

"Don't look so happy," Timaeus told her, whizzing past. "Consider whose magic keeps us up."

She lost her grin.

"I only hope," muttered Father Thwaite, "that he doesn't forget where he's taking us before we get there."

The pigeon fluttered desperately to keep up.

Sir Ethelred Ethelbert sat forlornly on the coverlet of the four-poster bed. He brushed his hand over a tassel. Part of the coverlet was sticky with coagulated blood. Sir Ethelred looked away from it.

They'd taken Mortimer away. Sadly, Sir Ethelred looked toward the French doors that led to the balcony. The doors banged, swinging in the wet breeze.

Since Mortimer had never had children, the heir presumptive was Baron Harald of Meep, Mortimer's nephew. Sir Ethelred sighed. Harald was nineteen and a complete fool. His main pursuit was hunting, both deer and the local peasant girls. Sir Ethelred gloomily considered the prospect of being foreign minister to such a lout.

At least, he supposed, it should be possible to get Harald to go to Ishkabibble's aid. It would probably be more difficult to prevent the loon from going to war with everyone else.

Sir Ethelred looked at the pitiful pile of clothing by the bed. Damn Veronee. He hoped his men found her, but feared they would not. She was a wily one.

Gods knew, Mortimer had been a trial at times. Still, whatever his drawbacks as a monarch, he had been a superb mycologist, among the best in the world. He had been passionate about his subject. And he had been sensible enough to leave the governance of the realm in reasonably capable hands.

Most of the time, anyway.

Well. Time to get moving. Someone had to see that the Fifth Frontier got fed. And to initiate funeral proceedings. And see that the barons and the populace were informed. And put out an announcement on the news crystal. And send a messenger with a fast horse to Baron Harald. . . .

Sir Ethelred got to his feet. Where the devil was Jameson when a man needed him?

"Egad," said Sir Ethelred, peering out toward the terrace. What was the heroic statue of Roderick doing out there?

He went to the French doors and studied the bronze in amazement.

"I sit here in Castle Durf with the best espionage bureau in the human lands," he muttered to himself, "and I still haven't the foggiest notion what goes on."

Part III.
ANOTHER QUEST

I.

Soaked and chilled, they fluttered to the landing of the Cloud Club.

The club was a cloud. It was not built *on* a cloud, it was built *into* a cloud. The cloud was tethered by thick rope cables to one of the bridges over the River Jones. The walls of the club were fleecy; parts white, parts gray, parts rosy with magically captured sunset light. The architecture was fanciful and airy.

The Grand Hall of the club was built into the lowest layer of the cloud; its floor and one entire wall were constructed of solid air, permitting the diners a glorious view of the city of Urf Durfal and Athelstan's rolling hills —at least, when it wasn't raining cats and dogs.

Access to the aerial club was, necessarily, by air. Some members could fly to it of their own volition. Others hired flying carpets. The club itself maintained a ferry service, a flying carriage pulled by swans. The concierge was therefore not surprised when thirteen persons of assorted races tumbled to the soft, white cloud deck which served as a landing strip.

The group moved toward the reception desk.

They were uniformly soaked. Several were wounded. The only reason the concierge didn't order them tossed over the edge was that—well, they *had* flown here under their own power. Obviously, there must be more to this group than met the eye.

Vic trudged up to the desk. Behind it, the concierge stood resplendent in a brilliant crimson uniform with golden tassels. Behind him was a pegboard. Small metal circles hung from the pegs. Inside each circle, the name of a club member was engraved. "How may I help you, sir?" the concierge said.

"I'm a member," Vic said. "Theshe're my gueshtsh."

The man leaned over the desk and peered at Vic's garb. "Ah," he said skeptically. "And your name, sir?"

"Vincianus Polymage," Vic said.

The concierge turned to the pegboard and scanned it. How was he going to get rid of this lunatic? The fellow's friends looked frightfully well armed. The board of directors would have his neck if he disturbed the club's members in the process of evicting this clown. He cleared his throat. "I'm afraid there's no Vinc—by Dion," he said. He reached up. From the left-most, highest peg on the board hung a rusty metal circle. He tugged at it. It was rusted to the peg, which itself was nearly rusted through; the peg broke off. The doorman brought the circle close to his eyes. He swallowed. Vincianus Polymage was indeed a member. Moreover, according to the code on the rusty circle, his dues were paid up. In fact, they were paid in advance—for the next ten thousand years.

"Yes, sir," said the concierge faintly. "Everything appears to be in order, sir. Will you and your companions be dining tonight?"

"Hi," said the waiter. "My name is Jeremy, and I'll be your waiter for this evening."

The ancient geezer stared at him malevolently. "You tell your true name to everyone who asksh, shonny?" he said. "You do that around here, you'll get turned to a frog fashter'n you can shay 'ribbit.' They shtill got frogsh' legsh on the menu?"

The waiter was somewhat at a loss. "Ah . . . no, sir, but I can ask the chef . . ." He noticed with a start that a pigeon was standing on the linen tablecloth.

"Shoo!" said Jeremy, waving his hand at the pigeon. "Shoo!"

"Cut it out, mac," said the pigeon.

Jeremy's eyes bugged out.

"Leave him alone," said Vic, waving a liver-spotted hand. "Get ush three bottlesh of Château d'Alfar."

"Very good, sir. The ought-nine?"

Vic stared at him. A confused look came into the oldster's eyes. He started counting his fingers and mumbling.

"The ought-nine is fine," said Timaeus.

"What year ish it, anyway?" the geezer hissed in a loud stage whisper.

"Never mind," Father Thwaite said gently. "Ought-nine was a good year for the northern elvish appellation."

"Would you like to hear about the specials?" said Jeremy.

"Can I have some bar nuts?" asked the pigeon.

Jeremy blinked. "I'll see what I can do," he said faintly.

"I vant roast boar," said Kraki.

"A portion of roast boar," said Jeremy, jotting the order on his pad.

"No," said Kraki. "Vone roast boar."

"That's what I said, sir," said Jeremy. "One roast boar."

"He wants the whole boar," said Nick.

"Sir?" said Jeremy.

"Is right," said Kraki. "Vone roast boar."

"Yes, sir," said Jeremy. He gulped.

"I'd like to hear about the specials," said Sidney.

Jeremy cleared his throat. "Very good, madam," he said. "Our specials tonight include filet of dragonelle pan-fried in *beurre noir* with asparagus; roc egg omelet with shrimp, fresh tomatoes, and coriander; and a greep bouillabaisse."

"Isn't bouillabaisse a fish dish?" asked Garni.

"Yes, sir," said Jeremy.

"I thought greeps were nuts."

"Sir? By no means, sir. They are indeed *fruits de mer . . ."*

GREEP BOUILLABAISSE

"They are indeed *fruits de mer,* flown fresh at great expense by dragon riders from the southern seas.

"I can claim a certain expertise in this matter, for I was born in southern climes.

"Ah, how I yearn for the clean breeze of the south! For the salt spray, the azure skies, the crystal sands!

"I was raised on a remote coral isle. Few other humans lived nearby, so I made my friends among the merfolk. Oh, happy were they! And happy was I, to watch them frolic among the waves. Though I was clumsy in the sea, lacking webbed fingers, gills, and flukes, I learned from them to swim as best a human may. Together, we explored the reefs and grottoes of the shore.

"And I fell in love.

"Oh, do not be shocked, good sirs, good ladies! Though I was a man and she but a fish, our love was strong and true!

"Thalassa was her name. We hid our love from everyone, for both of us knew the penalty for miscegenation. We knew, too, that any issue we might have would be an unhappy hybrid, clumsy in both water and air, unable himself to breed. Yet we persisted.

"We'd meet on the rocks by the eastern shore, and I would strip and join her in the sea. She'd tell me of the beauty of the reef and of the strange unity of life beneath the waves; I'd tell her of the people and the creatures of the land. Once, I brought her a bouquet of flowers; their beauty, strange to her, entranced her. She took them with her when she left. The next day, she was crying when we met. 'They cannot survive in salt water,' she said dolorously. 'Nor can you.'

"I knew it was true. I knew how hopeless was our love. But there was nothing to be done, so I thought.

"I thought wrong. For she knew . . .

"One day, she appeared, eyes shining. She kissed me and told me she'd found a mermage who'd taught her a spell. She could, she told me, turn me mer.

"How we rejoiced! How happy I was! At last, we could be together.

"She recited her spell. Gills appeared along my neck. My legs merged into a single fluke. And webbing appeared between my fingers. I plunged into the sea, and together, webbed hand in webbed hand, we swam into her world.

"Thalassa was of simple birth, as was I; she introduced me to her parents. I joined a gang of fishermers to make my living; and, respectably employed, gained the favor of her folks. Soon, we were engaged.

"We lived in beauty. You who have never seen below the waves, I cannot tell you of its glories. The fish that populate the reefs are like flowers in their prime. Strange life waves gently in the currents. There are no storms, no drastic cold or heat, no need for shelter. We drifted across the ocean, hearts and hands entwined.

"I loved my work. The merfolk raised seaweed, as we raise grain. But mostly, they eat fish. Each morning, we ventured forth, with nets and spears, in search of prey. We sent out scouts to locate schools of fish for our nets.

"Swordfish, we hunted with spears. Fluke, lobster, conch, and crab, we harvested; but above all else, we sought the greep. For the merfolk prize the greep's flesh above all others.

"Have you ever seen the greep run? In the spring when they school, they turn the sea silver with their bodies. They leap into the air and plunge back in again. There are so many, sometimes, that the splashes of their leaps sound a constant roar, like that of a waterfall.

"Each spring, the merfolk gather and hunt the greep while they can. For once the greep have bred, they scatter across the ocean and can be caught only by ones and twos. But while they run, they can be captured in their thousands. For the merfolk, the greep run marks the springtime.

"Well I remember their small silver bodies, thrashing against the net. Well do I remember my fellow fishers, laughing bubbles in the water as we gathered up our catch. Well do I remember dolphins, gamboling through the school, eating their own fill of the ocean's bounty. Ah, the greep run was a time for rejoicing.

"Greeps are not large fish; no more than six inches long. But the merfolk have a legend of a monstrous greep, a greep cubits in length. The Old Greep of the Sea, he is called. And it is said that whosoever captures him is granted a single wish.

"I heard the legend, but thought nothing of it.

"Not all the fishers in our group were male. The merfolk think nothing of sending merwomen to the hunt. Our gang had several; but the one I knew best was Mare.

"She was a lithe little creature, a faster swimmer than any of us. She was positioned to my left on the net, so we saw much of each other. We became friends and used to joke as we swam toward our prey.

"One day, during the greep run, we labored home with a monstrous catch. Everyone was exhilarated and exhausted. We'd do well off the catch; and the next day promised a catch just as fine.

"We went to celebrate at a grotto where merfolk purchase essences. They do not drink as humans do; instead, they uncork small bottles, release the liquid contents into the sea, and inhale this through the gills. The effect is both like and unlike bibulation.

"I overindulged. And Mare swam alongside me. She kissed me, and we left the grotto for a private niche among the reefs.

"Once the deed was done, I began to choke. Mare looked at me with horror and revulsion. My fluke, which she had thought handsome, had separated in twain. My gills were scabbing over. She fled from me in fright.

"I barely surfaced before I could breathe the waters no more. I was miles from the island, but I'd been a good swimmer virtually from birth. I made it to land with the last of my strength.

"I stumbled to my parents' house. They had given me up for dead. 'Where have you been?' my father asked.

"I gasped out my tale. Horror passed across their faces.

" 'You slept with . . . a fish?' my mother asked.

" 'Get out of my house,' my father said.

"I slept on the beach. The next day, I went to the special place where Thalassa and I used to meet. She never came.

"But her father did. 'You have ruined my daughter,' he screamed, and threw a trident at me. It missed. He could not pursue me on land. 'Animal!' he yelled, thrashing about the bay.

" 'What happened?' I asked. He told me the tale.

"Driven by her love for me, Thalassa had sought out and captured the

Old Greep of the Sea. She had asked that I be made mer, and he had agreed. 'But,' the Old Greep said, 'the enchantment is powered by the love between you. Should you ever be unfaithful to him, or he to you, he will revert to human form.'

"Laughing, Thalassa told him that would never happen. We were too much in love.

"Too much in love.

"And I betrayed her.

" 'She will find no suitor now,' said her father, cursing me. 'No one will marry a lover of animals.'

"My love was lost. My parents disowned me. And so I fled my land, fled for the cold north, away from Thalassa, away from the merfolk, away from the greeps, away from everything I knew."

. . . sobbed Jeremy. He ran toward the kitchen, crying.

"Well," said Jasper after a pause. "I can't say I think much of the service here."

Vic was sprawled in his chair, his head hanging back, his mouth open, revealing toothless gums. He snored.

"Vhat about my boar?" asked Kraki.

"Waiter!" Wentworth yelled. Reluctantly, a white-coated young man approached. "Sir?" he said.

"We want to order," said Wentworth.

"This isn't my table . . ."

"Right," said Wentworth. "It's the table of your weepy young friend Jeremy. After you take our order, you may go console him in the kitchen."

The waiter blinked. "All right, sir," he said, mystified. "Can I tell you about our specials?"

"Absolutely not. We want one whole roast boar."

"Sir?"

"A whole roast boar. Are you having any difficulty understanding me?"

"No, sir. Will you have salad with that?"

"Pah!" Kraki spat. "Is for rabbits."

"No, I think not," said Wentworth. "The boar is for him. And I'll have fish."

"What sort of fish, sir?"

"Any sort at all, except greep."

"And you, madam?" the waiter addressed Sidney.

"I'd like a chop," she said.

"What kind?"

"Any kind, other than greep."

Father Thwaite ordered a salad, of any type, as long as it contained no greep. Nick ordered a stew, failing to specify type, other than a complete absence of greep. Jasper ordered mineral water (without greeps), and the filet of dragonelle, subject to the waiter's firm assurance that the sauce contained not the slightest smidgen of greep. Morglop ordered the roc egg omelet. "No greep," he muttered. Timaeus, going with the tide, ordered steak tartare.

"Without greeps, sir?" asked the waiter.

"Correct," said Timaeus.

Garni had a pastrami on rye. Without greeps.

"Sidney," said Wentworth, "wake Vincianus and find out what he wants, will you?"

Vic wanted greeps.

Everyone stared at him.

"Are you sure?" Jasper said.

"What'sh the matter with you guysh?" said the old man querulously. "Never had greepsh?"

Everyone shuddered, except for Timaeus, who was rather partial to a greep now and again.

"Now, Vic," said Sidney. "Why don't you tell us how you stole the statue?"

"Shteal?" said the old man. "Never shtole anything in my life." He sounded highly offended.

"Appropriated," Timaeus suggested soothingly. "Absconded with. Borrowed."

Vic stared at him as if he were mad. "Where'sh the wine I ordered?" he said.

"Wine!" said Wentworth, slapping his forehead. "Damnation. I knew I'd forgotten something."

"We'll order some when he gets back," said Sidney. "Tell us about the damn statue!"

Vic looked at her with a wounded, puzzled expression.

"The statue," she said slowly. "The statue in Roderick Square."

Vic began to mumble. He took a piece of bread from the basket, and began to gum the crust.

"Father," Sidney said, "he's drifting. What can we do?"

Thwaite looked up. "Nothing," he said. "Vic's like that. He'll clear up in a little while. To a degree."

"You know the gentleman?" Jasper asked.

"For many years."

"But you didn't know he was a polymage?"

"Certainly not. He never displayed any magical powers in my presence."

"What do you know about him?"

"He's lived on the streets of Five Corners Parish for longer than anyone can remember. He's kind to children. His mind wanders. He tells long, pointless stories."

"I can vouch for that," said Timaeus.

"You mean," said Wentworth, "that he's senile?"

"That's about the size of it, yes."

They stared at the old man.

"Copper for an old man?" Vic said to a passing waiter. The waiter stared at him strangely.

"This," announced Wentworth, "is insane. He's got more magical power than the entire local chapter of the Sodality combined, but he can't remember what year it is. We're never going to get a coherent story out of him."

"Well," said Father Thwaite, after a silence, "I've found that if you begin to tell Vic what you remember of one of his stories, he sometimes picks up the thread—"

"But we don't *know* what the story is!" said Wentworth with exasperation.

Nick took a sip of his water. "Well, the orcs told me a little bit about it," he said.

Everyone looked at him. "Go on," said Sidney.

"They said that it came from the Orclands. The orcish colony in the Caverns of Cytorax was established by a group of refugees, fleeing some civil war. They brought the statue with them."

"Civil war? Among the orcs?" said Wentworth frowning. "I've never heard of such a thing. Usually, Arst-Kara-Morn keeps a pretty tight leash on things. . . ."

"Ah," said Timaeus, "but there was such a civil war. In the late 3700s, I believe. Shortly after Stantius III was captured in the battle of Durfalus— *and then taken to the Orclands!*"

"Yes?" said Wentworth, leaning over the table and peering at Timaeus through his cracked monocle. "And then?"

Timaeus shrugged. "Nobody knows," he said. "I talked to a professor of history at the university. He says that there are rumors that some great ritual magic was to be performed on the plain of Arst-Kara-Morn, but no one knows why or what it involved."

Everyone looked at Vic. "Do you know anything about that?" said Father Thwaite in a calm voice.

" 'Bout what, Geoffrey?" asked Vic. A bit of saliva-soaked bread adhered to his chin.

"Ritual magic in Arst-Kara-Morn?"

"Sho what elshe is new?" Vic shrugged.

Thwaite sighed. "I guess not," he said.

"Hmm," Jasper mused. "Suppose you had an enemy king. What would you do with him?"

"Hold him for ransom?" suggested Nick.

"I was always told that the health of the king is the health of the mountains," said Garni. "At least, that's the way it is among dwarves. Could you torture the king to weaken your enemies or something like that?"

"Of course!" said Timaeus. "Nothing quite so crude, but . . . the fundamental principle of magic is the Law of Similarity. There is no distinction, magically, between, say, a woman and a lock of the woman's hair; the objects are similar, so that the lock of hair can be manipulated magically to affect the woman. A king *is* the health of the land, in a literal sense. A king *is* his species. By capturing the king, *you may capture his people!*"

Jasper bounced up and down over his chair. "By Cuthbert!" he said. "Do you mean to say that the ritual magic in Arst-Kara-Morn was the Dark Lords attempting to bind humanity to their will through Stantius?"

"Why not?" said Timaeus. "That would certainly tip the balance of power in their favor, don't you think?"

"This is a great deal of speculation built upon a rather flimsy basis of fact," said Wentworth. "Why didn't it work, if this is true? Why do we not have a king who leads us in the services of darkness?"

At this moment, the waiter arrived with food. He unfolded a stand by Vic's seat, set his platter on the stand, and began to remove dishes from it, placing them before the diners. Sidney was the first served.

"Something went wrong," Sidney suggested. She was tempted to begin on her chop, but decided to wait until the others were served. "The ritual got screwed up. Maybe Stantius was killed, but instead of binding the new king to his service, the Dark Lord stopped *any* king from being chosen."

"There is a spirit in the statue!" said Jasper excitedly. "Stantius's spirit!"

"Do you *know* that it's Stantius's spirit?" said Wentworth.

"Er, well, no. But if it *were* Stantius's spirit, that would explain why there has been no king for two millennia. Stantius's spirit has not departed this plane of existence; therefore he is, in some sense, living; so the gods have not chosen a new king."

"Perhaps," said Wentworth. "But all you have is the word of a couple of orcs (we know how reliable *that* is) and a great deal of supposition."

"I'm sorry," said the waiter. "Who's having the greeps?"

"Him," said Kraki, pointing to Vic.

"Vic," said Father Thwaite, "does the statue contain Stantius's spirit?"
Vic looked at Thwaite. "Shorry, Geoffrey?"

"I said, does the statue contain Stantius's spirit?"

"Doesh the shtatue contain Shtantiush'sh shpirit?" He appeared to mull
this over for a minute. The waiter leaned beside him to set the plate of
greeps on the table.

"Yesh!" shouted Vic, springing to his feet. The plate went flying. The
waiter hurtled into the stand. The rest of dishes spilled to the ground.
"The shtatue!" shouted Vic, wild-eyed, rising from his chair and quivering
in excitement. "For a thousand yearsh have I shought the shtatue, the
shtatue that containsh the shpirit of Shantiush Human King. It musht be
freed!"

"I am most dreadfully sorry, sir," said the waiter, trying to mop the
greeps off Vic's filthy shirt with a napkin. "Extremely clumsy of me. I do
beg your pardon."

"Freed, Vic?" said Father Thwaite. "What do you mean?"

"Get away from me, boy," shouted Vic, pushing at the waiter petulantly. "I musht find the shtatue and take it to Arsht-Kara-Morn to un-
work the Dark Lord'sh shpell and releashe the shpirit of Shtantiush, that
humanity may once again have a king!"

All eyes in the restaurant were on the shouting, gesticulating old man.

"I musht gather companionsh to join me on my quesht," he bellowed.

Suddenly, he stopped. He looked around the Cloud Club querulously,
then frowned. "Where'sh my wine?" he said.

The waiter was on hands and knees, trying to scrape up the greeps.
"Wine, sir?" he said, looking up.

"Château d'Alfar," Vic said automatically, sitting back down. The
waiter stood up and headed for the kitchen.

"What quest?" said Father Thwaite.

"Quesht? Quesht?" said Vic. "I shaid wine, not quesht."

"The quest to take Stantius's statue to Arst-Kara-Morn," said Father
Thwaite.

"Oh, *that* quesht," said Vic. "Never happen. Damn shtatue'sh been
losht for two thoushand yearsh. What happened to my wine?"

"Would you need companions for such a quest?"

"Yesh, of courshe," muttered Vic rubbing his eyes. "Alwaysh need companionsh for a quesht. Pain in the neck, really, but it'sh traditional. If
anyone found the damn thing, they'd be the onesh to take." He yawned
widely. "Time for a nap," he said, and leaned back in his chair.

"Vic?" said Father Thwaite. There was no reply. "Vic?"

"Let me get this straight," said Sidney. "He wants us to go to Arst-Kara-Morn with him."

"A place," said Nick, "where they'd rather gut you like a trout than say hello."

"Lugging a statue that weighs a ton," said Garni, "across three thousand miles of hostile terrain."

"A statue," said Timaeus, "that we're suppose to hide from the opposition while it pumps out magical energy like a whole pantheon of gods."

Vic began to snore.

"Vith," said Kraki, "a senile geezer who can't even remember vhat year it is as our guide."

"Your wine, sir?" said the waiter, presenting a bottle.

Vic snored.

Everyone stared at him.

"Never mind the damned wine," snapped Wentworth. "What about our food?"

THE END

OR, AT ANY EVENT,
THE SHAMELESS CLIFF-HANGER

Notes

The main trade currency of the human lands is the pound *argentum*— which is equal to one pound of silver, as the pound sterling was originally. Different polities mint their own coins, but all coin is hard money, and the pound-shilling-pence system has been universally adopted. There are twenty shillings to the pound and twelve pence to the shilling, meaning that each penny weights one-twentieth of a (troy) ounce. Nick says that one ounce of gold is worth one pound *argentum;* if he is correct, gold is somewhat more common in his world than in our own. On earth, gold usually goes for fifteen to sixteen times as much, per ounce, as silver; but there are only twelve troy ounces to the troy pound, not sixteen. Perhaps Nick is confusing the troy pound with the pound *avoirdupois*—a supposition suggested by the fact that he talks of Father Thwaite's weight in the same passage.

"Essence of belladonna" is, in fact, atropine, a drug refined from the belladonna plant. Its appearance here is, of course, not in keeping with the otherwise Renaissance technology of the world; in our world, it was first extracted in the mid-nineteenth century. I posit that the fascination of witches and alchemists with medicinal plants and herbs leads to alternative, magical methods of extraction. The symptoms and dosages described are correct; however, I believe atropine is no longer used as an anaesthetic. It is still sometimes used in the treatment of certain poisons.

The orcish Hymn of Propitiation can be sung to the tune of Beethoven's *Ode to Joy* (if anyone cares).

* * *

Several archaic units of measure are used. A cubit is traditionally the distance between the tip of one's middle finger and the elbow—about eighteen inches. A stone is a unit of weight, that, depending on type, can vary from eight to twenty-two pounds; the traditional English stone is fourteen pounds.